PRAISE FOR HA JIN'S

A MAP OF BETRAYAL

"A poignant novel that portrays the emotional drama of an immigrant torn apart by conflicting loyalties and 'bone-deep loneliness.' . . . [Gary] may be a traitor and a super-spy, but his tragedy is relatable. . . . It should strike many close to home." —*Los Angeles Times*

"Ha Jin has captured the painful, often humdrum essence of the hidden agent. . . . We see America through the eyes of a Chinese émigré, torn between an old loyalty and growing affection for the adopted land he is betraying." —*The New York Times Book Review*

"One of the great triumphs of *A Map of Betrayal* is how it uncovers and underscores the similarities between the domestic and the political, the family and the larger cul-ture. . . . Lilian strives not to judge but to understand. She searches for a capacious, forgiving, and subtle interpreta-tion of a struggling soul." —*The Boston Globe*

"With one foot in China and the other in the United States, Ha Jin is the quintessential Chinese-American writer. . . . In his absorbing new book, *A Map of Betrayal*, the author offers his most searing portrait yet of divided loyalties." —*Chicago Tribune*

"The book stands out for the way it straddles a number of worlds—China and the U.S., family life and adultery—and in Shang's case, the torturous inner life of a man torn between loyalty to two nations." —*NPR*

HA JIN
A MAP OF BETRAYAL

Ha Jin left his native China in 1985 to attend Brandeis University. He is the author of six previous novels, four story collections, three volumes of poetry, and a book of essays. He has received the National Book Award, two PEN/Faulkner Awards, the PEN/Hemingway Foundation Award, the Asian American Literary Award, and the Flannery O'Connor Award for Short Fiction. In 2014 he was elected to the American Academy of Arts and Letters. Ha Jin lives in the Boston area and is a professor of English at Boston University.

INTERNATIONAL

A
MAP
OF
BETRAYAL

A
MAP
OF
BETRAYAL

HA JIN

VINTAGE INTERNATIONAL
Vintage Books
A Division of Penguin Random House LLC
New York

FIRST VINTAGE INTERNATIONAL EDITION, JULY 2015

Copyright © 2014 by Ha Jin

The Library of Congress has cataloged the Pantheon edition as follows:
Jin, Ha.
A map of betrayal : a novel / Ha Jin.
pages cm
1. Chinese American women—Fiction. 2. Fathers and daughters—Fiction.
3. Moles (Spies)—Fiction. 4. Espionage—Fiction. 5. Family secrets—Fiction.
6. United States. Central Intelligence Agency—Fiction.
7. China—Relations—United States—Fiction.
8. United States—Relations—China—Fiction. I. Title.
PS3560.I6M37 2014   813'.54—dc23   2014008892

Vintage Books Trade Paperback ISBN: 978-0-8041-7036-9
eBook ISBN: 978-0-307-91161-2

Book design by Iris Weinstein

www.vintagebooks.com

Printed in the United States of America
10 9 8 7 6 5 4 3 2

FOR LISHA

A
MAP
OF
BETRAYAL

My mother used to say, "Lilian, as long as I'm alive, you must have nothing to do with that woman." She was referring to Suzie, my father's mistress.

"Okay, I won't," I would reply.

Nellie, my embittered mother, had never forgiven my father for keeping another woman, though he'd died many years before. I kept my promise. I did not approach Suzie Chao until my mother, after a tenacious fight against pancreatic cancer, succumbed last winter. Death at eighty—I can say she lived a long life.

Still heavy with grief, I got in touch with Suzie, first by letter and then by phone. She lived in Montreal, far away from my home state, Maryland. When forsythia began to bloom in my backyard, she mailed me my father's diary, six morocco-bound volumes, each measuring eight inches by five. I hadn't known he kept a journal, and I had assumed that the FBI seized all the papers left by him, Gary Shang, the biggest Chinese spy ever caught in North America. The diary recorded his life from 1949 to 1980. He hadn't written every day, and the journal was more like a personal work log. One of the volumes bears a quotation from Nietzsche on its first page: "Preserve me from all petty victories!" Another opens with Franklin Roosevelt's words: "The only thing we have to fear is fear itself." The last volume starts with a claim from Martin Luther King Jr.'s "I Have a Dream" speech: "Unearned suffering is redemptive." My father was fond of aphorisms and filled a notebook with hundreds of them, but that little trove of wisdom was in the FBI's possession now.

Once I was done for the spring semester, having graded my students' finals and papers, I began to pore over my father's diary to piece together his story. I also reread all the newspaper articles about him, which I kept in my file. By the end of the summer of 2010 I had a substantial grasp of his life, but there were still holes and gaps. Those troublesome spots tormented me, and try as I might, I couldn't figure them out. That was why, in mid-November, as soon as I heard I'd been granted a Fulbright lectureship, a one-semester appointment at Beijing Teachers College for the spring of 2011, I contacted Suzie again and asked to see her.

"Your mother was a bitch," Suzie said, looking me in the face. She was seated across from me in Starbucks in downtown Montreal. Her feet were tucked under her legs on a chair while her eyes, bleary with age, peered at me without blinking. She was so old that she reminded me of a puppet, loose-jointed with dangling arms and a silver mane. It was hard to imagine the pretty woman she'd been forty years before.

"My mother could be difficult sometimes," I admitted, "but she had her reasons. My dad might not have loved her."

"Well, Gary wouldn't divorce Nellie to marry me," Suzie said, pursing her lips smeared with a bit of cappuccino foam. When young, she'd been charming, vivacious, and quick-witted. I could think of several reasons my father had fallen for her. Above all, she'd brought to mind the kind of seductress the Chinese call "fox spirit."

I went on, "My mother often said Gary loved nobody except for himself and me."

"Bullcrap. Gary loved Nellie in the beginning, I'm sure. But the love went sour." In spite of Suzie's annoyance, her voice still had a pleasant low timbre.

"Thanks to you," I said with studied levity, trying to smile but feeling my face tighten. I don't think my father ever loved my mother, though in the later years of their marriage he developed an attachment to her.

"If not me," she continued, "there'd have been another Chinese woman in his life. Your father was always lonely and couldn't share everything with your mother."

"Because she was white and American?"

"That's part of it. I was more useful to him than Nellie. Believe it or not, I'm still proud of being his mistress. I could do anything for him and he trusted me."

That caught me off guard. For a moment we fell silent. She lifted her cappuccino and sipped. I was lost in thought, musing about her and my father. Here was another slave of love. I admired her for that, for holding on to the remainder of her lifelong passion and for her total self-abandonment to the man she loved and cherished. How many of us are capable of that kind of devotion without the fear of being hurt or ruined? I turned to gaze out the window at the clean wide street, which was quiet with just a few pedestrians passing by, as if we'd been in a suburban town. It was overcast, the low clouds threatening snow.

I switched to the topic that had been on my mind for a long time. "Suzie, I know my father had another family in China. Did you ever meet his first wife?"

"No, I didn't. Gary missed her a lot."

"What's her full name?"

"Yufeng Liu."

"I wish my mother had known that," I blurted out, surprising myself, because the awareness of his other family could hardly have mollified Nellie.

"That would've made her crazier, and she would have hated Gary and me all the more," Suzie said.

"Do you think Yufeng is still alive?"

"I haven't the foggiest idea."

"She might have remarried long ago, don't you think?" I asked.

"Maybe. Who knows? I had a feeling you might bring up Gary's first wife. I only know her name and that they married in their mid-twenties. Last night I looked everywhere but couldn't find her address. She used to live somewhere in Shandong, in the country-side, and I don't know if she's still there. But there's somebody in Beijing who might help you track her down."

"Who's that?"

"Bingwen Chu. Goodness knows if that's his real name. Perhaps he's gone too. Here's the old address of his office."

She gave me a slip of paper bearing her slanted handwriting. I liked Suzie in spite of her barbed words. She had moved to Canada in her mid-fifties and married a Malaysian businessman, but the marriage fell through a few years later. She seemed content living alone now.

HENRY, MY HUSBAND, was staying behind while I went to Beijing so that he could continue managing our apartment building in College Park. The three-story property consisted of eighteen units and sat at the end of a quiet street; it was always fully occupied thanks to its fine amenities and bucolic setting. We'd bought the building four years earlier and were living in a corner apartment on the first floor. I had a studio in the basement where I read, wrote, and prepared my lectures for the history classes I taught at the university. Before we married, Henry had recently been widowed, while I'd been divorced for nearly a decade. Neither of us had children, much as we loved them. Henry was sixty-one, seven years older than me. We often fantasized about adoption, preferably a baby girl, but we also knew that our ages would disqualify us, so we never filed an application.

The spring semester wouldn't start in Beijing until mid-February. I arrived three weeks early, intending to give myself plenty of time to settle down and look into my father's past. The teachers college's campus was empty, like an abandoned village, but every day I would run into a colleague or two. The few people I spoke with were excited about the democratic demonstrations in the Arab countries. They seemed to believe that the tides of the political tsunami in the Middle East would soon reach the Chinese shore and wash away some parts of the bureaucratic system of their own country. I'd been to China before, had followed its affairs for decades, and knew changes wouldn't come here easily. In 1988 I'd taught at the same school, and my mother had come to visit me toward the end of my stint. Her view of this country could be summed up in one word, "brutal," which she had modified with a nervous giggle and this remark: "Like your father's lot in life." Yet she was deeply impressed by the people she met here, particularly by their optimism, their hunger for learning, their industriousness, their patriotism. Unlike my Chinese colleagues, I wouldn't raise my hopes for the arrival of the global democratic waves. China was China and had always done things its own way, though this shouldn't be an excuse for its resistance to change. I kept reminding myself that I was here just to teach two courses and would head back to the States in the early summer, so I'd better avoid getting involved in politics of any kind. Instead, I wanted to unravel my father's past and locate his first wife, Yufeng, if she was still alive.

Bingwen Chu, the lead Suzie gave me, had been my father's sole handler on and off for three decades. In his diary Gary referred to him as the Torch, probably because the Chinese character *bing* means "burning bright." After I settled down on campus I called his number, and as I'd expected, it was no longer in service. I went to the old address in Chaoyang district, but the four-story building was now occupied by a law firm, a British education agency, and other business offices. I asked a few people. Nobody had ever heard of Bingwen Chu.

In spite of the impasse, I continued perusing my father's diary and pondering his life. I'd also brought with me a book on him, which had come out a few years before. Titled *The Chinese Spook,* by Daniel Smith, it portrays him as a brilliant spy, a longtime mole in the CIA, who sold to China a huge amount of intelligence and did immeasurable damage to U.S. national security. The book offers a plethora of information on my father: his education, his unique role in the Chinese intelligence apparatus, his friendship with some American officials in the DC area, his ways of handling money, his tastes in food and drink, his fondness for petite women with abundant hair. But it doesn't touch on his first marriage and his family in China; his life before he started working for the Americans remains a blank.

There was no denying that my father had been a top spy, but the more I worked on his materials, the more I was convinced that money hadn't been the primary motivation in his espionage for China. He was a man with a sizable ego; to me, he seemed too big for his boots and full of delusions. By professional standards I wouldn't say he was a skilled spy, and his role had largely been thrust upon him by circumstances. As his life was gradually taking concrete form in my mind, I came to believe that he'd been not only a betrayer but also someone who'd been betrayed. Before school began, I immersed myself in reconstructing his story. A historian by profession, I wanted to tell it in my own fashion while remaining as objective as possible.

1949

At the beginning of that tumultuous year he arrived in Shang-hai from the north. His first name was not Gary but Weimin, and he was a young secret agent working for the Communists. He had come with the task of worming his way into the Nationalists' internal security system, specifically into the Eighth Bureau, which had been executing a large-scale plan code-named the Trojan Horse. It trained hundreds of agents who were to remain in the city after the Nationalists retreated to Taiwan. The Communists were eager to apprehend all those dangerous elements, who would sabotage factories, disrupt transportation, manufacture counterfeit currency, upset social order, gather intelligence, and would also coordinate with the Nationalist army when it came to retake the mainland. Weimin was a novice in the business of espionage, but as a graduate of Tsinghua University, he was intelligent and better educated than his comrades. In addition, having attended a missionary school for three years, he spoke English fluently and could mix with foreigners.

He had married a month before, and his bride was still in the countryside in northern Shandong. The marriage had been arranged by his parents, but he liked his wife, Yufeng, even though he didn't feel deep love for her yet. She had a fine figure, abundant hair, glossy skin; her large eyes would twinkle when she smiled. For the time being he wanted to keep her in his home village so that she could help his mother with housework and take care of his parents. The Shangs were well-to-do and owned seven acres of farmland. Weimin believed that eventually he might end up living in a city, Beijing or Tianjin or Jinan, and he had promised his bride he would come back to fetch her in the near future. As a northerner, he didn't like the south, despite the better food and the foreign influences in the coastal cities. But living in Shanghai didn't bother him that much, given that he was supposed to be here for only a short period. The political situation in the country was getting clearer every day; anyone could see that the Communists were defeating the Nationalists roundly and would soon take the whole country. It was very likely that Beijing, where Weimin would prefer to live, would become the new capital.

He hadn't made it into the Eighth Bureau. He lacked the practical skills required for the police work: he couldn't shoot well, nor could he drive or dismantle a bomb, and he failed the hands-on test miserably. But he aced the political exam, in which his answers all hit the bull's-eye, and he wrote a concise, lucid essay on the Three Principles of the People put forward by Sun Yat-sen (nationalism, democracy, and the people's livelihood). The colonel reviewing the results of the exam was impressed and summoned Weimin to his office.

Opening the applicant's file, Colonel Hsu said to the young man seated before his desk, "Why are you interested in this kind of work, Mr. Shang? As a Tsinghua graduate plus an English major, you can do much better than this. You must agree that none of the jobs we advertised are for someone of your caliber."

"I need to eat and have to take whatever is available," Weimin answered, looking at the officer in wonder.

"I like your attitude, young man. You're able to stoop or straighten up according to circumstances. Tell you what." The colonel was beefy and had a gold-capped tooth. He wriggled his forefinger to get Weimin closer to his desk. "You should look for employment in foreign services, for example, the U.S. embassy or an international bank. They pay much better."

"I'm new here and have no idea how to do that."

Colonel Hsu uncapped his silver fountain pen and wrote something on an index card. He pushed it across the desk to Weimin and said, "Here's a place where you might try your luck. They need translators, I heard."

Weimin took the card and saw the name of a U.S. cultural agency and its address. The colonel added, "They give tests regularly nowadays, on Monday mornings. You should get there before nine o'clock."

Weimin thanked the officer and took his leave. He wasn't sure he should try foreign services. For such a change of direction he'd have to get the Party's approval. But to his amazement, when he told his superiors about the opportunity, they encouraged him to apply, saying that the Communists too had something like the Nationalists' Trojan Horse plan, designed to penetrate all levels of the enemy's military and administrative systems, including the diplomatic ranks. Yes, he must apply for such a job and do it under an alias, Gary Shang, which sounded savvy and fashionable for a young Chinese man. From now on he must go by this name. The legal papers would be prepared for him right away.

So Weimin became Gary. He went to take the test at the U.S. cultural agency. It was to translate a short essay by the writer Lao She into English without the aid of a dictionary. This wasn't very hard for him, except that he couldn't spell some words, such as "cigarette" and "philosopher." For those two, he put down "smoke" and "thinker" instead. He was certain he had made a number of silly mistakes. Feeling embarrassed, he avoided mentioning the test in front of his comrades.

But the following week a notice came in the mail summoning Gary Shang for an interview. Did this mean he had passed the test? "You must have done pretty well," said Bingwen Chu, a round-faced, hawk-eyed man, who was just one year older than Gary but was his immediate leader. Bingwen was a more experienced agent, sent over directly from Yan'an, the Communists' base in the north. Gary figured that the foreign employer probably wanted to interview him because there hadn't been many applicants—clearly the Americans would flee China soon, and few Chinese were willing to get too involved with them.

Winter in Shanghai was damp and gloomy. Gary had been miserable, always chilled to the bone, because most houses had no heat and it was hard to find a place where he could get warm even for a moment. At night he and his seven comrades would share beds in a single room, sleeping head to foot. And worse still, people in the city were apprehensive as the civil war was raging. The Communist field armies were advancing from the north steadily and poised to cross the Yangtze to capture Nanjing, China's capital then. Every day dozens of ships left Shanghai for Taiwan, transporting art treasures, college students, officials' families, industrial and military equipment. Unlike Gary, his comrades all enjoyed the cosmopolitan life, especially the cafés, the nightclubs, the cinemas. Some of them even secretly frequented gambling houses. Gary liked movies too, but preferred tea to coffee, which he drank with three spoons of sugar for every cup. When the other men talked about Shanghai women and girls, most of whom looked down on provincials like them, he'd shake his head and say, "They put on too much makeup." He missed Yufeng and every night thought of her for a while before going to sleep.

A junior American official, George Thomas, interviewed Gary at the American cultural agency. The man, in his late twenties, was wide-framed and had a head of woolly auburn hair. He gesticulated with his large hands as he spoke. He asked the applicant which English books he had read. Gary gave a few titles: *The Good Earth, Sister Carrie, Main Street, The Scarlet Letter,* and *Gone with the Wind.* He was a breath away from mentioning Edgar Snow's *Red Star over China,* a book that he'd enjoyed reading and that had inspired tens of thousands of young people to join the Communists, embracing the revolution as the only way to save the country, but just in time he thought to bring up Ibsen's *A Doll House* instead, though he'd seen it only onstage, not on the page. Except for Pearl Buck's novel, he had read all the others in translation. Thomas appeared pleased with his answer and said, "You speak English better than you can write. This is unusual among Chinese."

"I went to an American missionary school."

"What denomination was it?"

"The Episcopal Church. They were from North Carolina."

"Well, Mr. Shang, there're some errors in your translation, but you did better than the other applicants. We believe that your written English will improve quickly once you start working for us."

"You mean you want to hire me?"

"At the moment I can't promise anything because we'll have to run a background check."

"I understand."

"You'll hear from us soon."

The interview went so smoothly that Gary felt he was just a step from a job offer. That evening he briefed Bingwen on his progress, and Bingwen said he was going to report to their higher-ups immediately to get further instructions. He was pretty sure that the Party would have Gary take the job and stay with the Americans for some time. This opportunity looked like a windfall, though neither of them could surmise what it might entail.

Meanwhile, Gary was getting nervous, knowing the Americans were preparing to pull out of Shanghai. He wouldn't mind working for them for a short period, but what if they moved to another country, say Australia or the Philippines? Would he have to go with them? He would hate to live overseas, because he was his parents' only child and had promised Yufeng he would come back to fetch her. Within three days Bingwen got instructions from above: "Comrade Gary Shang must seize the opportunity to work at the American cultural agency, which is actually an intelligence unit in disguise. He must stay with them as long as possible and collect intelligence."

George Thomas mailed Gary a letter a week later, informing him that he had been hired as a translator with a salary of $145 a month. As inflation was skyrocketing all over China, U.S. dollars had become a sought-after currency, and in some business circles they were the only money accepted, save for gold bars. Gary was pleased about the pay, some of which he assumed he'd be able to send home.

Once he started working for the Americans, he was able to gather very little intelligence because he was allowed to translate only unclassified documents, such as information on shipments of merchandise, public speeches given by officials and noted figures, scraps of news. But his English was improving rapidly. When he counted things, he found himself saying numbers in the foreign tongue, and he also began to dream in English. The Americans liked his work, particularly the clarity and accuracy of his translations. His written English had a peculiar cadence and fluency that sounded foreign but elegant. With his first month's pay he bought himself a new suit and a pair of oxfords. In half a year, he calculated, even after sending his family fifty dollars a month, he'd save enough for a radio set.

Then the Nationalist regime began collapsing like an avalanche. Nanjing fell in late April, and eight Communist field armies were approaching Shanghai from different directions. One day in mid-May, George Thomas called Gary into his office and asked if he could leave with the Americans since his service was "highly valued." Gary couldn't answer on the spot but said he'd have to speak with his family.

He reported this to Bingwen. The directive came from above the next day: "Follow the Americans wherever they flee."

Gary wanted to see his parents and wife before leaving with the agency. He hadn't heard from his wife for three months; in the turmoil of wartime, the mail had of course become erratic. He'd written Yufeng several times but never got a reply. How eager he was to go back and find out how his family was doing, but his Party superiors wouldn't grant him permission. Even the Americans disapproved of such a trip; their Chinese employees had often used home visits as a way to quit quietly. Caught in the whirlwind of the retreat, Gary hardly had a moment to think about his future and only executed the orders his higher-ups issued. He was upset, not only because of the prospective long separation from his family but also because he wouldn't be able to directly participate in building the new country. His future immediate contact would be Bingwen, who promised to have his salary from the Communist payroll sent to his family every month during his mission abroad. The man gave Gary a German-made pocket camera, a Regula, saying it might come in handy.

Gary left Shanghai with the Americans in late May. The whole cultural agency stayed in Hong Kong briefly and then moved to Okinawa.

The spring semester started on February 15 at Beijing Teachers College. In my American history class, a survey course for undergrads, six or seven students were from Hong Kong and Taiwan. They didn't stand out among their peers except that they spoke English better, not because they were smarter or better at memorizing the vocabulary and expressions but because they'd begun to learn the language in their childhood. Twenty years ago it had been unimaginable that such students would go to college in China. I gave lectures in a large room with sloped seating, and the class was always well attended. I noticed that many students were taking the course mainly to learn English, since they planned to go abroad for professional school or graduate work. One girl, an anthropology major, told me that her parents would pay for her tuition and living expenses if she was admitted by a decent graduate program in the States. I asked what her parents meant by a "decent" program, and she said, "At least a state's flagship university, like Rutgers or UMass-Amherst. Any of the UC schools would be great too." I was impressed by her parents' savvy about American universities.

Many Chinese had quite a bit of cash now, in part because they spent mainly on food and didn't pay property taxes. Of course, if you stepped off campus, you would encounter all kinds of people who struggled to scrape together a living. Not far from the school's main entrance there was a job agency beside a billboard that advertised shampoo. Under the gargantuan ad, which displayed a charming female face smiling over a bottle spouting pink bubbles, migrant workers, young men and women who had just arrived from the countryside, would gather in the mornings, waiting to be picked up as day laborers or temporary hands who made five or six dollars a day. Some of them smoked and wisecracked, and some stared at the ground. If you went to the train or bus stations, you'd find people lolling around, and some of them were homeless.

I was also teaching a graduate seminar and met a group of fourteen students once a week for three hours. We discussed issues in Asian American history and culture. I'd taught both courses numerous times and could do them without much preparation, so I had a lot of time for my personal project of reconstructing my father's story. These days Beijing's atmosphere was tense because the government was nervous about the popular democratic movements in the Mideast and Africa. But on campus people could talk freely in private. I told a few colleagues about the impasse in my personal investigation. One of them was in the Philosophy Department, Professor Peng, an older man I had known for many years; he said I shouldn't give up the hope of locating Bingwen Chu. Professor Peng believed we could track Chu down if he was still alive. Chu used to work in the Ministry of National Security, which must have a file on him. Given his age, he must have retired long ago, so there should be no rule forbidding him to meet with me. Professor Peng said that a former student of his was working in that ministry and might be able to help me. He called the young man, a junior official, and told me to go see him.

I went to the headquarters of the Ministry of National Security, which was a brownish seven-story building encircled by a high black steel fence. The sentry at the front gate phoned my contact inside, and the young official strolled out to meet me. He had a soft-skinned face and an urbane demeanor. I told him I was looking for an uncle of mine, which was true in a sense since Bingwen Chu had been my father's longtime friend of some kind. I showed him Chu's snapshot, which I had Xeroxed from *The Chinese Spook*. A photo was necessary because I was clueless about his real name. The young official was delighted to know I was teaching at his alma mater for the second time and to hear me speak decent Mandarin, a language I had never stopped learning since I was a child, so he was more than willing to help. He jotted down the information on Bingwen Chu and promised to get someone to look through the archives. He'd give me a ring if they found anything about the man.

He called at the end of February to tell me that Chu was living in a suburb of Beijing, in a residential compound for retired cadres. I phoned Chu that very evening, saying I was Gary Shang's daughter from the United States and would love to see him. After a long pause, Chu said in a voice that suggested a clear head, "All right, I have plenty of time nowadays. Come any day you want to."

We settled on the following Wednesday afternoon, since I'd teach only in the morning that day. Before visiting him, I reviewed some questions essential for reconstructing my father's story. I took a taxi to Chu's place, intimidated by the packed buses and subway. Two decades ago, when I was in my early thirties and teaching in Beijing, I'd ridden a bike or taken public transportation whenever I went out, but it was hard for me to do the same now, because the buses and trains were far too crowded and because I was no longer young.

Bingwen Chu was a small withered man with a bush of white hair and a face scattered with liver spots, but his eyes were still bright and alert. Given his age, eighty-seven, he was in good shape. He appeared at ease and glad to see me.

We were seated in his living room, its walls decorated with framed certificates of merit, all bearing the scarlet chop marks of the offices that had issued the commendations. After his youngest daughter, a forty-something, had served dragon well tea, he said to her, "Can you excuse Lilian and me for a moment?"

The stocky woman nodded and left without a word. Although he addressed me by my first name and I called him Uncle Bingwen, I felt a palpable barrier between us. He'd been my father's sole handler for three decades, but not an unfailing friend. I reminded myself to be composed and that I was here mainly to ask him some questions. Chu allowed me to take notes but not to record our conversation. That was fine with me.

"Sure," he said, "Gary and I were comrades-in-arms, also buddies. I was his recommender when he was inducted into the Party."

"When was that?" I asked.

"The summer of . . . nineteen fifty-two—no, fifty-three. He was voted in unanimously."

"Uncle Bingwen, in your opinion, was my dad a good Communist, a sincere believer?"

"Well, it's hard to say. But I know this: he loved China and did a great service to our country."

"So he was a patriot?"

"Beyond any doubt."

"Did it ever occur to you that he might have loved the United States as well?"

"Yes. We read about that . . . in some newspaper articles on his trial. I could sympathize with him. No fish can remain . . . unaffected by the water it swims in. In a way, we have all been shaped . . . by forces bigger than ourselves."

"That's true. How often did you meet him?"

"On average, we met every two years. But sometimes we lost touch . . . due to China's political chaos. Sometimes we met once a year."

"Did he ever come back to China on the sly?"

"No, never. Our higher-ups wouldn't let him . . . for fear of blowing his identity. Gary was always eager to return for a visit. He often said he was lonely and homesick. The people in the intelligence service all know . . . what those feelings are like. For his suffering, bravery, and fortitude, Gary had our utmost respect."

"Then why didn't China make any effort to rescue him when he was incarcerated in the States?"

"He was a special agent—the type we call 'nails.' "

"Can you elaborate?"

Chu lifted his teacup and took a swallow, his mouth sunken. He seemed to have only a few teeth left. He said, "A nail must remain in its position . . . and rot with the wood it's stuck in, so a spy of the nail type is more or less a goner. Gary must've known that. There was no help for it; it's in the nature of our profession."

I felt he was hedging by categorizing my father's situation. Perhaps he couldn't go into detail about his case, which involved some thorny issues, such as the diplomatic relationship between the two countries and Gary's future usefulness or uselessness to China. I veered the conversation a bit, asking, "To the Chinese government, how big an agent was my dad?"

"Gary was in a class all his own, our highest-ranking spy."

That was a shock. "But—he was a general merely on paper, wasn't he?"

"Not at all. The intelligence he sent back . . . helped China make right decisions that were vital to our national security. Some of the information from Gary . . . went to Chairman Mao directly."

"So for that he earned his due?"

"Yes. His rank was higher than mine, although he had started later and lower than me." Chu paused as if to gather his strength. He resumed, "In intelligence circles, very few can reach the rank of general . . . purely by their abilities and contributions. Gary was an exception. He got promoted to general, well deserved. I couldn't catch up with him."

"You didn't become a general?"

"I'd been a colonel . . . for more than twenty years before I retired. I thought they might give me the big promotion, but they did not, because I didn't have enough pull and resources."

"What do you mean by 'resources'?"

"Basically money and wealth. You had to bribe the people in key positions. At any rate, Gary was different from the rest of us . . . and earned his promotions, granted directly from the top.

To tell the truth, in the seventies, my colleagues would pronounce his name with reverence."

"You mean they regarded him as a hero?"

"Also a legend."

Again my father's gaunt face appeared in my mind's eye, but I suppressed it. I looked through my list of questions and asked again, "Uncle Bingwen, did you ever meet my father's first wife, Yufeng Liu?"

His face fell as if I had hit a wrong note. He said, "I met her once, in nineteen sixty . . . when I went down to the countryside to attend . . . your grandfather's funeral. We used to mail her money every month, but later we lost contact. She left their village in the early sixties. I have no idea where she is now . . . or if she's still alive."

"You have no information on her at all?"

"I have something." He stood and went over to a bookcase. He pulled open a drawer, took out a spiral notebook, and tore off a page. "Here's her old address in the countryside. Like I said, she relocated, so we stopped sending her Gary's salary."

I folded the paper and put it into my inner jacket pocket. "Why wouldn't she let you know her new address so that she could get paid?" I asked.

"Money became worthless during the three famine years. I guess that could be a reason. Or maybe she got married again . . . and wouldn't want to be tied to your dad legally anymore."

We went on to talk about my father's personal relationship with his handler. Chu insisted that the two of them had been bound together "like a pair of grasshoppers on one string." It was Gary's role as a top agent in the enemy's heart, the CIA, that helped Chu, Gary's sole handler, survive the political shifts and consolidate his position in intelligence circles in Beijing. For that he was still grateful to my father. In his view Gary was undoubtedly a hero, whose deeds all the Chinese should remember.

Chu seemed to be carried away by his remembrances, growing warmer and chattier as he went on. Evidently he had few opportunities to speak his mind like this. While I was wondering if it was time to take my leave, he said, "Do you know . . . you have some half siblings?"

"My father mentioned them in his diary. But he spent only a few weeks with Yufeng before he left home. Are you sure they're his children?"

Chu chuckled. "Absolutely. Yufeng gave birth to twins, a boy and a girl, in the fall of 1949. I told your father about them. The two kids really took after him."

His words, though casually said, struck me, and my cheeks heated up. I had known about my half siblings but questioned their paternity. Something like a wash of shame crept over me as I realized I had unconsciously attempted to distance my half siblings from our father ever since I came to know of their existence. Before saying good-bye, I held Chu's blotchy hand with both of mine and thanked him for speaking to me.

Now I was more determined than ever to find my father's first family.

1950

Gary had been in Okinawa since the previous winter, working for a U.S. radio station with which his former cultural agency had merged. It was early summer now and rained almost every day. He liked the climate on the whole, mild in the winter but damp in the spring. The clouds, fluffy like cotton candy, looked low enough that you could reach out and snatch a piece. Once in a while he'd sit at the seaside, gazing at the turquoise ocean, its color turning brighter toward the horizon, and as he breathed the fetid whiffs that wafted over from rotten seaweed, he'd sink into thoughts about his homeland. When the tide was coming in, small whitecaps would lap the coral reefs, sloshing up scummy foam. The open flattish landscape hardly changed color through the seasons and could be drab. It was here that for the first time he'd seen palm-tree groves and sugarcane thickets. He enjoyed strolling along the trails on hillslopes alone. On those short excursions, he often ran into locals walking barefoot, women carrying bundles of susuki grass on their heads and small boys, naked above their waists, tending goats or looking for artillery shell fragments, each holding a straw basket. They'd greet him with a smile or a cry of recognition, as if he were Japanese.

Gary liked the rural feel of this place. Seafood was daily fare, though he still couldn't eat raw fish and would avoid sushi whenever he dined out with Thomas and his other colleagues. If they happened to end up at a Japanese restaurant, he could manage a few fish rolls wrapped in nori, but absolutely no sashimi, which had once upset his stomach. "Food poisoned," he'd told the others. Nor would he drink sake with ice in it like his colleagues; he preferred to have it the Asian way, just the plain liquor. To avoid overspending, most times he ate at the canteen that served American food. He disliked cheese, undercooked steaks, meat loaf, and funny-tasting salads. Once in a while he went to a local eatery that offered decent noodles, usually covered with a hard-boiled egg cut in half and five or six slices of pork or calamari, accompanied by half a dozen pot stickers as a side dish. Thank heaven Okinawans used soy sauce and bean paste.

His workplace was close to the U.S. military base, the vast airfield bringing to mind a townscape at night, but during the day the planes droned and roared continually. He was an official translator now, gleaning and compiling information from Chinese-language periodicals published in Hong Kong, Taiwan, and the mainland. On occasion he also translated articles from English into Chinese, mostly short propaganda pieces that the radio station broadcast to Red China. His English was excellent by now, and in his free time he read the novels of D. H. Lawrence, cheaply printed editions from Hong Kong. He liked the novelist's poetic prose, the spontaneous narrative flow, the earthy myth, and also the daring eroticism.

Unlike him, his American colleagues would frequent bars and nightclubs, where they picked up girls. Gary seldom went out and was known as a bachelor. He missed his wife and wished he had spent more time with her. How he regretted having left Shanghai in a hurry without writing her another letter. Now any kind of communication was out of the question. Lying in bed at night with crickets exchanging tremulous chirps (*chee chee chee chee*) and dogs barking fitfully in the distance (*wow wow wow wow*), he would ask himself why he hadn't thought about the consequences of leaving his homeland and why he hadn't voiced to his higher-ups any misgivings about his assignment. Perhaps deep in his heart there'd been the desire to leave home to see the broad world so that he could grow into a man with a wider vision and a mature mind. A professor of his had once told him that he had to read ten thousand books and travel a hundred thousand miles to become a real man. But that couldn't be true; not everyone had to leave home to grow up.

Every night before going to sleep, he'd think of Yufeng for a while. The more he thought about her, the more excruciating their separation felt, as though her absence had only tightened the tie between them. He would replay her words and actions in his mind. Some of her phrases and facial expressions had been growing mysterious and more vivid, pregnant with meanings he couldn't decipher. Sometimes in the middle of the night he'd awake with a start, feeling his wife standing at the head of his bed and observing him. Her breathing was ragged while her eyes radiated resentment. He wondered whether his preoccupation with her was due to his sense of guilt, but concluded it was not. He cherished Yufeng, believing he couldn't have found a better wife. If only he could again hold her in his arms, caress her silky skin, and inhale the musk of her hair.

At the radio station there was a Filipino man who spoke Japanese fluently and a Vietnamese man who knew French well. Both of them were formal and polite at work but turned foulmouthed like the Americans as soon as they called it a day. They had their families with them, yet once in a while they'd go to nightclubs to see local girls dance. They would wave dollar bills and packets of chewing gum at the performers while crying, "Shake it! Shake it!" Gary went with them once but regretted having spent ten dollars in less than two hours. He blamed himself for such extravagance as he remembered the rustic life his parents and wife had been living back home. He wouldn't go to a place like that again.

As the only Chinese translator here, he handled all the Chinese-language publications and could follow events in China. Time and again the Communists declared they would liberate Taiwan in the near future, but their plan for the liberation was thwarted by the lost battle on Jinmen, an island about six miles east of Amoy. The previous summer the People's Liberation Army had launched an attack with three regiments—more than nine thousand men in all, assuming that the Nationalist troops hadn't been able to build their defenses on the island yet. Under cover of darkness the assaulting force landed on a vast beach, but right after they arrived, the tide began falling away and made it impossible for the three hundred boats to go back to fetch reinforcements and provisions. As a result, the landed soldiers, some having seen the ocean for the first time, had no choice but to charge ahead at the defending positions. When it was daylight all the attackers were fully exposed on the beach, so the Nationalist army shelled them with artillery and raked them with machine guns. Then bombers came and destroyed all the stranded boats, a few of which were even loaded with live pigs and chickens, jars of rice wine, crates of liquor, and boxes of cash for the expected victory celebration.

Before dusk, the invading troops were routed, and some fled to the hills, but they were either killed or captured. All told, about three thousand men were taken prisoner. The lost battle was a huge blow to the Communists' plan to cross Taiwan Strait, and Mao had no option but to put "the liberation of Taiwan" on hold for the time being. If they attacked any island again, they'd have to be able to crush the defenders with overwhelming force. Gary realized that so long as the People's Liberation Army was preparing to capture Taiwan, his superiors might not call him back, because they would need military intelligence from him. He dreaded getting mired in Okinawa for good.

Through reading reports, interviews, and private talks, Gary could see that the Americans didn't trust Chiang Kai-shek. They believed that the Nationalist government and army were too corrupt to have any future. Just a few years back the United States had granted them two billion dollars in aid, assuming they'd be able to hold the Communists in check, if not to root them out. But all the money vanished in the fire and smoke of lost battles and in some top officials' pockets, and the whole of China went Red in just four years. It was whispered that the White House had been seriously looking for someone in the Nationalist army to replace Chiang. Gary could also see that the Americans had no plan for defending Taiwan at all. This meant that on their own the Nationalist forces could hardly defend the island state, so mainland China should attack it as soon as possible.

In addition, the native Taiwanese didn't like the Nationalist regime, which had been ruling the island with terror and blood. Thousands of educated natives had been rounded up and killed; many disappeared without a trace. Even some mainlanders who'd fled to Taiwan resented the brutality. The previous summer hundreds of middle schoolers from Shandong, to whom the Nationalist government had promised uninterrupted education, had been forced to join its army; a number of student representatives had protested to the officers but only got bayoneted. Later the military court tried the activists involved in resisting the coerced service— two middle school principals and five students were sentenced to death. The deaths of those men and teenage boys from his home province made Gary hate the Nationalist regime all the more.

Everything in Taiwan indicated that the government was quite shaky and could be toppled easily. Gary wanted to see his country unified soon so it would be more powerful in fighting imperialism and colonialism. He was excited by the tidbits of intelligence he had gathered, considering them valuable to the mainland, and he even wrote a long summary of what he'd found, a kind of analysis of the current situation in East Asia, but since he was still altogether isolated, he had no idea where to send the intelligence. He felt frustrated and even wondered if his comrades, consumed with building the new country, had forgotten him.

In the meantime, the storm of war was gathering on the Korean Peninsula. It was reported that Kim Il Sung had claimed he was going to overthrow the U.S.-backed puppet government in Seoul, but no one took his threat seriously. Then, in late June, he launched a full-scale attack with ten divisions, all equipped with Russian-made weapons. Seoul fell in three days. The South Korean forces and the U.S. troops couldn't stop the invading army and began retreating south toward Pusan. Kim Il Sung proclaimed that his soldiers, "Stalin's warriors," would drive the enemies all down into the Pacific in a matter of weeks. But his army soon became battle-fatigued and depleted, unable to break the U.S. final defense line—their T-34 tanks' rubber-clad wheels were melted by napalm, their troops were slaughtered by American bombers that came from the ocean, and within two months they'd lost more than fifty thousand men. Although they managed to surround Pusan in late August, they couldn't finish the battle; their offense bogged down.

Then, in mid-September, General MacArthur succeeded in landing eighteen thousand marines at Inchon. From there the American troops proceeded to cut the North Koreans' supply lines and attack them from the rear. The Communist army crumbled instantly and had to retreat helter-skelter. MacArthur declared that the U.S. forces would go after them and wipe them out wherever they were. In no time Seoul was taken back, and all Kim's soldiers were fleeing north. Still, the U.S. army wouldn't stop pursuing them. It looked like the war would soon reach the bank of the Yalu. In response to the crisis, Zhou Enlai, the Chinese premier, told K. M. Panikkar, the Indian ambassador to Beijing: "China will not sit back and watch if the U.S. army crosses the Thirty-Eighth Parallel to invade North Korea." His warning was dismissed by the White House. Indeed, how could a weak, war-battered China confront a global superpower? Who wouldn't take Zhou's words for a mere bluff?

But Gary understood how the Chinese Communist leaders' minds worked—in general, they wouldn't have said anything they couldn't back up with force. He didn't want to see a war break out between the United States and the new China, which was only a year old and couldn't afford such a confrontation. It was time to keep peace, reconstruct the country, and let the populace recover from the destruction of the civil war. Yet the two countries seemed unable to understand each other, heading toward a frontal clash. Two days after the Korean War broke out, President Truman had declared that he'd decided to dispatch the Seventh Fleet to block-ade Taiwan Strait. To Gary, as well as to most Chinese, this was a blatant affront, because evidently the United States dared not confront the Soviet Union and vented its spleen on China instead. The American warships steaming toward Taiwan Strait shattered China's plan for imminent national unification, since there was no way it could fight the powerful U.S. navy. Outraged, a Chinese delegate at the UN asked the world: "Can you imagine that because Mexico has a civil war, the United Kingdom is entitled to seize Florida?" Zhou Enlai also announced that Truman's declaration and the U.S. navy's blockade constituted an armed invasion of China's territory. But all the announcements and warnings were ignored by the West.

In translating the Chinese warnings in the intelligence report he compiled for the CIA, Gary deliberately toned up the original a bit, and whenever possible, he'd render the wording more striking. If there was a choice between "will" and "determination," he would pick the latter; or he would pass over "resist" for "fight back." Deep down, he knew no politician or general might notice the nuances of his word choices. Indeed, who would pay attention to his little verbal maneuvers? The sense of futility depressed him, though some of his American colleagues were agog, thrilled that the United States was flexing its military muscles again. Everybody at the agency had more work to do all of a sudden. Gary resented some of his colleagues' bragging about the might of the aircraft carriers and the battleships equipped with sixteen-inch guns, but he had to keep a straight face. If only he could get in touch with the Chinese side and let them know they should find another way to get their intentions across to the United States.

Thomas and Gary were eating dinner together in the canteen one evening. "Jesus, it's hot here," said Thomas, his face so pale that tiny blue veins were visible beside his nose. His annual furlough had just been denied, and he was upset.

"The sun's intense," Gary echoed. Indeed, at six p.m. the sun was still as fierce and stinging as it was at noon.

"It looks like we might stay here for another couple of years. I hate Kim Il Sung, the bloodthirsty bastard!" Thomas put a piece of roast chicken in his mouth, his strong jaw moving up and down.

"I miss home a lot too," Gary confessed and forced a grin.

"If I'm stuck here too long, my fiancée might send me a Dear John letter, hee hee hee hee."

"No, she won't," Gary said, wondering why Thomas laughed like that, as if he were suppressing a hacking cough. The man must feel sick at heart and might go berserk if he lost his woman.

Unlike Gary, the other Asians on staff were elated by the war on the Korean Peninsula, because it would enable them to work here for a longer time. The pay was good and the food rich; they had PX privileges and free medical care; better still, their children could go to the American school. Gary couldn't help but envy those men who had their families with them, each living in a cozy Japanese bungalow that had glossy wood floors and black ceramic tiles on the roof. If only he could speak and act freely like others, especially like the GIs, many of whom kept local girlfriends.

Henry and I emailed each other every day, but I didn't call him very often. On average we spoke once a week. When he wrote, he sounded at ease and cheerful. He was a large man, six foot one, and weighed more than 210 pounds. I often reminded him not to overeat and to watch his weight. Also, he mustn't forget to take lisinopril in the morning for his blood pressure. In all likelihood he enjoyed being alone, reliving his bachelor days for a spell. He was fond of reading books, particularly war histories, and must have had more time for them now. In his messages he called himself "a grass widower." I missed him, his carefree laugh, his small talk, the touch of his hands. I hadn't slept alone for years, and at night my body was still unused to the discomfort of solitude.

My father's home village had been on my mind ever since my meeting with Bingwen Chu. I was my parents' only child, half Chinese and half Irish; that made me American. I couldn't stop wondering what my half siblings were like. Already in their early sixties, they must have grandchildren. Even if they were no longer in Shandong, there must be relatives on my father's side down in the country. That's where I would start to look for them. I scrapped the thought of telephoning the village, which I wanted to see with my own eyes to have a concrete sense of the place and the people. Moreover, there would probably be many Shangs in the countryside, and I might find family connections. I'd go first to Maijia Village in Linmin County, Shandong.

I bought a SinoMap from Spring Rain Bookstore and perused it. Linmin is approximately two hundred miles south of Beijing, just beyond the border of Hebei province. It's near the expressway that runs from the capital to Shanghai. Perhaps I could make a quiet trip on a weekend I thought, but I didn't have a Chinese driver's license and couldn't rent a car. Should I borrow one from a friend or colleague? Or ask somebody to rent one for me? No, I mustn't drive with my Maryland license. If caught, I'd get others and myself in trouble. Should I take a bus then? That might be too much hassle. I was sure there was no direct bus service from Beijing to Linmin. If I took a bus, I'd have to go to a city first, say, Dezhou or Jinan, then switch buses. That would be a long detour. If a train had run through Linmin, I'd have taken it and made a secret trip on my own, but the town had no railroad. In fact, I enjoyed traveling alone in China, where people tended to view me as a Chinese as long as I didn't open my mouth to speak at length. Somehow since my early forties, my Irish features—sharp cheekbones, grayish eyes, chestnut hair—had begun to fade, and I looked more Asian each year, as if my Chineseness had been pushing out from within and manifesting itself on my face.

In my graduate seminar I had a student named Minmin, who always wore stone-washed jeans and teardrop earrings. She happened to have a car, a China-made Volkswagen Santana, a popular model among low-level officials and white-collar professionals. I'd seen her drive the green sedan. After class one afternoon I called her into my office and asked whether, as a favor, she'd make a trip with me in her car. Without hesitation Minmin, slender and with dark round eyes, agreed to accompany me to Shandong.

"I'll pay you two thousand yuan for three days, plus gas and all the other expenses," I told her.

"No need for that, Professor Shang."

"Uh-uh, call me Lilian."

"Okay, Lilian, I'd be happy to go and see the countryside with you. You don't need to pay me."

"You'll work for me for a few days, so I've got to pay you. Make sure the car is in best running condition, will you?"

"It's my older brother's car. He has four of them and keeps them all serviced regularly."

"That's good. Don't let anyone know of the trip. I just want to see what my father's home village is like."

"I won't let it slip, of course."

The college wouldn't want foreign teachers to move around freely, because it was responsible for our behavior and safety. Minmin and I decided to meet at my place early Saturday morning. She was one of those grad students who I suspected planned to go abroad eventually to work toward a PhD or professional degree, so I assumed she might want to have me as a reference in the future. I liked her for her vivacious personality and her tinkling laughter, which often raised her classmates' eyebrows.

We set out around seven a.m. on Saturday. I was wearing a plain flannel jacket and no makeup. This way I looked like a professional Chinese woman. Actually, I'd just given away my new parka (bought at Macy's specially for my Fulbright stint), because a fine long coat was inconvenient in China—wearing it, you couldn't sit down freely on dingy buses and subways, or walk on a bustling street where automobiles might spatter dirty water on you, or mix with pedestrians casually, running, pushing, and jostling to get where you wanted to be.

It took Minmin and me almost an hour to get out of Beijing, where many streets were jammed and the area near the Great Hall of the People was blocked by the police to make way for a motorcade. But once we got on the expressway, traffic became sparse and we started cruising with ease. The new eight-lane road, four lanes each way, was well built, washed clean and shiny by a rainsquall before dawn. Minmin was at the wheel, her narrow hands in the nine and three positions. She said she'd never driven such a long distance before; at most she'd spun to Huairou, a town about forty miles north of Beijing, so she was excited about this trip. The roadsides were hardly used, and only a couple of billboards appeared along the way. I noticed that the tolls were expensive. The ticket Minmin had picked up at the entrance to the highway stated seventy-six yuan from the capital to Tianjin, about twelve dollars for ninety miles. That might account for the scarce traffic.

It was warm for mid-March, and patches of distant woods were just in leaf, the fuzzy branches shimmering a little. Spring seemed to be coming early this year. It had been a dry, warm winter in the Beijing area, and it had snowed only once, lightly. Somehow since getting out of the city, we hadn't encountered any of the police cars that were omnipresent in Beijing. I gathered that only on the highway could you escape the police's surveillance, though the absence of the slashing strobes and blasting bullhorns gave me more discomfort than ease.

As we were approaching Tianjin, we saw a brand-new billboard that declared: WELCOME MIGRANT WORKERS!

"That sounds fishy," Minmin said, flicking her fingers dismissively.

"Unconvincing at least," I agreed, knowing how migrant workers were viewed by common Beijingers—like underclass citizens; their children couldn't even go to public schools. It had always bothered me that the Chinese were not born equal in spite of their constitution that guarantees every citizen the same rights. People from the countryside, greatly deprived compared with city dwellers, had to own real estate in a city in order to become its legal residents. Even though this was an improvement over the former policy, which did not allow country people to become legal urbanites at all, it was still discriminatory. It reminded me of the investment immigration practiced in North America, where a large sum of money can buy a U.S. green card or a Canadian maple leaf card. Yet I'd never heard a Chinese complain about the discrimination against the country people. As a matter of fact, most Chinese viewed the current policy as a progressive step toward reducing the gap between the country and the city. I once asked a reporter why this inequality hadn't raised any public outcry, and he merely shook his head and gave a resigned smile.

I had not expected to travel so fast. Within three hours we'd almost reached the border of Shandong province, so we pulled off the expressway to grab a bite. We found a restaurant called Jade Terrace, where the waitstaff wore tangerine-colored shirts and white aprons. A thin young waiter with a raw, new haircut seated us and asked, "What would you two beauties like for lunch?"

"I'm no beauty," I said. "I'll become a senior citizen in a few years, so save that word for a nice-looking girl."

Nonplussed, he looked at Minmin inquiringly, then they both laughed out loud. I had a problem with the term *meinü*, a beauty, employed indiscriminately by the Chinese. Every young woman was called that, whether she was homely or beautiful. I disliked such a careless use of language, which blurred the actual forms of things and ideas. The word "beauty" ought to refer to someone who at least had some pretty features. My objection to the waiter's greeting also implied I knew I was average-looking.

We ordered steamed fish, spiced tofu skin mixed with mustard greens, and sautéed lotus root to go with rice. I calculated that we should be able to reach Linmin in less than two hours. "Let's relax and take our time," I told Minmin, who was fanning herself with a menu. It was warm inside the dining room, the air thick with the smell of frying oil.

Our order came, all at once. To my amazement, the fish was a sizable salmon fillet, garnished with a few slivers of daikon and two sprigs of cilantro. I told Minmin, "I don't think I ever saw salmon in China twenty years ago."

"This fish was imported," she said.

"But they sell the dish for only twenty-two yuan here. How can they make money?"

"I don't mean the full-grown salmon were imported. The fry were originally bought from Europe and then sold to domestic fish farmers. So this salmon must have come from a local farm."

"I see." I noticed that she didn't touch the fish and served herself only the tofu skin and the vegetables. "You don't like salmon?" I asked.

"I like it, but it's not safe to eat fish randomly. Don't ever eat fish heads and innards at restaurants. A fillet might be all right, less contaminated."

"Contaminated by what?" I asked in surprise.

"Chemicals. My brother saw local farmers feed their fish lots of antibiotics to keep them alive in polluted ponds."

"Oh, I see," I said. Food contamination was indeed a major problem in China. Just a week ago I had read in a newspaper that a small boy died after eating two pork buns bought at a food stand. It was also common knowledge that contaminated baby formula and poisonous milk were still rampant in some cities and towns. Word had it that thousands of infants had been sickened by drinking milk adulterated with melamine, a chemical used in making plastics. But I was nearly fifty-four and wasn't terribly bothered by the problem. I told Minmin, "By Chinese standards I'm an old woman and shouldn't worry too much. But you youngsters should be more careful about what you eat."

"Especially when you want to get married and have a baby," she said.

Minmin mentioned that her sister-in-law had been on a strict diet to detoxify her body so that she could have a better chance of giving birth to "a clean, healthy baby."

"What does she eat? Vegetables and fruits only?" I asked.

"No. Some vegetables aren't safe either, like napa cabbage, leeks, bean sprouts, tomatoes. Leeks are the worst because you have to use a lot of insecticide to keep worms from eating the roots."

"What vegetables are safe then?"

"Potatoes, taros, carrots, turnips. This is okay too." She picked up a perforated slice of lotus root.

"How long will your sister-in-law continue to detox?"

"A whole year. Besides the diet, she must drink an herbal soup every day."

"Ugh, I'd rather eat contaminated food." It gave me a chill just to think of the bitter medicinal liquid.

Minmin went on to say that her brother, a real estate developer, had urged his wife to go live in L.A. so she could give birth to their baby there. "Besides the better living environment," Minmin said, "the child would become a U.S. citizen. But my stupid sister-in-law won't go, saying she's afraid of America and doesn't mind living and dying in China, blah blah blah. What she really fears is that my brother might shack up with another woman in her absence, so she claims she doesn't want to be a new member of the Mistress Village in L.A."

I laughed but immediately covered my mouth with my palm. Hundreds of young Chinese women, mostly mistresses of wealthy businessmen and powerful officials, had been living in a suburb of L.A. where they could get around without speaking English and where a whole support system was provided for those expectant mothers. The gated community was nicknamed the Mistress Village, a moniker that often cropped up in the Chinese media.

We left more than half the salmon untouched. I picked up the tab and gave the waiter two five-yuan bills for a tip, which made him smile gratefully now that most Chinese diners, as was the custom, didn't offer a gratuity. We hit the highway again around one p.m., and the drive was so smooth that we arrived at Linmin just after three o'clock. The county seat was like a small city, new mid-rise buildings everywhere, a few with gray granite-like façades. The streets were noisy and smelled of boiled peanuts, baked yams, popcorn, deep-fried fish. At a farmers' market the last few produce vendors were still hawking their wares. Cars were honking, tractors' two-stroke engines puttering, horses and donkeys pawing the ground, all eager to go home. On a busy street a couple of neon signs flickered here and there, beckoning people to beauty salons, foot spas, karaoke bars, massage parlors. At a tea stand I asked an old man for directions to Maijia Village, and he said it was south of the town, about three miles away. We avoided regular hotels, fearing they might request my ID. If they discovered I was a foreigner, they would report me to the local police. We checked into a family inn, or a guesthouse as the locals called it. Minmin told the young receptionist that I was her aunt, so the girl didn't ask for my ID card, which every Chinese citizen had. We shared a twin room.

1953

By the spring of 1953 Gary had been in Okinawa for three and a half years. He had learned to drive and bought a jeep from an officer who had returned to Hawaii. Sometimes he drove along the military highway to a beach spread with white sand or to a bay lined with red pines and banyan trees, where he'd sit alone, breathing the briny air, lost in his thoughts. He'd begun to smoke and liked American cigarettes, particularly Chesterfields and Camels. In the summer he would don a perforated straw boater, but he wore a felt derby in the other seasons. His hats, fine suits, and patent-leather shoes made him appear a bit dashing, though he always gave off a solitary air and the impression of being absentminded—something of a loner who was careful about his appearance but didn't know how to blend in. By now his homesickness had grown into a kind of numbness, a dull pain deep in his heart. He felt its heaviness constantly but took it as a sign of maturity, as though he at last had the fortitude needed for fulfilling his mission.

The semimilitary life gave him a sense of discipline, while his daily work helped him keep at bay the memories of his family and homeland. During the past two years he had also developed a love for popular American singers, above all Hank Williams. He borrowed the records from the radio station's library and played them on a phonograph with a trumpet speaker that he'd bought second-hand. He learned some of the lyrics by heart and couldn't help letting the tunes reverberate in his mind. When strolling on a beach or along a winding trail, he would croon to himself, "Well, why don't you love me like you used to do? / How come you treat me like a worn-out shoe?" Or with a measure of cruel self-mockery, "No matter how I struggle or strive / I'll never get out of this world alive." Or touched by a fit of self-pity, "As I wonder where you are /

I'm so lonesome I could cry." Those songs would bring tears to his eyes as though he were a jilted lover whose moaning and pining didn't make any sense to others. Yet he would force himself to hum them as a way to toughen himself.

He'd been devastated in late October 1950, when the Chinese army ambushed and mauled the U.S. troops east of the Yalu. Hearing the news, he hurried out of his office and stood behind an Indian almond tree in the backyard, hiding his face in the glossy leaves while tears streamed down his cheeks. He pressed his forehead against the damp trunk and stayed there for almost an hour. He could not explain why he reacted so viscerally. By instinct he must have sensed that because the two countries had virtually gone to war, he might become more valuable to China, which would, he was sure, assign him dangerous tasks. In other words, he might have a long spying career ahead. He hated to be put in such a position and felt marooned, but he kept reminding himself to be more patient. Indeed, every worthy spy must have iron patience, being capable of taking refuge in solitude while biding his time. Ultimately everything would depend on how much he could endure.

The Chinese army's initial victories didn't hearten Gary, because he knew China was a weak country and couldn't fight the war for long without the Soviets' backing. When news came of the horrendous casualties the Chinese had suffered, Gary suspected that his countrymen had been used as cannon fodder for the Russians. His suspicion was verified later on. Through translating articles and reports, he chanced on information unknown to the public. The Soviets had provided a great quantity of weapons for the Chinese troops in Korea, but Stalin gave them only limited air cover east of the Yalu, just down to the Ch'ongch'on River. Consequently, most of the Chinese and North Korean army units were exposed to the U.S. air attacks and dared not move around in daylight. Only by night could their vehicles get on the road. Still, American bombers devastated the Communist forces. That was why Lin Biao, the most brilliant and experienced of Mao's generals, foreseeing this horrifying slaughter, had refused to take command of the Chinese army in Korea, and Beijing had no choice but to appoint Marshal Peng Dehuai the commander.

Summer in Okinawa was sultry in spite of the cool breeze coming from the ocean at night, but this year Gary didn't have to put up with the heat and humidity of the dog days again. In late July he was dispatched to Pusan to help interrogate the POWs held by the UN side. He was pleased about the assignment, believing that once in Korea, he might be able to find a way to contact his superiors back in China. Also, he was eager for a change. The armistice had just been signed, and no more large-scale fighting would be likely, because every party involved seemed too exhausted to continue. The war had reached its tail end. Gary boarded a C-119 one early-August morning and landed in Pusan four hours later.

There were too many POWs for the UN personnel to interrogate. From the Chinese army alone, more than twenty-one thousand men were held prisoner, mostly captured in the spring of 1951. The Chinese had been mangled severely in their fifth-phase offensive, and a whole division, the 180th, was liquidated. That forced North Korea and China back to the negotiation table with the UN. But the talks dragged on and on owing to the thorny issue of the POWs. Many of the Chinese prisoners had served in the Nationalist army before (they'd been caught and then recruited by the Communists) and dreaded returning to the mainland because they'd been instructed never to surrender in Korea, even at the cost of their lives. Fearful of punishment, they wanted to go to Taiwan and rejoin the Nationalist army there. Chiang Kai-shek was badly short of soldiers, so he welcomed these men, whose return to their former ranks would also make the Communists lose a battle on the propaganda front. So some Nationalist officials flew in to persuade more Chinese prisoners to sail for Taiwan.

Gary served as the interpreter when the top U.S. prison officers received the Nationalist emissaries, who were not allowed to enter the jail compounds. At most they could meet the POW representatives with barbed-wire fences between them. Nevertheless, they managed to deliver to the prisoners Chiang Kai-shek's personal presents: cigarettes, playing cards, toffees, books, musical instruments, and a wool overcoat for every man willing to go to Taiwan. Though Gary was not a POW, the Nationalist delegates gave him some presents as well, including a trench coat and a canvas rucksack.

Gary stayed in a makeshift cottage in the POW collection center on the outskirts of Pusan. The ocean was within view, and large ships in the harbor loomed like little hills in the morning mist. On a fine day fishing boats would bob on the distant swells. The water was uneven in color, some areas yellow and some green. To the north, outside the immense prison camp, spread endless rice paddies, some unsown, choked by algae and weeds. The bustling city was full of refugees. All kinds of Korean civilians had swarmed here and put up temporary shelters; even the nearby slopes were dappled with patches of tents and shacks built of straw, plywood, and corrugated iron. Gary could see that the soil here was rich and the climate congenial. He saw giant apples and pears for sale, much bigger than those in China, and he couldn't help but imagine how good this place could be in peace. Fluent in both English and Mandarin, he was appreciated by his superiors and peers. He also mixed well with the officers from Taiwan who were here to help the UN with the prison's administrative work. Most of these officers would stay just a few months. Gary often sat at their tables at mealtimes and also shared cigarettes and beer with them.

One day at lunch, as Gary was eating a Salisbury steak with a dill pickle, Meng, a broad-shouldered Taiwanese officer in his mid-thirties, came and sat down across from him. The man's bold eyes shone with excitement while he gave a cockeyed grin. He said to Gary under his breath, "Mind you, I'm having low back pain."

That sounded familiar. Then it hit Gary that those words were part of a code for initiating contact. He responded according to the script, "Your kidneys must be weak. Herbal medicine might help."

"What kind would you recommend?" Meng asked calmly.

"Six-flavor boluses."

"How many should I take?"

"Two a day, one in the morning and one in the evening."

A knowing smile emerged on Meng's face. Gary's heart began thumping as he was convinced that this man in the Nationalist army's uniform was an agent working for the mainland. With practiced casualness Gary looked around and saw two American officers eating a few tables away, but they didn't understand Mandarin.

"Brother"—Meng leaned in—"I know you meet prisoners every day. The boss wants you to get hold of the photos of the diehard anti-Communists among them."

"I'll see what I can do, but they all go by aliases," Gary said.

"We know that. That's why we need their pictures."

"When should I give you the goods?"

"I'll return to Taipei soon. You should contact Hong Kong to see how to deliver them."

"Using the old communication channel?"

"Correct."

That was their only meeting, and Meng left Pusan three days later. Gary continued to join the U.S. officers in interrogating the Chinese POWs. He was respected by his colleagues for knowing some of the prisoners' dialects and for understanding their psychology. In the beginning he had sympathized with those POWs who still had unhealed wounds, but he was jaded by now. Some prisoners would weep wretchedly like small boys and beg the UN officers to send them to Generalissimo Chiang's army in Taiwan. Some kept complaining about being bullied by others, particularly by their prison-compound leaders, handpicked by their captors. Some remained reticent, only repeating, "I want to go home." A few, the minute they sat down, would curse their interrogators and even call Gary "the Americans' running dog." There was a fellow, his face and limbs burned by napalm, who would make a strange noise in response to the interrogators' questions, and Gary couldn't tell whether he was giggling or hissing or crying. One of his eyes never blinked; maybe it was already sightless. The files on the POWs were messy because the prisoners would frequently change their names, also because they were often regrouped in different prison units. And no staffer would take the trouble to set the files in order, everybody being overwhelmed with the work he had to do.

A number of POWs were leaders within the prison compounds and worked hard to persuade others to desert the Communist ranks. These men were quite obedient to the Americans and eager to curry favor with the prison administration. Whenever possible, Gary would strike up conversations with them, sharing cigarettes or candy or peanuts. He learned from them the calisthenics that the Chinese army had designed for its soldiers. He found many of these men using names different from those in their files. The prison administration wouldn't bother to straighten this out, or perhaps even encouraged them to adopt aliases as a disguise. Occasionally Gary would take a photo with one of those men as "a keepsake." Whenever it was possible, he'd bring their files back to his room, which he shared with an officer who'd always go out in the evenings. With his German camera Gary shot photos of some anti-Communists' files and kept a list of their names with cross-references to their current aliases.

When his Pusan stint was over, in late October, he returned to Okinawa with six films of the prisoners' files and resumed his work as a translator at the agency. He could have had the photos developed, but that might be too risky, so he put the films into a cloth pouch and tied its neck with a shoelace. He wrote to Hong Kong, to the old address, a Baptist seminary, which he'd been told to use in case of emergency.

To Gary's delight, Bingwen Chu wrote back two weeks later, saying in the voice of a fake cousin that Gary's family in the countryside was well and missed him, and the two of them should spend some time together in Hong Kong in February. As for the "medicine," Gary should go to Tokyo as soon as possible and deliver it to "a friend" there, who was an overseas Chinese. Bingwen provided the man's address in Shibuya district and described him as "a short, thickset fellow with a balding head and a Sichuan accent." Gary wondered why Bingwen and he couldn't meet somewhere in Japan. Then he realized that few Chinese agents, unable to speak a foreign tongue and unfamiliar with the life and customs of another country, would dare to undertake a mission in an environment where they had little control. This realization made him smile with a modicum of complacence, feeling he must be quite outstanding compared to his comrades back home, perhaps one in a thousand. Like his American colleagues who often went to the capital on weekends, he took a three-day leave, flew to Tokyo, and delivered the intelligence without incident.

Minmin and I started out for Maijia Village early the next morning. Once we got out of Linmin Town, I was amazed to see that most of the country roads were well paved, some new. The villages and small towns in this area seemed all connected by decent roads, though the asphalt was often littered with animal droppings. The drive was pleasant; there was little traffic at this early hour. We passed an immense reservoir fringed with reeds and sparkling in the sunlight, and then some wheat fields appeared, the stalks, their heads just developing, swaying a little in the breeze. Approaching Maijia Village, we saw a pond to our right, in which flocks of white ducks and geese were paddling. An old woman, a short sickle in her hand, was sitting on the bank, tending the fowl. We pulled up. As we stepped out of the car, she cackled, "Goosey, goosey, qua qua qua." We went over and asked her where the village chief's home was.

She pointed to the slanting columns of cooking smoke in the east and said, "There, beyond those houses. His home has red tiles on top."

We thanked her and drove over.

The village head was a man around fifty, with a strong build and large smiling eyes. He introduced himself as Mai after I said I was Weimin Shang's daughter and Minmin was my student. He seemed pleased to see us and asked his wife to serve tea. Seated on a drum-like stool in his sitting room with his ankle rested on his opposite knee, he told me that there were still more than a dozen Shang households in the village, but none of them was my father's immediate family. "Weimin Shang's parents died and his wife moved away," Mai said. "Nobody's here anymore."

For a moment I was too flummoxed to continue, my nose

became blocked, and I had difficulty breathing. Mai went on to say that because of a famine, Yufeng had left the village in the early 1960s for the northeast, where her younger brother had emigrated.

"Who knows?" Mai resumed. "Perhaps it was smart of her to leave. After the three years of famine came all the political movements, one after another, endless like all the bastards in the world. Your father's situation was a mystery to us. There were some rumors that said he'd taken off to Taiwan with Chiang Kai-shek, and some people heard he had died in a labor camp somewhere near Siberia. So if Yufeng hadn't left, she might've become a target of the revolution. There was no telling what might happen to her."

"Is there a way I can find her contact information?" I asked.

"Matter of fact, a cousin of your dad's is still around. He must know something about her whereabouts."

"Can you show me where he lives?"

"Sure thing, let's go."

Mai stood and we followed him out. Without extinguishing his cigarette butt, he dropped it on a manure pile in his yard. He said we could leave the car behind because we were going to walk just a few steps. I was unsure about that, but Minmin felt it was all right. "It's an old car anyway," she said. Together we headed toward the southern side of the village. It was quiet everywhere, and on the way all I saw were two dogs slinking around; they were so underfed that their ribs showed and their fur was patchy. The street was muddy, dotted with puddles of rainwater, some of them steaming and bubbling a little as if about to boil. There was trash scattered everywhere—instant noodle containers, glass bits, shattered pottery, rotten cabbage roots, candy wrappers, walnut shells, paper flecks from firecrackers that looked like the remnants of a wedding or funeral. A whiff of burning wood or grass was in the air and a few chimneys were spewing smoke.

We stopped at a black brick house behind an iron-barred gate, which Mai, without announcement, pushed open and led us in. The instant we entered, two bronze-colored chickens took off. One landed on a straw stack while the other caught a top rail of the pigpen, both clucking and fluttering their feathers. An old man was weaving a mat with the skins of sorghum stalks in the cement-paved yard. At the sight of us he tottered to his feet, his gray beard scanty but almost six inches long. Mai explained that I was Weimin Shang's daughter from Beijing. At that, the old man's eyes lit up and his mouth hung open. He turned away and whispered something to his wife, a large-framed woman with a knot of hair at the back of her head. He then said to me, "This is my wife, Ning."

"Very glad to meet you, Aunt Ning. I'm Lilian." I held out my hand, but she drew back a bit, then gingerly shook my hand, her palm rough and callused.

"Welcome," she mumbled.

"Come on, Weiren," Mai said to the old man. "Don't keep us standing like this."

So the host led us into the sitting room, which was also a bedroom. A large brick bed, a *kang*, took up almost half the space. On the whitewashed wall hung a glossy calendar that displayed the Golden Gate Bridge, and next to the picture was a garland of dried chilies, a few of them fissured, revealing the yellow seeds. Minmin went over to the picture of the bridge and blurted out, "Wow, this is gorgeous. Do you know where this is?" As soon as she said that, she bit the corner of her lips as if to admit a gaffe in assuming the host's ignorance.

Mai laughed while Uncle Weiren smiled, showing that only three or four teeth were left in his mouth. "Sure I know," the host said. "It's in the American city called Old Gold Mountain." That's the Chinese name for San Francisco.

Aunt Ning came in holding a kettle and served tea while Uncle Weiren offered us Red Plum cigarettes. Mai took one; Minmin and I declined. I lifted the mug and sipped the tea, which had a grassy flavor. The old man told me that his name, Weiren, meant he and my father were cousins. In other words, he was a real uncle of mine. All the males of their generation in the Shang clan had the same character, *wei,* in their personal names.

"I'm your grandpa's nephew," he added. "Your father and I are cousins."

"Do you remember my dad, Uncle Weiren?" I asked.

"You bet. He taught me how to dog-paddle when I was a little kid. I knew your first mother pretty well too. She was a kindhearted woman and once gave me a full pocket of roasted sunflower seeds." He was referring to Yufeng. Traditionally a man's children by his second and third wives also belonged to his first wife, who was the younger generation's "first mother."

"Where is Yufeng now? Do you know?" I said.

"In the northeast. Your sister used to write me at the Spring Festival, but her letters stopped coming after a couple of years."

"Why did they have to leave?" I asked. I had been plagued by the question for a long time. "Didn't the government provide for them?"

Uncle Weiren sighed, then took a deep drag on his cigarette. "They used to send her your dad's pay every month, but money became worthless during the famine. Rich or poor, folks all starved, and only the powerful had enough food."

"By docking others' rations," Mai said.

I asked Uncle Weiren, "But didn't my grandparents leave Yufeng some farmland?"

"Their land was taken away long ago, in the Land Reform Movement in the early fifties. Since then, all land belongs to the country."

"I see. So there was no way Yufeng could raise her kids here?"

Uncle Weiren stared at me, his bulging eyes a little bleary. He cleared his throat and said, "It was hard for her indeed. Your brother died of brain inflammation, but it was also believed he starved to death. All the Shangs in the village got angry at Yufeng, because the boy was the single seedling in your father's family. The old feudalistic mind-set, you know, that doesn't allow girls to carry on the bloodline. It wasn't fair to Yufeng really. She was an unfortunate woman, alone without a man in her home. How could she raise the kids by herself? To make things worse, your brother was weak from the day he was born. The Shangs here were all upset about his death, and some blamed Yufeng for it, but every family was too desperate to give her any help. It was not like nowadays, when we can afford to spare some food or cash."

"About a third of our village died in the famine," Mai said. "I remember wild dogs and wolves got fat and sleek feeding on corpses."

"That's awful," Minmin put in.

"So you drove Yufeng out of the village?" I asked Uncle Weiren, bristling with sudden anger.

"It didn't happen like that," the old man said. "She had a younger brother who was a foreman or something on a state-owned farm in the northeast. He wrote and said there was food in the Jiamusi area, so he wanted her to come join his family there. It was generous of him to do that. Also good for Yufeng."

"Especially when she was of no use to the Shangs anymore," I said.

"That's not what I mean. Lots of bachelors would eye her up and down whenever they ran into her. Many would whistle and let out catcalls. Even some married men wanted to make it with her. She was a fine woman, good-looking and healthy enough to draw a whole lot of attention. Some wicked men even tried to sneak into her house at night. Your father hadn't been around for such a long time, we didn't know whether he was dead or alive, so the village treated her more or less like a widow."

"Did she marry again in the northeast?" I asked.

"That I don't know. Truth to tell, I respected her. She was a good woman and had a sad, sad life."

Mai broke in, "My mom used to say that any man should feel blessed if he could have a wife like Yufeng. Folks really looked up to her. She had dexterous hands and made the thinnest noodles in the village. She could embroider gorgeous creatures like a phoenix, mandarin ducks, peacocks, and unicorns. Lots of girls went to her house to learn embroidery from her."

"Do you still have her address, Uncle Weiren?" I asked.

"I might've kept a letter from her daughter. Let me go check." He stood, pushed aside a cloth door curtain, and shuffled into the inner room.

I turned to Mai. "Doesn't Uncle Weiren have children?"

"He has a son and a daughter. Both are in Dezhou City and doing pretty well. The daughter teaches college there."

"So most of the Shangs are doing all right?"

"You bet. Yours is a clan that always valued education and books and has produced a good many officials and scholars. The Shangs have been respected in this area for hundreds of years."

That was news to me. Uncle Weiren came back and handed me a white envelope, partly yellowed with damp. As I took out a pen to copy the address, he stopped me, saying I could keep the letter. I thanked him and put it into my pocket. We went on conversing about the other Shang families in the village, some of whom were rather well-off now. I told them I was living and working in Beijing, though I'd grown up overseas, having a white mother. Minmin and I exchanged glances, her eyes rolling as if to assure me that she wouldn't breathe a word about my American citizenship. Such a revelation would only have complicated matters, drawing officials and even the police to the village, so I'd better let them assume I was a Chinese citizen and had lived in China for many years. I said my father had remarried because the Party wanted him to start another family abroad. When I told them that he had died in America long ago although he'd planned to retire back to China, they fell silent and didn't raise another question.

I learned that my grandparents' graves were outside the village. "Can I go and pay my respects to them?" I asked Uncle Weiren.

He appreciated the gesture, so we two set out with a shovel, a bunch of incense sticks, and a basket packed by Aunt Ning. Mai left for home, saying he had a business meeting; he owned two chicken farms and planned to start another one. Minmin went with him to fetch her car. She would stay behind to rest some since Uncle Weiren and I would soon come back for lunch. We were walking east and passed a poplar grove partly swathed in haze, some of the boles glowing silver in the sunlight and some of the leaves still damp with dew. Uncle Weiren told me that poplars had been in fashion in recent years because the trees were hardy and, fond of sandy soil, they grew fast (they can be ready for felling in eight or nine years), and the timber could bring a good price. Many families in the village had cleared patches of wild land and planted them with poplars. An acre could produce more than two hundred trees. Uncle Weiren had two acres of them, which was a virtually risk-free investment after the saplings had survived the first winter and spring. Once his poplars grew up and he sold the timber, he planned to expand his house to two stories. As long as the Party didn't change its current agricultural policies, he felt that the country folks' livelihood might improve some. In spite of my skepticism, I didn't contradict him. I had read that some poor families in the countryside couldn't pay taxes and abandoned their homes.

I didn't see a single child, and only a few middle-aged men and women greeted Uncle Weiren. When I asked him why there were so few children in the village, he said that all the young people had left to work in the cities and would come back only once a year, mostly at the Spring Festival. People didn't want to raise many children anymore, especially those young couples who already had a son. The one-child policy was still in place, but you might have more children if you were willing to pay heavy fines. "It costs too much to bring up kids," he continued. "There're still five or six tots in the village, in their grandparents' care. The others are all gone. Our elementary school closed down two years ago 'cause there weren't enough pupils. Parents pull their kids out of school earlier nowadays, even before they finish middle school."

"They won't send them to college anymore?" I asked.

"Way too expensive. Besides, after college they can't find good jobs. So why even bother?"

We passed a few mud and straw adobes, dilapidated and deserted, some overgrown with dried brambles. Uncle Weiren was silent while I lapsed into thought. This place seemed to be dying and might disappear in twenty years. Clearly there were people who'd gotten a raw deal in the national economic boom. In some poor areas more villagers had uprooted themselves to make a living in cities, and they might never return to their native places. I had read that in some regions in western China, entire villages were deserted. The demise of the village would surely transform the country from within. But how would this massive migration affect Chinese society as a whole? Who would benefit? At whose expense? What might be the consequences in the long run?

The decrepit scene reminded me of eighteenth-century Europe, where rural people were driven off their land and drawn to industrial centers to work in factories. China was a capitalist country in the making and was relentlessly consuming the young blood from the countryside.

My grandparents' graves were at the base of a foothill, where all the Shangs of the village were buried. Hundreds of mounds of earth spread to the side of a dried brook, many of them covered by wild grass. A few had wooden signs at the heads, but there wasn't a single headstone. We stopped at a pair of graves near the southern end of the burial ground. These two were unmarked and appeared identical with some others.

"Here they are," Uncle Weiren said.

"How can you tell?" I asked.

"We come here every spring to clean them up."

Indeed, the two graves looked just tended, so I added a few shovelfuls of earth to them. We lit the joss sticks and planted them before the mounds. Out of the basket Uncle Weiren took a half bottle of liquor and poured some in front of the incense. In the alcohol something whitish swayed like a stringy ginseng root; then

I was astonished to see that it was a tiny snake. Why did he offer snake liquor to my grandparents? Grandma couldn't have been fond of drinking, could she?

Uncle Weiren saw the shock on my face and said, "This is good stuff for old folks who have joint pains and backache. Your grandparents both had arthritis, I remember. I use a cup of this drink every day, so I thought they might like it too."

I didn't know what to make of that. Probably the bottle of liquor had just been handy. He could have brought along a new bottle without a snake in it. In any case, I thanked him, as if these graves had been my charge, not that of some relatives I'd never met. I took the apples and pears out of the basket and placed them in front of the graves, on two small flattish rocks I had picked up nearby. I stood and stepped aside to gather my courage. Then I returned to the graves, held my hands together before my chest, and said in Mandarin: "Dear Grandpa and Grandma, I came all the way to see you. We live far away, thousands of miles from here. My dad, your son, cannot come, so I am here on his behalf. He missed you and loved you. I love you too. Please forget your worries and rest in peace . . ."

As I was speaking, tears trickled down my cheeks. There was so much I didn't know how to say. I knew they had died in 1960, within three months of each other. My father had recorded this in his diary. After being informed of their deaths, he was laid up with grief in a hotel room in Hong Kong for two days.

To our right, about twenty feet away, was a pile of earth like a giant loaf. It had also been tended recently.

"That's your brother's grave," Uncle Weiren said.

I went over and added a few shovels of fresh dirt, then left an apple and a pear at the front of his grave. Though heavyhearted, I couldn't conjure up an image of him. If only I'd seen his photo.

Uncle Weiren and I went back to the house for lunch, which consisted of dough flake soup, fried toon leaves, and scrambled eggs. I was grateful for the simple meal, though I knew it might have become a banquet if I were a male family member. Both Minmin and I enjoyed the lozenge-shaped flakes used in place of noodles in the soup. Our good appetite pleased Aunt Ning, who continued to ladle more into our bowls. On the back of her hand was a tiny burn covered with ointment to prevent a blister from forming. This was the first time I'd eaten toon leaves, which were fragrant and had a mellow aftertaste. Their texture in the mouth reminded me of collard greens.

"Where did you get this, Aunt Ning?" I asked.

"From those trees." She pointed to the backyard, then to the dish. "This is from last year. In a month or so we can have fresh toon leaves."

I had assumed they were a vegetable grown in a field. My father had mentioned them several times in his diary, in addition to some herbs, such as amaranth, purslane, and shepherd's purse. In a late May entry he said that toon leaves were in season back home, and he must have been craving them.

After lunch I took two sets of Legos out of the trunk of Minmin's car and gave them to Uncle Weiren and Aunt Ning for their grandchildren. Then we said good-bye and drove back to the county seat. It wasn't three o'clock yet, the sky was streaked with only a few high clouds, and it would be a fine evening. Minmin and I decided to check out of the inn and head back to Beijing.

On our drive north, Minmin asked me about my father. I told her that he had worked for China, living in Japan and then America. I even said he had planned to retire back to his homeland, but he died of an illness in DC. "Don't let anyone know my family background," I said.

"Of course I won't," she promised. "I guess your father might have been bamboozled by the Chinese government. It must be a sad story."

"His life was very complicated. I'm still trying to piece it together. Don't let anyone get wind of this trip, all right?"

"Sure, I'll keep my lips sealed."

1954

For the first time, Gary took a vacation. George Thomas, recently married and having just returned from the States, had granted him three weeks off. Gary went to Hong Kong in early February, hoping to be able to cross the border to enter Guangzhou; though he didn't have a passport from Red China, he was still holding the one issued by the Nationalist government. He also had his refugee papers, which permitted him entry to the United States. For five years he hadn't heard a word from his family and only joined them now and then in his dreams. Were his parents still able to work in the fields? Did Yufeng resent his long absence from home? What could he say about his unfulfilled promise to go back and fetch her in a year or two? What a lousy husband he had been. If he got to see her this time, he would try to give her a child so that she might feel less lonely when he was away, and so that he could have a solid reason for requesting discharge from his overseas mission.

He wasn't sure whether his superiors would allow him to go home for a visit. All his planning might turn out to be wishful thinking. But in spite of the uncertainty, he was full of hope and couldn't stop indulging in reveries about a family reunion.

On the very afternoon he checked into a small hotel on Queen's Road in downtown Hong Kong, he called Bingwen, who was delighted to hear about his arrival and eager to see him. They agreed to meet the next morning, around eleven, at a restaurant near the ferry crossing to Kowloon. Bingwen reminded Gary not to eat too much for breakfast because they'd have an early lunch. Gary didn't get up until ten thirty the following day. After washing, he set out for the waterfront unhurriedly. On his way he stopped at a bakery stall, bought a small bun stuffed with red-bean paste, and ate it ravenously while strolling. Like anywhere in China, nobody here took notice of his eating on the street. He felt at ease, though he hardly knew this city, having once lived here for only a month (in the barracks at Stanley Fort), and was unable to understand the peddlers' cries in Cantonese.

When he arrived at the restaurant, Bingwen was already in there, at a window table that commanded a full view of the room and a part of the terrace outside and the harbor. At the sight of Gary, he stood and rushed up to him. The man wore suede boots with brass buckles and a gray wool vest over a white shirt. They hugged, overjoyed to see each other at long last. Gary found that his comrade hadn't aged in the slightest, having the same bright eyes and the same smooth, vivid face. After tea was served, a willowy waitress handed them each a small warm towel, with which they wiped their faces and hands.

They ordered lunch and resumed chatting. Bingwen pulled an envelope out of the pocket of his cashmere coat draped over the back of another chair. Dropping his voice, he said, "This is a little token of thanks from our country."

"For what?" Gary asked in bafflement.

"For the information you provided three months ago."

"Was it useful?"

"Certainly, it helped us smash a clique of spies disguised as returnees from Korea. We nabbed them all, executed a few, and put the rest in jail."

Gary was shocked but didn't say another word. He slipped the envelope into his rear pocket. He had assumed that all those anti-Communist POWs would go to Taiwan.

Their food came. The crabmeat dumplings, which Bingwen had ordered for the benefit of Gary's northern palate, were steaming and puffy. Together with the entrée were some side dishes, all Mandarin. Gary lifted a dumpling onto his plate, cut it in two with his chopsticks, and put half into his mouth. "Oh, delicious," he said, sucking in his breath because of the heat. "This makes me more homesick."

A ferryboat blew its horn like a mooing cow, chugging away from the waterside and dragging a frothy wake. Bingwen said, "You're from Shandong, so we're having dumplings for this welcome-home lunch."

"Thanks. When can I go back? You know I haven't seen my family for five years."

"Ah, that's another matter I'm supposed to discuss with you." Bingwen smiled cunningly, his hawk eyes scanning, as if to check whether the other seven or eight diners were eavesdropping. They were all out of earshot. He said to Gary, "Your family's fine. We've been taking good care of them."

"Can I go back to see them, just for a short visit?"

"No, you cannot, because the moment you cross the border, the Brits will inform the Yanks about you and that will blow your cover. The Party wants you to stay with the U.S. agency in Okinawa and to gather as much intelligence as you can. For this mission your identity must be kept secret. Brother, I know it's hard for you. You've been making a tremendous sacrifice for our country. For that you have our highest respect."

Hearing that, Gary felt touched and disarmed, unable to push his request further. A dull pang seized his heart again while a hot lump swelled his gullet. He lowered his eyes and asked, "What if the agency moves back to the United States? There's been talk about that."

"Go with them. That's the instruction from above."

Gary frowned, breathing hard as though something were stuck in his throat. "Look—I'm going to be thirty in a month, and this celibate life isn't easy for me." His voice took on a petulant note. "I won't say I miss my wife terribly like a newlywed. My parents picked her out for me. But I feel bad, guilty—I shouldn't have treated Yufeng this way. Besides, I miss home."

"We know Yufeng is a good woman, and she understands you've been doing an indispensable service to our country. As for your personal life"—Bingwen blinked meaningfully and gave a tight smile—"the higher-ups deliberated about that too. If neces-sary, you should consider starting another family abroad. This also means you must prepare to live overseas for many years."

"So mine is a protracted mission?"

"That's right."

Gary was stunned, but he managed to say, "Okay, I under-stand." He came within a breath of protesting but realized that would only make matters worse and might jeopardize his family. He heaved a sigh, unable to fathom the full implications of the directive.

As much as he was happy to see his friend and handler and to know he was a Party member now, the welcome-home lunch was a huge letdown. In addition to the $500 in the envelope, Bingwen notified Gary that he'd been promoted, now holding rank similar to a captain's in the army. From now on he would earn two salaries a month—$230 from the American agency and 102 yuan, about $50, from China's Ministry of National Security. He was sure that few of his comrades were paid so well. That lessened his despon-dency a little. If he lived frugally and saved, someday he'd be able to return home a wealthy man. Still, hard as he tried, he couldn't reason away his misery.

Hong Kong was warm in February, and there was a scent of spring in the air. The streets were overflowing with pedestrians, many of them in rags, apparently refugees from inland. Yet few wore cotton-padded clothes or heavy coats as people did in the north. Walking back to his hotel, Gary heard pigeons cooing and raised his head to look around, but he didn't see any birds. Instead, he saw colored laundry fluttering on bamboo poles stretched between the balcony rails. Along the street endless shop signs swayed like tattered banners. A uniformed Indian guard appeared, standing at the entrance to a grand stone building, his head turbaned and his beard trimmed. The air was musty and felt a little sticky. Sum-mer must be insufferable here, Gary thought. Perhaps hotter than Okinawa.

A small cleft-lipped boy in a patched gown accosted him, stretching out his cupped hand, but Gary recognized him—on his way to lunch he'd given this same beggar two coins, so he shooed him away. An old woman was limping over from the opposite direction, holding an oil-paper umbrella under her arm. A rickshaw caught up with her to see if she needed a ride, but she waved it off. As Gary was nearing a street crossing, a midnight-blue Rolls-Royce with chrome lights and bumpers emerged, honking petulantly while the pedestrians jumped aside to make way. Still, the sedan spattered muddy water on some people and on the stands selling hot soy milk, magazines, flowers, fruits, deep-fried fish balls. A middle-aged woman in green slacks and rubber boots waved her arms vigorously while yelling at the bulging rear of the car, "Damn you, foreign devils!"

Gary had seen only the Chinese chauffeur and another Asian face in the Rolls-Royce, but he was sure it was a foreign car since it had a U.K. flag on its fender. This reminded him that he'd been engaged in fighting imperialism. China had to drive all the colonial powers off its soil, and he'd better stop indulging in self-pity and fretting about his personal gain and loss. He ought to be more devoted to the cause of liberating the whole country. He stopped to pick up the *South China Morning Post*, which he'd found had better coverage of international events than Chinese-language newspapers.

During the rest of his vacation, he tried to enjoy himself and felt entitled to spend a bit of money. He dined at restaurants that offered northern food and frequented some bars, where he developed a taste for fruit juices, some of which he'd never had before. He liked mango puree, pineapple smoothie, kiwi slush, squeezed guava drinks. Restless with stirrings and with a knot of lust tightening in his belly, he even went to some nightclubs, where girls danced provocatively, their red flapper dresses flaring out from their waists. At one of the clubs he picked up a twenty-something, speaking only English to her, partly because he'd been instructed never to disclose his mainland background and partly because he meant to impress her with his U.S. affiliation. (Indeed, after he'd stayed more than four years with the Americans, his body language had changed enough that some people wouldn't take him for a real Chinese anymore. He would shrug his shoulders and hold doors for others behind him.) The young woman of mixed blood, Brazilian and Cantonese, called him American Chinaman when they were both tipsy. She kept calling him that even in his hotel room.

As if suddenly liberated, he felt a kind of transformation taking place in him, and during the rest of his vacation he didn't hesitate to seek pleasure, as though he meant to drop a cracked pot again and again just for the madness of it. He knew that once he returned to Okinawa, he would become the tame, quiet clerk again. Aware that this kind of dissipation might deform his personality and lead to a disaster, he made a vow that after his thirtieth birthday, on March 12, he would stop indulging himself.

Before Gary's vacation was over, Bingwen gave him a lavish dinner at Four Seas Pavilion, a send-off attended by just the two of them. He told Gary that he should try to work his way up the ladder in the U.S. intelligence system. He needn't collect every piece of useful information but should gather only what he considered vital to China's interests and security. If possible, he should come to Hong Kong once a year so they could catch up and make plans. From now on he'd have an account at Hang Seng Bank, and the reward money would be deposited into it regularly.

"You're our hero on the invisible front," Bingwen told Gary in total earnest.

"A nameless hero," Gary said with a tinge of irony. That was the glorious term used in the mainland media to denote a Red spy.

"Brother, I can't say how much I sympathize with you. But I know this: you must feel like you're living in captivity all the time, like a caged tiger. If I were in your shoes, I would crack up or die of homesickness."

"Thanks for understanding," Gary said. His comrade's words

dissolved his bitterness a little. He swallowed. Again the pain was shooting up his throat. He wanted to say he might be out of his element once he landed in America, but he thought better of it. He wouldn't want Bingwen to report his words to their superiors, in whose eyes Gary was reluctant to devalue himself. What's more, he believed there was glory in serving his country.

Bingwen resumed, "Please always remember that China has raised you and appreciates your service and sacrifice."

"I shall keep that in mind."

"Also, under no circumstances must you contact your family directly. That would put a lot of people in danger."

"I won't do that." Gary knew that "a lot of people" would also include his family.

They lifted their shot cups and downed their West Phoenix. The strong liquor was making Gary giddy and teary. They polished off a whole bottle of it.

As soon as I returned to Beijing, I wrote Yufeng a letter. I told her who I was and that I'd like to meet her. The address Uncle Weiren had provided might be out of date, so my letter was hit or miss. All the same, I expected to hear from my father's first wife and checked my mail eagerly every afternoon.

By early April I still hadn't heard from Yufeng, and I grew more anxious. I talked with Henry about it. He suggested going to the northeast personally to find out what had happened to her, so I began making plans. I moved my seminar from the next Thursday afternoon to Tuesday evening (pizzas provided) so that I could have six days for the trip.

On April 7 I quietly set out. It would have been faster and easier if I'd flown, but I'd have had to present my passport to purchase plane tickets, and then the police might keep an eye on me and throw up obstacles. So I decided to take the train. At the station, to my surprise, I was asked to show my ID too. This was something new. I had traveled on trains in China before, on my own, and never needed to produce my papers for the tickets. With no way out, I handed my U.S. passport to the woman clerk behind the window, saying I was going to Heilongjiang to see my aunt. To my relief, she didn't ask any questions and just gave me the tickets and the change, perhaps because there was a snaking line of people behind me. Plus, I spoke Mandarin well enough that she might have taken me to be an overseas Chinese, belonging to a different category of foreigners, who travel frequently in China to see families, relatives, and friends.

The trip was long, more than twenty hours, including the layovers in Harbin and Jiamusi. I didn't go deep into the two cities while waiting for the next trains but merely strolled around a little to stretch my legs. Both places still had traces of the Soviet Union's urban layout—massive buildings, broad boulevards, and vast squares. In the food stores I saw bread the size of a basin, bulky meat loaves, stout sausages. There were also a number of Russians on the streets, probably tourists and businesspeople.

The train rides had been humdrum but not tiring, thanks to my sleeping berth. I'd brought along a pocket *New China Dictionary,* which I enjoyed reading to brush up and learn some characters. The final leg of the trip was different, though. From Jiamusi I took a local train to Fushan County, and for two hours I sat among Chinese passengers, some of whom looked like peasants. Opposite me were a couple in their late forties, the man with a bald patch on the crown of his head and the wife with ruddy cheeks. Next to me a young woman sat with a toddler on her lap. She was obviously an urbanite, with a pallid face. After a male conductor had poured boiled water from a large galvanized kettle for the passengers who held out their mugs, I looked out the window, gazing at the shifting landscape, which reminded me of the midwestern American countryside. In a vast field two tractors were pulling harrows to pulverize the soil to prepare it for sowing, tossing up dust like teams of back-kicking horses. In another field a seeder was rolling. Beyond the machines, wildfires were sending up swaths of smoke. All the while I'd been holding my tongue to avoid revealing my accent, but now, unable to keep silent any longer, I asked the couple opposite me, "What are those fires for?"

"They're probably clearing land for farming," the man said. "They also burn the weeds to fertilize the soil."

"What are they sowing? I mean those seeders."

"Corn and wheat."

"Soybeans too," added his wife.

"Where are you from?" asked the young mother, my seatmate.

"Beijing," I said.

"You don't sound like a Han."

"I'm half Uigur" came my stock answer. "But I live and work in the capital."

Uigurs, a minority people in western China, are light-skinned and nicknamed the Whites of Asia. The passengers all bought my answer, and we began chitchatting. Soon the young woman next to me dozed off with her arm around her boy, who seemed in the deepest of sleeps. The man opposite me said that he and his wife had just gone to Nanjing to visit their son, who was a truck driver in an artillery regiment. The young man might get promoted to officer. If not, he should be able to make a decent living as a cabbie or trucker after being demobilized. I remembered that it used to be a sort of privilege to join the army and wondered if it was still so. The man said that military service was popular, but not everyone could afford it.

"What do you mean by 'afford it'?" I asked in wonder.

"You have to pay," his wife pitched in.

"Pay whom?"

"The recruiters," the man said.

"How much did you pay for your son?" I was all the more amazed.

"Well, eight thousand yuan, the standard fee."

That was about twelve hundred dollars, a hefty sum to a common Chinese family. His wife added again, "If you have a girl who wants to join up, that'll cost you ten thousand."

I said, "I guess military service might be the only profession where girls are more expensive than boys."

That made both of them laugh. I wondered what would happen if a war broke out. Perhaps many soldiers would pay their superiors to get discharged or to avoid being sent into battle. The Chinese are a pragmatic people, most of them not interested in politics or principles. For them, survival has to take priority. The common people's main concerns can be summed up in four words: food, clothing, shelter, and transportation. Nowadays they also talked a lot about health care and children's education.

The station of Fushan was a new yellow building topped with a clock tower, which read 2:50. The platform was paved with concrete slabs and swarmed with people, many of whom were there seeing off family members or friends. The toddler whose mother had shared my seat refused to get off the train and burst out crying. He wanted to keep on riding. That got the grown-ups laughing and his mother embarrassed. Her eyes widened in panic as she said to no one in particular, "Forgive us. This is his first train ride."

Outside the station stretched a line of taxis, and young women were holding signs that displayed hotel prices and amenities, all including free cable TV. I got into a cab and told the driver, "Take me to a guesthouse in town."

"A cheap one?" He started the ignition and pulled away.

"No, a good quiet place."

We were going north. Along the roadsides the young trees, birches and aspens and acacias, were sprouting leaves like tiny scissor blades and spearheads, all their trunks lime-painted from the roots up to four feet to protect them from insects. The town felt empty, with only a handful of pedestrians in sight. This was the first time I'd seen a town in China that looked as if there'd been more houses than people. It brought to mind a small U.S. midwestern town on a quiet day, though Fushan was a county seat. I asked the cabdriver why so few people were around. He said there'd just been a peasant uprising, which was suppressed by a contingent of riot police sent down from Harbin, so most country folks weren't coming to town for the time being. Even the marketplace had been closed, and had just opened up again the day before.

"What for?" I asked the cabbie. "I mean the uprising."

"Some officials in the county administration leased thousands of acres of land to local peasants and pocketed the money. But the land is public property and belongs to the state. This outraged the country folks. They sent delegates to the provincial capital and then to Beijing to lodge their grievances, but they got manhandled in both places. All the officials turned a deaf ear, so the villagers came back and started a demonstration. The local police tried to break up the crowd but got roughed up by the demonstrators. Then the whole thing grew into a huge uprising, roads blocked and trains stopped, and more than a thousand cops were rushed down from Harbin."

"Did anyone get killed?"

"No, but hundreds were injured. Some cars and tractors were smashed and burned. The cops fired lots of tear gas and rubber bullets."

"No pepper spray?"

"What's that?"

"Some police in foreign countries would spray peppered water on demonstrators. It can be effective for breaking up small crowds." I moved my hand left and right to show how to apply an aerosol can. He saw my demonstration in the rearview mirror, wagging a toothpick between his lips.

"More like a toy, isn't it? Tell you what, the country folks eat hot peppers every day and wouldn't give a shit about something like that."

I chuckled. Actually, my question about pepper spray wasn't frivolous—I wanted to see how sophisticated the Chinese police had become in crowd control. The government was unlikely to send out the standing army to quell uprisings again, having learned from the fiasco of Tiananmen Square. That was why in recent years they'd been building a huge police force (2.5 million in total) and spent more on "internal security" than on the military. I often wonder, without that astronomical budget, how much China could do for its people, for the children in the countryside who are underfed and deprived of decent schooling.

We stopped at a two-story inn called Home for Everyone. I handed the cabbie a fifty-yuan bill for a thirty-five-yuan ride and let him keep the change. A fortyish woman at the check-in counter gave me a multibed room, just for myself, as it was a slow time of year. I went upstairs, unpacked, took a quick shower, and lay down on a bed that smelled of tobacco. Though exhausted, I was in a good frame of mind because the woman downstairs hadn't asked for my ID and I might be able to stay here peacefully. I had not expected the trip to go so smoothly.

In the evening I went out for dinner at a nearby eatery, a cubbyhole that had only three tiny tables below a cyst of a low-watt bulb, but it offered spicy noodles and succulent steamed buns stuffed with pork and cabbage. I wished I could eat noodles like a full-blooded Chinese, heartily slurping the broth and sucking in the wheat ribbons noisily and then, halfway through, holding the big blue-rimmed bowl to my sweaty face to bolt down the remainder. But whenever I ate noodles, people could tell I was a foreigner who used chopsticks clumsily and was afraid of lifting the bowl to my mouth. So I bought two small buns and a bowl of soup instead. The old man at the counter pointed his stubby red finger at me and said good-naturedly, "Just two buns? You eat like a kitten." Behind him a stack of huge bamboo steamers was swathed in a cloud of vapor. He must have taken me for a Chinese woman fastidious about food, so I said, "Thanks," then carried my purchase to a table and sat down to eat.

In China I liked being viewed as Chinese, though in the States I always insist I am American. For me, similarity is essential— I want to be treated equally. In elementary school I had once come to blows with a girl who called me "mongrel" instead of "bitch." I looked up the word in a dictionary to see if it was related to "Mongol." It wasn't. I also examined a photo of my family and could see that I had my father's nose and mouth, but I had white skin. Strangers tended to regard me as a brunette. Clearly it was my last name that singled me out. Yet intuitively I had always known I was different. Later my father would urge me to date only Chinese boys, saying they were more reliable than white or black boys. That sounded anachronistic to me. I was so annoyed by his harping that once I retorted, "Why don't you find me a suitable Chinese boy? I don't want a nerd, though." I said that thinking of Francie Wong, the only Chinese boy in my prep school. After my father died, I often wondered what he would have thought of my first husband, who was Hispanic. Carlos was quite nerdy, even bespectacled, but he had his charm and, as an insurance broker, maintained a large clientele.

Back at the inn, I ran into its owner, a roly-poly man with a doughy face and a thatch of bushy hair, and I asked him how to get to Gutai Village, where Yufeng was supposed to live. He said it was far away, more than ten miles, and I should take the bus. But I wanted to go alone in a car so I could have a flexible schedule the following day. The man helped me book a taxi, for which I put down a one-hundred-yuan deposit.

I ARRIVED IN GUTAI around midmorning the next day. The trip was easy but turned out to be futile. The village chief told me that Yufeng had died a few years ago, and that the rest of her family was living in the county seat, running a seamstress shop. Her body had been cremated and the ashes were in her daughter Manrong's charge, so Yufeng had left nothing in the village. "Damn," I said to myself. "I hope this won't be a wild-goose chase." Without further delay I headed back to Fushan Town.

In the afternoon I went out in search of my half sister. The village chief had told me, "Just ask about Seamstress Shang, everybody knows where her shop is." I was glad she and I still shared the same family name. My mother used to tease me, not without malice, saying, "You're probably the last Shang on earth." True, even in China, Shang, meaning "esteem," is an uncommon name, but in a nation of 1.3 billion people, there must be many thousands of Shangs. The seamstress shop was easy to find indeed. It was on a cobbled street in the commercial section downtown, the part

closed to automobiles. After passing the few vendors selling produce and poultry along the sidewalk, I entered the shop.

"Can I help you?" a resonant voice asked from a corner. Following it emerged a sixtyish woman in a green turtleneck sweater.

At the sight of her I felt my heart lurching. She was the spit-
ting image of my father, although a female version and four or five
inches shorter, with the same elongated eyes, wide nose, full forehead, and roundish cheekbones. She was a bit plump but glowing
with health.

"Are you Manrong Shang?" I asked.

"Yes, I am."

"Your father's name is Weimin Shang."

"Who are you?" She stared at me in amazement.

"I'm Lilian Shang, his daughter too. Can we speak inside?"

She called over a younger woman, obviously her daughter, and
told her to mind the front counter. Then Manrong led me into the
back room. After we sat down at a table strewn with scraps of cloth,
stubs of French chalk, and a measuring tape, she kept looking at
me as if she hadn't yet recovered from the astonishment. I took a
small album out of my purse and handed it to her, saying, "Here
are some photos of our father."

"I never met him," she said. "All I know about him is that he
gathered lots of important intelligence for our country but couldn't
come back to join us. He died in the line of duty. That's what
the Internet says." She couldn't access uncensored Google or she'd
have known that our father's life had ended wretchedly. As she was
thumbing through the album, her eyebrows now joined and now
fluttered. Then her thick lips stirred, a smile emerging on her face.
She said, "This is him. We have a photo of him as a young man."

Holding down the turmoil inside me, I tried to explain calmly,
"Our father died thirty years ago. He had never forgotten your
mother. He loved her but couldn't come back, so he married my
mother, a white American woman, and they had me. I'm their only
child."

Manrong broke into tears, rubbing her nose with the back of her hand. I began crying too, my fingers gripping her forearm. "I'm so happy to find you at last, Sister."

She wiped her face with a hand towel, got up, and went to the front room. She called out, "Juya, come and meet your aunt!"

1955

In February 1955, a month before Gary's thirty-first birthday, he was notified of the agency's imminent departure for the States. Thomas asked him to move with them, and Gary agreed, saying he was a refugee anyway and had better hold on to his current job. Now, most of his personal belongings had to go. He sold his noisy jeep for two hundred dollars to a local businessman, a Taiwanese merchant of wine and liquor. He gave away his tatami mat, his two chairs and sideboard, his kerosene stove and utensils, but he was possessive of his books, which, for as long as possible, he wouldn't let go. He even kept those he had read and marked up.

In early March they boarded a large rust-colored ship. A month later they reached San Francisco, then took the train across the American continent. Gary had read quite a bit about the States but was still awed by the immense land, which looked sparsely populated in many places despite the abundant water supply and the farmable soil. No wonder the Chinese called this country the Beautiful Land. The sky looked higher and deeper blue, a match for the boundless landscape. He was struck by the sight of forests, mountains, deserts, lakes, meadows, vast crop fields, and farms. On every farmstead stood a house, a barn, a silo, sometimes a windmill; viewed from the distance, they brought to mind a set of toys. There were also a lot of cattle and horses that looked content, lazing around without a harness on them. The animals seemed to have a lot of leisure. The fields were flat, and some stretched beyond the horizon. What's that for? Gary thought about a tall gleaming structure that slid by, but he couldn't figure it out. Probably it was a water tower or some sort of refinery. Passing a prairie in Nebraska, he saw a herd of bison and wondered if they were domesticated. He had read somewhere that bison had been wiped out by the European settlers by the end of the nineteenth century, but George Thomas assured him that those were wild.

Their agency settled down on a quiet backstreet in Alexandria, Virginia, as an extended unit of the CIA, for which it provided translation services. Gary had his own office in the small three-story building; to the east spread a wood of spruces and oaks. He lived just a few blocks away and walked to work. His apartment, for which he paid forty-two dollars a month, had a bedroom and a den, which he used as a study. Against a side wall of the den stood a pair of bookcases, their bottom shelves filled with a set of *Encyclopaedia Britannica,* the 1913 edition, left behind by a former tenant. The bathroom was shabby, the mirror stained with coppery blotches and the slats on the venetian blind drooping with age, but the claw-foot bathtub surrounded by a new shower curtain pleased Gary and made him feel like a man of means whenever he ran a hot bath. What's more, the tap water tasted good, better than anyplace he'd been before.

American life amazed him, particularly the good wages (some jobs even paid by the hour); the fabulous libraries, out of which he could check as many titles as he wanted; the streets, big or small, all illuminated by lamps at night; and the supermarkets, where even spinach, celery, and mushrooms were wrapped in cellophane. He liked the fruits here, especially bananas (fourteen cents a pound) and oranges (a quarter a dozen). He was also fond of American nuts, their kernels full and plump. But he didn't like some meats, farm-raised fish, and vegetables, which tasted bland.

In spite of everything, Gary was sure he'd feel miserable if he lived here for long. Wherever he was, he couldn't shake his wariness. Twinges and jolts of fear often galvanized him. Sometimes when passing a street corner, he was afraid that a hand might stretch out to grab him. Walking home alone from work, he had to force himself not to spin around to see if he was being shadowed. He hoped he could return to China soon and again walk on solid, familiar ground. In his first letter to his handler he insinuated that he felt homesick and out of place, but Bingwen replied that they had to "stick to the original plan."

Soon after Gary settled down, a tallish young woman walked into his life. That was Nellie, who waited tables in a small restaurant where Gary often went for lunch. She noticed him because of his quiet disposition and gentle demeanor. Unlike other men, he never raised his voice and seemed to prefer to eat alone. Yet whenever he saw someone he knew, he would greet them warmly. He seemed easygoing and good-natured. One day toward the end of the busy lunch hour, Nellie got up her nerve to speak to him, to see if he could talk at length like a normal man, especially with a woman. For a brief moment, he looked perplexed, his eyes intense, staring at her. Then his face relaxed into a smile that showed his square teeth.

He said, "I don't think I've introduced myself. I'm Gary." He stretched out his hand.

"Nellie McCarrick." The second she said that, she felt stupid to have mentioned her last name. She must have sounded as if she was at a job interview, but Gary didn't seem to have noticed her unease. The grip of his hand felt forceful, and she liked that.

There were few customers around, so she sat down across from him and put her elbow on the table, her face rested on her hand to check the shivers of excitement and to keep her lips from trembling. Yet she managed to hold his gaze while a pinkish sheen crept up her face. Even the tops of her ears turned red and hot.

Already done with lunch, he took out a pack of Camels and offered her a cigarette. She declined, saying she didn't smoke. He put it into his mouth and struck a match, shielding the flame in his cupped palm. After taking a deep drag, he let out a puff of smoke. He seemed at ease and spoke to her as casually as if they'd known each other. They went on to converse a little, about the DC area, new to both of them, and then about Japan, where Nellie's older brother, Jimmy, had fallen in the Battle of Savo Island thirteen years before.

"Was he in the army or the marines?" Gary asked.

"On the *Astoria,* a cruiser," she said. "The U.S. Navy had lots of casualties in that fight, thousands."

"I'm sorry about your loss. Was he your only brother?"

"Yes, my parents took it very hard."

"I can imagine."

That started their acquaintance. Sometimes he seemed deliberately to come late for lunch so that he could chat with her after the busy hours. She got more and more interested in him despite his accent and Asian face, which was smooth but energetic. He spoke English with impeccable grammar, but everyone could tell he was a nonnative speaker, lacking ease and spontaneity. Some words seemed too wayward for his tongue to manage, and at times he missed the interdental sounds, mixing "th" with "s." Yet he was a professional translator, something of a learned man, working for the government. This made Nellie eager to know him better and to find out how old he was. He looked youthful, probably in his mid-twenties. No, he might be older, because his bearing, polite and composed, indicated that he must have lived quite a bit. He seemed to have a steadfast character, which Nellie appreciated. In truth, at twenty-six, she didn't have many prospects, and still had no real job. She looked neither plain nor pretty, with a broad forehead, fair skin, and gray eyes, which were a little wide-set, giving her a preoccupied look. Her bones were thick, though she was thin, as if undernourished. Her mother often said to her on the phone, "Find yourself a man soon or you might end up an old lady." Nellie had gone to a two-year community college in Miami, and though her major was economics, it hadn't helped improve her livelihood one iota. Her father would tell her, "You'd better find a guy who's qualified for a mortgage and can make an honest woman out of you."

Gary, isolated and lonely, was predisposed to friendly conversations, which brought the two of them closer and closer. Soon they began to go out. One night she let him kiss her outside a movie theater after they'd watched *Singin' in the Rain,* but before saying good night, she warned him that she'd give him hell if he jilted her. He hung back, his lips parted. That thought had never occurred to him. He'd been dating her in earnest, as if looking for a wife, though he felt he might be able to handle it if she said no. He was used to losses and thought he could manage a new one with some equilibrium. He assumed that an American woman was entitled to drop a foreigner like him on a whim. Not in a position to choose, he always viewed himself as a married man and couldn't date a woman without qualms.

He perceived Nellie as a windfall. She was a good bargain indeed. She wasn't a looker but had blond hair and glossy eyes. In a way, her ordinary looks could be an advantage, making her less likely to flirt and less distracting to him. Her slightly freckled face, strong arms, and solid bone structure all suggested a reliable character that could become a backbone in a household. Over and above these qualities, she was not demanding—in this respect she was totally different from George Thomas's bride, Alicia, for whom the man frequently had to buy flowers and gifts. Yet Gary wouldn't say he loved Nellie; his heart was numb and unable to open to another soul. He was pleased that he didn't even have to go out with her on weekends. More often they just spent time together, sharing a meal cooked by themselves at his or her place, or taking a long walk on the waterfront or in the parks, where bullfrogs squawked like crazy after rain. He liked the pasta and lasagna she made, while she loved the chicken and fish he cooked. "The best Chinese food in town," she often enthused. Once in a while they'd go to the movies. He was fond of Westerns, having seen all the John Wayne movies despite knowing the actor was a die-hard anti-Communist. In secret he was also enamored of Audrey Hepburn but was content to watch her on the screen—he wouldn't talk about her in front of others, afraid that his praises of her fearsome beauty might make him sound silly and unbalanced.

By September 1955, three months into their relationship, Gary began to introduce Nellie to his colleagues as his girlfriend, but she wasn't happy about the slow progress. It had taken her some trouble to persuade her parents to consider a Chinese man for a prospective son-in-law. They didn't like Gary that much; not only was he too starchy but he also had an unclear background. Worse yet, he didn't belong to a church. He'd told Nellie that he had no family in China anymore and had only a cousin in Hong Kong. Now that her parents had finally given the green light, why was Gary so hesitant about popping the question? It was so tiresome having to come up with plans for every weekend and holiday. Nellie believed that together they could make an outstanding couple. She'd be a good wife and they would raise husky sons. Time and again she hinted they should get engaged, the sooner the better, but Gary didn't want to rush.

"Give me some time, please," he said one day on their drive back from shopping. He was steering with one hand.

"Tell me, what part of me d'you still have doubts about?" She stared at him from the passenger side.

He didn't turn to her but felt her eyes boring into his cheek. He said, "Not because of that, I've told you so many times."

"Then because of what? What's there to worry about? You've no parents to ask for permission and no siblings to consult. I can't see why you're so wishy-washy. Tell me the truth, am I not good enough for you?"

"Please don't get fired up like this."

"You can't dump a girl after sleeping with her, you know. It's not like in China or Japan."

"I am serious about us. Just give me a couple of weeks."

She sighed. "Guess I've gotta bite the bullet."

"If that's too hard on your teeth, you don't have to do it."

"Gimme a break!" She swatted his shoulder, and they both laughed.

A few months back he had applied for a green card so that he wouldn't have to get his visa renewed every year, which he'd heard could be a hassle. Also, the U.S. permanent residency would make it easier for him to travel abroad. His plan was to get naturalized as soon as possible so he'd be able to access more-classified documents at his agency. By doing this, he also meant to take a part of his life into his own hands, to have some legal protection here. There was no telling what might happen between the United States and China, and the two countries were likely to have another military confrontation, probably somewhere in East Asia. If that happened, his higher-ups might not call him back in the near future.

He had constantly agonized about that possibility, which seemed unavoidable in light of some recent events. In January 1955, the People's Liberation Army had launched a massive attack on the Yijiangshan Islands, off the Zhejiang coast. It was a coordinated operation of the air force, the navy, and the infantry—the first in the PLA's history. The overwhelming forces crushed the National-ist defenders and wiped out the whole regiment deployed on the islands, whose commander, Colonel Shengming Wang, fought with his men doggedly and in the end blew himself up with his last grenade. Tactically Gary believed the Communists had scored a complete victory, but politically it was a disaster. Within ten days of the battle, the U.S. Congress passed the Formosa Resolu-tion and granted Dwight Eisenhower the power to protect Taiwan and its adjacent islands against invasion from the People's Repub-lic of China. The legislation made the liberation of Taiwan much more difficult, if not impossible. From now on, the PLA would have to fight the U.S. forces if it attempted to cross Taiwan Strait. That would be unimaginable, given that the Chinese air force and navy were both in their infancy. Eisenhower even declared that he might authorize the use of nuclear weapons if necessary. In response, China's premier, Zhou Enlai, claimed that the Chinese people were not afraid of atomic bombs and would continue to confront the American imperialists. Gary saw the attack on the Yijiangshan Islands as a political mistake that had widened the gulf between Taiwan and the mainland. While the hostility between

China and the United States was escalating, he felt plunged into deeper isolation. In his heart he couldn't stop blaming the Chinese Communist leaders and generals, some of whom he believed were too shortsighted. "What a bunch of idiots!" he'd say to himself.

Since the early summer of 1955, he had noticed a spate of documents from Taipei that touched upon the role of General Sun Li-jen, who had been the commander of the Nationalist land force in Taiwan. Gary was fascinated by this man partly because Sun and he were fellow alumni, both having attended Tsinghua University, though the general had been many years ahead of Gary. At college Sun had played basketball and even joined China's national team briefly. Then he went to Purdue on a scholarship, majoring in civil engineering. After earning his BS, he worked in a New York architecture firm for a short while. Later he enrolled at Virginia Military Institute (class of 1927) and studied military science for two years. He then returned to China and served in the Nationalist army, in which he rose rapidly through the ranks.

He fought numerous victorious battles against the Japanese and the Communists. Among Chiang Kai-shek's generals, Sun was the most capable, feared by the Red Army and dubbed the Eastern Rommel by Joseph Stilwell, the U.S. commander of the China-Burma-India Theater during the Second World War. But Sun was isolated in the Nationalist army, whose generals were mostly graduates of the Huangpu Military Academy, which Chiang Kai-shek had once headed. Owing to Sun's American background, Chiang had never trusted him and, in the summer of 1954, removed him from the command of the army and appointed him a staff general in the president's cabinet without any commanding power.

Through translating some reports and conversations, Gary suspected that Chiang Kai-shek might have begun purging Sun Li-jen, who was suspected of attempting a coup to seize presidential power and to set himself up as a U.S. puppet. Groundless though the accusation might be, Sun was fired in August 1955 and soon placed under house arrest. Gary could see that the CIA might actually have engineered the alleged conspiracy, though he wasn't sure how deeply Sun had been implicated. His instinct told him that Sun's career might be over. If so, Chiang's army would be weakened considerably, if not in disarray. He checked out the documents concerning General Sun's situation, telling the clerk in charge of classified materials that he had to translate parts of them at home. That was common among the translators when they had to work late into the night. Gary took photos of many pages about Sun's case, believing these were significant intelligence.

In mid-October he took a two-week leave and went to Hong Kong. He met Bingwen and handed him the films. His handler was thrilled, since the mainland was still dead set on liberating Taiwan, and the loss of Chiang's top general might open a window of opportunity. Gary also reported on his relationship with Nellie and asked for instructions from their superiors.

Two days later he and Bingwen met again at a teahouse. His handler told him, "As for this woman, do whatever is necessary. You must live in America as long as you can."

"You mean I should marry her?" Gary asked.

"Yes, that will make your life easier. We all understand the situation. Besides, that'll make you appear more normal among the Americans."

"How about my wife and parents back in Shandong?" Gary muttered, his heart gripped by a numbing pang, even though in recent months he had managed to suppress most of his memories of Yufeng.

"Our country will take care of them. You can set your mind at rest."

So Gary spent ninety-four dollars for an engagement ring with a tiny pear-shaped sapphire. He flew back to the States three days later. He had no idea that he already had two children. His superiors must have instructed Bingwen to withhold the information so that Gary could settle down more quickly in America.

My sister, Manrong, insisted that I stay with her family, so I checked out of the inn late in the afternoon and left with my niece Juya for her mother's house. Juya, a strapping woman with an ample chest and wearing a purple kerchief on her head, was carrying my stuffed suitcase with as much ease as if it were empty. On the way, whenever we ran into acquaintances of hers, she'd tell them I was her aunt, and I just nodded at them without speaking.

Manrong's husband, Fanbin Liang, greeted me warmly and shook hands with me. His palm felt thick and meaty. He had been a low-level official in the county administration and had just retired. In China the retirement age for men is sixty and for women fifty-five. I often half-joked with my colleagues in Beijing that I wished I were a Chinese woman so I could retire at fifty-five, which meant I'd have only one year left. By and large, China was still a good place for older people—in some areas life could be slow and easy. At age sixty-one, Fanbin didn't look that old, though his eyes were pouched and his mustache and temples grizzled. He kept saying to me, "What a happy day this is for our family." Indeed they were all in festive spirits. Manrong had called over her son-in-law and granddaughter, a small girl who was a bit rambunctious, wearing a tiny pigtail on either side of her head. The six-year-old gaped at me and brought out, "You don't look like American."

"Shush, Little Swallow!" Manrong scolded the girl, then turned to me. "She hasn't started school yet but is already a big mouth."

"I just told her what I think, Nana," Little Swallow cried back.

That made the grown-ups all laugh. I touched the girl's apple face and patted her hair. In response she placed both palms on the back of my hand. This indeed felt like a family reunion, as if every one of them had known me for ages. I was moved—rarely had I been among so many relatives. My mother had an older sister who had a son my age, but I'd met him only twice in my whole life.

Manrong's home was clean and spacious, the floors made of fine bricks sealed with cement. A large flat-screen TV stood against the back wall in the sitting room, a stainless-steel floor lamp inclined its gooseneck from a corner, and framed family photos were propped up on a long oak chest against another wall. "This is my mother," Manrong told me, pointing at a black-and-white picture. I leaned over to see Yufeng in her mid-forties: a smooth egg-shaped face, narrow cheekbones, a straight nose, bright but pensive eyes, a mole above the left corner of her mouth, and graying bangs covering a part of her forehead. She looked healthy and somewhat citified, like a nurse or schoolteacher. She must have been very capable both inside and outside the household. Next to this photo stood another one, a wedding portrait, in which she and my father, shoulder touching shoulder, were smiling blissfully. They were a handsome couple, lean-faced and rather elegant, a veil over the bride's head while the groom's hair was pomaded shiny and parted on the side. In his breast pocket was stuck a fountain pen. Above their heads, toward the right-hand corner, was a sloping line of characters: FOR WEIMIN AND YUFENG'S HAPPY UNION, JANUARY 16, 1949.

"Your mother was very pretty," I said to Manrong.

"Yes, she was voted the number one beauty back in our home village in Shandong."

"Voted by whom?"

"By some men in the village, secretly."

"No wonder it was so hard for her to live there." I remembered the proverb and quoted, " 'Gossips always cluster around a widow's house.' I mean, without her husband around she must have lived like a widow."

"You really understand the Chinese, Lilian."

"Our father always demanded that I learn Mandarin. One of my fields is Chinese history."

I saw a bottled watercooler stand in a corner, similar to the one in Henry's superintendent's office in our apartment building back in Maryland. Fushan County is right on the Songhua River, whose water must have been quite polluted. The bottled drinking water also indicated that Manrong's family was doing well, though I noticed she used tap water for cooking. In the back of the house was a low-ceilinged office, where I saw a computer, a scanner, a fax machine, and a laser printer. I was impressed that even in such a backwoods town the family was savvy about electronics. Juya said that she went on Weibo, the Chinese microblogging site, every night. She had online pals in other provinces, even one in Mongolia. I told her I didn't blog. That was a surprise to her, because she thought that most Americans were bloggers.

"Why don't you blog, Aunt?" Juya asked me in her throaty voice.

"It's too time-consuming. I prefer to spend my idle hours reading books. That's part of my job besides."

"It's really wild out there. You can make all kinds of friends through blogging. Also, it's fun and helps me follow what's going on in the world."

"I have many students already. I might lose my mind if I have to deal with more people."

She gave a chesty laugh. I admired her carefree manner that showed she was pretty content and got on well with her parents. My sister was lucky to have a daughter like Juya, not to mention her granddaughter, Little Swallow. I had always regretted not having children. My first husband disliked kids, and my second marriage took place too late, when I was already forty-eight.

At dinner I learned that besides Juya, Manrong and Fanbin had two more children, Juli and Benning, twins in their mid-twenties who were both working in the south. (My sister and her husband had been fortunate: their firstborn was a girl, and at the time the one-child policy wasn't strictly implemented in the region, so they were allowed to have another child, but the second-born turned out to be twins.) How the family all wished those two could join us. We were seated at a lower dining table on the long brick bed, heated from underneath, which was very warm due to the cooking of the big dinner—the heat and smoke from the kitchen range went through under the bed before reaching the chimney flue. I couldn't sit cross-legged like they did, so I bent one leg and let the other one hang over the edge of the bed. I apologized for my bad manners, but Manrong said, "Just make yourself comfortable. You're at home now."

They kept putting food into my bowl: a chunk of fried catfish, or a piece of chicken, or a spoonful of sautéed mung bean sprouts mixed with baby shrimp and wood ears. I liked the food but couldn't eat much. They all had better appetites. I wished I could eat heartily without being concerned about my weight. Even though I wasn't on the heavy side, I was always wary about overeating. In my mind's ear would ring my mother's voice, "Lilian, don't stuff your face."

That night Manrong chased her husband to another bedroom, saying she wanted me to stay with her so we could talk about our father and also "girl to girl." In fact, we had hardly mentioned him during the day. I would not confide to my sister that he'd been a Chinese spy caught by the FBI, or that he'd been a lousy husband. I told her instead, "He missed your mother a lot but couldn't come back."

"We all knew he was on an important mission overseas," Manrong said. "Did he know about my brother and me?"

"Yes, in the late fifties his higher-ups informed him about the two of you. When he died, he assumed our brother was still alive. He often mentioned your mother in his diary."

"My mom had a hard life." She paused, as though expecting my response, but I didn't know what to say. We were lying on the brick bed in the dark, two feet apart. The room was so quiet that there was only the tick-tock of the wall clock.

Manrong continued, "Mom often said my dad was a distinguished man with a degree from Tsinghua University. That was really something. I don't know who else in our home county went to Tsinghua. On her deathbed my mother said to me, 'When you see your dad someday, tell him I was a good daughter-in-law to his parents and a good wife to him.' Well, I wish I could've let him know that."

"I went to Maijia Village in Linmin last month," I said. "I was told that you and your mother had left because our brother died."

"He was born runty, not like me, although we were twins. In the fifties we lived decently on the money from the government. But when the famine struck, we became worse off than the villagers, because we couldn't grow crops and money became worthless, like straw paper. Our brother and I were eleven that year, both skinny like bags of bones, hungry all the time. It was reported that lots of people had died of hunger, so Mom was terrified. Then our brother died and my mother almost lost her mind with grief. When Uncle Mansheng asked us to join his family here, we left Maijia right away."

"It was a smart move," I said. "More than two hundred villagers starved to death in the following years."

"As a matter of fact, later Mom told me there was another reason we'd moved."

"What's that?"

"There was a man in the village, Uncle Weifu, who was from our Shang clan, a distant cousin of our father's. I remember him, a quiet, humble man. He was a bachelor and very kind to us. He often came to help Mom with household work, like thatching the roof, digging ditches to drain rainwater out of our yard, killing a hog for the Spring Festival. He was a handsome man, tall and muscular, with a straight back and sparkling eyes. His family was so poor he couldn't find a girl willing to marry him. The village was whispering about him and Mom. The two were fond of each other for sure. Mom later told me that Uncle Weifu had asked her to marry him, but she'd never do that because she was still married to our dad. She said to him, 'What if my husband comes back one day?' In spite of everything, she couldn't help but develop a soft spot in her heart for Uncle Weifu and would get heady with joy whenever he was around. She confessed to me that if we hadn't moved away, soon enough she might not have been able to restrain herself. She dreaded a scandal."

Something surged up in my chest, and tears welled out of my eyes, bathing my face. I covered my mouth with my palm, but still Manrong heard me sobbing.

"Why are you crying?" she asked.

"I feel so sad for your mom. She was a good woman. I wish she had lived differently."

"You're a good woman too. The moment I saw you I knew you were someone I could trust." She stretched out her hand and gripped my arm.

We went on talking. Manrong said life was much better now, but most people were unhappy because of "the unfair distribution of wealth." I was impressed by her use of that phrase. She hadn't even gone to high school, but she liked reading books, especially romance novels from Taiwan and Hong Kong, so she was articulate and at times could be eloquent.

I WENT TO MANRONG'S SHOP the next morning, eager to spend more time with her. She had hired two full-timers and also farmed out work to housewives in the neighborhood, paying them piecework rates. The sewing machines were purring in the side room as Manrong and I sat at the counter chatting. Now and then a customer stepped in, and she turned away to handle business while I resumed watching the street. People passed back and forth, and there were also panniered donkeys and mules, whose hooves clip-clopped on the cobbles. As a three-horse cart loaded with stuffed gunnysacks was wobbling by, I noticed a Mongolian pony branded with "283" on its haunch; perhaps the little shaggy nag had served in the army and had been decommissioned. Across the street some vendors squatted behind their wares along the sidewalk. They were selling chickens and ducks, tobacco leaves, hothouse vegetables (mostly cucumbers, leeks, bell peppers, and oyster mushrooms), wicker cages, and willow baskets. From time to time a voice cried out at potential buyers.

Through our conversation I learned that Manrong's twin daughter, Juli, was a migrant worker in Guangdong province. She was in Dongguan, a city near Guangzhou, doing a factory job. The girl used to come back once a year, at the Spring Festival, but this year she had not returned, saying she'd have only a week off and the long trip would have tired her out, so she decided just to send her parents money and to get some rest in her dorm during the holiday. As for her son, Benning, my sister was unclear about where he was. He seemed to be based in the south and traveled a lot, sometimes on ships going abroad and sometimes in different Chinese cities. Perhaps he was with the merchant marine. His mother hadn't seen him for more than two years but was certain that he was doing fine. Among her three children, he was the smartest, had gone to college, and might have a bright future. In the past his letters had been forwarded to his parents by his sister Juli, so Manrong never had his address and phone number.

Around midmorning the next day, my niece Juya took me to the Songhua, saying we should watch the river opening its frozen surface, which she assured me was a one-of-a-kind spectacle. It was still chilly in mid-April, and many people were wearing heavy coats and wrinkled calf-high boots. On the streets some men still wore fur hats. Juya and I headed north, taking shortcuts whenever we could. She was walking ahead, picking the way. The backstreets were a wholly different scene from the downtown, many houses ramshackle and enclosed by slapdash wooden fences, some windows still covered outside by tattered quilts, and heaps of trash everywhere, some four or five feet high. Besides muddy puddles there were half-thawed feces on the narrow streets, and it was hard to pick our way through the sludge. The down and dirty alleys brought to mind a swamp of compost giving off miasmic fumes. Just a few blocks from the bustling commercial district, the back alleys were like a ghetto without any drainage or sanitary service. If all the garbage and waste remained here, disease might break out in the summer. I'd seen similar scenes elsewhere in China—behind the shiny façade were the hapless people jettisoned by the ship of success.

It was blustery on the river; howling gusts of wind buffeted trees and people's hair and coats. Time and again large chunks of ice were tossed up and splashed the dark greenish water. I saw a number of fish, carp and pike and bass, floating by, belly-up, crushed dead by the ice. The river was roaring, and if I closed my eyes, it sounded like an ancient battle in full swing with all the clangs and clatters of blood-drawing metal. It was terrifying to see the immense body of water churning small icebergs and rushing them eastward, smashing whatever they met along the way, and gliding against the backdrop of gray woods on the other shore, where patches of snow were still visible.

Behind us, the sloping riverbank was covered with rocks, and up beyond the slope, on the esplanade, some kiosks stood, though they were unmanned. There was also a restaurant that would open to tourists in late May. Atop that structure squatted a loudspeaker that must have remained voiceless for the whole winter. On the west of the pavement spread a small cemetery, and in its center stood a tall bronze statue of a Russian soldier against an obelisk, wearing a rain cape and holding a submachine gun that had a thick, round magazine. A flock of crows perched on his helmet, shoulders, and arms, cawing hungrily. Around us people were all excited, some jabbering, some shouting, and some snapping photos of the floating ice blocks. Downriver to the east, across the water, was a cement factory where two smokestacks were spouting whitish fumes.

Juya said the riverbank was a hot spot for social gatherings in the summer and also a place where young people would come for a date. You could rent a rowboat, and if you were willing to spend more, could take a two-day cruise downstream to the Russian border in Tongjiang and Fuyuan.

"We used to pick up fish from this water when the ice was breaking open," Juya said.

"You don't do that anymore?" I asked.

"Uh-uh, it's too dangerous. Besides, a lot of farmers raise fish now, so folks no longer eat fish from this polluted water. My brother, Benning, was once trapped on a block of floating ice while he was reaching out for a killed bullhead. He was scared and hollered like mad."

"At this spot?"

"No, down the river, close to our village."

As we were speaking, a flock of oil drums bobbed past, some glistening with patches of grease in the glare of sunlight. "He was rescued?" I asked about her brother.

"Yeah, an off-duty firefighter jumped into the water and brought him to the bank, but the man's leg got crushed. He became a local hero for a couple months."

"Where's Benning now?"

"I wish I knew. He only told us he travels a lot. He's been in touch with Juli, though. They're very close." There was a trace of petulance in her voice.

"I'd love to meet him," I said.

"He used to be based in Guangdong, but I'm pretty sure he sometimes goes to Beijing."

Her father also mentioned Benning before I took my leave the next morning. His parents wanted me to meet him when he went to the capital the next time, and they asked me to urge him to find a girl, start a family soon, and give them a grandchild. "Treat our son and daughters like your own kids," my sister told me. At her repeated request, I promised to visit them again in a year or two.

Their warmth and hospitality moved me and made me reflect again on my parents' secluded life. Both Gary and Nellie had been loners and rarely mixed with others except for a few relatives. Although I loved my mother, I often felt uneasy when spending time with her alone. Unhappy and frustrated, she tended to take her anger out on me, perhaps because she believed I was closer to my father than to her. When I finished my PhD and was hired by the University of Maryland, Nellie appeared underwhelmed and closemouthed, as though to show I could never live up to her expectations. She had wanted me to go to medical school, but I hated medicine. When I published my first book, a monograph on the U.S. role in the Opium War, and got tenure, she remained unimpressed. I used to tell Henry that my mother was a troubled woman; yet the two of them got along and were fond of each other. Whenever Nellie came to visit, Henry would make shrimp scampi or chicken Parmesan for her. He was much better at cooking Italian than I was. My mother often joked about me, saying, "A slow girl can have a late blessing." That was her way of approving my second marriage. I think she envied me.

1956–1957

Gary and Nellie got married in the summer of 1956 and moved into a bigger apartment in north Alexandria. It was on the third floor and had a living room; two bedrooms, the smaller of which he used as his study; and a narrow balcony—more than eleven hundred square feet total. For the first time in her life Nellie lived in a place that felt like her own. Her parents, despite having accepted the marriage, still could not appreciate Gary, who in their eyes was too introverted and too tense. He seemed never to let his guard down and even at parties wouldn't touch alcohol, giving the excuse that he was going to drive afterward. (Grandpa Matt often said about Gary, "Jesus Christ, the dude kept a poker face even at his own wedding. I wonder what can make him happy." Grandma Beth would counter, "Gary couldn't loosen up like you 'cause he and Nellie were gonna leave early the next morning. He had to keep his head together." The newlyweds spent their honeymoon the following week in St. Petersburg, Florida.)

Yet unlike the McCarricks' other son-in-law, Gary was responsible and generous to his bride. Better still, he had not expected anything from her parents. Before the wedding, Nellie had talked to Gary about whether she should ask her parents for a few thousand dollars to pay for the wedding party, but he urged her not to, saying he was already grateful that they'd given her to him, that in China the groom's family had to take care of all the expenses. That was true, but it could also have been his way to ease his guilty conscience about bigamy. He believed that, with the help of the Chinese government, he could explain and justify things to Yufeng eventually. But what could he say to Nellie? There was no way he could reveal himself as a married man to her without being exposed. This realization made him more considerate to her.

After their wedding Nellie had stopped waitressing because she wanted to raise a family. With Gary's salary, $680 a month, she was happy she needn't go out to work anymore. In the early days of their marriage, they enjoyed having sex, so much so that he stopped using his study at night for weeks. At times they'd go to bed even before ten p.m. ("He was like a wild animal," Nellie confided to Lilian many years later. "He was a little rough in bed in the beginning. I had to teach him how to slow down with some foreplay and how to follow my lead.")

Nellie found herself pregnant in the late fall of 1956. In spite of his excitement, Gary was unnerved. Now remarried and with a child on the way, he realized he'd begun putting down roots in America. More unsettling was the prospect that the longer he lived here, the deeper and wider his roots might reach. He often shuddered at such a scenario: China summoning him back and his having to leave without delay, abandoning Nellie and their child without warning. He hoped nothing like that would happen. If a departure came, he'd like to have enough time to make arrangements and untangle himself.

Nellie's pregnancy made her moods swing capriciously. She complained a lot and often threw fits, but Gary was tolerant and solicitous. If he couldn't stand her anymore, he would lock himself in his study, working or reading. Nellie had few friends. She spent most of her days in front of the TV and wouldn't miss a single episode of *I Love Lucy* and *Lassie.* She even dyed her hair fiery red like Lucy's, and when she didn't like what Gary said, she'd grunt "Eww" in imitation of that funny woman. At dinner she would brief him on what she had watched that day, but seldom did he show much interest. She suspected that her words went in one of his ears and out the other. Once in a while she felt so frustrated that she would lash out at Gary, calling him a "swot," a word her grandfather had used to refer to someone who stuck his nose in a book all the time. Indeed, nowadays Gary read and wrote a lot, often deep into the night, in the study that he kept strictly to himself. In there everything was in order, and he wouldn't let Nellie tidy up the room for him. Every morning he made sure to lock his two file cabinets before going to work. Whenever he found she had entered the study in his absence, he'd blow a fuse, insisting that the nature of his job allowed nobody but himself admittance to his work space. That annoyed her, but bit by bit she gave up cleaning that room.

What troubled her more ever since her pregnancy was that he had stopped making love to her, giving his fear of damaging their baby as an excuse. According to the Chinese custom, he argued, a husband was not supposed to have sex with his pregnant wife, because it was believed that sex might not only hurt mother and baby but also bring on bad luck to the man. Gary even added his own little spin to this common practice, saying, "It's unnatural to have sex when a woman is expecting. Look at all the wild animals. They copulate only to breed. Once a female is impregnated, the males will leave her alone until she's in heat again."

Nellie wouldn't buy that nonsense. One evening at dinner when the topic of sex came up again, she asked, "What if your pregnant wife is still in heat?" Her voice was full, a bit gravelly.

Gary stared at her in disbelief. "That's just an assumption, isn't it?"

She went on with a teasing smile. "By your Chinese standards such a woman must be abnormal, a shameless broad, right?"

"Oh, come on, let's not talk like this. After our baby is born we'll sleep together again."

In fact, she wasn't eager for sex either and was also afraid of damaging the baby. Nellie was just anxious about his avoiding her bed at night. Worse, seldom did he spend time with her during the day. If she could, she'd have smashed his study, which was becoming his bedroom. She continued, "My obstetrician said sex is okay during pregnancy as long as we're careful."

Gary's eyes blazed, widening at her. He couldn't believe she had discussed such a matter with Dr. Nelson, that dumpy man wearing a thick gold band on his tapering finger. Gary remembered the obstetrician's smirk while the man was assuring him that the baby was healthy after he had examined the young mother privately, as if to insinuate to the husband that he'd just had fun with his wife alone despite the clean johnny wrapped around her body. Gary spat out at Nellie, "I don't believe him. I don't trust that quack. He's a schmuck!"

"Jeez, you're such a crank. You always have a chip on your shoulder." She stood and returned to the living room while he rose to clear the dining table. They had divided the kitchen work: she cooked and he washed dishes. He took out the trash every morning as well.

Nellie was also afraid that Gary might go after other women during her pregnancy, especially those Asian females at Voice of America. He often freelanced there, translating articles from English into Chinese for broadcast. She knew he rubbed elbows with them. Whenever they were together, Gary's rear end would turn too heavy to get up from a chair—he'd gab with those women for hours on end. Nellie had seen a handful of them, who were attractive and had suave, syrupy voices. Unlike other Chinese men, who spoke little English and preferred to live on the West Coast or in Chinatowns, Gary blended well with Americans. That made him stand out, and he was probably more attractive to those Asian women. The more Nellie chewed over his aloofness from her, the more embittered she got.

The baby was born on July 16, 1957. Nellie was a bit disappointed when a nurse told her it was a girl, because she had bragged to Gary that she'd give him husky sons who would make him proud. But this was just the first child; there'd be the second, the third, and maybe the fourth. She shouldn't feel hopeless or afraid of facing her husband. To her relief, he looked genuinely happy and held their daughter in his arms, cooing and rocking her gently. Like Nellie, he believed that the baby was only his firstborn, which partly accounted for his happiness. Yet in the back of his mind lurked a vague thought he avoided clarifying: if the baby were a boy, Gary might have cherished him more, and it would be harder for him to pull up stakes when he was ordered to retreat from the States. The arrival of the baby girl was good and appropriate because she might not tie him to this place.

At home Nellie and Gary talked about what to name the child. They both liked Lilian, though he suggested Yu as her middle name, claiming that was his mother's maiden name. It was actually the first character in "Yufeng," as if by his adhering to the traditional Chinese custom, his first wife could somehow own a part of this American baby. Knowing Gary didn't like her parents that much, Nellie agreed to let Yu stand between Lilian and Shang. (Three decades later, the daughter had Yu replaced with McCarrick on her own.)

Meanwhile, Gary followed international events closely. So many things happened in the USSR that 1957 could be called the "Soviet year," the year the number one socialist power triumphed over the West. The Soviets had succeeded in firing an intercontinental ballistic missile that could deliver nuclear warheads. (They possessed both atomic and hydrogen bombs by then.) They sent into orbit two satellites, the second one carrying an animal passenger, a dog named Laika. In December the Soviet Union launched its first nuclear submarine. In contrast, the United States, having suffered the recent setback on the Korean Peninsula, seemed on the defensive. In late May in Taipei a large mob broke into the American embassy after the U.S. military court acquitted an American officer who had murdered a major of the Nationalist army. The mob breached a safe in the embassy and made off with the classified documents that laid out the U.S. plan to replace Chiang Kai-shek with a new puppet leader. It was widely believed that Chiang's son Jingguo had a hand in the attack on the embassy. Chiang immediately apologized to the White House, emphasizing that this was not an anti-American act condoned by the Taiwan government. As a gesture of reconciliation, he allowed the U.S. military to deploy surface-to-surface missiles that could launch nuclear strikes on most cities in mainland China.

Through handling the information, Gary could see that his motherland was an underdog compared to the two superpowers. Although in 1957 China produced its first bomber and jet fighter, modeled on the MiG-17, the country was largely in a shambles. The rural collectives could not increase food production as expected, and the common people's standard of living was deteriorating. Many things were rationed now—grains, cooking oil, meat, cloth. In south China each urban resident was allowed to buy ten feet of cloth a year, whereas in the northeastern province Heilongjiang, each person could get twenty-four feet because they needed more for winter clothes. The scarcity was so severe that throughout the country even some basic necessities, such as tofu, matches, cotton thread, wool, cigarettes, tea, sugar, soda, eggs, and soap, required coupons. All the bad reports saddened Gary, though from time to time there were snippets of heartening news. One piece that excited him quite a bit was about a Chinese swimmer who'd broken the world record in the one-hundred-meter breaststroke (1'12"7, held by a Czech) by one second. Somehow that man's accomplishment touched Gary and reassured him that sometimes it took only one individual to make a difference and bring honor to the country. This sentiment was bolstered by his reading of Nietzsche. He began to believe in the superman, though he never succeeded in mastering his own life or outgrowing the herd values ingrained in him long ago.

Gary didn't go to Hong Kong that year, having little valuable intelligence to deliver. In his letter to Bingwen, he said he couldn't leave his postnatal wife alone at home and it was "business as usual" here. His handler wrote back that everything was in tip-top shape in Hong Kong, where it was uncomfortable for summer vacation anyway, so Gary needn't come. Bingwen promised to "keep an eye on the old folks." By that Gary knew he meant to look after his family back home. He felt vaguely dubious about his handler's words, but he stifled his misgivings. The man represented the Party and the country and couldn't possibly have promised anything they could not deliver. As long as they took care of his family, Yufeng and his parents should be able to live decently. That was the only way of helping them for the time being, so he'd better trust his superiors. After reading the letter once more, Gary flicked his lighter, set the sheet aflame, and dropped it in a jade-green porcelain bowl, which he kept under the window in his study for this purpose.

I asked my grad students to write two papers during the semester, one for the midterm and the other for the final. I was unhappy about the first ones they had turned in. They were surprisingly long-winded but too cynical to think hard about real issues. Many indulged in boilerplate, writing pages without saying anything substantial. Few could offer something interesting and original. In discussing the topic of one's proper relationship with the collective, almost without exception they claimed they had to serve the country and the people heart and soul. As an individual, you could find the meaning of life only in "a harmonious relationship" with the people around you. In other words, the individual had to be subsumed under the collective. Only one young man insisted that he serve his mother first because she'd given birth to him. I couldn't tell how serious he was, nor could I believe they all meant what they said. Some of them were fond of purple prose. They mistook verbosity for eloquence and ambiguity for beauty, worshiping the evasive and the fuzzy while looking down on lucidity and straight-forwardness. I had read enough of their nebulous writings to see the absence of sincerity as the crux of the problem. I told the class, "If you cannot write clearly, that's because either your head is mud-dled or you are too afraid to reveal your true feelings and thoughts. To me, clarity is a great virtue of intellect."

Some of the faculty members auditing my seminar looked doubtful, although they wouldn't say anything against me openly. I could see, though, that they had their reservations and might think I was too hard on the young people and had neglected the particu-larity of their conditions.

One grad student said, "We've been taught to write like that."

"We cannot say everything too bluntly," another chimed in. "That's not the Chinese way."

"Nothing's absolute besides," said Hongbin, a student Party member. "So we ought to avoid getting too explicit and too excessive."

I told them, "Your explanations don't hold water. What I cannot abide are cynicism and intellectual relativism. A punch in the face means pain, to open fire on peaceful demonstrators is a crime, incarceration without charge is a violation of a citizen's rights, a home torn down without enough compensation is a loss, selling recycled sink grease as cooking oil is profiteering, to borrow others' ideas without acknowledgment is plagiarism. You must call things what they are. Many of you will teach high school and college after graduation. How can you be good teachers if you have no firm convictions? If you cannot tell right from wrong or good from evil, how can you expect your students to respect and trust you?"

"I totally agree," Minmin said. "Whether wearing a condom or not, to force a woman to have sex is rape."

The class exploded into laughter. Just a few days earlier it had been reported that a county official in Guizhou province had assaulted a young schoolteacher after a banquet. The woman pressed charges, but the local police refused to investigate, claiming it was not rape because the man had worn a condom. The incident provoked a national uproar.

I WAS DELIGHTED that my niece Juli came from Guangzhou to see me. She was so svelte, with a narrow waist, that it was hard to imagine her as the sister of the thickset Juya. Already twenty-six, Juli looked as if she was in her late teens, wearing black chinos and plaited leather sandals. She'd been to Beijing several times, so when I offered to take her sightseeing, she said, "I can go to town to see friends by myself. You don't need to keep me company, Aunt Lilian. You must have a lot to do at school." So I gave her some cash and asked her to come back for dinner.

The next evening Juli and I chatted over decaf coffee. She was fond of cappuccino, espresso, latte, all the drinks offered at Starbucks, but like me, she couldn't consume too much caffeine in the evenings for fear of insomnia. Sprawled on a canvas-covered sofa in my living room, she looked like a carefree child, smiling and blinking her brown eyes. She took after her mother, with round cheekbones, a pug nose, but a delicate neck. With her around, my apartment felt warm and cozy, and I enjoyed the homey ambience, in which we could relax. Juli said she worked with a troupe now, acting small parts in plays and singing with its band. Her goal was to break into a movie or TV series. "From the stage to the screen," she told me. "They might give me a part or two. I know some people in the local TV business."

"Your parents still think you're a factory worker," I said.

"Oh, I was, a long time ago."

She went on to mention several places where she had worked. She'd left home seven years ago for Dongguan, a boomtown about forty miles southeast of Guangzhou. With a fellow townswoman's help, she got her first job at a zipper factory, earning four hundred yuan a month. But she couldn't get along with some roommates in the factory's dorm, so she jumped ship and found a job at a textile storehouse, where she mostly handled inventory. The work wasn't heavy, mainly processing paperwork and driving a forklift, but she had to do long shifts, sometimes putting in sixty hours a week, with no overtime pay or benefits, though the food wasn't bad—there was meat at lunch, usually two dishes plus a soup. She'd eat as much as she could at noon so that she could spend less for dinner, which was on her own. She was homesick and miserable all the time, but everyone said she was lucky because her job was good by comparison and paid almost six hundred yuan a month. Still, she was constantly nagged by the thought of working in a warehouse for the rest of her life, so she moved on again. This time she was hired by Wal-Mart as a cashier, with similar pay but fewer hours.

"For a low-end job, Wal-Mart is as good a place as you can find," she told me. "People prefer to work for foreign companies. The wages are guaranteed and never delayed, and they also pay you overtime. On top of that, the foremen are not as mean as those in the local companies, and they won't treat you like you're shirking if you take a bathroom break for more than ten minutes. Still, it was hard for me to stand at the cash register punching numbers and making change day in and day out. What's worse, you had to smile at customers no matter how tired and unhappy you were."

"How long did you work there?"

"Eight months. Then I joined a nightclub because they found I had a good voice. I became a bar singer, but I didn't stay with them for long. Customers were rude and kept harassing me. They treated a girl like a prostitute, like you were supposed to let them have their way with you if they offered you a price. For most customers a girl was just a piece of meat, like a live fish or chicken available for consumption. It was there that I realized I'd never be happy if I worked only for money. What prompted me to quit was that one night, on her way home, a girl got battered and lost a tooth because she refused to go out with a customer."

"So you joined the troupe?"

"Yeah, I want to perform onstage or to become an actress in movies or TV no matter how poorly I'm paid. I know I'm not pretty enough to become a star, but I'll be happy to settle for small parts."

"I'm pleased to hear that," I said. "I'm proud of you, Juli. What's a good life? A combination of vocation and avocation—to make work and fun one thing. That's from Robert Frost."

"Who's he?"

"An American poet."

"That's cool—the way he put it."

"It's wisdom, simple and clear."

"Thanks, Aunt Lilian. This is the first time somebody has said such heartening words to me about my wild life. I've never dared to tell my parents about this; they might send someone to bring back their bad daughter on the loose."

We both laughed. We also talked about her twin brother, Benning, whose exact whereabouts Juli didn't know. She was sure he'd been working for the government, often in other countries. That was all she knew. Sometimes Benning seemed quite aloof and secretive. Juli told me that he was the scholar of the family, the only one who'd gone to college. He also spoke English well; he had learned it as a foreign-language major. The more she talked about him, the more mystified I became by this nephew of mine, who seemed like a phantom my mind couldn't grasp. I asked if Juli had a photo of him. She had some but not with her.

"Benning used to be a wild thing," she said. "In high school he was obsessed with automobiles, but he was underage and couldn't get a driver's license. Whenever possible, he'd sneak into a car or tractor, monkeying with the gearshift and the dials on the dashboard. One evening our granduncle, my grandma's brother, gave a dinner party at his home. We all went. When most of the men had gotten drunk, Benning slipped out and stole a truck that belonged to one of the guests. He drove it away, but the minute he got out of the village he lost control and ran into a pond used for soaking hemp. Lucky for him, the water wasn't deep and he could get out of the flooded cab. My parents spent five hundred yuan repairing the truck."

"I'd love to meet him," I said. "He's the only nephew I have."

"I'll send you his email address."

"Please do. Do you have a scanner?"

"I have one."

"Email me some of his photos."

"Sure I will."

Juli asked me what my father had been like. It struck me that part of her purpose in visiting me might have been to find out something about her granddad. I would not reveal his true profession; for the time being I was reluctant to introduce him to his granddaughter as a top Chinese spy. Instead, I told Juli that my father had missed her grandmother Yufeng all the time (which might have been partly true). I added that he'd been a loving father to me but a feckless husband to my mother, that he had lived a displaced life because of the separation from his original family, and that he'd also made many sacrifices for China and should be regarded as a hero by the Chinese.

I didn't share my thoughts and questions about my father with Juli, though my mind had been full of them lately. In the center of his plight may have resided this fact: mentally, he couldn't settle down anywhere. It was true that in his later years he began to like America and grow attached to my mother, but he could not imagine spending the rest of his life with Nellie. His heart was always elsewhere. Wherever he went, he'd feel out of place, like a stranded traveler.

1958

Gary and Nellie didn't have many friends, but that didn't bother them, since they preferred a quiet life. They were no longer in close touch with her parents, who had come to see their grand-daughter the previous winter but stayed only three days, having to head back for the endless work on their vegetable farm. Since the birth of Lilian, Gary and Nellie seldom went out together, because they were reluctant to hire a babysitter. Once a man who had dated Nellie many years before phoned and chitchatted with her for more than an hour. Gary blew up and exchanged angry words with his wife. He threatened to move out if she kept answering that man's calls. She caved and told her ex-boyfriend to leave her alone. She knew that her husband's threat was not idle. Sometimes when Gary worked late into the night, he'd sleep in his little cage of a study, on a futon that he had insisted on buying over her objection. She was alarmed, afraid he might have lost interest in her, revolted by the ten pounds she had gained after giving birth. (In reality she was still trim with long limbs and a twenty-eight-inch waistline. She took great pride in her figure, and it would easily outshine her daughter's in the future.) Nellie noticed that Gary was sometimes absentminded, seated at his desk doing nothing. That made her wonder why he looked so sad.

Indeed, his mind was elsewhere, shadowed by the memories of his other wife. One of those moments he always remembered was an evening soon after their wedding. Yufeng was sitting cross-legged on the warm brick bed, needle in hand and thimble on finger, mending a tear in his quilted overcoat. She was wearing a green tunic printed with tiny jasmine blossoms, which set off her smooth face, calm and shiny with concentration. He was lying with his head in her lap and observing her raptly, though she kept urging him, "Close your eyes and take a nap." The light thrown by an oil lamp was soft but sputtered from time to time, and the bridal chamber was so peaceful that he felt he'd love to repose like this for the rest of his life. If he died then and there, he'd be happy. This tranquil image of Yufeng plying her needle would rise in his mind every now and then, haunting him and misting his eyes. If only he could rest his head in her lap again.

He felt she must still love him, but in a perverse way of thinking, he hoped she had betrayed him by finding another man. That would have made her life easier and assuaged some of his guilt, though it might cause her to lose his salary. It was too cruel to let her wait for his unforeseeable return. She'd be better off if she stopped being his wife. On the other hand, without her in the household no one was there to take care of his elderly parents. Like him, Yufeng was misused relentlessly. Someday he'd have to find a way of making it up to her, if he could.

Yet his thoughts about Yufeng did not totally incapacitate him in his current marriage. He was fond of Nellie, and once a week they still had sex, even with abandon. He would kiss her on the mouth and nibble her earlobes, and when inside her, he would move slowly and gently, feeling her blood pulsating in his loins, so that they both could reach climax. He'd do anything to make her come and loved to see her ecstatic face clench as if she were in pain. Much as he enjoyed her body, sometimes he preferred to sleep alone, giving the excuse that he had to work late into the night and was reluctant to disturb her. In a sense that was true, but he also meant to keep a clear head for his day job and secret mission.

In DC's intelligence community Gary had gradually acquired a reputation as the best translator of Chinese. He was nicknamed the Linguist. His good name was partly thanks to his friendship with George Thomas, who was in charge of Chinese affairs in the CIA's East Asia Division and often assigned Gary projects. To further his own career, Thomas had resumed his work toward a PhD in Chinese literature at Georgetown, writing a dissertation on the Tang poet Du Mu, whose lyrical poems he loved so much that he could quote some exquisite lines off the top of his head, especially those about mist-swathed Nanjing, the capital of many dynasties. Besides the primary texts, Thomas needed to read some secondary sources written in classical Chinese, but his grasp of the language wasn't up to the task, so he asked Gary to translate some key passages of the conventional poetry diaries, which had been left by many major poets and had over the centuries become an essential part of Chinese poetry criticism. This was easy for Gary. He checked out a thick anthology of the diaries from the Library of Congress, a place he loved and visited at least once a month. Thomas wanted to pay him out of his own pocket for the translation, two dollars an hour, but Gary adamantly refused to take money from him. He did the work out of gratitude, and also to deepen their friendship now that Thomas was a senior officer in the heart of the U.S. intelligence business.

In return, Thomas invited Gary to a club named Bohemian Alley that offered live music. The place smelled of cigars and whiskey and had a poolroom in the back. The waitresses were young and lovely, wearing high heels, knee-length skirts, and tiny flowers, mostly forget-me-nots, in their hair, though the fluorescent lighting made their faces appear a little greenish. Gary and Thomas would drink beer and munch nuts and chicken nuggets. Thomas would ogle the waitresses' behinds unabashedly while Gary tried to bridle his own impulses, and soon his neck grew stiff. He wished he could have Thomas's bold wandering eye. Once in a while the two also had dinner there, steaks or barbecued pork chops or chicken enchiladas. When eating, Thomas would pick Gary's brain about problems concerning the Far East.

It was there in the summer of 1958 that Gary discovered jazz. He enjoyed the spontaneous ebb and flow of the music, the swings and plunges, and the assured improvisation by the black musicians, one of them wearing dreadlocks, a hairstyle Gary hadn't seen before. In spite of the mercurial notes, the music was so comforting and relaxing. Unpredictability—that was what he loved about jazz—everything was freewheeling, unprepared, yet always under control. He was so enamored of it that he began collecting jazz records, in particular those of Louis Armstrong and Benny Goodman.

One evening Thomas told Gary over a glass of Chablis, "You'd better get naturalized soon." His green eyes were snapping meaningfully, as if to hint that once Gary became a U.S. citizen, there'd be more lucrative work for him.

"I'll do that," Gary said.

Since he wasn't naturalized yet, Thomas could give him only less classified documents to translate, mainly the type listed as Confidential. Above that there were levels, such as Secret and Top Secret, to which Gary, as a noncitizen, was denied access. Nevertheless, every once in a while Thomas would use Gary for rendering secret orders for the spies in China that could not allow any ambiguity or inaccuracy. By translating these directives, Gary came to know some agents' code names, their missions, their communication plans. He just kept notes on them and did not attempt to send out the intelligence right away, because he remembered the instructions from Bingwen: he was a strategic agent, not a petty spy specializing in sabotage or stealing technology. In addition, time is a determining factor in the espionage business. Generally speaking, the information before an event takes place is intelligence, whereas the information on an event that is already unfolding has become news. If the event is over, any information about it is nothing but archival material. Without a direct delivery channel, Gary couldn't pass urgent information to Bingwen quickly, so he didn't make an effort to collect the kind of intelligence whose value hinged on a time frame.

At the same time, his mind had been preoccupied with the ongoing events in China. At the end of July 1958, Khrushchev visited Beijing, and the two countries signed a joint communiqué that highlighted the cooperation and solidarity between them. A month after the Soviet leader had returned to Moscow, Mao ordered a massive bombardment against the Nationalist troops on Jinmen Island. One evening five hundred artillery pieces—cannons, howitzers, heavy coast guns—fired all at once, shelling the military positions, wharves, airfields, supply lines. Within hours hundreds of soldiers were killed outside the bunkers and in the trenches. Three generals, all vice commanders of the Jinmen defense, were also among the casualties. The top brass were eating dinner in a dining hall when a barrage of shells landed on them. Two generals were killed on the spot and the other one died on arrival at the field hospital.

For days the Nationalist army was too crippled to fight back. Then the United States gave them twelve 8-inch M55 self-propelled guns, which were delivered under cover of darkness. With the deployment of these heavy howitzers, the Nationalist troops began to fire back and managed to suppress some of the Communists' artillery (though one of the big guns was blown up by a hostile shell that landed right in its barrel). Soon mainland China declared that it would bombard the island only on odd-numbered days to give the civilians and the defending troops a breather. Such a practice, which was also a way to dispose of expiring shells, continued till 1979, when China and the United States finally reestablished a formal relationship.

Following the events after the attack, Gary came to know that John Foster Dulles and Chiang Kai-shek had recently held secret talks about how to deter Red China's aggression. The secretary of state suggested using nuclear weapons, which Chiang agreed to in principle, saying that a handful of small tactical bombs might do the job. But when Dulles revealed that the warheads should be at least as powerful as those dropped on Hiroshima and Nagasaki, Chiang was aghast. After the talks, his government informed the White House that nuclear weapons should not be an option—the fallout might endanger Taiwan and the U.S. military bases in East Asia.

Another piece of information also took Gary by surprise. Some

political analysts in Southeast Asia believed that the Communists'
artillery attack served two purposes: one was to sabotage Khrushchev's new policy of promoting world peace because Mao, an advo-
cate of confrontation, was always spoiling for a fight against the
imperialist West; the other was to form a link with Taiwan—in
other words, the bombardment signified a territorial claim. It was
reported that the moment Chiang Kai-shek heard of the attack,
he'd said in praise of Mao, "What a marvelous move!" That was
because he didn't want to see an independent Taiwan either, still
viewing himself as the leader of the whole of China. Initially Gary
was baffled by Chiang's words. All three of the generals who had
died were noted for their ability and bravery, and Chiang must have
known them personally. So how could he call the bombardment "a
marvelous move"? Evidently, to the top commander, even generals were expendable. The whole affair felt as if Mao had stretched
out his hand and Chiang had shaken it with appreciation, so that
Jinmen Island would serve as a link between the mainland and
Taiwan. The two sides seemed to have worked in tandem, and only
the soldiers were the losers.

Gary took photos of the documents, specifically the conversation between Dulles and Chiang. He wanted the Chinese leaders
to be more cautious when they decided on military action in the
future. They ought to take into account possible nuclear attacks in
retaliation.

After telling Nellie that he wanted to travel back to Hong Kong
to see his cousin, Gary went in early December, a good time of year
for a vacation there. He gave thought to the possibility of being
noticed by U.S. counterintelligence. "Let them follow me," he said
to himself. "If that happens, I'll go home sooner." But nothing
happened, as McCarthyism had been publicly condemned and foreign travel was more common now. In Hong Kong, Gary handed
his films to Bingwen. For this intelligence he was paid a thousand
dollars, deposited directly into his account at Hang Seng Bank.

It was on this trip that Bingwen revealed the existence of Gary's twins back home. The news made his stomach heave. He was speechless, staring at the photo in which Yufeng and their son and daughter were smiling at him. They all looked content: his wife had aged a little and was fleshier than before, while the children both had his eyes and mouth. The boy was bonier and shorter than the girl; if only they could have traded bone structures so that he might grow up more strapping. The photo must have been recent because the twins looked eight or nine years old. They had started school the previous fall, according to Bingwen. After examining the three faces in the grainy picture for a long while, Gary sighed and said, "If only I had known Yufeng was already a mother."

Bingwen lifted his cup of oolong tea, his pinkie sticking out, and took a sip. He asked, "Your point being?"

"I would've had second thoughts about getting married abroad." Eyes glazed in pain and smitten with regret, Gary wanted to add, "What a terrible mess!" but he held back. Furrows gathered on his broad forehead and his ears buzzed. He swallowed, wheezing and pushing down a wad of misery in his windpipe. Unconsciously he lifted his cup, but the tea splashed, leaving brown drops on the white tablecloth. He put it down without drinking it.

"I see," Bingwen said. "You want to be more devoted to Yufeng and to your kids. That's why our higher-ups did not allow me to disclose the truth to you—they feared you might want to come back soon. Our Party and country need you to stay in the enemy's camp."

"They ordered you to keep me in the dark?"

"Yes, my friend."

In shock, Gary realized he might have to live in the United States for a long time. In spite of his bitterness, all he could do was to ask his handler to take care of his wife and children back home. Bingwen promised, "Rest assured, their well-being is guaranteed, in the hands of our country." He picked up a succulent shrimp ball with his red chopsticks, dipped it into the satay sauce, and put it in his mouth.

✧✧✧

When Juli was back in Guangzhou, she sent me her brother Benning's email address and two photos, which, though somewhat blurry, showed he had a rectangular face and curly hair like my father's. I wrote him, saying I was his aunt and would like to meet him if he lived nearby or came my way, but I got no reply. He used a Hotmail account, so it was impossible for me to surmise where he might be, in China or abroad. His sister sent him messages as well, and she did not receive a response either.

Then Juli mentioned that she was going to perform in a concert. It would be her debut, her "first big event," which I felt I ought to attend since her parents wouldn't be there. I decided to fly down to Guangzhou to spend a day or two with her, and also to see her sing. I had a friend from Wisconsin, Stacy Gilmour, who was teaching international finance at a business school in that city and said she would be happy to put me up in the two-bedroom apartment she had to herself on campus. I flew south on the third weekend of May.

I'd been to Guangzhou two decades before to do archival work for my book on the Opium War, and now the city was much brighter and brisker in spite of auto exhaust and the floating smog clouds. To my amazement, there were a lot of Africans living here, many with businesses in the area called Chocolate Town; they were involved in importing and exporting, mainly buying Chinese products and selling them in Africa and the Middle East. I guessed they must like the semitropical climate, which was too sultry for me. It wasn't summer yet, but the downtown at noon was already sweltering like a busy kitchen. Juli was ecstatic to see me and introduced me to her boyfriend, Wuping, a tall man whose shoulder-length mane and disheveled appearance brought to mind the French philosopher Descartes, although the fellow wasn't interested in philosophy. He managed the troupe whose band had taken Juli on. Like her, he was a northerner, from Jilin province, and his family had moved here many years before. He looked much older than my niece, perhaps on the verge of middle age. He drove a black minivan, the type nicknamed "bread box," but his resembled a coffin on wheels.

After dinner with the two of them at a Vietnamese restaurant, where we had vermicelli noodles and seafood sautéed with napa cabbage and cayenne peppers, I spent some time with Juli alone, seated outside a bar on the Pearl River. A yacht with a boat-length TV screen attached to its side chugged back and forth in the shadowy water, displaying a series of commercials, while to our right, about two hundred feet away, a crowd of middle-aged women and men were clapping their hands and singing a Mongolian song: "In the blue sky float white clouds / Below the clouds horses are galloping . . ." A distant drumroll went on throbbing spasmodically as if a show was under way. Behind us a high-rise residential building loomed, silhouetted against the starry sky and leaking columns of lights through the undersize windows. The air smelled of overripe banana and was vibrating with a faint din like firecrackers exploding far away. Over iced tea Juli and I talked about inflation and boyfriends. I confessed that I had dated a dozen or so men in my life and married twice, but only two of them still meant something to me, Henry excluded.

"How about your ex-husband?" Juli asked me.

"Carlos is one of the two. He's a good man, but we didn't get along." I stopped there, reluctant to talk more about him.

Juli said she'd been called "nympho filly" in high school, though in reality she had dated only one boy in her teens. "Or one and a half actually," she said. "My second boyfriend dumped me as soon as he left for college. We'd been friends for less than a semester, and I didn't do anything with him, so he shouldn't count."

I asked her how serious she was about Wuping. "I love him," she told me.

"Does he love you back?"

"I think so."

"What is it that makes him so attractive?"

"I feel happy and confident around him. I like mature men who have lived a bit."

"How old is he?"

"Thirty-eight."

"My, don't you think he might be too old for you? Twelve years is a big age difference."

"That's not a problem. The problem is he's still married and has a nine-year-old son."

"Well, does he plan to get a divorce?"

"He's been separated from his wife, and they'll reach a settlement soon."

"What does that mean?"

"He's going to file for divorce."

I started having a sinking feeling. "Juli, in this situation, try to use your head, not your heart. You're not a teenage girl anymore. Don't let love eat you up."

"You mean I shouldn't be too serious about Wuping?"

"I'm afraid he might be taking advantage of you."

"You're so prehistoric, Aunt Lilian. The fact is, you could say I've been using him—he can help me advance my career. He's well connected in show business here. On top of that, we love each other."

"Are you sure he loves you enough to leave his wife and son?"

"Not a hundred percent yet, but it doesn't matter. Truth to tell, whenever he spends time with me, I feel he's doing me a favor. So long as he allows me to hang around, that will be okay with me. As a matter of fact, he says I've been sucking him dry, but he won't mind. That's the price for love he's willing to pay."

Basically she was telling me she was content to be a "little third," a term referring to a young woman who specializes in seducing married men and wrecking families. There are additional monikers for such a woman, like "fox spirit," "evil flower," "professional mistress." Juli admitted that she had joined the online club called Little Thirds, whose theme song proclaims that their mission is to take men away from dull, obtuse wives. One of their slogans is "If you can't take care of your husbands, let us help." They'd just held their first conference on March 3, a covert event in Shanghai attended by scores of "little thirds" from all over the country. Some of the twenty- and thirty-somethings were quite brazen. One young woman posted five of her photos online and even boasted that her beauty had "startled the Party," as if she'd swept numerous high-ranking officials off their feet. Her pictures showed nothing out of the ordinary.

Juli was a good woman, I was sure, but she could have found a better man than Wuping, who I felt was too smooth. I always believe that if you love and marry someone, that person will become a kind of investment, because together you two will build your home, your family, and if you are lucky, your wealth. But the Chinese dating scene is quite unusual. Most girls won't consider any young man without his own housing. In a city like Beijing or Guangzhou, an eight-hundred-square-foot apartment costs over three hundred thousand dollars, but the wages of a regular worker or clerk are around six hundred dollars a month. How on earth can a young man come to own any decent housing by working an ordinary job? So a lot of men are kept out of the dating scene. To make matters worse, most well-off older men are interested only in twenty-somethings, and as a result, many professionally accomplished women have been excluded from the dating arena as well. There are pretty, well-educated, financially secure thirty-somethings galore, but they won't date younger, poor men. These young males, disenfranchised and sexually frustrated, can be a major source of social unrest.

Juli's concert was to take place in a small theater near the city's stadium the next evening, and I was looking forward to it. During my teens I'd been fascinated by Woodstock—the star performers, the crazed audience, the camping tents, the VW buses, the drugs, the sex, the freedom, the harmony, but I was too young to go to the festival by myself. (Although there was a coterie of budding hippies in my prep school, they were so full of themselves that I couldn't get close to them.) Neither of my parents liked that kind of wild music. I always wondered if my mother was tone-deaf—she hardly enjoyed any song. My dad had never outgrown his attachment to Hank Williams. He often said that all the other singers were too mannered and self-conscious, without the spontaneous magic of Williams's voice, which came out of him as naturally as breathing. The only other singer Gary was fond of was Frank Sinatra. During my grad school years, I'd attended some open-air concerts in New England and enjoyed them immensely. Now I was looking forward to Juli's performance.

The event was much smaller than I had expected. It wasn't Juli's concert exactly. She and her band were to play for only fifteen minutes, and the rest of the show would feature other groups of artists. The theater was like a lecture hall that could seat four hundred people, but it was only half filled. As I was walking down the aisle, the walls seemed to be quavering and thumping with music that sounded familiar—earthy, tumbling, raucous, and forceful. It was rock, probably American, but I couldn't place it.

Juli came over the moment I sat down in the second row. She told me that the song was called "Summertime," performed by a Ukrainian band named the Mad Heads.

The lights dimmed and the audience was quieting down. A pudgy emcee in a pin-striped suit and a crimson tie sashayed to the lip of the stage and called out, "Ladies and gentlemen, may I have your attention, please!" He clapped his hands and repeated the request. When the hall hushed, he began to describe the program, which was titled "Mad in Love," saying this was going to be an unforgettable night for everyone. He promised that the show would be nothing shy of bona fide dramatic art and asked the audience to silence their cell phones. As the stage turned dark he faded away.

The first group to perform was a heavy metal trio. The music was too loud, virtually thundering from start to finish. The audience seemed puzzled and hardly responded; perhaps many of them had no clue what to make of this cacophony. Next, Juli's band went onstage. She was sporting a scarlet hip-hugging miniskirt and fishnet stockings and began strumming an electric guitar. On her right arm, near the shoulder, was a tattooed butterfly. She started singing, "All the years I've been looking for you / In my dream and in my memory / You are so close by, yet beyond reach . . ." She looked jittery, and her voice was a bit harsh, halting now and again. But little by little she got more confident. The music, somewhat like rock, wasn't impressive, but the lyrics were pretty good, full of pathos. Her voice was becoming more guttural as she belted out, "Till then I won't say good-bye / And I won't say good-bye." The audience was moved, especially the young people, and started clapping their hands. Some got to their feet, swaying with the music and waving their arms while colored bars of lights ricocheted above their heads. By now Juli and her fellow musicians were playing and singing with total abandon. I was impressed—onstage my niece appeared more daring than in life. She was in a way like her grandfather, demure in appearance but bold at heart.

Two other local groups took the stage after Juli's band, but neither was as good. A pair of young men did a break-dance routine, but they were out of sync with the music and didn't move in unison either. When one was done and stood up, the other was still spinning on the floor like a top. Following them was a kind of strip show—four girls, all wearing sooty eye shadow, spike heels, and canary two-piece swimsuits with frills, strutted, wiggled their hips, and frolicked around. Every one of them seemed to be a bundle of nerves. Their fists were drawing tiny circles in front of them as if they were boxing with someone invisible. Now and again they kicked their feet high, revealing the pale undersides of their legs. Someone in the audience gave a shout of laughter. "Take it off!" a male voice boomed from the right front corner of the hall. I noticed that no matter how erotic the girls' movements were, their faces remained wooden, slightly worried, as if they'd been alert to someone, their director or boss, observing them from the side. The performance felt robotic, though loud catcalls rose from the back.

Then the emcee stepped onstage again and announced, "Dear friends, brothers and sisters, let me remind you that tonight's show is called 'Mad in Love,' so our finale is going to be enacted by two performance artists who will demonstrate our theme to the max."

The stage went dark while the room kept buzzing. When the lights came on again, a couple, both sporting red underwear, the man in his mid-twenties and the woman a few years older, were making out on a large mattress on the stage. The audience was too transfixed to let out a peep. When both performers seemed aroused, they got into a sitting sex position. The woman, straddling the man's lap with her back to his face, peeled off her cherry-red bra and dropped it to the floor. She went on to bump and grind her fleshy backside while they both faked orgasmic cries. Some in the audience grew disgruntled, swearing under their breath. A few snickered and hooted.

Then the two performers changed positions—the woman got on all fours, swaying her hips a little, ready to take the man. As they were slowly stripping off their underwear with exaggerated gestures, a team of police arrived. They rushed onstage, pulled the couple to their feet, and shoved them. The male actor swerved to escape, but a cop tripped him. At once another two pounced on him and pulled him up. One slapped his face while the other punched him in the gut. "Ow!" The man doubled over, holding his sides with both hands.

The two performers had sheets wrapped around them but were still barefoot. The police handcuffed them to each other, led them offstage, and proceeded toward the side exit. Though shaken, the couple kept shouting, "Long live artistic freedom! Wipe out oppression!"

Juli was close to tears, muttering that she too was in hot water now. I wrapped my arm around her shoulders and tried to calm her. Wuping was frantic and hurried up to the emcee to demand an explanation. Why hadn't they informed him of such a hare-brained finale beforehand? Why had they invited that pair of freaks to enact sex publicly? Who was supposed to take responsibility for this show now? Several others also surrounded the chubby emcee, who apparently hadn't breathed a word about the finale to them either. I took Juli out of the theater and hailed a cab.

We went to Stacy's apartment, afraid that the police might be after Juli. My friend was out with her students, so I sat Juli down at the dining table and put the kettle on the stove. She was still in a daze and kept saying, "They'll haul me in tomorrow for sure. Aunt, I'm in big trouble." She shielded a part of her face with her narrow hand, which had callused fingertips and square nails.

After a few mouthfuls of pomegranate tea, she calmed down some. She asked me whether what the performance artists had done was art. "Certainly not," I said. "Millions of people are doing the same thing every day in this province alone. How in God's name can they justify the crude sex act as art? At best it's part of life, an experience but not art."

"So the cops should nab them?" Juli asked, her cheeks still tearstained.

"I don't think they deserve to do jail time. At most they should be charged with public indecency."

"So even in the United States people are not allowed to make love onstage?"

"Not like that. It was too vulgar, beyond the pale."

The more we talked, the more distraught Juli became. She was so terrified by the prospect of getting arrested that she dissolved into tears, sobbing in my arms. Patting her shoulder, I murmured, "I won't let that happen. I won't leave until you're safe."

She hugged me tighter. "Aunt Lilian, you've been so good to me, like my mother."

I wouldn't let her go back to her place that night, afraid that the police might turn up there, so we slept in the same room, sharing a queen-size bed.

The next morning when we saw Wuping, he said that the two performance artists were a married couple, notorious for being flaky, but their marital status might help lighten their penalty, because the charge might simply be public exposure. His prediction turned out to be correct. Rather than being treated as serious criminals, the couple were each given half a year in forced labor, and the chubby emcee lost his job.

I spent three more days keeping Juli company. Convinced that the police were not after her, I returned to Beijing. But the week after I was back, they summoned her. They asked her a host of questions, which she answered truthfully, so they were convinced that she'd had no inkling about the sex performance. She insisted she too had been outraged by it. Lucky for her, they let her go.

1959

The electric fan whirled while Gary slept in his study. Suddenly his daughter burst into tears in the living room. He sat up with a start, rubbing his eyes. He hadn't gone to bed until three in the morning, having to finish a report for Thomas on China's covert campaign to root out the remnants of the Dalai Lama's followers. The Tibetan leader had fled to India a few months before.

"Mommy, I can't get up! Help me!" hollered two-year-old Lilian.

Gary ran into the living room and found his wife lounging on the sofa, watching *Leave It to Beaver*. Her blond hair was in ruby rollers that made her head twice its normal size. Lately Nellie had been so moody that she often threw tantrums. Their baby was lying faceup on the floor in a flowered pinafore and a diaper, one of her legs motionless, apparently in pain, as her other leg kicked the air.

"Leave me alone," Nellie grumbled and pushed Lilian with the side of her slippered foot.

Gary rushed up to his wife and asked sharply, "Why don't you help her?"

"I'm just tired of the little bastard."

"What did you say?"

"I'm tired of her and you!"

He slapped her, then grabbed hold of her forearm and pulled her off the sofa. She yelped. He went on beating her. "Don't ever abuse my children again!" he hissed and kicked her thigh and rear end. Her denim sundress was disheveled; her pink panties showed. Then he caught himself using "children," the plural, and that brought back his presence of mind. He reached down, picked up their daughter, and carried her into his study. The girl kept gulping down her tears. Gary looked at her shin, on which was a bruise the size of a nickel. She had just tripped over a kiddie chair.

From the living room came his wife's wailing. "Goddamn you, Gary! I know you have lots of bastards elsewhere!"

It was out of the question that she could know about his first family, because he'd left their photo in his safety deposit box in the Hong Kong bank. Wait, had he let slip the truth in his sleep? Impossible—Nellie didn't understand Chinese. But couldn't he speak English about his twins? Damn, anything could happen in a dream. He pushed back those unanswerable questions, went into the kitchen, and opened the freezer for ice cubes. He wrapped them in a hand towel and pressed it on Lilian's shin. As his anger subsided, he regretted having beaten Nellie. How could he have lost his head like that? How had he degenerated into a wife beater? A surge of shame sickened him, but he remained unapologetic.

That was the only time he beat his wife. In their twenty-five years of marriage they often quarreled, but he would just walk out if he couldn't stand her fits of temper anymore. He would roam the neighborhood and the parks until he thought she'd cooled off. Yet neither his wife nor their daughter could forget that beating. Even long after he died, Nellie would remind Lilian of the humiliating episode, saying, "It was all thanks to you." Lilian, then in her forties, would remain silent, knowing her mother might blow her top if she responded.

Ever since Lilian began teething, Nellie had been complaining about their apartment, calling it a "henhouse." Their neighbor's television was on most of the time, blasting music and commercials through the poorly insulated wall. The Jamesons, in the unit overhead, would squabble raucously even in the middle of the night, shouting out obscenities and threats. Even their kitchen knife would continue to chop chop chop above Nellie's head every afternoon. She'd given up on the couple, who would never mend their ways however much she pleaded with them. She was sick of all the scuffles and the noise, including that from the front street, where cars would whoosh by even in the early hours of the morning. Just a week ago an old Hungarian woman had broken her hip while descending the stairs, which were worn and slippery. There was also the recent four-dollar increase in the rent, eighty-one dollars a month now. It would surely go up again the next year.

Nellie wanted "a real home," a house on a quiet street where their child could ride a tricycle without their needing to watch over her. Gary agreed to move, but he said they had to wait until they had saved enough for the down payment on a house. Nellie suggested selling their car, but he wouldn't do that. They had a good part of the loan for the Buick yet to pay, and they needed that car. He didn't trust Nellie's opinions about financial matters and often said to her, "You're so extravagant. I never thought you were such an expensive girl when we were dating." Indeed, in spite of her modest origins, she wouldn't hesitate to splurge on clothes, cosmetics, groceries, and toys for their daughter. To be fair, Nellie didn't have fancy taste. When dining out, she didn't mind having hamburgers or fish and fries. Even burritos would do. Her spendthrift ways might have been due to her years of waitressing in bars and restaurants, where she'd seen rich people throw cash around. To some extent, she was pleased that Gary took charge of their money, because he was frugal by American standards and also prudent about household expenditures. Sometimes she joked that she wished her father were a Chinese man. (Grandpa Matt would uncork a bottle of Jack Daniel's or Johnnie Walker on any excuse, and money burned a hole in his pocket.)

Gary also had a good head for investment. Enlightened by a hurricane that had blacked out parts of the DC area for two days the summer before, he'd bought some electricity stocks, which had been rising in value ever since. Nellie was impressed that it was so easy for him to make money.

In truth, he took a casual approach to the investment, which eventually didn't yield much. His mind was preoccupied with other matters. Following the news in his homeland, he came to know that the previous year China had scored a bumper harvest. Then the collectives called "the commune" began to be formed in the countryside. He had misgivings about that, knowing the kolkhozy, the commune system in the Soviet Union, had turned out to be a nightmare. The collectivization in China went to such an extreme that even household kitchens were banned. The country folks began to have meals at communal dining centers, where free food was plentiful enough that everyone could eat their fill. People seemed too optimistic and giddy with fantastic visions, which promised to realize a Communist society soon, a utopian world where everyone would work diligently while taking whatever they needed free of charge. ("You can eat beef stewed with potatoes as much as you want," according to Khrushchev's depiction of Communism.) The Chinese government propagated this slogan nationwide: "Surpass the UK in ten years, catch up with the USA in fifteen."

Gary had been to England and was very impressed by its order, efficiency, and affluence, though it was still recovering from the war. China's official slogan appeared too simpleminded to him, based on the assumption that the United Kingdom and the United States would stop developing. Worse, the Chinese seemed unaware that the West's development had relied on the elaborate building of infrastructure and resulted from centuries' worth of accumulation of wealth and knowledge. Also, of course, from exploiting underdeveloped nations. Bo Yibo, the vice premier in charge of industry, even reported to Chairman Mao that China would surpass England in outputs of electricity and steel in 1959. Mao was so exhilarated that he declared, "We shall definitely get ahead of the Brits in three years, but for now we must keep this secret." That sounded silly to Gary, because to maintain a bigger household you must pay bigger bills—the same went for countries.

Though beset by uncertainties and doubts, Gary was riveted by the tremendous changes in his homeland—evidently the nascent socialist country was developing at a record pace. Growing up, he had seen how destitute the people were—many county seats would be teeming with beggars in the springtime, and some folks were so desperate that they sold their children and headed south to beg. By any criterion China was poor. More than half the population was illiterate, and everywhere the land was exhausted after sustaining the population for millennia. Granted, the socialist system might have unleashed the potential of the country, but most Chinese seemed unaware how shabby their land was compared to many other nations. At the same time, Gary could sense a kind of desperation in Mao, who'd just spoken about the necessity of reaching economic preeminence in the world, saying, "If you have no rice in your hand, even chickens won't respond to your call." The chairman's analogy, devoid of his habitual pompous rhetoric, seemed to show his knowledge of their country's plight; on the other hand, it also implied that Mao might aspire to become the leader of the Socialist Bloc, like the late Stalin. The chairman's ego must be too inflated.

Unlike his American colleagues, who were amused by some Chinese posters designed to promote the Great Leap Forward in developing the country's economy, Gary felt downhearted about them. He resented David Shuman's flippant remarks about "the propaganda crap." The young man, a graduate of the University of Chicago, had joined the translation agency two years before; he was over six feet tall with sloped shoulders and in the habit of carrying to work a red water bottle that resembled a miniature fire extinguisher. He hated Communism with a passion because his paternal grandfather had perished in a Soviet labor camp on Sakhalin Island. David and Gary often argued about the rift between China and the Soviet Union. Most times Gary could get the upper hand, believing that the two countries were not on congenial terms in spite of their apparent friendliness. But nowadays, when they looked at the Chinese propaganda graphics together, he could hardly say anything against David's gibes and smirks, because the pictures were indeed preposterous, some even farcical. In one, a plump young woman sat atop rice plants to prove that the crops were thick enough to support her weight. Obviously the plants had been put together for the photo shoot. Every province had begun bragging about their increased grain production; some counties even upped the number to twenty or thirty times more than the previous year. (This in turn made the state demand doubled or tripled grain contributions from them, and consequently, more country people starved to death.)

Many of the posters showed wild imaginings: pigs as large as elephants; enormous bundles of rice plants launched into space in the form of satellites; a new breed of corn that grew so gigantic a railroad flatcar could carry only a single ear; the same with wheat, but two ears per flatcar. (The caption claimed: "Shipping Our Harvest to Beijing for Chairman Mao.") Even the photos of actual things and events were incredible. To promote steel production, smelting furnaces were erected all over the countryside like small granaries constructed of mud, more than thirty thousand of them lighting the skies day and night. Commune members, besides being deprived of their poultry and animals, were ordered to surrender their utensils to the stopgap furnaces—every piece of iron and steel must go. Even metal gates and fences were dismantled and taken away. Their leaders told them, "Whatever we have belongs to the public, even our bones." In some areas it was a crime to hide any iron tool or vessel—"the same as harboring an enemy soldier in your home," an editorial claimed. The makeshift smelting furnaces emerged in cities as well, where citizens were also mobilized to join the steel production. One stood in the very compound where Mao resided. With a broad smile the chairman watched his young colleagues pouring out molten steel. Gary couldn't help asking himself: Can steel be produced that easily? Something must be terribly amiss.

Oddly enough, despite the distance of an ocean and a continent, he now could feel China's pulse, which beat irregularly, racing feverishly, as though he could at last grasp intimately his vast homeland in its entirety. For his superiors back home he compiled information showing that even the Americans believed China might implode if it continued with all the reckless experiments.

Gary shared his concerns with Bingwen when they met in Hong Kong in late August. His comrade sighed deeply and said, "People seem to have lost their senses. In my hometown everyone enjoyed free meals last fall and began to laze around because they didn't need to work hard to support themselves and their families anymore. The crops were bountiful but left to rot in the fields. The villagers ate the whole year's food in just three months, so they had to starve afterward. If the harvest is bad this year, they'll face a terrible time."

"How about all the activities promoting steel output?" Gary asked, taking a drag on his Peony cigarette.

"That was a mess too. Most of the makeshift furnaces can produce nothing but low-quality pig iron. So there's no substantial increase in steel production to speak of."

"I hope Yufeng and my kids are all right. Can you ask our leaders if I can go back and see them and my parents?"

"Don't think about it for now. The higher-ups made it clear again that you must stay in America as long as possible. By crossing the border back into China, you'd blow your identity. We cannot afford such a loss. But don't worry about your family—we take good care of them."

"This makes me feel like an exile, banished by my own comrades," Gary said with some bitterness.

"Be patient, brother. I know how great a sacrifice you've been making for our country, but you're in a unique position to perform such a service. Among us you're the only one destined for greatness. Believe me, someday you will come home with honor and glory."

Gary didn't argue further, knowing his request would be denied. As a matter of fact, he had recently concluded that his twins back home could be a blessing, because by the time he was withdrawn from the States he might be too old to raise a family. It was better to have children now. This thought comforted him some and made him more determined to have Yufeng and their kids well provided for and protected. For that, he'd better keep a cordial relationship with Bingwen.

Bingwen relayed their superiors' instructions: Gary must Americanize himself as thoroughly as possible and remain a mole in the U.S. intelligence system. He also told Gary that from now on he mustn't come to Hong Kong directly for their meeting. He should take a vacation in Taiwan, and from there he could make an excursion to Hong Kong for a day or two. This was to preempt the CIA's suspicion.

Gary took all the cash, six thousand dollars, out of his Hang Seng bank account. When he came back to the States, he told Nellie that he now had the down-payment money for a house—his cousin had just repaid an old debt. In the past she had often chafed at his taking a vacation alone in Asia and once said, "I know you'll chase some pussy there." But this time, Nellie deduced that he hadn't seen any woman, otherwise he couldn't have come back loaded with cash, plus two fine silk dresses for her. Nellie felt relieved. Before long they started house hunting.

My seminar on Asian American history was over at the beginning of June, the grad students left alone to write their final papers, but my undergrad class continued. These days the campus was tense because the anniversary of the Tiananmen Square incident was approaching. The Party cadres had been attending meetings to make plans for keeping order and peace at the college. Like elsewhere in China, every department of the school had two lines of leadership, one of the Party and the other of the administration. The real power was the Party secretary, sometimes called "chancellor" in foreigners' presence because the word "secretary" had a negative ring, whereas the department's chairperson was more like a manager who had to report to the Party boss. With few exceptions, the administrative heads were also Party members, so the Party controlled everything. A number of my Chinese colleagues told me that they had just received phone calls from the police, who warned them about June 4: on that day they mustn't speak publicly, mustn't hold any gathering larger than six people, mustn't wear black armbands or white clothes, and mustn't take to the streets. One old professor was so annoyed by a midnight phone call that he joked, "Hell, I shall go out in the raw on that day."

On June 2, the president of a communications college in Beijing, Professor Wei Fang, came to give a talk. He was an authority on cyberspace control. A technocrat, he held a number of patents on Internet policing devices. Out of curiosity I went to his talk; the topic was "Managing China's Cyberspace." The auditorium was filled almost to capacity, with about six hundred attendees. A vice president of our college introduced Professor Fang, saying the man was a pioneer in China's Internet technology, revered as a founding father of the Great Firewall. Then Fang, a potbellied man with wire-rimmed glasses, lurched to his feet and waddled to the podium. He opened a yellow folder and started his speech with a long preamble, his head bobbing up and down.

A smile played on his pudgy face while his beady eyes almost disappeared. He was small-boned but heavy-fleshed. His hair, dyed raven black, was so lustrously gelled that it might have been too slippery for a fly to land on. "Dear students and comrades," he said in a jubilant voice, "I am here today to reminiscence about the arduous process of protecting our national sovereignty in cyberspace. In addition to talking about the great feats and ingenuity my colleagues performed, I would like to share with you our experiences—our glory, frustration, and gratification—in serving our motherland. We all know that the Internet has never been a neutral space like the high seas. Numerous foreign powers hostile to China have been utilizing the new technology to penetrate our communications systems so as to disseminate rumors, incite civil unrest, sabotage our Party's leadership, and undermine the foundation of our socialist country. The Internet is a new weapon used by international reactionaries, so we must seize it and fight back with it.

"As early as 1992, the Party Central Committee, wise and prescient, assembled a group of more than twenty experts to deliberate about the dangers that might arise from the Internet and to search for ways to regulate its use and monitor the traffic online. Truth be told, I am still amazed by how astute our national leaders were. As time goes by, the advantages of our Internet supervision system grow more and more conspicuous. Some of you might be aware of what has been happening in Russia, where the government hasn't implemented any online intervention at all, and as a result, any skilled blogger or Facebook user can start a public gathering easily—"

"Get offstage!" a male voice cried from the audience.

"Shut your stinking trap!" another called out.

A sneaker passed the speaker's head. Another one hit his chest and stunned him.

"Shame on you!" a few voices bellowed together.

"Running dog, get out of here!" a girl yelled.

Some students in the front began throwing eggs at Professor Fang. One hit his flat forehead; instantly his face was streaked with the yolk. He was so shocked that wordlessly he took off his glasses and polished them on the corner of his jacket, their gilt stems flailing. Without the glasses on and with his eyes bugging out a little, he looked ten years older, as if he were in his seventies.

"Give us online freedom!" a voice boomed. Some of the audience repeated the demand in unison.

"Tear down the Internet Berlin Wall!" another man cried. More people roared together.

Two security guards turned up, leapt onto the stage, and whisked the speaker away. The moment Fang appeared in the aisle heading to the back exit, slippers, loafers, sneakers all were hurled at him. A few hit his head and roundish shoulders. Some students raised smartphones to snap photos of him in flight. Shuffling away with the guards, Professor Fang became furious, hollering with one eye closed, "You all will face legal consequences! You'll be kicked out of college! Damn you, I'll get back at you!" His voice was booming through the lavalier mike still on his lapel while he waved his hands, giving the audience the finger and for some reason also the victory sign.

"Students, don't lose your heads!" shouted the vice president of our college. "Don't put our school to shame!"

"Shameless scumbag!" someone responded.

"Strike down the lackeys!" screamed another.

The minute the speaker vanished beyond the door, the audience began to break up, filing out through different exits. Amazingly, I saw Minmin holding an empty bucket and heading to the platform. I intercepted her and whispered, "Did you plan to bust up the talk beforehand?"

"No, I wasn't with them at all." She shook her permed hair. "I'm just going to pick up the shoes so those who threw them can have them back. My friends are setting up a lost-and-found corner in the front lobby."

"That's very thoughtful of you," I said.

She smiled and proceeded toward the front. Then her classmate Hongbin appeared, a smile fanning out across his face and his nostrils dilated. He was the only Party member among the students I knew, and he often challenged me in class discussion. "Serves him right!" he panted. "The shameless toady!"

"You don't like our guest speaker either?" I asked, a bit nonplussed.

"I hate his guts! Every time my fiancée emails me something interesting from Japan, it's blocked. That man is my enemy; he's the enemy of all the netizens in China."

"We'd better leave," I reminded him.

Without delay I left the auditorium, afraid of being spotted by the campus police. On the same day the incident became national news across the Internet. Although no student was identified as an egg or shoe thrower, there were all kinds of rewards offered to them online: Nike shoes to be shipped from Amazon, gift cards for bookstores, dozens of Alaska snow crabs, Apple iPads, one-night stands, vacations at beach resorts, porcelain toilets, whole sets of Haruki Murakami's novels, even girlfriends and boyfriends. It was hard to tell what percentage of the offers was genuine, given that no one could claim any of them.

My colleagues and I were worried about the students' safety. The following day the security on campus was stepped up, but fortunately the college didn't take measures to discipline the rabble-rousers—it would be too risky to ignite another outburst of anger right before the anniversary of the Tiananmen Square incident.

June 4 saw plenty of police patrolling the campus, though the tense atmosphere was eased by the French Open in Paris, at which the Chinese tennis player Li Na was to play the final match with the Italian defending champion. Most students gathered in the dorms watching the game. When Li Na finally won the Grand Slam, they came out in force, lit chains of firecrackers, and played instruments and thumped drums and basins in celebration. No one ran amok, though. Some shouted "Li Na, offense!" as if she were still fighting on the tennis court. Some teachers joined the celebration as well, and the police didn't interfere. The young people regarded Li Na as a hero, partly because she had quit the national tennis team long ago and won the championship on her own. What's more, her victory made history—no Asian player had ever won the French Open.

In her acceptance speech Li Na didn't thank China or any leaders. Instead she said, "My thanks to my sponsor, to the staff here, to the ball kids, and to my team." She also took the opportunity to wish a friend a happy birthday. That was extraordinary to the Chinese and certainly grated on the bureaucracy. On another public occasion she had insisted, "Don't talk about bringing honor to our country. I'm competing for myself." She once cried into a mike held by a reporter, "I love you, Jiang Shan!" That was her husband, who couldn't accompany her to the tournament. She also openly claimed she played tennis for money. Regardless, when the band started the Chinese anthem at the medal ceremony, she turned tearful and mouthed the words. To the students, Li Na embodied a rebellious, independent spirit. Hers was a new face of China, open and confident and smiling, so for the moment she became an icon, an inspiration to the young people.

At last I heard from my nephew, Benning. Evidently he and Juli had just exchanged emails, and he knew I was American and a history professor. He wrote his message in solid, effortless English, which struck me as extraordinary. Yet when I suggested meeting him in person, he became evasive, saying he was too far away from Beijing at the moment. But where was he? I didn't get a clear answer. The more he hedged, the more curious I got.

Then one day he confessed, "I am in the United States, on the East Coast." That was a shock, and I wanted to know more. "Don't interrogate me, please," he wrote. "I am sure we will spend a lot of time together in the future."

I wouldn't let it go at that and kept asking him. He avoided answering fully but would reveal something from time to time. I tried to form a picture of him with the scraps of information I had. He'd been in the States for more than two years, running a small business outside Boston that dealt in software and computer parts. He'd been assigned there by a Chinese company and seemed to be enjoying himself. The reason he hadn't told his family his whereabouts was that he felt he might be called back or sent elsewhere after his current assignment; also because he came back to China for business or vacation every two or three months. I said I'd love to see him remain in the States for many years, which he said was what he wanted too. I was excited that I would have a family member on my father's side living near me after I went home. The world suddenly felt smaller and more mysterious. If only my father could have seen his grandson in America.

1961

The Shangs were living in a quiet cul-de-sac at the end of Riverview Street in Alexandria. Their home was a raised ranch with an attached carport; a huge rock sat beside the house, and holly hedges demarcated the property. A pomegranate tree, rare in Virginia but already more than ten years old, stood in a corner of the backyard, reminding Gary of the same kind of tree back in his home province. He had paid twenty-three thousand dollars for this place, a little higher than the market price, but he loved the tranquil location, the brick exterior of the house, the living room with oak-paneled walls, and the finished lower floor, where the windows were just above the ground and where he could have a room for a study, so without haggling he had clinched the purchase. Nellie also liked the home, particularly the bay window in the kitchen and the French doors between the living room and the dining room, which made the house feel more spacious than it was. She was fond of the peaceful neighborhood too and devoted herself to taking care of Lilian and to the housework. The girl was going to be four in July, and once she started preschool, Nellie would look for a job, doing something she liked. But what did she want to do? She wasn't sure yet, though she thought about it now and then.

Gary would mow the half-acre lawn and trim the shrubs. All the work outside the house belonged to him, including digging out the weeds in grass—dandelions, creeping charlie, mallow, clover. He hated slugs and would get rid of every one he saw. He was good with his hands and maintained their car and household appliances. Sometimes when he was free, he'd take a walk in the nearby park, where the air would quiver with scattered birdsong. He'd bring along his daughter if the weather permitted, either holding her in his arms or leading her by the hand, and once in a while he would carry her piggyback. He'd teach her some Mandarin words or phrases. To some extent he was a good family man, gentle to his family and polite to their neighbors, who were all impressed by the chrysanthemums he had planted around his house. Yet he was detached from what was going on around him and wouldn't mix with others, except for the fact that he followed the NBA on his own and could talk with his colleagues about the games. Try as he might, he couldn't get excited about baseball; the game was too slow for him. Fortunately, his wife never complained about their lack of social life. Rarely would the Shangs invite people over. Not until their daughter was old enough to make school friends and to hold a pajama party once a year, around Halloween, did they begin to have a few visitors.

Although Gary was calm in appearance, 1961 was a tumultuous year for him. In the spring he was naturalized. At the citizenship ceremony he pledged allegiance to the Star-Spangled Banner and swore he'd bear arms to defend the U.S. Constitution, a document he had read with great admiration for its careful attention to the citizens' rights defined and protected by the amendments. It was like a contract between the country and the people. He went through the whole ceremony with a numb heart, though he was deeply impressed by its solemnity and forced a smile when he showed a woman official his expired Chinese passport. With a pair of scissors she cut a corner off its front cover, handed it back to him, and congratulated him on his brand-new citizenship. By now Gary could honestly say he loved some aspects of American life— the orderliness, the plentitude, the privacy, the continuity of daily life, the freedom of travel (domestically with a car and internationally with a U.S. passport or green card). Nevertheless, his mind couldn't help but wander to the distant land where his other family was. He had decided not to have more children with Nellie, not wanting further complications. For him, happiness lay elsewhere, and he could visualize it only in his homeland and in the reunion with his original family.

With his U.S. citizenship in hand, he had to pass a lie-detector test in order to become a regular CIA employee. He read about how the polygraph worked and knew that as long as he wasn't disturbed by any question and didn't make the needle jump, he should be able to fool the machine. To keep himself calm, he began to put into his teacups two herbs—schisandra fruit and tuckahoe, both of which he'd bought in San Francisco years before. For days the herbal tea made him slightly sedated, and a week later he passed the test without difficulty. Now he had access to documents classified as Top Secret, some of which were sent to him for translation directly from George Thomas, who had earned his PhD the year before and was now addressed as Dr. Thomas by his colleagues. He and Gary, though, were still on a first-name basis. They continued to frequent jazz bars together. Most times Thomas would talk while Gary just listened. Afterward he would recall their conversations, write down snippets of intelligence, and squirrel them away.

Now able to read more reports on the Far East, Gary could see that China was in shambles. The Great Leap Forward had been a catastrophe, and the whole land had been ravaged by a continuous famine. The collectivization in the countryside ruined the agriculture. People wouldn't work hard anymore because they were no longer paid and could eat for free. During the previous fall a lot of crops were left in the fields, to be eaten by birds and animals or just to rot. Even fruit was not picked in some orchards. When people had consumed all the food before the winter set in, they began to eat the seeds. As a result, many fields couldn't be sown in the spring. This reduced grain production drastically. Now in both cities and the countryside people were starving and dying. Many secretly left their villages for provinces where the famine was less severe.

Bad news came from all over China, but Gary focused his attention on his home province, Shandong, because he wasn't sure whether some of the information had been doctored by Taiwan's intelligence service to influence the White House and the Pentagon. (They were always eager to present a chaotic China to the Americans.) By following the events in a place he knew, he might be more capable of assessing the severity of the situation. Yet he could find little news about his hometown, though he gathered quite a bit of information on some nearby counties. Most country folks there suffered from dropsy, with swelled bellies and their legs puffed out like small barrels. Many women had prolapsed uteruses; even those in their twenties and thirties underwent menopause. An official in charge of birth control admitted that she no longer needed to hand out contraceptives because people were too feeble to conceive. The government tried to help some, issuing six ounces of grain per day for a grown-up and four for a child. But the emergency rations were distributed through echelons of cadres, many of whom would embezzle some for themselves and their families. As a result, country folks received hardly any food. According to one account, in the Huimin area, the prefecture where Gary's home county was located, tens of thousands had died of hunger and some villages were deserted.

For a whole summer he followed the reports anxiously, still a tad incredulous. How could it be possible for the China that used to be poised to surpass the United Kingdom to collapse into such havoc in the blink of an eye? When dining at Chinese restaurants, he would prick his ears to catch bits of conversation and would talk with others about the situation back home. One day, he saw Suzie Chao, a Mandarin broadcaster at Voice of America, sitting alone in Bamboo Garden, an eatery that had only six tables and offered a lunch special for seventy-five cents. He asked her, "Can I join you?"

"Of course, welcome," she said pleasantly, her almond-shaped eyes smiling as she waved her slim hand.

He placed his bowl of noodles on the table and sat down opposite her. She looked worried in spite of her bright face. She had a vibrant voice, which had struck Gary as tinged with yearning whenever he heard her on the air, as though she were speaking to somebody she knew well but couldn't reach. They talked about the famine back in China. She was also anxious to learn more about it. Gary told her about the reduction of population in Shandong but added, "A lot of folks fled their homes or just disappeared, so the figures we got might have been exaggerated. Still, it looks awful."

She sighed and flipped back her hair to keep her pageboy in shape. "I've just heard that my uncle's family lost their home. The villagers went to tear down his house and used the bricks and timber to build a pig farm."

"Why would they do that?" Gary asked, thinking it might have been because of her relatives' connection with her family, who had fled to Taiwan.

"All the houses belong to the commune now. This makes me sick." She sniveled, on the brink of tears.

"But can they still raise pigs—I mean, do they have something to feed to the pigs?"

"Actually, the pigs are all gone. Either died of disease or were slaughtered for food. People were too desperate to think about their future livelihood. They even ate grass and elm bark. A lot of them starved to death. I heard there was cannibalism in my home county."

That came as a surprise. Suzie was from Jiangsu, a province known for its fertile paddies and abundant water supply, generally called "a land of fish and rice." If the famine had wreaked havoc in a place like that, then the whole of China must have become hell.

After that lunch, Gary and Suzie often met at noon or talked on the phone. Initially he was cautious when speaking with her and suspected she might have a complicated background, with her family both in Taiwan and on the mainland. She was poised and somewhat pretty and had a fine figure and a distinct voice. As they got to know each other better, he was surprised to find her single. Unlike most young women, she was not in a hurry to look for a man, though she was already thirty-one. She even claimed she could never make a good wife ("Domesticity is not my strong point," she confessed), so it would be better for her to remain single. She'd once had a boyfriend in Kao-hsiung, a journalist who'd died in a ferry accident seven years before. That man was an overseas Chinese from Indonesia but had lived in Taiwan most of his life. These days whenever Suzie heard something about the famine on the mainland, she would share it with Gary, who was good at analyzing the information and could see numerous implications. She was impressed and said, "If I had your brain, I'd go to law school or do a PhD in the history of science."

The more time they spent together, the more intimate their conversations became. One day over dinner Suzie revealed to Gary that a few years ago she had dated an American man, an audio engineer at the Capitol, but they broke up because he looked down on things Chinese. She told Gary, "In the beginning Michael was all right, but he got spoiled. I was too easy on him, I guess. One evening I made rice crust soup and he said under his breath, 'It's impossible to eat Chinese shit every day.' I heard him and shot back, 'If you sleep with a Chinese woman, you ought to eat Chinese food.' We had a row, and I just couldn't stomach it anymore, so we split. Afterward I gave up dating altogether."

Gary chuckled softly. Her story reminded him of Nellie, who never complained about the food he liked. For that he was grateful. Then Suzie sighed and said, "No matter where I go, I always feel I'm Chinese."

For some reason her words moved him, though he pressed on, "But you're a U.S. citizen, are you not?"

"I am. I don't mean I can't be a citizen of another country. I mean something inside me cannot be changed, was already shaped and fixed in China. In that sense I'm damned."

"To be honest, I feel the same," Gary said. "If you had come to the States before your teens, you might have been more adaptable."

"Probably."

They slept together a few weeks later on a late fall evening, in her apartment on Duke Street. After an early dinner she had

invited him to tea at her place. Her apartment had one bedroom
and a living room, a tidy cozy nest decked with flowered sofa cov-
ers and sage-colored window curtains that had big rings at the
tops. They didn't drink tea but shared a jar of rice wine instead,
which a friend of Suzie's had brought back from Taipei. Then one
thing led to another. The sex that followed was bone-shaking and
tempestuous. Her pillows dropped on the hardwood floor, next
to their clothes crumpled in a pile. They panted out coarse words
that neither of them had ever heard spoken here. "Ah!" she gasped,
her mouth open like that of a fish just out of water. Holding her
nipple in his mouth, he kept plunging, his back arched. They'd
been raising a tremendous din, unafraid of being heard by others,
assuming nobody in the building could understand their love cries.
Engulfed in the whirlwind of desire, they'd lost the sense of shame
and shed the armor of self-respect. The vulgar expressions gushed
out of them with force, as though the words were forgotten incan-
tations, coming back with a vengeance to drive them to copulate
for the sake of self-preservation. They fucked like animals.

Suzie was in tears after she came for the second time. Her hair
was mussed, but her flushed cheeks gave her a youthful glow. For
a moment even her neck was ruddy. She confessed, "You made me
feel like a woman again. Guess I won't be able to sleep well for a
couple of days. I will miss you."

Her words unsettled Gary, and he checked his impulse to ask
in jest what part of him she would miss. Then it struck him that
she too was a lonely soul, homesick and restless in spite of her composed façade. What amazed both of them was that, lying shoulder
to shoulder in bed, they became chatterboxes, as if there were endless things they could talk about—from their childhoods in the
provinces to their college years in Beijing, from the local foods they
missed to the mountains and beach resorts they had both been to,
from the family members persecuted in the Land Reform Movement to the class statuses in China's countryside now, from the
differences in the sense of beauty between Asians and Westerners to

some plain-featured Chinese women married by handsome foreign men. They talked and talked until around one a.m., when he had to climb out of bed and go home.

It felt chilly outside. Gary fastened the middle button on his light duffle coat. A thin blaze of moon was high in the sky, which was thick with stars, a few twinkling through the spiky branches. An oak tree dropped an acorn on a nearby roof, the nut thrumming down the shingles until it hit the ground with a tiny thud. Walking in the limpid moonlight to his car parked behind Suzie's building, for some reason Gary remembered the English expression "talk a blue streak." And he envisioned the two of them caged like a pair of birds that could chirp and warble only to each other.

IN THE PRACTICE OF ESPIONAGE, gathering intelligence is just the first step. After that, there is the task of analyzing the information, and then comes the challenge of how to make the best use of it. So much intelligence had gone through Gary's hands these last few months that he couldn't possibly photograph all the valuable pages, so he had adopted the role of analyst as well. He chose what he believed were important passages, and compiled and synthesized them to make a coherent report. In his analyses he highlighted the U.S. awareness of the catastrophic situation in China. He meant to convey to the Chinese leaders that if they didn't get out of their mess soon, China might open itself to attacks from other countries. Unlike the United States, with oceans on the east and west and no powerful country to the south or north, a weak China, surrounded by hostile neighbors, many of which had territorial disputes with it, would be like an exhausted body floating in shark-infested water. He knew his analyses might sound a little far-fetched at times, but he couldn't help himself and even mentally cursed the stupid Chinese leaders.

He went to Taipei in late December 1961 and from there made a short trip to Hong Kong. He told Nellie that his cousin's mother-in-law had just died, so he felt obligated to pay a visit, but his cousin was living with his in-laws in Taiwan now. Bingwen was in Hong Kong to meet him again. The man looked sickly and emaciated, which further convinced Gary of the severity of the famine. But his friend shook his bushy head and said, "I just had hernia surgery and haven't fully recuperated yet. Everything's swell back home."

That couldn't have been true and must have been what Bingwen had been instructed to tell Gary. Plainly the man had a famished look, and when they dined in restaurants, Bingwen would order a tableful of food for just the two of them and would wolf down whatever he could. He informed Gary of a big promotion—now his rank was the sixteenth, which was equal to a major's in the army. Gary was pleased, and together they downed three shot cups of Maotai in a row. Bingwen assured him that Yufeng and the twins were well but that his parents had passed away the previous winter—his father died first, then his mother, three months later. Both of them had been slowed by rheumatism in recent years and coughed some during the winter, but other than that, they'd had no major health problems. Bingwen assured Gary that their deaths were due not to hunger but to old age. They'd been in their sixties, so Gary believed they'd met their natural ends, even though his mother's was caused by a bout of fever. Bingwen told him that he'd gone to the countryside personally to see to their funerals, whose expenses the local government had paid. Gary's parents were interred in the Shang clan's burial ground, both clad in new clothes, and a dozen or so wreaths were presented to them. Everything was handled in a proper manner.

Before the trip, Gary had thought about writing to his family and asking Bingwen to mail his letter in China, but now he quashed the notion, certain that such a letter would never be delivered. He was not allowed to communicate directly with his family back home. In addition, he'd feel uncomfortable letting others read what he wrote to his wife. Since his salary went to Yufeng every month, she and their children should be able to live decently.

He hadn't shown much emotion when Bingwen told him about his parents' deaths, but once back in the hotel room alone, Gary felt the waves of grief surging in him, paralyzing his will to do anything. He lay on the bed and wept from time to time, immersed in the memories of his parents. As a teenager, his father had gone to Siberia with a gang of villagers to seek his fortune. They'd ended up in Vladivostok, where by luck he was hired by an old Chinese couple who owned a small emporium. Literate and quick, he soon could manage the business on his own, and the childless couple loved him so much that they adopted him as a son. Three years later they both caught typhoid and died after bequeathing to him everything they owned. He sold the shop, returned to his home village, and bought four acres of good cropland. The next year he built his house of five rooms, which boasted a ceramic-tiled roof, and he married a girl from a well-to-do family. The bride wasn't pretty but had finished elementary school, which was rare among girls at the time. The young couple planned to raise a big family, but somehow they could have only one child.

Gary would say that his parents had lived a decent life, though the old man had always toiled in the fields alongside his hired hands. His father and mother were so overjoyed when he had passed the entrance exams and enrolled at a top university in Beijing that they went to a lakeside temple to burn incense and donate twenty silver dollars to the local god, who had once been a chieftain of bandits but always protected the common people. It was in Gary's junior year at Tsinghua University that his parents chose Yufeng for him. They believed that the girl, amiable and healthy, could bring good fortune to the household. Out of filial duty Gary went back to see his bride-to-be, who, to his delight, was lovely and well mannered, so he agreed to the engagement. Now, lying in the hotel bed and breathing the moldy air, he was tormented by grief and anger, seething at his superiors, who had kept him from his family. He was sure that his wife had been a conscientious daughter-in-law to his parents. If only he could have seen his mom and dad before they died. The sorrow yanked at his heart again and again, and for two days he didn't step out of the hotel.

✧✧✧

Summer vacation at the teachers college would not begin until early July, but because my classes were over, the final exam and papers all graded, I could head home in mid-June. Knowing that my nephew, Benning, was in the States, I was eager to go back and see him. I also missed home and my husband.

I found that Henry, though sixty-one, appeared younger than when I'd left half a year ago. I joked that he might live to be a hundred if I stayed away from him. He said, "That I don't know, but for sure you'll outlive me." His was a family of longevity. His father had died at ninety-four, and two months prior to his death, the old man had still taken evening walks in the state forest south of his house. His mother, eighty-nine now, refused to go to a senior home and was able to care for herself. Most of their relatives, the Cohens, were in Europe, and some had migrated to Israel. Henry often said I sucked his energy, probably because he felt tired easily when I was around. In contrast, living with him, sharing the bed and the dining table, I always got refreshed. This may be a matter of chemistry. In my early thirties I'd had a brief but intense affair with a Chinese man, who I felt drained my energy whenever I spent time with him. He was a decent fellow and might have loved me. But because of the insurmountable obstacles—he'd have had to give up his career, his Party membership, his wife and son to marry me—we parted ways. I won't say I loved him, but the affair left a deep wound in me. Yet bit by bit I managed to push him out of my mind, and I was healed. Even when I was last in Beijing, I hadn't looked him up, but every once in a while my memory of him still crinkled the placid surface of my contentment.

Henry was delighted to see me back, following me from room to room so we could talk without letup. Though half Jewish, he looked a bit Mongolian, with heavy eyelids on his oval face, and wore his hair in a mullet. He had on a T-shirt and jeans, which set off his long limbs and little paunch. He had attended Northwestern Law School but had quit after a year because by then he no longer wanted to be a lawyer. Unlike his two siblings, a financial planner and an editor at *The Wall Street Journal,* he enjoyed working with his hands and was good at fixing things. We rarely hired others for the landscaping and maintenance of the building. He was as capable as any professional. Moreover, maintaining the property helped keep him in shape. We were a good team for the work—I handled the bills and kept the books.

We went to Seven Seas for dim sum the day after my return. Ironically, those Cantonese appetizers were what I had missed most in China, where food was more diverse and often better prepared, but ever since my student Minmin told me about the antibiotics and pesticides overused in food production there, I had grown more apprehensive and avoided dining out as much as possible. Whenever I saw giant pears for sale, each weighing over a pound, I'd feel uneasy. Later I discovered that many powerful and wealthy Chinese had their own food supplies that came direct from restricted gardens and farms. Some officials even had hills sealed off so that they could grow tea unaffected by insecticides and have it harvested manually. There were also organic grocery stores throughout the country serving only senior officers and officials. Henry and I sat in a booth, enjoying the meal at leisure. When I mentioned I had a nephew in Massachusetts, his eyes brightened.

"Take it easy," I told Henry. "Benning is not a kid, he's twenty-six."

"That's a kid to me. Why didn't you tell me he's in the States?"

"He just told me, and I haven't figured him out yet. Let's try to get to know him step by step, okay?"

"Sure, no need to rush."

"It's so good to be back and make a pig of myself again."

Despite saying that, I hardly ever overate. In my childhood my mother would weigh me every week, saying that if a girl's figure was gone, she'd lose her prospects. She allowed me to eat ice cream once a week, but I could have cookies more often, perhaps because she got them at a discount. I don't know why she thought weight might be a problem for me; neither she nor my father was on the heavy side. At present I was five foot eight and 132 pounds. Of course, after a hearty meal of dim sum, that would be a different story—I'd be pushing 135.

That evening I phoned Benning. He sounded cheerful, calling me Aunt time and again. That pleased me. His sister Juli must have assured him that I was not an impostor but a real aunt of theirs. Still, when I said I'd like to come and see him, he paused, his breathing audible. Then he said, "By all means, I'd love to meet you in person, Aunt Lilian." He gave me his address and the directions, which were unnecessary because I knew Boston well.

I loved riding the train between DC and Boston, especially when the ocean came into view in Connecticut and when I saw swans cruising in lakes, most times in pairs. Even Baltimore could appear beautiful after snow, like an abandoned battleground swathed in white serenity. In China, whenever people asked me what the biggest difference was between their country and the United States, I'd tell them that America had a different landscape—simply put, the land is more suitable for human habitation and more abundant in natural resources. They might not have believed me, but I said the truth. Chinese land by comparison seemed overused and exhausted. I suggested they take the Greyhound across North America if they came to visit this continent. Then they might see how much China could benefit from keeping a good relationship with the United States and Canada, considering both countries' vast natural resources and plentiful agricultural products.

Benning was standing outside when I emerged from the subway station at Quincy Center. He beamed, as if we'd met before (in a way we had—we'd exchanged photos via email). He came up and took over my small suitcase, saying, "Welcome, Aunt Lilian." I was struck by his resemblance to my father, the same kind of elongated smiling eyes, wide nose, round cheeks, and strong jaw. His legs were slightly bandy too, making him walk with splayed feet like his grandfather. He looked five foot nine, a bit shorter than Gary. He must have come directly from work, a brown leather briefcase hanging over his shoulder from two hooked fingers of his other hand.

He told me he had dropped "ning" in his first name, so I should call him just Ben. He lived by himself in an apartment building six or seven minutes' walk from the train station. His unit had four rooms, and he insisted that I stay with him when I mentioned I wouldn't mind spending the night in a motel. After I washed up and sat down in his living room, he said, "Aunt Lilian, for dinner, should we go out or eat in here? I can cook or order takeout."

"Let's go out. I did graduate work at BU. I want to see what Quincy's like now."

It was a cool day for late June, a steady breeze blowing from the northeast. My skin could feel the ocean as we ambled along Hancock Street toward downtown. The city had changed quite a bit—there were more Asian faces now. A few shop signs even displayed Chinese characters beside the English words. Small wonder I was told that Quincy was becoming Boston's second Chinatown, but that seemed unlikely, because it was a city, sprawling in every direction and with four subway stations, and the Asian population was scattered everywhere, without a center. At most, some Chinese immigrants and expats might be settling in pockets of this big town. Ben and I decided to enter a restaurant that specialized in Taiwanese cuisine.

While waiting for our order, he told me about his life here. He'd been in the Boston area for a year and a half and had just gotten a green card, but he traveled a lot, going to Asia and Europe eight or nine times a year. "I might not be able to live here for long," he said.

"Why?" I asked. "Don't you like it here?"

"Love it. But my business is a branch of a state-owned company. I might get transferred anytime."

He turned to speak Cantonese to a moonfaced waitress, who had greeted him in a friendly manner. I was impressed by his fluency in the dialect, and when the woman moved away, I asked him how he knew the language. "I lived in Guangzhou for a while" was his answer. I remembered that my father had complained in his diary that he couldn't make head or tail of Cantonese when he visited Hong Kong. Once he observed, "They seem to call everyone a devil."

Ben wanted to know how his parents and siblings were doing. I assured him that they were well but anxious to know what he was up to. While talking, I couldn't help wondering how much he knew about my father. I hadn't mentioned Gary to him yet, unable to bring myself to give him too much all at once. Our order came—he had steamed chow mein and I fish congee. We shared two dishes, sautéed green beans and orange chicken. I enjoyed such a simple, good meal and was glad to see that Ben wasn't eating like a glutton. He said what he disliked most in China were banquets, which tended to be too wasteful. Indeed, I had noticed that some Chinese, particularly the nouveaux riches, identified lavishness and swank luxury with a high-quality life. Many young women wouldn't hesitate to blow a whole month's wages for a brand-name bag, a Louis Vuitton or Gucci or Kate Spade. They cared too much about appearances and price tags. I was often bemused by the way my young colleagues in Beijing spent money—"like running a tap," in their own words. Given the pragmatic nature of the Chinese, they should have been more practical.

Ben went on to say about banquets, "After three or four dishes you can hardly taste any difference in what follows. What's the point of eating course after course? It's just wasteful. I knew people who were nicknamed different types of gluttons, like Great Eater, Expert Eater, and Indiscriminate Eater. Without exception they were proud of their nicknames. A genuine Chinese reform must start with the dining table." Ben laughed, and so did I.

"The eating culture there bothered me too," I admitted. "At some sumptuous dinners in Beijing I couldn't stop wondering whose money we were spending. I once spoke with an official seated next to me at a table, and he said he would dine out five or six evenings a week. It was his job to accompany his bureau's guests."

"And the taxpayers would foot the bills, of course," Ben said.

"So dining reform is a serious business, like political reform?"

"Number one priority to me, because most people, regardless of their ideologies, will support such a concrete change."

When we were done with dinner, I waved for the check, but Ben was adamant about picking up the tab, saying I was his guest. I let him. He also asked for a doggie bag, which I appreciated. (Many Chinese, ostentatiously lavish, wouldn't bother about leftovers at restaurants. The truth is that poverty and extravagance often go hand in hand.) Together Ben and I headed back to his apartment.

Over tea, I shared with him some photos of my father. One of them showed Gary hosing down his Buick Century. "So he had a luxury car," Ben said, the corners of his mouth tilting up a little.

"He always drove a Buick."

"I love American cars too, roomy, sturdy, and powerful. I have a Mustang."

"A gas guzzler, isn't it?"

"I don't mind."

Most Chinese expats and immigrants would have a Toyota Corolla or Hyundai Elantra for a first car; Ben seemed to have unusual taste. In another photo Gary was blowing at the conical flames of candles planted on a cake, the smile on his face crinkling the corners of his eyes. Nellie and I were standing by, clapping our hands while singing "Happy Birthday." Ben put down the picture and breathed a small sigh.

I took a sip of high mountain tea (one of my favorite Taiwanese teas), amused that we were still using handleless cups like those in a Chinese restaurant. "You look sad," I told Ben.

"Your mother had blond hair and blue eyes."

"Her eyes were gray actually."

"She was blond."

"She and your grandfather made a handsome couple, in some people's opinion. His American name is Gary, by the way."

"I used to think he had lived a miserable life here, if not in destitution, and he sacrificed himself for our country."

I didn't know how to respond, unable to grasp what Ben meant. I managed to say, "He loved China of course."

"Like him, I've been working hard for my country."

"I hope you're not a spy, though," I said. He laughed.

Gradually our conversation shifted to patriotism, which seemed to have possessed some young Chinese, who often claimed they wouldn't hesitate to sacrifice themselves for their motherland. They insisted that their love for the country was unconditional, and many of them were proud of being nationalists. Ben and I couldn't see eye to eye on this issue. I told him that I loved America, but not more than I loved my husband. I believe that a country is not a temple but a mansion built by the citizens so they can have shelter and protection in it. Such a construction can be repaired, renovated, altered, and even overhauled if necessary. If the house isn't suitable for you, you should be entitled to look for shelter elsewhere. Such freedom of migration will make the government responsible for keeping the house safe and more habitable for its citizens. I went on to say, "It's unreasonable to deify a country and it's insane to let it lord over you. We must ask this question: On what basis should a country be raised above the citizens who created it? History has proved that a country can get crazier and more vicious than an average person."

My argument caught Ben by surprise. He muttered, "Still, I love China unconditionally."

"What if you have joined the church?" I asked. "A good Christian must never place his country above God. According to Christianity, God created humans first, so a human being is more sacred and must come before a country."

Ben stared at me. I went on, "See, patriotism has become a religion to you. That's dangerous. Now, come to think of it—what if your country has betrayed you or violated some basic principles of humanity? Will you still love it unconditionally?" Seeing him wordless, I added, "Loyalty must be sustained by mutual trust. It's a two-way street. To be honest, many Chinese are ardent patriots because their existence depends on the state. As a result, they cannot envision an existence outside their country, and to them, nothing can be bigger and higher than China, which is actually a historical construct. Two centuries ago if you asked the ordinary Chinese about their nationality, they'd go blank, because they didn't even have the concept of citizenship. China has never been a fixed entity, and its borders have changed constantly. So have its ethnic groups."

"You're American while I'm Chinese," Ben said, his upper lip curled a little as if my remarks irritated him.

"Don't let nationality stand between us. We are family," I responded, flinging up my hand and then scratching my temple.

He grinned. "Sure we are. I'll always have you as my aunt."

I realized Ben might be ignorant of China's treatment of his grandfather. Reluctant to share the whole story with him at the moment, I said, "Ben, I want you to remember this caveat: 'The unexamined life is not worth living.'"

"Is that from a philosopher or a sage?"

"Socrates. Please be aware of the forces around you and assess yourself constantly. Your grandfather was an intelligent man, but he didn't examine his life carefully and lived blind as a result."

"Okay, I will remember," Ben said offhandedly.

Before going to sleep that night, I thought about giving him a full account of my father's life, but I decided to wait. The truth might be too upsetting to him, I thought, so I'd better disclose it gradually.

Around midmorning the next day, I went to Ben's company, which was on the top floor of a small concrete building on Washington Street, near the public library. He had three employees, two women and one man. The man, screwdriver in hand and wearing an earring and a pink button-down, was at a desk working on a computer, its innards fully exposed. One of the female employees was a young Ukrainian named Sonya, whom Ben introduced to me as his girlfriend. She was slightly thick-boned but looked smart and energetic with straw-colored hair and hazel eyes. When we were alone again, I asked Ben what kind of women he was fond of. He seemed abashed. "Gosh," he said, "you think I treat women as a commodity? That's a capitalist mentality." He gave a half laugh. "Sonya is somebody I can trust. When I travel abroad on business, I need a person to cover my bases."

"It's not easy to find someone trustworthy," I admitted.

Sonya joined us for lunch at a noodle joint. I found that she used chopsticks more skillfully than I did; what's more, she could use them with both hands. She said she was ambidextrous and could also write either way. I'd never met such a person before. Sonya grew more vivacious as we were conversing. She confessed she'd been "seduced" by Ben because he was a gourmet and used to take her to all the cheap but good restaurants. Ben protested, "Please, don't be so forgetful. I've never been stingy to you. Didn't our company help you apply for a green card?"

"I've been working my butt off for that," she replied.

Sonya told me that her parents and two younger sisters were all back in Donetsk. She'd gone to Brandeis University on an international scholarship, and after college she decided to stay for a few years in the States. At this point she wasn't sure how long she would live here, though she had applied for permanent residency. There was a possibility she'd go to Europe, to either the Netherlands or

Denmark, where she had relatives, to see if she might like it there. She spoke about emigrating as if it were as simple as changing jobs. I was impressed. Her life must have been full of adventures.

After lunch Sonya returned to work while Ben drove me to a yacht club behind a mid-rise tenement whose flattish, undersize windows brought to mind a jailhouse. He said he was going to give me a boat tour. He unlocked the gate to a private dock and strolled along the pier, taking me to the waterside. When we had reached the end of the dock, he leapt onto a motorboat, shouting, "Let's have a ride!"

I followed him and jumped aboard. He took a Nikon camera out of his shoulder bag and strapped it around his neck. The boat rocked a little while a rush of delight ran through me. Ben started the engine, and we sped out toward the greenish ocean. The wind was rushing by, tousling our hair. I felt a sophomoric thrill and began letting out happy cries. Ben handed me a pair of mirror sunglasses, and I put them on. The subdued light at once rendered all objects closer.

We stopped near a lighthouse, of which Ben shot a few photos. He also snapped pictures of seabirds and a passing ferryboat. He gave a few lusty shouts and waved at the passengers aboard. From a distance people might have taken us for a couple—with the shades on I would appear younger, my figure accentuated by the fluttering dress that hugged my body. Then we proceeded toward a shipyard, where some ships were docked for repairs. I thought we were taking a shortcut back to the pier, but a long destroyer emerged, nobody visible on its deck. Ben stopped our boat, its engine idling. He went to his knees to steady the camera and began snapping photos of the warship, its satellite dishes, front cannon, missile launchers. I stood stupefied, and he veered and took a picture of me. I must have looked silly in that one, my mouth perhaps agape. Before I could say anything, he revved the engine and we raced away, going back by the route we had come. I suspected he might just have committed an act of espionage, using me as a camouflage. On second thought, that destroyer, looking obsolete and docked there without being guarded, might no longer be a secret. The Chinese must have known everything there was to know about its type. Nevertheless, I couldn't shake my misgivings.

That evening I spoke to Ben about what he'd been doing for China. He was unwilling to level with me and said, "You're over-sensitive, Aunt Lilian. How could I run the risk of doing anything illegal? I'm not that stupid. If I can't settle down in the States, I'll be worthless to China. That's why I've been trying to persuade my company to let me live in America for another couple of years. Once I'm naturalized, I'll be able to act more freely."

"I hope I'm wrong," I said. "I've always been sensitive about espionage activities, because your grandfather was a top Chinese spy."

"I know. He sacrificed himself for our motherland and became a nameless hero."

"What's that supposed to mean?"

"Very few Chinese know about his heroic deeds."

He seemed to have in his head an official version of Gary's career. I felt as if I were chewing on something rotten but not daring to spit it out in front of others, so I steered the conversation away from my father, talking about American life instead. Ben said he'd buy a sailboat someday, or even a yacht if he had the wherewithal. One thing he felt uneasy about was that America had been growing more attractive to him. "This place can be very seductive and corruptive," he said. "It can suck you in and make you forget who you are and where you're from."

"That's why conventionally this country is called a 'melting pot,'" I replied. "So you must fight your love for America from within?"

"It's not love but attraction."

"But attraction can develop into other feelings and can be the first step toward love."

"Well, that's what I fear." He smiled thoughtfully.

1962–1963

B y the end of 1961 the construction of CIA headquarters was completed in the suburb of Langley, Virginia. Many of its support units in the DC area were moved into the immense new compound, and so was Gary's translation agency. After February 1962, he'd go there to work every day. This relocation marked a significant rise in his spying career, because in his Chinese superiors' eyes he was at last physically at the heart of the U.S. intelligence system. His value as a spy soared, and now the Ministry of National Security in Beijing could brag about this breakthrough to the Party's Politburo.

Gary loved his new office, which overlooked a juniper wood. In a way the whole compound resembled a park in a forest, every side of the colossal building shielded by trees. He often stood at his window, gazing at the tranquil setting. Sometimes a pair of rabbits would come, chasing each other or sharing something they found in the woods, a tuber or a dried fruit; they would nibble on it unhurriedly. Gary noticed that all the squirrels, chipmunks, and rabbits were plump with sleek fur. In the mornings blue jays and cardinals would land on the grass, pecking around or fluttering their brilliant feathers in the sunlight. He enjoyed seeing the birds and animals so at ease, yet sometimes the fat rodents unavoidably reminded him of the famine back home.

It bewildered him that the catastrophe in China had drawn so little international attention. Indeed, the world tended to be galvanized by more inflammatory events. In the fall of 1962 the Cuban Missile Crisis brought the United States and the Soviet Union to the cusp of a nuclear war. Gary followed the news raptly and was relieved when President Kennedy announced that the Russians had agreed to ship their missiles away from Cuba. The whole of

America breathed a sigh of relief, and some were jubilant, since in appearance this was a huge victory for the United States. In truth, as Gary saw it, the Soviets had gained as much as the Americans, because the White House had promised, as an exchange, to remove all the intermediate-range missiles deployed in Turkey and Italy and not to invade Cuba. To Gary's mind, Khrushchev had guts just as Kennedy did; both were willing to shake hands with the enemy and strike a deal for peace. Gary felt grateful that a world war had been averted. For that he admired Kennedy and would vote for him when he sought a second term.

Then, border clashes between China and India broke out in south Tibet. The Chinese troops crossed the McMahon Line and overran the Indian brigades. Though the victorious army had advanced dozens of miles into the disputed territory, it soon pulled back to its original positions. The world was amazed and finally relieved, because few countries would so easily give up land seized through bloody battles. As Gary translated the reports sent over from Taiwan, he began to see why the Chinese had retreated. Internationally China had become a pariah of sorts and had lost most of the prestige gained from the Korean War. The aftermath of the Great Leap Forward and the famine had reduced the country to an underdog, one that both the United States and the Soviet Union held as an enemy. Even most of the Third World nations preferred India to China, because Nehru had a better reputation and more personal charisma than Mao. Above all, there was no way China could have provided for its troops if they had occupied the seized land permanently. The roads to the front were arduous and unreliable, often disrupted by torrential rains, landslides, heavy snowfalls, and avalanches. (The ammunition and provisions for the Battle of Walong had been transported by mules and packhorses for months.) It had been wise of the Chinese leaders to withdraw in a timely manner. As a matter of fact, Chairman Mao claimed at a meeting, "With this victory we hope to have peace on the Sino-Indian border for a decade." To Gary's mind, when it came to international affairs, Mao seemed more astute and prudent, perhaps because he couldn't wield absolute power in that context as he did domestically.

That was Suzie's opinion as well. Gary could talk with her freely about the political and economic situations back home, since she also followed the news and was eager to compare notes with him. Yet their conversations would without fail shift to their own ongoing affair. Suzie seemed on edge lately and often insinuated that their relationship could not continue as it was.

"What are your true feelings about me?" she asked him one afternoon in her living room, staring him in the face.

Her question threw him. He said, "What do you mean?"

"Who am I to you? Do you plan to keep me as your whore forever?" Her eyes flashed with the smolder of hurt.

"Suzie, I've told you many times that I can't leave Nellie. If I filed for divorce, I'd lose my daughter. I wouldn't be able to pay the alimony and child support. Nellie wouldn't go out to work—she'd be hell-bent on bankrupting me."

"Heavens, you can think only in terms of money!"

"I don't want to be a deadbeat, I have my responsibilities."

"Don't you have any of those for me?"

"We're friends. You're an independent woman."

"You have a heart of stone."

In silence he picked up his hat and made for the door.

"Where are you off to? Come back!" she cried.

He ignored her and dragged himself away.

She had often complained he was "a cold fish"; yet in bed he could be warm and tender, especially after sex. He could melt her without making deliberate effort. He'd even say something that jolted her. Once he whispered to her, "I'm your dog, totally at your disposal. If you want to kill me, you can do it now. You can use a knife or gun, or whatever." She could tell he really didn't care and completely surrendered to her mercy. She couldn't avoid wondering what was wrong with him.

But the moment their lovemaking was over, he became his normal self again, collected and detached. She couldn't possibly fathom how messy his life was—his first family was back in China, waiting for him to come home. But here, he had another wife and another child. Torn, hardly able to juggle the two families, he wouldn't bring a third into the mix. Yet the more he resisted Suzie's insinuations and suggestions, the more frustrated she became. She put his stubbornness down to his lack of ability to communicate. He would remain silent when she said she couldn't understand why a professional translator was unable to render his own thoughts and feelings into words. If only he could spill everything to her. If only there'd been no children involved. If only China and the United States had not been hostile nations so that he could travel back and forth easily. If only he could become a citizen of both countries, a man of the world.

He was sure that Suzie was a good woman, but his inability to explain his predicament had widened the rift between them and made her more cantankerous. One day in mid-December, as he was leaving her place, he resolved not to see her again. Yes, he'd better extricate himself in time and stop seeking pleasure outside his family. He had to endure the bone-deep loneliness alone.

At home he and Nellie seldom talked about anything outside their household. Their daughter was a first grader now, a shy girl but full of beans. Recently Nellie had found a part-time job, keeping books for Outstanding Fences, Inc., a small business run by two men, father and son. She'd go to their office near a crossroads three mornings a week and do the rest of the bookkeeping at home. She made $1.95 an hour. The wages she pulled in were almost enough for her family's groceries. Although Gary discouraged her from working outside their home because he made enough to support the family, she wouldn't quit, saying, "I can't depend on you." Deep down, she felt he didn't love her and might walk out on her one of these days. Indeed, even in bed he rarely used the word "love," and lately sometimes she couldn't turn him on however she tried. "You're such a cold man," she would mutter, wondering if it was true, as he'd told her prior to their marriage, that she was the only woman he'd ever slept with. How could that be possible? What a liar.

Only to his daughter was he attentive and lively. Every morning on his way to work he'd drop her at George Mason Elementary School. Before the girl clambered out of the car, he'd say, "Give Daddy a kiss." She'd give him a smack on the cheek and then scamper away, her heavy book bag bobbing on her back. If there was no car behind him, he would wait until he saw her disappear beyond the entrance of the brick schoolhouse.

WHEN GARY WENT TO HONG KONG by way of Taipei in late September 1963, Bingwen told him that the famine was over—things had turned around and China was on the right track again. The national leaders had rectified their mistakes and introduced new policies, so people continued devoting themselves to building the new society. As for Gary's family in the countryside, everybody was well. He should set his mind at ease and just focus on his mission overseas. The intelligence he had provided this time was invaluable, especially the international perspectives on China's domestic troubles and the CIA's operation in Indochina. After depositing five hundred dollars into Gary's account in Hang Seng Bank, Bingwen told him, "We know this small amount is far from enough to compensate you, but we did our best. In the future, when our country's rich and strong, we'll give you more."

"It's an honor to serve our motherland. Please don't mention compensation," Gary said with feeling, his eyes hot and moist.

Bingwen gave him the contact information for Father Kevin Murray, a priest at a Catholic church in downtown Baltimore. From now on Gary could go to that man for help in case of emergency. "Rest assured," his handler said, "Murray grew up in the Philippines, but his mother is Fujianese. His father is an Englishman. If you want to send us something urgent, he can handle that too."

After lunch at a restaurant called Old Shanghai, the two got on a cruise boat heading out to the ocean. Gary was refreshed, as if the land and the water around him were more invigorating than those in Virginia. Indeed he hadn't felt so alive for years, and there was a stir of joy in his heart that for the moment soothed the pang of homesickness. He gazed at the distant shoreline and the wooded hills, on which a few villas were shaded by shifting foliage and beyond which spread the land he had so often returned to in his dreams. A flock of seabirds were wheeling above the flickering waves, letting out cries like children in a game. Far away in the northeast a sampan with bronze sails jumped a little on the horizon.

To help Gary relax, during the following three days Bingwen took him to a waterfront club, two performances of traditional operas, a floating restaurant that served fresh-caught seafood, and arrays of stores in Sham Shui Po and Western Market, where Gary bought presents for Nellie and Lilian. He had a lot of fun on this trip and came back loaded with stuff that amazed his wife and daughter.

Among the things he'd brought home for Nellie were a necklace of pearls and a bamboo-handled back scratcher with a tiny ivory hand at its end. There were also two packs of smoked sausages, fiery red like shriveled hot dogs, which neither Nellie nor Lilian would touch. His wife and daughter were afraid of the fat visible in every slice like specks of cheese, but he ate the meat with relish. Several nights in a row he'd have a glass of whiskey while savoring the sausage on a butter plate alone.

TWO WEEKS LATER, Gary attended a small meeting at which eight of his CIA colleagues, all East Asia hands, deliberated on the military situation in Vietnam. Thomas took an internal report out of his chestnut portfolio and began to read some information on China's involvement in the region. China had secretly sent thousands of engineering troops and several antiaircraft artillery regiments to help the Vietcong. Some Chinese infantry units, disguised in the North Vietnamese army's uniforms, participated in battles against the Americans. There was also a supply line, maintained by Chinese personnel, winding from Yunnan province through the mountains and across the rivers all the way to Hanoi. Moreover, some Chinese army hospitals south of Kunming City had been treating wounded Vietcong soldiers. It looked like China was becoming the rear base of North Vietnam. If the Chinese continued backing up the Vietcong on such a scale, there'd be no way the Americans could win the war.

"We must figure out how to stop Red China," Thomas said to the analysts around the oblong table. "The Pentagon wants us to give them some suggestions so they can make action plans to deter the Chinese."

While the others were expressing their opinions, Gary's mind wandered. He was thinking about how to get hold of that internal report, which obviously contained vital intelligence that showed how the United States considered China's role in Vietnam and what measures it might take against China. Apparently the Americans regarded his country as a major opponent in that region; they might launch attacks on the Chinese troops there, and might even bomb some cities beyond the Sino-Vietnamese border. At any cost Gary wanted to make a copy of the report. He had planned to meet with Father Murray soon and ought to pass some valuable intelligence to the man as his first delivery.

One of his colleagues seated next to Thomas picked up the report and began leafing through it. He kept tapping his forehead with his fingertips while he read. As he was coming to the last page, Gary said, "Can I have a look?"

The man handed it to him. Gary started skimming it while listening to the others. Then he placed the report next to his manila folder as if it were something he'd taken out of his own file. He joined the discussion and threw in his suggestions now and then. He said that the Chinese were expert in night fighting, so the American barracks in Vietnam should be equipped with search-lights and flares; that our troops should stay out of the firing range of Chinese artillery, which was quite accurate, agile, and powerful; that we should consider a naval blockade since a large quantity of weapons were shipped from the Soviet Union to North Vietnam by sea.

Then a bespectacled man seated across from Gary asked, "Can you pass that to me?" He was referring to the report, and Gary had no choice but to hand it over.

For the rest of the meeting he tried to think how to get it back, but to no avail. Eventually it returned to the head of the table. When the meeting was over, Thomas gathered his documents, including the report, and put them back in his portfolio. He left the conference room with it under his arm. Watching his boss pad down the hallway with his stiff legs, Gary knew he'd have to pilfer it.

The next day, carrying his manila folder, Gary went to Thomas's office on the pretext that he needed his authorization for some travel expenses for which the treasurer's office wouldn't reimburse him. Recently he'd gone to San Francisco to interview potential recruits, and while he was there he'd rented a car for two days. It was this item that the accountant refused to accept. Gary told Thomas the truth, that he'd driven to Berkeley to use its Asian library and also to meet with Professor Swanson, a noted transla-tor of ancient Chinese poetry, whose work both Thomas and he admired. "Sometimes Sharon can be a tightwad," his boss said about the chief accountant. "But we need someone who can keep our budget under control." Without further ado, he uncapped his fountain pen and began to look through the sheet of paper with Gary's receipts attached.

At this point the phone rang and Thomas picked up. The call was from his wife, Alicia. "Excuse me for a moment," he said to Gary and went into the inner room, where he could speak privately. Seizing the opportunity, Gary opened his boss's chestnut portfolio, which was lying on the sofa, found the report, and slipped it into his own folder. He had planned to create a small mishap, upsetting an ashtray or coffee cup, so that Thomas might go to the bathroom for a paper towel and give him a moment alone in the office. If that didn't work out, he would come again with a pair of birdlike tropical fish, since Thomas and his wife kept an aquarium at home. Now Alicia's phone call had come at an opportune time. Somehow Gary had always had luck with Thomas—never had he failed to lift a document from him.

Thomas came back two minutes later and wrote a brief note to the chief accountant, stating that Gary had gone to Berkeley on behalf of the agency and should be reimbursed for his expenses there.

That night Gary photographed the report, eleven pages in all. But afterward he grew anxious, unsure if Thomas was aware that the document was missing. There was a remote possibility that his boss had purposely let it circulate at the meeting so that it might prompt Gary to commit the theft. Did this mean he was already a suspect? Had they begun to lay traps for him? That was unlikely. He managed to quell his misgivings, believing he couldn't possibly become a target of the mole hunt being conducted by the CIA's counterintelligence staff. In recent years that unit had concentrated on searching for Soviet penetrations at the CIA. Despite the secrecy of the operation, it was whispered that many officers in the Soviet Division, particularly those of Russian extraction, had severe cases of nerves. But Gary was merely a translator in the East Asia Division, far away from the scrutinizing eyes, and had always managed to stay under the radar.

It was too bad he'd left his fingerprints on the report. What should he do about that? Then he remembered that several people had touched the pages at the meeting, so he might not be singled out. Now he had to figure out how to return the report to Thomas. There was no hurry. As long as his boss was unaware of the loss, Gary would have plenty of time to put it back. He'd done that a couple of times before and knew it would be easier to return a document than to steal it.

He called Father Murray from a pay phone on his way home the next evening. This was the first time he'd spoken with the man, who sounded resonant in spite of his subdued voice. They agreed to meet at Baltimore's Inner Harbor in disguise as anglers. Gary told Murray that he'd wear a gray polo shirt and jeans and carry an olive backpack.

Two days later, on Saturday afternoon, Gary arrived at the waterside. He saw a fortyish man of medium build leaning against a wrought-iron rail and holding a glinting fishing rod. But the fellow didn't look Asian. That made Gary hesitate for a moment; then he remembered that Murray was only half Chinese. Indeed the man's round eyes and pale skin suggested mixed blood. Still, Gary had to double-check. He went over and put down his backpack and his beige enamel pail, which contained earthworms covered in damp topsoil. After dropping his line into the water, he rested his elbow on the rail, next to the man.

"Nice spot," Gary said. Then he spoke the code words in an undertone. "How did you get here?"

"I drove," the man answered casually. He turned to Gary. A knowing smile wrinkled his face, which had high cheekbones and a smooth slender chin.

"What kind of car do you drive?"

"An old Dodge."

"What year is it?"

"Nineteen fifty-two."

"What color?"

"Chocolate brown."

Gary held out his hand, which the man grabbed firmly. The

priest's grip was sinewy and forceful. He must exercise a lot, Gary thought.

Gary offered him a cigarette, which Murray declined, saying he didn't smoke. But Gary pressed the half-used pack of Camels into his hand anyway, whispering that it contained a film. He began to speak Mandarin, while the priest answered in English, saying he understood the official Chinese but his pronunciation was terrible, incomprehensible, so Gary switched back to English. They went on talking about their future work. Murray said he was merely a sidekick whose task was to help Gary communicate with China. This modified Gary's perception of their relationship somewhat. He'd thought that Murray was his superior in charge of China's espionage operation in the DC area or on the East Coast.

"No." Murray shook his round head. "My job is simple—I just serve you. You're the boss."

"How often should we meet?" Gary asked, not fully convinced because Murray would pass orders from above to him and was at least a liaison.

"It's up to you."

"Okay, I'll call when I have something to deliver."

"Sure. I'll be at your service."

Murray had only a rubber tadpole attached to his hook. When he reeled in the line, Gary said, "Here, use an earthworm." He pointed at his enamel pail.

"No way. I won't touch any live worm or insect. They're too creepy."

Gary laughed, picked up a thick earthworm, and fixed it to Murray's hook. "Fish don't like dead bait. If you use a fake creature, you'd better keep it moving in the water, to make it appear alive." He dangled the three-inch worm, which was wiggling a little. "This will fetch you a big shark."

They went on fishing and chatting. In the distance, on a sprawling dock, the windows of a low-rise brick building flashed now and again. Beyond it, a tugboat crawled westward, dragging a plume of white smoke and an expanding triangular wake on the metal-blue water. "Gosh, I forgot to bring a bottle of soda," Murray said, apparently thirsty. Gary took a fat tomato out of his bag and gave it to the priest, who started munching it ravenously. Behind them a truck sounded its horn like a guttural squawk, which spun Murray around. Gary realized that the man was jumpy, probably uncomfortable about this meeting spot.

The sun was broiling in spite of a fitful breeze, and perspiration stood out on both of their foreheads. Gary opened a new pack of cigarettes and lit another one. Suddenly the priest's rod trembled and curved. Murray gave a yelp, pulling and reeling in the line. "I caught a fish, it's a big one!" he cried out. His brown eyes sparkled like a young boy's.

"Jesus, it's just a baby bass." Gary chuckled and shook his head. Indeed, the fish, writhing on the ground now, was less than half a foot long. "Man, you'd better throw it back or it'll die."

"Can . . . can you help me take it off the hook?" stammered Murray.

"You don't know how to unhook a fish?"

"Never done it before."

Gary picked up the striped bass and pulled the hook out of its mouth. "Here, hold it for a picture." He thrust the fish toward the priest. "I have a new camera here." His other hand pointed at his backpack.

Murray shook his head. "I don't need such a keepsake."

"All right then." Gary dropped the bass into the water. After zigzagging a few yards, it vanished. "So you haven't done much fishing before?" Gary asked Murray.

"Nope, this is my first time."

"No wonder you have the brand-new gear."

"I picked it up at Sears yesterday."

"Probably we shouldn't pretend to be anglers then."

"I agree. The water's so dirty that few people fish here. Besides, two Chinamen fishing together at the harbor can be too eye-catching."

They decided to treat each other like buddies from now on and would not adopt any conventional method of spycraft—no code names and no secret drop. They both believed it would be safer just to keep everything simple and natural, misleadingly transparent. In front of others they should appear casual and relaxed to avoid drawing attention. Murray said he'd tell people at his church that Gary was his friend so that the two of them could meet at a moment's notice.

✧✧✧

My niece Juli wrote to me two or three times a week. She was still singing with the band, which had begun to get attention and often went to nearby towns and cities to perform. I once asked her if she'd like to come to the States. She replied: "Maybe for a visit. Honestly, I'm different from some of my friends who have the emigration bug in their heads. I feel too old to uproot myself. Besides, I can't speak English."

I wished she could come and stay with me for a few months. She was still carrying on with Wuping and perhaps kept dreaming that someday he'd leave his wife. I was worried and wanted to tell her that he might be an empty suit, not worth her love and devotion, but I refrained.

Then Juli informed me that two officers from the local National Security bureau had come to question her about me. Besides my "activities" in Guangzhou, they wanted to know what I'd told her about my father. To my amazement, I couldn't recall telling her anything about Gary. My prudence turned out to have been prescient, because full knowledge of her grandfather might have confused her and prompted her to act rashly. The officers warned her about me, urging her to keep some distance from this American woman who was biased against China, even though they didn't deny that I was her aunt. They also demanded that she notify them immediately if she heard anything unusual from me, such as an odd query or an unreasonable request. Juli had no option but to agree to do that. "Of course, I don't believe a word of what they said about you," she wrote me. "The instant I saw you, I could tell that you were my aunt. You and my mom really look like sisters, only you are in better shape and have light-colored hair. Family is family, right?"

She also revealed that the National Security people had questioned her parents about my visit to them. Her father urged her to be more cautious when communicating with me. "Lilian is American and might have another pot to boil," he said to her on the phone. Father and daughter had a heated exchange—she was arguing that I was innocuous, while he insisted that she mustn't tell me too much about China. He got impatient but conceded, "I won't say Lilian is bad. I like her and believe she's a good person, harmless. Just be careful and keep in mind that there're other eyes to read what you write to her and other ears to catch what you say."

I told Juli: "I don't blame your dad. His concern is entirely justified. Do take precautions."

But from then on I felt too self-conscious to speak freely when I emailed or phoned Juli. I was uncertain about to what extent the National Security people monitored our communications. I just told her to let her parents know I'd keep an eye on her brother and give him a hand whenever he needed it.

MY HUSBAND WAS FASCINATED by my nephew, so I invited Ben to visit us. There was another reason for my invitation—I needed his advice about how I could communicate with his family in China without compromising them. I didn't want to ask him on the phone; his line might have been tapped by the FBI. Even his cell phone might not be safe. I suspected he was an agent of some kind, but perhaps involved only in some borderline espionage activities—at most a small-time spy.

I invited Ben to join us for Independence Day, but his girlfriend Sonya's parents would be in Boston for a short visit that week. He arrived on July 8 instead, and we went to pick him up at the train station, driving my two-year-old Toyota Prius. This was his first trip to DC, and at the sight of me and Henry, Ben waved spiritedly. He hurried over, beaming, with a blue suitcase in tow.

He hugged me, then my husband. The two of them had spoken on the phone.

Stepping out of the station, Henry asked him about the train ride, and Ben said, "Everything was splendid except for Baltimore."

That made us laugh. On our drive home, Ben was impressed by how quietly and smoothly my Prius was running. He said that his Mustang, with 230,000 miles on it, was noisy and jerky whenever he accelerated, but he'd just found a used engine and would have his old one replaced soon. He'd never trade his Mustang for another car unless it was a Chinese model. Too bad China hadn't produced safe, quality cars yet.

"How about a new Volvo?" I asked. "A Chinese company acquired Volvo from Ford last year."

"Hope they won't bungle the product," Ben said. "But a Volvo is not for a bachelor like me. It's more like a family car, isn't it?"

"Why d'you say that?" Henry asked him.

"If I had kids I might consider a Volvo."

"It's expensive," I put in.

"Sure, assuming I can afford it," said Ben.

We ate at home that evening, mixed greens salad and boiled dumplings stuffed with shrimp, pork, and chives, which I'd bought ready-made at Maxim Super Market in Silver Spring. Ben liked red wine, so we uncorked a bottle of Merlot. As we were eating, all using chopsticks and mashed-garlic sauce mixed with balsamic vinegar, Henry asked Ben, "Don't you miss home?"

"Sometimes I do," Ben said, smiling with his top lip curled a little, as if the food were too hot. "But New England is quite similar to northeast China in climate and landscape. It could have been worse if they had sent me to Miami or Houston. I'm a northerner and not used to the hot humid weather. I lived in Alabama for half a year, and my first American summer down there was pretty miserable."

"So you feel at home in Boston?" Henry pointed his chopsticks at his own plate as he spoke.

"Not really. I must learn to be detached, because at any moment my company might call me back or transfer me elsewhere."

"If you had your druthers," I said, "would you like to settle down in the States?"

"Absolutely, I like America. Life's good here."

"What d'you like most about American life?" asked Henry.

"Believe it or not, I like the order and peace you can have as long as you're law-abiding."

"And can pay your bills," I said.

"Of course. For that matter, I've found Americans work too hard, harder than the Chinese, perhaps because there're too many bills to pay here. I have friends who are doing two or three jobs at the same time. That's crazy. They all believe that only by working hard can they get rich. I don't see how they can get out of money troubles by making ten or eleven dollars an hour. On the other hand, this shows another positive aspect of American life—hard work is always rewarded more or less."

Henry and I chuckled, amused and impressed by his remarks. After dinner, we retired to the living room and resumed our conversation. Both Ben and Henry loved hockey, so, teacups in hand, they turned to watch a rerun of the final match between the Canucks and the Bruins, while I retreated to my study in the basement to revise a paper on the depiction of Asians in Hollywood Cold War movies. There was a hard deadline for the submission, so I'd have to complete the piece within three days.

BEN TOLD ME I ought to avoid talking about politics when I phoned Juli, because her line was definitely tapped by Chinese National Security. In addition, I should be careful about what I wrote to her. The Internet police there monitored the online traffic and could break into your email to gather evidence against you. Recently they had banned a good number of bloggers and shut down their accounts because those users had grown too outspoken, their voices gaining too many readers. Whoever could hold the attention of the multitude might be suppressed sooner or later. Ben was worried about his twin sister, who could easily get carried away.

After breakfast the next morning Henry and I gave Ben a brief tour of our property. We took him through the three floors of the building and then to the grounds behind it. On the boughs of a sycamore hung two transparent bird feeders filled with mixed grains and sunflower seeds. We stopped to watch some goldfinches, red crossbills, and robins eating the feed. A handful of birds, already done with breakfast, were chattering while bathing and grooming at a granite birdbath next to a kidney-shaped flower bed, but most of the other birds stood quietly on the maples and hornbeams nearby, waiting for the two at the feeders to finish and fly away— then another two would go over to the plastic tubes and eat. They'd mostly been standing in line patiently, though a few scudded from branch to branch.

"Gosh, they're more polite than the subway riders in Beijing," Ben quipped. A red-breasted robin fluttered its wings as if in response.

Henry laughed. "They know each other."

I joined in, "They're not as tough as birds in China for sure, poor competitors."

This time it was Ben who broke into laughter. He said, "They're blessed without the need to compete."

On the eastern side of the backyard spread a tennis court surrounded by a high chain-link fence; a few balls dotted the green court, some tattered and mildewed like overripe fruit. "Wow, you two are real landlords," Ben blurted out at the sight of the court.

For a moment I was at a loss for words. Then I said, "Henry keeps everything in order. We take care of the property by ourselves."

"You know I'm pretty good with my hands too," Ben said and then turned to Henry. "If someday you want to retire, please hire me. I can do carpentry and plumbing. Last fall I helped my friend Deon fix his roof."

"Can you really do those things?" I asked.

"Sure I can. I can do basic masonry too. You saw the floors in my parents' home, didn't you?"

"I did."

"I laid the bricks in all the rooms."

"That's impressive. Tell me, why didn't you use grout instead of cement to seal the bricks?"

"That was too expensive."

No doubt Ben was a handyman of sorts, but I wasn't sure he knew how to do all the maintenance jobs here. It wouldn't matter—he always could learn.

After rush hour, Henry took Ben into DC to visit some museums, while I returned to my study to finish the paper on Cold War movies. These days I had also been perusing my father's diary, on which I'd spent hundreds of hours but which I still had to read time and again, especially some fragmented sentences, to connect all the dots, though by now I had grasped his story on the whole. Today, however, I had no time for my father's journal, having to provide dozens of endnotes for the paper. That would take several hours.

Late in the afternoon Ben and Henry came back. My nephew couldn't stop raving about the museums on the National Mall, which were all free to the public. He told me, "We even saw many original pieces by Rodin—they all stand in the sculpture garden, in the open! Amazing. I can imagine how privileged the people living in that area must feel. All those great museums must be like amenities in their lives. This is unbelievable. I wish I could live in DC so I could take friends to those museums when they come to visit me."

"Which of the museums do you like most?" I asked.

"The air and space museum. I had never seen one like that."

Before dinner I showed him my study. He looked through

my little library, shelves crowded with books floor to ceiling, and admitted, "I've read only seven or eight of these books. I wish I were a scholar like you, Aunt." He was seated in a rattan lounge chair, drinking almond milk.

"You've been doing pretty well in your computer business. I'm just a woman of books, not suitable for anything else."

I showed him the six volumes of diary left by Gary. He opened one and began skimming some pages. I said, "I'm still working on your grandfather's story. Once I'm done, I'll let you have his journal."

"Well," he replied thoughtfully and put down the volume, "I might have to know more about his life to make sense of this."

"I've been trying to understand him too."

Ben and Henry seemed to have hit it off. They talked a lot about basketball and football games; both were fans of the New England Patriots. After Ben had left, my husband kept saying about him, "What a fine young man. I wish I had a nephew like that on my side."

"You've met him just once," I said.

"Look, Lilian, I'm about to be sixty-two. In a couple of years I won't be very active anymore. If Ben can manage this building for us, that will make our remaining years free of lots of trouble. Don't you think?"

"Can you trust him entirely?"

"Not yet. Like I said, we can try to get to know him better. I'm fond of him, that's the honest truth."

I was pleased to hear that. Sometimes I did feel a stirring of maternal feeling for my nieces and nephew and couldn't help but try to get involved in their lives. Yet Ben seemed too ambitious to become a building superintendent. He'd once told me that he dreamed of living on Cape Cod, in a colonial home with a garden and a dog. And a boat, if he could afford it.

1964–1965

This was the third time Gary had resolved not to see Suzie anymore. He wanted his life to be simple and focused, but a few weeks later she called him and wanted to meet again, saying she missed their "confabulations." Could he see her just one more time? She promised she wouldn't misbehave or yell at him again. He did not agree at first and urged her to find something that could fill her idle hours, like yoga or meditation, both of which had come into fashion recently. Or it would be better if she could see another man, a bachelor. He wouldn't give her the illusion that he'd leave his wife, non-Chinese though Nellie was, and abandon his child on account of another woman. No, under no circumstances would he further complicate his life. But there was no way to communicate the deeper reason to Suzie. She kept calling him, at times even when he was in meetings. She knew he was a kind man at heart in spite of his phlegmatic appearance, so she was not afraid of pushing him. What she liked about him was that he wouldn't impose anything on her and always treated her as his equal, as a friend. When they were together, she felt at ease, didn't need to suppress a hiccup or a cackle, and could always speak her mind. Never had she been so relaxed and comfortable with a man. If only she could spend some time with him every day.

At last he agreed to see her just one more time. When they met in a café near Christ Church on an early summer afternoon, she said to him, "You must admit there's a lot of chemistry between us."

"Suzie," he countered, "please don't act like this, don't mess yourself up. My life is more complicated than you can imagine. You'll be better off if you stay away from me, a married man with a child."

"I'd have done that long ago if I could." She lowered her eyes, her lashes fluttering a little, as though she was ashamed of her confession. "Sometimes I wonder if this is due to bad karma. It feels like I owed you something in my previous life and came to this world just to pay you back."

"We've known each other for only a few years," he said.

"But I feel we'd met generations ago."

Her words touched him to the core, so the affair resumed and lasted till the end of his life. He'd go and see her once a week, usually in the evening, giving his wife the excuse that he had to put in extra hours at the CIA. Nellie never questioned him about the evenings he spent away from home. Besides the secretive nature of his work, she assumed that a man, especially a professional man, should have another life outside his home. As long as he brought back a paycheck every month and took care of their family, she didn't complain.

Yet in the early summer of 1964 she discovered the affair, informed by a neighbor, Mrs. Colock, a tall string bean of a woman whose husband had often bumped into Gary and Suzie together in bars and restaurants. Nellie and Gary fought that night, hurling furious words that frightened their daughter. This was the first time Lilian had heard her parents shout at each other profanities they had forbidden her to use. She locked herself in her room, crying and listening in on them.

The next morning her father drove her to school as usual. They spoke little, though the girl still kissed him before running to the school entrance. She was glad that summer break was about to start, that soon she wouldn't need her father to drive her to school anymore. But her mother seemed to have changed from that day on; she'd become more subdued and taciturn, as if she had a sore throat and had to save her voice. Actually, Nellie was thinking of divorce, which Gary said he would accept if she let him keep their daughter. In truth he couldn't possibly raise the girl alone, given his career and his absentmindedness; he insisted on sole custody of their child in order to save the marriage. That made Nellie hesitate, because she couldn't entrust Lilian to Gary alone.

But their fights had affected their daughter differently—the girl began daydreaming about leaving home. How she wished she could live far away. If only her piggy bank were full.

It was in the fall of 1964 when Nellie started her own affair with her boss, John Tripp, Jr., the manager of Outstanding Fences. John, a beefy man in his early forties with a lumpy face, would take Nellie to a nearby motel after they lunched together, and they would stay in bed there until her daughter's school was about to let out.

In fact, Nellie didn't enjoy the time she spent with Tripp, because he was too demanding in bed. He'd make her do difficult things for him as if she were "an entertainer." As a result, her body would grow sore and she feared there might be damage to her insides; still, she dared not refuse to give him what he wanted. Finally one afternoon, with a pounding heart, she asked him whether he might be willing to form a family with her if she asked her husband for a divorce. Tripp was taken aback, then said, "No, Nellie, I'm sorry I can't do that. I'm awfully fond of you, but I've been single all my life and it's too late for me to change my ways. But I'll be around."

She had asked that mainly to see how much he cared for her; she hadn't made up her mind about a divorce yet. His answer upset her and cooled her down. What a flameout.

The affair, which had been halfheartedly carried on by both parties for about three months, finally came to an end. Soon Nellie quit bookkeeping for the fence company and stayed home, knowing that for better or for worse Gary wouldn't abandon her and Lilian. He had promised her to keep the family together and wasn't a man who'd break his word.

Still, Nellie couldn't suppress her thought of divorce altogether and would talk about it with her sister, Marsha, on the phone. Lilian didn't like her aunt, a blonde with thin arms and long dimples on her cheeks. When the girl was a toddler, Aunt Marsha had called her China Doll, a nickname Lilian hated. It was good that the woman lived on the West Coast now.

One day after school, as Lilian was stepping into her house, she heard her mother talking on the phone. "To be honest, Marsha, I already feel like an old woman. It'll be too hard to find a man willing to share family life with me. . . . Okay, I'll think about what you just said. You know Gary's very stubborn about child custody. . . . Maybe he and I should be separated for a while, just to give each other more space. That might be good for Lilian too."

But that wasn't what the girl wanted. That evening after mother and daughter had sat together and read two chapters from *The Story of Crazy Horse,* Lilian told Nellie that she would stay with her father if they were separated. "I don't mind going to another school," said the daughter. Her mother looked stunned and remained pensive for hours.

Lilian later tipped off her dad that Nellie sometimes talked with Marsha about divorcing him. "Thanks for the info," Gary said with a weak smile. "Does your mom often drink beer or wine when I'm not home?"

"Uh-uh, I didn't see her drink."

"That's good. If she uses alcohol, let me know, okay? I don't want her to become an alcoholic like her father."

To her credit, Nellie wasn't fond of drink. Despite her many years of waitressing, she couldn't taste any difference between red wine and white wine. In contrast, Marsha often took a glass when chatting with Nellie on the phone. Once tipsy, Marsha would confide all kinds of unseemly domestic troubles, such as her husband's addiction to gambling—whenever he went to Las Vegas, a row would wait for him at home—and the couple's regular use of marijuana and other drugs. As a result, they often fought over money. And their son pilfered cash from his mother's purse (but she wouldn't tell his father, afraid he might beat the boy black and blue). Yet whenever Marsha urged her to leave Gary, Nellie would say, "Well, I mustn't rush. I must think more about this."

Without fail, Lilian would give her father an update on their chat.

THE PREVIOUS NOVEMBER John Kennedy had been assassinated. At first Gary was so overwhelmed by the news that he couldn't respond to it. Some of his colleagues grew emotional as they talked about it. David Shuman was mumbling about the event with his mouth slightly lopsided while tears glistened in his camel eyes. As he was listening to David, Gary burst out sobbing. He cried wretchedly, burying his face in his arms on his desk. That astonished his colleagues and convinced them that he was a true patriot, even more heartbroken and devastated than they were by the national tragedy. In fact, though saddened by the news, Gary wept also for another reason. He dreaded that the assassination of the U.S. president might trigger a world war if another country was implicated. His gut told him that the Soviet Union might have been behind it. Even China could have been an accomplice, if not directly involved.

For the whole spring and summer of 1964 he was restless, expecting the outcome of the FBI's inquiry into the case and hoping that Beijing had had nothing to do with it. After a ten-month investigation, the results were announced in late September: Lee Harvey Oswald had acted alone in the assassination. Many of Gary's colleagues shook their heads in disbelief, saying that the man couldn't possibly have done it single-handedly, that there must have been an organization behind him. If not the Mafia, it could have been a hostile foreign power. Unlike them, Gary in secret heaved a sigh of relief.

Nevertheless, China made big news that fall. In mid-October it shocked the world with the explosion of its first atomic bomb. The country, though ravaged by famine and revolutionary hysteria, began coming back to the arena of international politics with a vengeance. All at once Mao was feared and condemned as a monster, but he was also celebrated by some as a farsighted statesman who'd had the aspiration and determination to put his country on the map regardless of the odds against it. A major Japanese newspaper even proclaimed: "With the success of the nuclear test China has become the number one power in Asia."

Gary began to look into this matter and found that originally Mao had looked down on atomic bombs, though the United States had dropped two on Japan. In an interview conducted by the American correspondent Anna Louise Strong in August 1946, Mao said, "A-bombs are paper tigers that the U.S. reactionaries use to threaten people. The bombs appear fearsome but are not really that powerful." Mao's ignorant defiance alarmed even some leaders of the socialist countries. The French physicist Frédéric Joliot-Curie, a Communist who was Madame Curie's son-in-law, had these words passed on to China: "Comrade Mao Zedong, to fight against nuclear weapons, you must first possess them." That startled the chairman and set him thinking about how to make the bomb. He asked Khrushchev to help.

After long negotiations, the two countries signed an agreement in October 1957: the Soviet Union would provide for China a model of the atomic bomb, the blueprints, and the technical specifications. It would also send scientists to help China with the project. But the first expert did not arrive until the beginning of 1959, and he did nothing. More unfathomable and frustrating, in his pocket he always carried a handbook, which he would consult from time to time but wouldn't let any Chinese see. The other Russians who came after him didn't do much either. Then, in July 1960, quite unexpectedly, Khrushchev went back on his promise and withdrew all the two-hundred-odd Soviet experts serving in various areas of China's nuclear industry. The Soviet leader had never liked Mao, though he showed his respect because the Chinese leader was more experienced. "Comrade Mao Zedong always acts as if God must serve him," Khrushchev once observed.

Gary and his CIA colleagues all had thought that with the

Russians gone, China would abandon its nuclear ambitions, but to everyone's amazement, it pushed ahead. Hundreds of factories and thousands of scientists participated in the project. Many of these people lived in the desert in Xinjiang, working around the clock, totally dedicated though they were underfed and underpaid. Some died there, of illness or from becoming lost in the desert. The country was so resolved to build the bomb that Vice Premier Chen Yi declared at an industrial conference: "Even if we reach the point that we have to pawn our trousers, we must continue developing nuclear weapons!"

The relentless effort had finally produced a bomb and gave China a huge boost. The explosion also threw the United States a little off stride. More reconnaissance missions were flown by U-2s, but the planes were mostly shot down by Chinese SA-2 missiles. It was impossible to bring back photos of the nuclear base in western China. For months the White House had been pondering how to snuff out that dangerous program. Air strikes were no longer an option, a fact Gary gloated about in his diary. As an alternative, the CIA and Taiwan put together a contingent of paratroopers, all Nationalist soldiers specializing in demolition and night fighting and newly equipped with M16s. They would be air-dropped into the interior of China and proceed to destroy its nuclear facilities. This operation was code-named Thunderclaps. Together with the scores of commandos, some secret agents had already been sent to the mainland to prepare the operation.

While translating the exchanges between Taipei and Washington, Gary began to form a full picture of the undertaking. He also found its communications plans and the code names of some secret agents already in China. He checked out the documents, saying he'd have to work on them at night, and shot photos of them. In addition, he wrote a report that synthesized the information and described the operation in detail. He took an early vacation in June 1965 and went to Bangkok, a hot spot where, to Gary's knowledge, several CIA officers had spent their time off lately. From there, a week later, he flew to Hong Kong and delivered the intelligence to Bingwen. Immediately three more men came from Beijing to meet with Gary. They were convinced that he was infallible in his analyses and clairvoyant in his predictions, which had been proved correct time and again. Within a month China apprehended most of the secret agents and thus thwarted the Thunderclaps operation before it could get off the ground. The CIA was mad at Taipei, believing that someone in the Nationalists' rank and file had leaked the secret to Red China.

Later in the fall of 1965 Gary was notified by Father Murray that he'd been promoted to the fourteenth rank, similar to that of a lieutenant colonel. And along with the promotion came a first-class merit citation awarded by China's Ministry of National Security. His salary was 154 yuan a month now, about $70. That was a substantial amount, considering a worker usually made less than 50 yuan monthly. Gary assumed that his salary had routinely been sent to Yufeng. He had no idea that since she'd left their home village four years before, she hadn't received a penny from the government.

Minmin, my student in Beijing, wrote me that she was done with her master's and had just defended her thesis on the feminist movement in the United States in the 1970s. She wished I'd been there when "those fogies" on her committee were badgering her "with inane, outrageous questions." I emailed back and asked about her future plans. She said candidly that she was thinking about climbing Mount Everest, which for some reason had been on her mind of late. She could not explain why, but she couldn't stop thinking about the mountain. I liked that about her—she had the passion to follow her own vision, however silly and impractical it might seem.

In fact, I'd once told the students in my graduate seminar back in Beijing, "I admire many good qualities the Chinese have, such as diligence, resourcefulness, modesty, respect for old people, but I've found two characteristics I don't like about the Chinese, which I might also have since I am half Chinese. The two are petty cleverness and practical-mindedness, which tend to bring about expediency and compromise. These two shortcomings can erode the steadfastness of one's character and undermine one's will to do what's meaningful in the long run. George Bernard Shaw once said: 'The reasonable man adapts himself to the world; the unreasonable one persists in trying to adapt the world to himself; therefore all progress depends on the unreasonable man.' I hope that when you're young, you cherish your unreasonableness, which, like the fire of life, might dwindle as you grow older." The moment I said that, I realized I'd quoted those words from a volume of my father's diary, over which I had pored the night before. On its very first page he had put down that sentence by Shaw, whose plays, like D. H. Lawrence's novels, had helped him while away the long lonesome days in Okinawa.

I thought I might have offended some of my students, but a good number of them told me that my words made them think a lot, that they appreciated my candor. One even thanked me for reminding him not to become "a smart fool."

Minmin, unlike most young Chinese, didn't seem pragmatic. She was undaunted by the difficulties of reaching the summit of Mount Everest. (Of course she had fewer financial worries and family duties compared to other young people.) She might not be clever, but her vivacious personality set her apart from her class-mates as an individual who still showed a spark of life. For that I admired her.

She also told me about a dilemma she had to solve—a military college had just approached her with a job offer. If she accepted it, she might have to put off or abandon her Mount Everest dream. I didn't know how to advise her, since physically she wasn't that strong and I wasn't sure she could climb the mountain even though she had all the support she needed from her well-heeled brother. She might not even be able to go through the strenuous training for mountaineering, so I refrained from offering her any advice.

I HADN'T KNOWN Henry had been emailing with Ben directly. When he told me, I felt uncomfortable and asked, half in jest, "So you two can bad-mouth me behind my back?"

"Come on, Lilian," Henry said. "You know guys can chat more freely without a girl around."

"What do you talk about?"

"Ball games, girls, politics, military history, smart weapons. Also about how to make money."

"Ben already has a girlfriend. Why still talk about girls? Isn't Sonya good enough for him?"

"He's a handsome guy. There must be others falling all over him."

"You really think he's good-looking?"

"Absolutely."

By Chinese standards I'd say Ben had average looks—a bit too masculine, big-boned, rough around the edges. Conventionally, Chinese women preferred men with slightly feminine features—smooth skin, soft eyes, a delicate jaw, a refined manner. Some also liked bookish men, perhaps because the knowledge of books used to promise power and wealth, not to mention prestige. That has changed, though, as capitalism has penetrated every fiber of Chinese society and reshaped people's values and mentality. Most young men have a different sense of masculinity now. Two decades ago, my male Chinese friends had often said that their ideal man was the late premier Zhou Enlai or the great writer Lu Xun, both of whom were not strong physically. Nowadays many young men would pick Michael Jordan or Kobe Bryant or Tim Duncan (nicknamed Stone Buddha by his Chinese fans) as their male icon. And believe it or not, a lot of them also worshiped Allen Iverson because the six-foot basketball player embodied the possibility of stardom for men of average stature.

In late July I got a disturbing message from Juli. Wuping had jilted her and removed her from the band, and now she was at a loss about what to do. I urged her to keep a cool head. Since the relationship hadn't been going anywhere, it might be better to break up sooner than later. "You don't understand, Aunt Lilian," Juli retorted. "He has shacked up with another woman. The bitch just graduated from a drama college and started acting in a TV show. She knows how to put a spell on men and always sways her ass like it is a beacon in a lighthouse. There's no way I can compete with a slut like that. Heavens, my worst nightmare has come true!" The more we wrote back and forth, the more desperate and unbalanced Juli sounded. Then she told me that Wuping had beaten her and called her "a crazy cunt" when she went to his office to confront him. I guessed she must have made a scene.

I called Ben to see how much he knew about his sister's trouble. To my relief, he was up-to-date and said he'd met Wuping before and known from the outset that the man was unreliable. "He's a crook and a self-styled lady-killer," Ben said. "He uses every trick to turn a woman's head, but he's a smug good-for-nothing, the type we call 'an embroidered pillowcase.'"

"In English we say 'an empty suit,'" I told him.

"That's right. A big nothing or a bag of hot air."

I laughed out loud, amused that he could come up with those expressions. "He looked too smooth to me, like a top-notch schmoozer," I said. "But how can we help Juli? She seems to have lost her head over that jerk."

"Don't worry, Aunt Lilian. I'm heading back to Guangzhou tomorrow night and will settle up with him."

"What are you going to do? You must not resort to violence, okay?"

"Of course I won't touch him, but I'll talk with him. He knows I'm well connected in police circles there and can have him brought in anytime."

I couldn't grasp the full implications of Ben's words and asked, "Do you have enough money for the trip?"

"My company will pay. I'm also going back for business meetings in Beijing."

His ability to fly back and forth so easily made me mull over my father's life again. During his first years here, how poignantly Gary must have longed to go back to visit his family, even just once. Yet perhaps little by little he got accustomed to the pain of loss and jaded about homesickness. Did he always remember the streets of his village and the trails on the mountain slopes and along the rivers that used to be frequented by cranes, herons, mallards? And the endless chestnut groves on the hills? And the temples and shrines on the lakesides? Probably to a great extent he had managed to suppress the memories of home so he could function normally each day. Did he ever imagine adopting a new homeland so that he could restart his life here? Surely having "eaten all the bitterness" (as he phrased it in his diary), at last he could enjoy American life, given that he did grow to like this country. What a tangled existence he had lived. In recent months he had grown more enigmatic to me, because at times it was hard for me to penetrate the armor of detachment he had clothed himself in.

The thought came to me that I might put Ben in touch with Minmin. I liked Sonya, but my father's life had exemplified how difficult it was to live with a spouse of a different race, who spoke a different language, grew up in a different culture and social environment, and believed in a different religion. Actually, like my mother, Gary had gone to Mass regularly and even contributed ten dollars a month to our church, but I couldn't tell if he was serious about Christianity. In his diary he never mentioned the religion, and he seemed to have remained an atheist. In all likelihood he had joined the church as a camouflage. If he were a genuine Christian, he'd have owned up to his true identity in a confessional and some pastor would have entered his life, offering spiritual guidance. But his diary didn't mention any clergyman except Father Murray. I believed it was their common language and cultural background that had brought my father and Suzie together, and as a result, there was no way my mother could separate them. That conviction prompted me to call Ben again and tell him about Minmin. I wanted him to meet her in Beijing. I said to Ben, "You can buy a book for me and take it to her as my present. I will write her about this so she can know who you are."

The book I suggested was *The Search for Modern China,* by Jonathan Spence, which, though a hefty volume, might come in handy for Minmin. It was an excellent overview of modern Chinese history and a widely used textbook in American colleges. I told Ben that he could get the book at any good bookstore, and I would reimburse him. "No need for that," he assured me. "I will deliver the present to Minmin in person."

That night I talked to Henry about Ben's plan to intercede for his sister, afraid he might bungle the case, but I said nothing about Minmin. I did not intend to be overtly matchmaking, and my present for her was more or less a lark. "Don't underestimate Ben," Henry said. "He's very savvy about dealing with people."

"How can you tell?" I asked.

"I observed him when he and I went out together." Henry's eyes shone while a smile crossed his whiskered face. "He'll handle everything properly. I'm not worried about him."

"You sound like you know him better than I."

"That's why I hope he can manage our building someday. He'll be good at handling the troublesome tenants."

I couldn't help but laugh. Henry was always nervous when he asked for overdue rent from some tenants, above all two young women. I was the one who had to go to them and ask.

BEN CALLED A WEEK LATER. He was back from China and busy catching up on work. He assured me that Juli had broken up with Wuping peacefully and was out of trouble now. Curious about the word "peacefully," I asked him to elaborate. He said he'd met with the man and told him that if he'd jilted Juli without enough reason, there'd be consequences. Ben showed Wuping a page of information on the tax fraud committed by his father's garbage company. Every month his old man imported shiploads of trash from Japan and Australia for $1.5 a ton and then sorted it to get recyclable materials, which he sold to Chinese factories. He netted a two hundred percent profit. Aside from breaking the tax law, he had leased out some of his garbage dumps as ranches where thousands of cows grazed on nothing but trash, and as a result, their beef was heavily contaminated, even poisonous. The old crook's collusion with the cattlemen alone could get his company shut down and him put into jail. Despite denying any knowledge of the crimes, Wuping was shaken and came back to Ben on the same day. He offered Juli fifty thousand yuan, which settled their breakup and her unemployment.

I asked Ben, "How did you find out about his father's tax fraud?"

"I told you I was well connected in police circles there. No fat cat in China has a clean ass. All the successful businesspeople evade taxes, otherwise how could they get rich? The police have kept track of every one of them. If they don't behave, they'll be brought in."

I felt uneasy about Ben's way of handling his sister's affair but didn't press him for more details. I asked, "Is Juli all right?"

"Sure, she's back in Heilongjiang with my parents."

"You mean she gave up her musical career?"

"She was silly and lost her heart to that playboy. She isn't much of a singer to start with. It's time she came to her senses."

"You might be right." Somehow I had always avoided thinking poorly of Juli's musical talent. "Your parents must be happy now. Are they okay?"

"I didn't see them. I was busy attending meetings in Beijing. But I called them. They were well and sent their regards. By the way, I met Minmin and gave her the book. She loved it."

"She told me that."

"You should be careful when communicating with her, Aunt Lilian."

"Why? What's wrong with Minmin? You don't like her?"

"Not because of that. She is a fine person, but the military has taken an interest in her."

"I know they offered her a lectureship, but she doesn't want it."

"It might not be easy for her to turn it down."

"Really? Can't she choose her own career?"

"It's not that simple. Declining an offer from that kind of

school is like refusing to serve our country. She might have to pay for it if she can't give them a convincing reason."

"You mean she'll be treated as a dissident?"

"Something like that."

"That's ridiculous."

"A lot of things in China don't make any sense, but we have to accept them as part of life. In any event, she said she wanted to climb Mount Everest first. She's a bit nutty."

I didn't know what more to say. Minmin couldn't be that vulnerable; she had her own financial means and didn't have to take a day job. In a couple of years she might come to the States to do graduate work. So I felt I needn't worry too much about Minmin, to whom Ben seemed to have felt little attraction. That caught me off balance a bit, but there was no loss.

I thought more about Juli. She got fifty thousand yuan from her former lover. That was a small fortune. I remembered I had once asked my grad students at Beijing Teachers College how much scholarship money they received for living expenses. Typically each got seven hundred yuan a month, which was not much but enough for food, their major expenditure since they all had free beds in the dormitories. In fact, a small amount of money still could go a long way in China if you were thrifty and knew where to shop. Part of me was uneasy about the cash settlement Wuping had offered Juli. Didn't she once love him? How could she be compensated for her loss so easily? On the other hand, I knew that if she stayed with her family, she'd be all right and could recover from the heartbreak eventually. In my next email I urged her not to leave home again. I wrote: "There is nothing more precious than family in this world. Stay with your parents as long as you can. They are getting on in years and need you around."

"I understand, Aunt," she replied.

1966–1969

Since the summer of 1966 Gary had lost contact with Bingwen, who had been removed from his office and made to take part in the Cultural Revolution. Where was he now? Try as he might, Gary couldn't find out. He approached Father Murray, but the priest couldn't get in touch with anyone in China either. The country had fallen into total disarray. No one was in charge of the overseas intelligence work anymore. Gary had read that even the top officials in the State Council were brought down by the revolutionary masses, and that some of them were put on platforms and publicly denounced, made to wear dunce caps and placards around their necks. He followed the news with a sinking heart. Besides browsing through the periodicals in the library at CIA headquarters, every day on his way to work he would stop to spend five cents for the Chinese-language newspaper *The American Daily,* which, funded by Taiwan and printed in New York, published a good amount of disturbing news about China. The Red Guards were running the show now, able to travel around with free lodging and board to spread the revolutionary fire. They all wore Mao buttons and red armbands emblazoned with golden words and carried Mao's little red book. As a gesture of support, the chairman, in army uniform, had begun to review legions of Red Guards in Tiananmen Square regularly.

Like his friend George Thomas, Gary had bought a little red book at the campus bookstore on his visit to Georgetown University. He read it from cover to cover but was underwhelmed. He found Mao's thoughts rather crude and incoherent, though they were pithy and earthy, showing some solid horse sense. Most of them were incendiary ideas, more suitable for inciting and organizing the masses than for solving the nation's problems. No wonder so many hot-blooded college students in America also worshiped Mao, carrying the little book like the Chinese Red Guards. Some even wore Mao buttons. Gary couldn't help wondering where they'd gotten them. He and George Thomas talked about Mao's quotations one evening at Bohemian Alley, both of them in shirt-sleeves with their jackets draped inside out over the backs of their chairs. After releasing a belch, Thomas chuckled and said, "If I were thirty years younger, I might take the little red book as my bible too. It can misguide youngsters easily." Thomas was in his mid-fifties now, his hair sparse and half gray, but his eyes were still vivid and bright.

"Mao's brain seems wired differently," Gary said, pouring more beer into his glass. "He still has a young warrior's mentality, aggressive and ruthless."

"I have to say he has lots of gumption and charisma." Thomas spoke in a flat voice. "Mao is fearless and shrewd. Still, sometimes I was befuddled as I was reading him. How the hell could he say 'There is endless joy in fighting heaven, there is endless joy in fighting earth, and there is endless joy in fighting man,' as if he were a god of warfare? It's beyond me."

"He's being celebrated as a deity there," Gary said. "A septuagenarian war god, my ass. For me, Mao is China's biggest problem."

"Why's that?"

"His ego is so enormous that he can never swallow his pride in the interests of his country and his people. He sees China not as his responsibility but as his property. He doesn't understand that even though he's the head of the nation, he's still no more than its manager, its servant."

"Can you be more specific about his mistakes or shortcomings?"

"For example, he should have tried every way to retain the Soviets' aid for China, but he fell out with Khrushchev because he couldn't eat humble pie. He couldn't see how poor and underdeveloped China was, and couldn't sacrifice his personal pride so that the Chinese people could benefit more from the Soviets' economic help. In retrospect, I would attribute most of China's recent disasters to Mao's egotism. He has styled himself as a thinker and is never practical. He's too romantic to be a sophisticated and responsible leader. Worse yet, he has never kept his hands on small things, different from Stalin, who would oversee minute details in his economic plans. Even for a thinker, Mao's ideas are quite sloppy, and most of them are derivative." Gary caught himself and stopped short. Never had he spoken about the supreme leader like this. His loosened tongue disturbed him.

Thomas said, "I can see the difference between Mao and Stalin. Mao sometimes acts like a juvenile, lacking consistency and integrity. But you can also say he's more like a poet." Thomas ripped a packet of Sweet'N Low and emptied the powder into his iced tea.

"His poetry is okay," Gary said. He wondered why Thomas was so fond of the sugar substitute. He wouldn't touch the sweetener, because Nellie would not allow him, saying it contained too much saccharin.

A soaring saxophone note drew their eyes to the band. A trio of musicians was playing jazz, all swaying their bodies and tapping their feet. The music then went slow, dangling with a tumbling melody. Gary narrowed his eyes, and his facial expression became dreamy.

IT WAS AT THE END OF 1966 when he began to dye his graying hair. His wife thought he was too vain and told him that he actually looked better with salt-and-pepper hair, more respectable and even a bit professorial, but he wouldn't let his hair be ravaged by the hands of his biological clock. He joked by imitating Mao, "There is endless joy in fighting nature." He laughed at his own quip, which baffled Nellie. Once she grunted behind his back, "Crazy boob." Their daughter overheard her, but she too wanted to see her father look younger and more vigorous. She had once run into Gary and Suzie together in his car and found the small woman pretty with an angular face, clear skin, and delicate shoulders. At the sight of Lilian, they stopped talking. Gary waved at his daughter as if inviting her to get into the car, but the girl spun around and sprinted away, the hem of her plaid skirt fluttering. She never told her mother about the encounter. Somehow she couldn't hate Suzie, perhaps because she could tell that her dad appeared younger and more spirited when he was with her.

With his espionage activities suspended, Gary could relax some. He no longer needed to fuss over the secrecy that had almost become second nature, although he still wouldn't let Nellie enter his study. There was a plethora of useful intelligence going through his hands nowadays, but he didn't bother to collect most of it. What was the good of gathering the information if it couldn't be delivered? So he just let it slip by and picked only the items that might have long-term value.

These years, from 1966 to 1968, with his mission in the doldrums, were the most peaceful period of his life in America. He enjoyed the solitude and had acquired a taste for various kinds of cheese and California wines. He often walked in the parks alone for hours on end, carrying a twisted cane to keep away wild animals, especially snakes. His family life was uneventful despite Nellie's knowledge of Suzie. His wife realized that psychologically he might need a woman from his native land. As long as Suzie didn't pose a threat to their marriage, Nellie wasn't going to make a big fuss about the affair. Many years later, when her daughter asked her why she had turned a blind eye to her father's keeping a mistress, Nellie said, "Maybe that floozy could give him something I couldn't. I felt sorry for your dad. He was such a lonesome soul that he might've needed to find some comfort elsewhere. In spite of everything, I loved him."

Early in the winter of 1968, Gary came across a report sent over by Taipei, which stated that the Soviets had recently deployed more than thirty mechanized divisions in Mongolia besides those already in Siberia, perhaps with the intention to attack China. It was known that the two countries had border disputes, but never had Gary expected that their small-unit skirmishes would escalate into a confrontation of such a scale. He had no doubt about the validity of the information. Taiwan's intelligence service had a monitoring station in Mongolia, designed to follow the military activities inside China, but on the sly the listening post also kept an ear on the Soviet army's movements. And Taipei would routinely pass the information to the Americans. Gary was uncertain if China knew about all the Russian divisions and missile brigades placed along its northern border. He grew restless, being unable to send out the intelligence.

Then, in March 1969, military clashes broke out between the Soviets and the Chinese on the Wusuli River. In the two small battles, the Chinese troops got the upper hand even though they were not as well equipped and didn't use tanks. They'd been better prepared and ambushed the Russian soldiers who went in armored vehicles onto Zhenbao Island in the frozen river. The border fights galvanized the world. In China large public demonstrations against the Soviet chauvinists took place in many cities, while in the United States politicians and experts appeared on the radio, a few on TV, speculating about whether the two Communist countries might go to war. Most people in the West were glad to see the widening gulf between the two Red powers. For weeks Gary had been thinking about the possibility of a war, tormented by it. Everything inside China seemed a mystery now. The country was surely in disarray, yet it had been quite aggressive in confronting the superior Soviet army. Why would Mao authorize such a move? Didn't he understand that the Soviets might invade China just as they had occupied Czechoslovakia the previous summer? Was China ready for a war that might cripple, if not destroy, a good part of the country? Didn't Mao dread the Russians' thousands of nuclear warheads?

The information Gary had seen suggested a dire prospect. If war broke out, there'd be little hope that China could win. Perhaps there had been some domestic troubles that compelled Mao to externalize the tension by provoking the border clashes. Still, this could get out of hand. If only Gary had a way to make his Chinese superiors see the danger lying ahead and avoid acting rashly. If only he could meet Bingwen again. Gary talked to Suzie about the possibility of war between China and the Soviet Union. "Mao is a crazy warmonger," she said. She now hated the chairman, though she used to have mixed feelings about him and had even regarded him as the founder of the new China. To her mind, Mao was addlepated and should have retired long ago. The longer he stayed in power, the more harm would befall the country.

Gary just echoed Suzie's sentiments, unable to confide his true worries to her—that he'd lost contact with China and all the valuable intelligence he'd accumulated was becoming useless. On the other hand, he was by now accustomed to his isolation, which gave him an ease of mind that he had never experienced before. His life was growing more peaceful, and most of his old anxiety and fear were gone. He slept better and no longer felt like he was being shadowed when he walked alone. What's more, he'd begun to be fond of this place, where he had a secure, decent job and a comfortable home with a little flower garden. If he were a regular immigrant, he'd have felt like a success, like those who would brag to the people back in their native lands that they had made it in America.

In late July 1969 came the Apollo moon landing, a feat that astounded the world. Gary was riveted to the TV watching the astronauts, each carrying a bulky backpack and bounding in their white suits on the face of the moon. They also gathered around their vehicle and equipment as if working underwater. Gary took pride in this country (he wrote in his diary on July 20, 1969: "Truly a great feat!") and was happy to see the U.S. flag planted up there. Now this historic event was unfolding before the eyes of the world to demonstrate the U.S. supremacy in space technology. In the back of Gary's mind lurked the hope that the moon landing might shake the Chinese leaders back to their senses and make them see how far behind their country had fallen.

◈◈◈

On an early August afternoon, the postman delivered a bulky box to the super's office of our building. Henry had gone swimming at a fitness center, so I scrawled my signature on the scanner. Evidently it was something Henry had purchased from New Jersey, but usually he'd tell me before he placed an order.

That evening I asked him about the package, and he said, "Oh, that's something I bought for Ben."

"What is it?"

"We'll see." His eyes twinkled with a smile. He slit the sealing tape with a brass key and opened the flaps. Inside were foam peanuts, and he stirred them with his hand and fished out five blue boxes, each the size of half a brick.

"What are these?" I asked.

"Microchips."

I opened a box and took out a square chip, about two inches across and topped with a miniature cooling fan. My heart began to sink, and I asked Henry, "Are they expensive?"

"You bet. More than five hundred bucks apiece."

"Why did Ben want you to buy them?"

"He said because he had a Chinese last name, some salespeople often screwed up his orders and once in a while his purchases never arrived. If I could buy stuff for him, he'd pay me double price for everything I bought. So I thought it was a good opportunity to make some money. See these five little rascals? I paid twenty-seven hundred bucks for them and can get a one hundred percent profit."

"This doesn't sit well with me."

"C'mon, Lilian dear, don't be such a party pooper. Anybody can buy microchips. In actuality I think Ben's doing me a favor, letting me pull in a couple of bucks."

That night I surfed the Internet to find out what these chips were for. I spent about three hours online but couldn't figure it out exactly. Yet I came across several articles about Chinese nationals living in the States charged for shipping banned microchips to China. Some of the chips belonged to the category of embargoed technology because they could be used on aircraft and missiles. I was alarmed, though uncertain if Ben had been acquiring them for the Chinese military. I figured there was a fifty-fifty chance that this was illegal.

I talked to Henry about it again the following day and mentioned that some Chinese nationals had recently pleaded guilty to shipping banned microchips to China—two men had been sentenced to seven and five years in prison. "Please, Lilian," Henry said. "You're paranoid, still under the shadow of your father's case. First, if the chips I bought are banned technology, how can someone like me purchase them without any restriction? Second, it's not like I got hundreds of them. I ordered only five. There's nothing illegal in this."

I didn't know how to counter him. His reasoning sounded cogent, yet I couldn't feel at ease about this. I called Ben the next evening, and Sonya picked up. She sounded cheerful, her voice giggly. She had just moved in with Ben, and their relationship seemed to be going strong.

"Ben, Aunt Lilian's on the line," she trilled.

After a few words with him, I asked point-blank about Henry's purchase. "Please level with me, Ben," I said. "Is it illegal to do that?"

"No, anyone can buy Intel chips like those. For that matter, they're already obsolete. The manufacturer doesn't produce them anymore."

"Then why did you get Henry involved?"

"It's just easier for him to buy them directly. Besides, I want Uncle Henry to make some money. It's easy cash for him, don't you think?"

"So you can make a lot of profit acquiring microchips?"

"Yes, usually about three hundred percent. I give Uncle Henry a third of what I get."

"Thank you. But who are the ultimate buyers of the chips?"

"Some Chinese companies."

"Why do they pay three times more than the listing price?"

"Because they cannot acquire them by themselves."

"Does this mean the chips are embargoed?"

"In principle, yes."

"What do you mean by 'in principle'?"

"It's a long story. Ever since the Tiananmen Square incident in 1989, the U.S. has banned lots of technology from export to China. Some microchips are on the embargo list. But the problem is that many Chinese companies and labs have been using equipment made by American manufacturers, so some new chips are needed to replace the broken ones. This has nothing to do with cutting-edge technology. It is a matter of maintaining what the United States has already sold to China. The users of the machines can't buy any of the banned chips directly, so our company's service fills the need."

"I hope you're telling me the truth, Ben."

"Why should I lie to you? You're the only family I have on this side of the planet. You're my aunt by blood."

"Aren't some of the chips used on missiles and jet fighters?"

"Yes, they are."

"Clearly it's illegal to ship those to China. If the FBI finds this out, you might do jail time."

"Look, how many rich people are making money legally in this country, or in any country? It's not like I'm sending the chips back in large quantities. I sell only two or three at a time. The truth is, the chips are available elsewhere if not from the States."

Still unconvinced, I said, "Ben, you must stop doing anything illegal. In this country you have to keep your nose clean if you want to live a good, peaceful life."

"Okay, I hear you."

"I'm going to mail you some articles on your grandfather. You should read them carefully and see how he messed up his life here. Don't be a blind patriot like Gary."

"Thanks very much. Do send them along. I can't wait to know more about my granddad."

Should I mail him all the thirty-odd pieces in my file? I wondered. I decided not to. Instead, I Xeroxed seven major articles on Gary's case published in *The New York Times* and *The Washington Post*. Before stuffing them in an envelope, I looked through them again. My eye caught a passage I had underlined: "By Shang's own confession, he received cash for every delivery of intelligence, though at the moment it remains unclear how much he has actually been paid. According to a CIA officer, who spoke under anonymity, Shang had expensive taste and was a big spender. To date, the CIA has refused to comment and only insists that it has been participating in the investigation actively." I turned to another article, which said: "The Chinese have a different way of conducting espionage. They are extremely patient, and their secret agents tend to remain dormant for many years before they become active. Undoubtedly Shang was a master mole, a key source of intelligence for the Chinese. His spying activities have severely breached our national security, although at the moment it's impossible to assess the enormity of the damage."

I didn't want to give Ben the complete coverage of the story, figuring that some of the more devastating details should be disclosed to him step by step. I FedExed him the seven articles the next morning.

1969–1970

On August 28, 1969, *The Washington Star* published a frightening piece of news. A front-page article stated that the Soviet Union, tired of the border clashes with the Chinese, had been planning massive air strikes on China's nuclear installations. The Soviets had been sounding out the leaders of various countries on their reactions if it took such an extreme step. Although printed in the metro evening paper, whose reputation had in recent years fallen close to that of tabloids, the news unsettled the public. Gary had no doubt about the credibility of the report and was more interested in the motive behind such a publication. Even the U.S. State Department had been interviewed about the Soviets' air-raid plan, though its spokesman said this might be just "a rumor."

The news seemed to have been released through the usual channels, but some people in the DC intelligence community suspected that the report might be a maneuver by the White House—although there'd been discussions about destroying the Chinese nuclear arsenal in academic circles, this was the first time the topic had been broached publicly. The intelligence analysts surmised that by making this story appear in the media, the U.S. government might have been signaling and even making small overtures to the Chinese. In contrast, some others felt that the Russians might have a hand in this report, taking advantage of the U.S. media to put more pressure on China, because word of the story would surely get to Beijing and might help restrain Mao and his comrades. There were other speculations as well. Yet some military analysts dismissed the report as mere gossip, insisting that if the Russians had intended to bomb China's nuclear facilities, they'd have been quiet about it.

Like many of his colleagues in DC intelligence circles, Gary was convinced that the Soviet plan for the air strikes was by no means idle talk or a diplomatic gambit. He got agitated, wondering how China would respond. Bingwen was still absent from the scene, possibly no longer even alive, so Gary remained cut off from his homeland. He wondered if his comrades had given up on him. Why would nobody get in touch with him? Didn't China need a reliable source in the CIA? Even Father Murray had no idea how to communicate with Beijing anymore, though they both believed that through various channels the news about the Soviets' attempt must have reached China.

Sure enough, two weeks later Mao issued the internal order that the whole country "dig caves and store away grain widely." Gary did some research and found out that over the years the Chinese had actually been preparing for air raids, though they'd expected them to come from American bombers. Near every city caves and bunkers were dug and built, mostly in suburban hills and valleys. Then, right before October 1, 1969, the twentieth National Day, on which a large celebration was to be held in Tiananmen Square, China detonated two nuclear warheads in its western desert. One of them was a three-megaton hydrogen bomb. Gary interpreted these explosions as China's signal to the Russians that it was capable of dropping warheads of multiple megatons on the Soviet Union with the intermediate-range missiles the Chinese already possessed. Though the nuclear tests also showed that China might have overreacted, Gary felt relieved and even began to see that Mao was an astute politician, having foreseen China's need for nuclear weapons for self-defense.

Meanwhile, Gary's domestic life was quiet, even as his affair with Suzie continued. During the summer of 1969 Suzie had dated a Greek diplomat, a soft-voiced man with a handlebar mustache, but the relationship petered out after the man was called back to Greece, so she returned to Gary. Gary was pleased to have her back in his life, though he didn't say so. At home he and Nellie seldom quarreled now. They slept in the same bed at night, though he was a restless sleeper and often woke her up, speaking both English and Chinese in his dreams. Whenever he argued with someone in his sleep, he would yell out curses and warnings in his mother tongue, of which Nellie couldn't make out a word. But during the day he'd be quiet and gentle again, somewhat remote.

Now that he had more free time, he often played Chinese chess with Lilian, who had just started middle school. He'd taught her all the moves, which were incomprehensible to Nellie, who couldn't even tell a cannon from an elephant. One out of five games his daughter could beat him. Whenever this happened, he'd be elated, praising the girl for her "iron wit." He often said he wanted her to attend a prep school so that she could go to a top college. Occasionally father and daughter would communicate in simple Mandarin words and phrases. That annoyed her mother, who would scowl at her because she couldn't understand. She often muttered, "Like father, like daughter." Yet in spite of his love for Lilian, Gary planned to send the girl away in the near future to prevent her from getting in his way—he wouldn't have her enter his study when he wasn't home.

In the spring of 1970, Nellie went out to work at a bakery called Peggy's Kitchen. She enjoyed making bread, cookies, pies, cakes. Working for Peggy Loschiavo, a stout woman of sixty-two with fluffy white hair and thick glasses, Nellie became more energetic, in spite of her menopause, which she believed was too early for a woman who had just turned forty-one. She attributed the cessation to the stress Gary had caused her. Every day she brought back fresh bread that both her husband and daughter loved. And Gary grew fond of focaccia, onion rolls, challah, sourdough bread, croissants. He enjoyed munching fresh-baked bread with sausage, especially linguica, together with raw garlic. Sometimes Nellie also got leftover pastries for free: apple turnovers, chocolate rugelach, strudels, various kinds of cookies. Gary had never eaten so much sweet food, every piece of which was shot through with sugar and butter, so quintessentially American. He loved pastries with flaky crusts and fruit fillings. By way of joking he told his wife, "I'll put on twenty pounds by the end of this year." In reality, he couldn't get fat no matter how much he ate. He often said he wished he were a gourmet plus gourmand so that he could have enjoyed all the fine bread and pastries with gusto. A moderate eater, he was the type of person who was "born thin."

Nellie couldn't gain weight either, despite her hearty appetite. Something remarkable had happened to her over the years, and even she could feel the change in herself. She was calmer and more articulate than the young bride of fourteen years before. Perhaps this was due to her reading of books, hundreds of them, mostly paperback romances and detective novels. When her daughter was a pupil, Nellie had read everything the girl worked on in school, and had often kept her company while she did homework. She continued to do that until Lilian left for a prep school in Groton, Massachusetts, where she developed a passion for history thanks to a wonderful young teacher. In secret the girl had a minor crush on that sweet man, whose fingers she often fantasized caressing her budding breasts at night. Unlike most of her schoolmates, she did not return home very often, knowing her parents were estranged. For all its peace and quiet, their house had an icy feel, which Lilian dreaded. She was glad that her mother had begun working outside their home.

At the bakery, sometimes a cop or a lawyer on the way to the courthouse would stop by to shoot the breeze with Peggy. Some of the men would leer at Nellie and a few even attempted to tease her, but she had no clue how to flirt in spite of her looks, which had improved with age: a heart-shaped face, high cheekbones, glossy eyes, and a plump bottom lip. It was simply not in her nature. She always had a reserved manner that might come across as arrogant, as if she had a perfect family and a doting husband. She didn't use lipstick because she had to sample bread and pastries, but she put on delicate makeup that added a fine touch to her features. She'd wear an avocado green cardigan, a red apron, and a white hat.

Some people even mistook her, the only woman shop assistant, for a recent European immigrant who couldn't speak English. She would smile at customers timidly and wordlessly. In the beginning Gary disliked her going out to work, saying they didn't need the money, but she insisted she do something to make herself worth more. She referred to the fact that Gary had bought life insurance on himself whereas she couldn't do that because she held no job. "My life is so worthless," she used to mock herself with a tinge of bitterness. Probably she hoped that when she died, she could leave something to her daughter. She wasn't going to worry about her husband, who could take care of himself anyhow.

Ever since the newspaper's report about the Soviets' intention to attack China's nuclear bases, Gary had been trying to piece together the sequence of events that had led to the disclosure. Though a mere translator at the CIA, he had by the summer of 1970 heard enough about it to convince him of its validity. Word had gotten around that Soviet Ambassador Anatoly Dobrynin had approached Henry Kissinger on August 20 the previous year and requested a meeting. When they met, what Dobrynin said amazed the secretary of state: the Soviet Union wanted the Americans to stay neutral if it launched air raids on China's nuclear facilities. Before the Russians started the attacks, they'd like to know how the United States would respond. At first Kissinger was unsure how serious Dobrynin was, but the Soviet ambassador emphasized that the attacks would be surgical, only on military targets, and that there'd be no civilian casualties. The message finally sank in, but Kissinger still wouldn't respond directly, saying he'd have to consult the president. Then a week later, instead of a direct answer from the White House to the Kremlin, *The Washington Star* reported the Soviets' plan. Apparently the United States did not remain wholly neutral in this matter. Weak though China was, it still could help counterbalance the Soviet Union. Beijing got the message about the Russians' threat and responded by detonating two warheads.

Yet the Chinese leaders might not have seen the White House's intention in leaking the news, which could be twofold: to widen the gulf between Beijing and Moscow, and to extend a tiny olive branch to the Chinese.

Gary knew the U.S. policy of neutrality in regard to the Sino-Soviet split—"let the two dogs eat each other"—but he felt that the United States seemed willing to lean toward China within the realm of neutrality. This was a window of opportunity the Chinese ought to seize. To Gary's mind, Mao and the Politburo might need more details about this news leak to grasp its full significance. Above all, he wanted to see the two countries get closer and eventually become partners. Regardless of how others interpreted the news or rumor, he wanted to steer the Chinese leaders toward some reconciliation with the United States. For now this might be the only way China could avoid destruction at the hands of the Soviet Union.

Gary had to present a strong argument to his superiors back home. Assuming they still could receive intelligence from him, he wrote a report and gave a succinct account of the meeting between Dobrynin and Kissinger. He made it clear that there was no way to verify the contents of their conversation, but there must be a kernel of truth in the hearsay. He stressed that the published news might be a well-intentioned gesture the United States was making to China, and that in the long run Washington might be willing to join hands with Beijing against the Soviet Union. Now could be an opportune time for the Chinese leaders to develop a productive relationship with the West as a way to counter the Russian Polar Bear.

Gary wondered if he had painted too rosy a picture for his higher-ups. But he believed in his analyses, which he'd done as objectively as he could. By nature he was not an optimist, and there was no reason for him to lie to the national leaders about the U.S. goodwill. Yet it was possible that by now he had too much affection for this land, where life could be safe and comfortable and where few people died of hunger, and this positive feeling might have affected his judgment. Although he had always remained an outsider capable of stepping aside to observe life flowing by, he did love American movies and the NBA games—he was an ardent fan of Wilt Chamberlain of the Lakers. He was also fond of the American landscape—the mountains, waters, vast agricultural fields, highways. If he were a common immigrant, he might have felt at home in this place, adopting it as his homeland. He could see such a possibility. Yes, the U.S. Army had been mercilessly fighting the Communists and even slaughtering civilians in Vietnam, where the war actually gave the number one superpower a bloody nose, but there'd been protests and demonstrations against the war all over the country. Yes, racism was rife and prejudices everywhere, but racial segregation had been abolished and the country had been making social progress. This was a place where one could live with decency and some dignity. This was a country that protected its people, many of whom in return loved it. Gary tried to fight down all the digressive ruminations that might erode the spirit and integrity needed for fulfilling his secret mission. He went on to revise his report, trying to be as reasonable and objective as possible.

At long last Father Murray notified him that Bingwen Chu had returned to his office. When the pomegranate tree in his backyard had dropped its last fruit in mid-November, Gary flew to Hong Kong directly, too eager to make a detour through Taiwan or Thailand. His handler, absent for more than four years, had finally been summoned back to Beijing. To Gary's surprise, Bingwen had aged considerably: his hairline was higher, his eyes bleary, even his brows half gray, and dark lines meshed his face like a loosely drawn map. Worse still, he limped a little because one foot had been smashed by a cinder block at a construction site where he'd been made to labor. Hearing that Gary had flown to Hong Kong directly from America, his handler was disturbed and admonished him never to do that again. He even said that if Gary was caught by the Americans, their superiors would hold him, Bingwen, accountable. He'd be punished and might go to prison. Gary promised he'd be more cautious in the future.

After a shot of Scotch, Bingwen got buoyant, saying he was happy to have left the countryside of Jilin province, and his health had improved some due to his work as an apprentice mason. He thanked Gary for just being alive and continuing to do some espionage work on his own, evidently motivated by his profound love for their motherland.

Caught unawares by his friend's effusive words, Gary couldn't answer and only chuckled out of nerves. During the last few years he'd seldom thought of his love for their motherland but had done his duty routinely.

"Now we're a pair of mules harnessed to the same wagon. That's why they called me back to work," Bingwen said and lifted a spoonful of chocolate fondant to his mouth, shaking his head while chewing slowly. He also kept swilling rosé from his wineglass, its side stained with his finger marks. They'd chosen Café des Délices, a small restaurant in Tin Hau, because Bingwen missed a good French dinner, which Gary said he'd love to share with him. In fact, Gary no longer cared about food as most Chinese did, and he was conscious of this change in himself. Bingwen put down his spoon and went on, "You must take good care of yourself, brother. Your safety also means my safety. The higher-ups used me again only because you're irreplaceable and I'm familiar with your work."

Gary's intelligence, accumulated during the past four years, was rich and essential. Bingwen had reviewed it before dinner and been so impressed that he told Gary, "I don't know how much they'll pay you for this invaluable batch, but I'll try my best to get you a decent price."

"Don't bother about it," Gary said in earnest. "I know our country is in bad shape and don't expect to get paid. As long as my service is appreciated, I am rewarded and satisfied."

"I will report to our leaders what you just said. Who knows? Your words might bring you some high honor."

Contrary to Gary's expectation, Bingwen got him four thousand dollars this time. Half the money was an equipment fund that he should have received long ago.

My nephew paid Henry fifty-four hundred dollars for the five microchips he'd bought for him. Having pulled in a one hundred percent profit, Henry was rapturous and agreed to continue to purchase stuff for Ben. I had a lot of misgivings about that but said nothing. Henry kept saying that Ben would "make it big" one of these days. I asked, "How big?" He said, "A multimillionaire." That might just have come from his dream of getting rich. Intelligent though he was, Henry was very bad at handling money. I had to manage his paltry retirement plan for him.

One morning in mid-August, Ben called and thanked me for the articles I had mailed him. "What do you make of them?" I said.

"I knew my grandfather had done some important work for China's intelligence service, but I had no idea he had been that prominent. These days I've been thinking about him a lot. Truth to tell, I used to resent him for marrying a foreign woman and living a comfortable American life, which I assumed might have been part of the reason he abandoned my grandmother. After reading the articles you sent me, I felt his life here was very sad and complicated."

"I don't think he loved my mother. He might have had more feelings for your grandmother. He often mentioned her in his diary. Imagine, he never saw her again after he'd left China in his mid-twenties. He dreamed of her from time to time. Once she hurt herself and was hospitalized in his dream, and that made him downcast for days. He was also amazed that she spoke English to him in his dreams."

"She couldn't speak a word of English!"

"I know. That shows how deep she was rooted in his consciousness."

A lull fell between us.

Then Ben explained why he was calling: Sonya had been pregnant with his child for about two months. They'd found it out a week ago with a kit bought from a drugstore. For him the pregnancy posed two questions: whether they should keep the baby and what kind of relationship he should have with Sonya from now on. He and she couldn't see eye to eye on giving birth to the child and had exchanged angry words. He blamed her for going off the pill secretly, while she accused him of just using her and flirting with Minmin and other Chinese women who had joined his Weibo. He suggested an abortion, which Sonya would not consider.

"That's an awful suggestion," I told him. "How could you do that?"

"Don't take me to be heartless. I'm fond of children too, but these days I can't get my grandfather's life off my mind. I don't want to repeat his mistake."

"For God's sake, what has your problem got to do with him?"

"Well, if he hadn't started a family here or raised you, a daughter he loved, his life could have been much less tangled. He wouldn't have felt like a divided man, as he claimed in court, saying he loved both China and the U.S."

I was astounded, never having expected that the articles I'd sent Ben could set him thinking so deeply about Gary's plight. "Look," I said, "don't ever use your grandfather as a negative reference. You have your own life to live and must do what suits you best."

"All right, any suggestions?"

"Do you love Sonya?"

"Yes, I do."

"Do you think you'll be happy to sleep with her, only her, for the rest of your life?"

"Goodness, you sound as if I'm a connoisseur of women. To tell the truth, I've slept with only three girls to date, Sonya included. How can I say I'll be happy with her for the rest of my life?"

"So doesn't that mean you don't love her enough to marry her even though she's carrying your child?" Getting no answer from him, I continued, "I'm not blaming you. I just want to point out that you won't be able to wash your hands of her if there's a baby bonding the two of you."

"I don't intend to break up with her. I just want her to have an abortion."

"To be honest, it doesn't sound like you love her."

"I do love her, but I have more important responsibilities."

"Like what? Can you tell me?"

"I must be dedicated to my country. That's a bigger cause than my personal well-being."

"Bullcrap! Don't ever let China stand in the way of your personal fulfillment or lighten your personal responsibilities. You've been using your country as an excuse, as a big divisor to break your guilt into small negligible pieces so you can avoid facing it."

He didn't seem to fully understand me and remained silent, so I shifted the topic a bit. "Does Sonya demand you marry her?"

"No, she never said anything like that."

Ben seemed confused. I told him not to suggest anything to Sonya again. He first had to find out how she felt about their relationship and what she planned do with the baby if she kept it. Would she raise it by herself? Would she farm it out to her parents back in Ukraine if he wouldn't marry her?

Ben feared he might not be able to get Sonya to see reason, so that evening I spoke with her on the phone. She didn't deny that she had lied to Ben and stopped taking the pill on the sly.

"I just want to have a baby with him," she said in a guileless voice. "I'm almost twenty-six and shouldn't wait any longer."

"But you shouldn't have kept Ben in the dark to begin with."

"I won't become a burden to him."

"But a child will mean a lot of responsibilities to him as well."

"Well, I don't see it that way. I can raise the baby by myself. Besides, even though I'm not a regular churchgoer, I believe life begins with conception and nothing's more sacred than life."

"Sonya, let's be rational about this. I also love babies and so does Ben. Tell me, would you be happy if you two got married?"

"Of course, I'd be the happiest girl on the East Coast!"

"So you used the baby to keep your hold on him?"

She let out a small sigh. "Lilian, you're a smart woman and can see right through me. Let me say this: I can't stand to see him blabbing with those bitches on his blog all the time, and I will be jealous as hell if he ends up with another woman. I know he's just keeping me around as a girlfriend, but still I would do anything for him."

It was clear she loved him. But did he really love her as he claimed? I wasn't sure. How should I advise Ben then? In a way I was amazed to hear Sonya speak about her feelings like a young girl. Obviously she was not as sophisticated as her age and face might suggest. I liked her more for her innocence and bullheadedness.

I talked with Henry about Ben's trouble. He said, "What's the big deal? Get married. If the marriage doesn't work, get a divorce."

I wouldn't suggest that, because a divorce can be a big block in a young man's life, psychologically and professionally, a setback that can cripple his confidence. Perhaps it was unwise for Ben to attempt a solution right away. There are problems that are not supposed to be fixed once and for all but to be lived with. Sometimes a solution can give rise to a new problem—in other words, there might be no ultimate solution at all. We Americans tend to be self-proclaimed problem fixers of the world, and such a mentality is one of the causes of our tragedy—there are many problems we can't possibly fix.

I called Ben the next day and asked him not to impose his will on Sonya. He needn't rush. He had another two months to work with her for a solution. Once the pregnancy reached the fifth month, it would be too risky to abort the fetus. Then they might have to let the baby come into the world and figure out how to raise it.

"In fact, you should always take a child as a blessing," I told Ben.

"Okay, I'll try to think that way," he said, but he didn't sound convinced.

"You should also do some soul-searching."

"Why should I do that?"

"To answer the question of whether you'll be happy if you spend the rest of your life with Sonya."

"About that I have no doubt."

He sounded a little blithe, but I didn't press him to say more.

1971–1972

It was reported that Mao Zedong had been so impressed by Gary's analyses of the U.S. motivation in publishing the news about the Soviets' planned air strikes on China's nuclear bases that the chairman told his comrades in the Politburo, "This man is worth four armored divisions." Those words heralded an imminent rise in Gary's spying stature.

The intelligence he had sent back helped Mao see the Americans' motivations in a new light and make appropriate decisions in response to international events. For years the White House had been thinking about how to establish some relationship with Beijing, because the United States regarded the Soviet Union as the archenemy, more dangerous and destructive than China. The gulf between the two Communist countries was no longer news, but how could America exploit their animosity to reshape the world's political structure to its own advantage? No one at the White House could give a definite answer. All they knew was that they should engage China, with whom they might even cultivate some trade in the course of time, considering its huge population and vast market. At the moment this policy of engagement was the rule they would follow.

Who could have imagined that the rotation of the globe of international politics suddenly accelerated by the spinning of a tiny Ping-Pong ball? In early April 1971, the U.S. national team went to Nagoya, Japan, to compete in the thirty-first World Table Tennis Championships. By chance, an American athlete, Glenn Cowan, boarded a bus transporting the Chinese team to a stadium. When he saw his mistake, the door had already closed. He had no choice but to take the ride, standing behind the driver and displaying "USA" on the back of his dark blue sweater to the Chinese athletes. During the ride nobody said a word to the young American, but as the bus was approaching the destination, Zhuang Zedong, the three-time world champion then, was bold enough to say a few welcoming words to Cowan and even presented an embroidered kerchief to him. Though overjoyed, the American man had nothing on him with which he could reciprocate. But he waylaid Zhuang the following day and gave him a T-shirt with a U.S. team button attached to it. Their meeting was photographed by many reporters, and pictures of the American and Chinese athletes exchanging presents appeared in some newspapers that very evening. The incident became international news.

Toward the end of the tournament, the Chinese, having won three gold medals, invited a few Ping-Pong teams, including the Mexicans and the Canadians, to visit China. The Americans, an underdog team in the sport, approached the Chinese to see if it might be possible to get invited as well, since their southern and northern neighbors both were heading to China. Immediately the Chinese reported the request to their Ministry of Foreign Affairs, which suggested turning the Americans down. Then the matter was forwarded to Premier Zhou Enlai, who also believed there was no justification for a hostile country's Ping-Pong team to come for a visit. But when the Americans' request was reported to Mao, the chairman was amazed and cried out his admiration for the leading Chinese athlete. "My uncle Zhuang, what a diplomat! Smarter than the professionals." Mao gave instructions to invite the U.S. team without delay. But his aide, who was also his head nurse, wouldn't pass on the order because there was a rule that after Mao took a sleeping pill, his words would not count. Seeing the woman still sitting there, the chairman demanded, "Why won't you send out my order?" She answered, "You just took a sleeping pill and I can't break the rule." Mao burst out, "To hell with the rule! Go call the Foreign Ministry and tell them we invite the U.S. team right away. Go, go, I hope it's not too late."

Thus began the well-known Ping-Pong diplomacy, which

paved the way for the official exchange between China and the United States. A perceptive politician, Mao seized an insignificant occurrence, the casual meeting of two athletes, and turned it into an opportunity to effect a historic breakthrough in international politics. By inviting the American athletes, he meant to signify to the White House that China was ready to open itself to the United States. Three months after the U.S. Ping-Pong team's successful visit, National Security Adviser Henry Kissinger went to China secretly via Pakistan and mapped out the plan for President Nixon's official trip to Beijing in February 1972, which led to normalizing the two countries' relationship in 1979.

However, in the beginning, the Chinese leaders couldn't help but question the wisdom of receiving the U.S. president in Beijing. They were uncertain about Nixon's sincerity. The Americans were notorious for their deceptions and unscrupulousness, especially when their national interests were at stake. What if they went back on their word? What if Nixon got cold feet and at the last moment wouldn't come? That would be an international embarrassment. Even if he came, what if he refused to sign a joint communiqué? What if he demanded more than was reasonable? The whole thing could turn out to be a trick to humiliate China in the eyes of the world.

Those kinds of misgivings fed the intense debate in the Politburo. Even Mao couldn't make up his mind in spite of his eagerness to use the United States to offset the Soviet threat. Therefore, directly from the top came an order for Gary Shang: try your utmost to verify the U.S. intention in making overtures to China.

This proved easy for Gary. He'd been observing the Ping-Pong diplomacy intently, and the information flowing through his hands had convinced him that the United States was serious. He wrote a comprehensive report that argued for pushing forward to restore a normal relationship with the United States. He took photos of some key documents as evidence for his views. He delivered the intelligence through Father Murray, because he couldn't go to

Hong Kong in 1971. His wife, suffering from gallstones, had been housebound for months. Although urged by her doctor and her husband to have an operation, Nellie was terrified of the scalpel, and as a result, she had to bear more pain. If Gary had taken a vacation in the Far East under such circumstances, he might have aroused the suspicion of the CIA or the FBI.

Far away from his homeland, he was ecstatic to see the rapid progress in the two countries' relationship. Apparently the Chinese leaders had made full use of his intelligence, which had reinforced their resolve to receive the Americans with open arms.

IN THE SUMMER OF 1972, five months after Nixon's visit to Beijing, Nellie had recovered from an operation (she finally agreed to it because her pain had grown unbearable) and resumed working at Peggy's Kitchen, and Gary went to Bangkok again. From there he flew to Hong Kong a week later. This time, besides Bingwen, Hao Ding, who was the new minister of national security and in charge of China's intelligence work, received him. Gary knew of Ding, a squat man with a high forehead and fat ears, whose father had been a legendary figure in the Communists' intelligence community, a founder of the system. A sumptuous banquet of Mandarin cuisine was held at Phoenix Garden on a backstreet in Causeway Bay in honor of Gary, who had earned praise from the top national leaders. Five strange men, all from the mainland, were also present. One of them had no eyebrows, was as bald as a honeydew, and was chugging down cola instead of tea. Two of them seemed to be high-ranking officials, similar to Ding. Probably they had all taken this junket to Hong Kong on the pretext of honoring Gary. It was at this dinner that Gary heard about Mao's remark about him being "worth four armored divisions."

After two cups of Maotai, Ding gave a brief speech. He spoke solemnly in a subdued voice, saying that Gary's invaluable intelligence had enabled China to handle international politics and diplomacy with prescience and assuredness, so the country had awarded Gary a special merit citation. On behalf of the Politburo, Ding apprised Gary of a great promotion—now his rank was the eighth and he was appointed a vice minister of national security. In addition, twenty thousand dollars had just been deposited into his bank account. Ding ended by saying to Gary, "Now you and I are equal in rank. Congratulations, my comrade!"

Bingwen, overwhelmed by the announcement as if Gary's honors were his own, said with his mouth slightly awry, "Brother, you're a big man now. I'm so happy for you!"

Gary was stunned by the promotion and touched by his friend's words. He told them, "Whatever I did was out of my deep love for our motherland. A spy's life can be miserable and lonely"— his voice caught—"but when I think that hundreds of millions of people might benefit from my service and that our country might be safer because of the intelligence I have gathered, I feel that my personal pain and privation are no longer worth fretting about. Please let our national leaders know I am grateful and will serve our country more diligently." He had to stop, his throat constricting while tears filled his eyes.

All the men nodded approval. Ding, chain-smoking cigarettes out of an ivory holder, told Gary that they would love to see him retire safe and sound back in China someday so he could spend his remaining years happily with his family. That also meant their country would take care of him for life. The banquet continued for two more hours, until Ding got tipsy and began making smutty remarks about Hong Kong women.

On the double-decker tram back to Central, Bingwen was still excited and exuberant. He said to Gary, "You know, in terms of rank, you're a major general now. I'm so glad you made it."

Lounging on the hardwood seat the two were sharing, Gary replied, "Well, I was surprised when Hao Ding told me about the promotion. But come to think of it, it really doesn't mean much to me—it might not affect my life one bit there. I'm just a translator at the CIA, like a lowly clerk."

"But you are our hero!" Bingwen persisted. "Your feats will go down in our Party's intelligence history. You're a dagger plunged in the enemy's heart."

Gary twitched as his insides tightened. Through the window, a cinema flitted by, flaunting a garish ad for the Bruce Lee movie *Fist of Fury.* In the north a lone light kept flashing on the murky water as if it were signaling a message. Gary was a heartbeat from saying he'd trade any heroic name for a normal life, but he closed his eyes as if he were about to drift off to sleep. He stifled the urge to cry.

A moment later he managed to say, "Please make sure Yufeng and our kids will receive all the privileges that a vice minister's family is entitled to."

"Of course we'll do that," Bingwen said.

TWO MONTHS LATER, in a conference room at CIA headquarters, more than two hundred of Gary's colleagues were seated. George Thomas, now the chief of the East Asia Division, was presiding over the meeting, at which three employees were to receive a medal for distinguished service. He talked about the uniqueness of this year's awards, every one of them approved by Director Helms personally. Over the past decade Thomas's demeanor had grown somewhat senatorial, especially after he'd earned his PhD, and his tongue was more limber now—he could speak to an audience about any topic at length. One of the honorees was a woman of Cuban descent, an expert on Indochina; another was a Japan hand, a hulking man in his early sixties who had served as a captain in the U.S. Navy, had a Japanese wife, and would on a fine day canoe across the Potomac to work at the CIA; and the third was Gary Shang, recognized for his invaluable analyses and acumen, which had helped the United States find ways to engage China. Gary wore a blue double-breasted blazer, a red paisley tie, and tassel loafers, smiling while listening to Thomas praise the recipients for their work and dedication.

The moment Thomas read out the citation for the Indochina expert, the woman went over to accept her medal, contained in a small maroon box. She was somewhat rotund but wore wedges, teetering a little as she walked. Yet like a soldier, she turned to face her colleagues, clicked her heels together, and raised her hand to her temple in a salute. That evoked laughter from the room. Next went the Japan hand, wearing a brown corduroy jacket with leather elbow patches. His stooped back gave him a hump and also the nickname Dromedary, which nobody dared to use in front of him. He took the medal from their chief, wheeled around to the audience, kissed the box, and called out, "Thank you. Love you all!"

Thomas got emotional and long-winded when it was Gary's turn. After reading out the citation, the chief added a personal note, saying, "Gary Shang is a longtime colleague of ours and doesn't need an introduction. You all know he's one of the most accomplished translators and an expert in our profession. I'm proud of having known him for twenty-three years—that is to say, since he was a young man. In fact, I recruited him in Shanghai in 1949, after I interviewed dozens of people. He was the only one we took on. Gosh, how handsome and youthful the chap was. Every one of us at the cultural agency was impressed because Gary stood out in many ways. Smart, quick, prudent, and knowledgeable. Since then he and I have been working together, first in south China, next in Okinawa, then in the DC area. I'm not good at judging people, but one of the best things I did in my professional life was to hire Gary. He's a model of devotion, diligence, and loyalty. I count him not only as an outstanding colleague but also as a dear friend. Now, welcome Gary Shang."

Gary walked to the front with a slight spring in his step, his legs shaking a little, which was unusual for a man of his experience. It was George Thomas's heartfelt words that had unnerved him, but he forced a smile and hugged Thomas. They held each other tightly for a few seconds while applause broke out. Gary was moved, his eyes wet. He turned to speak to the audience. "I'm greatly honored by this award and touched by what George just said. Twenty-three years is a long time in a person's life, and for me, it has also been a transformative period, during which I first became a refugee, then an immigrant, and then a U.S. citizen. This country took me in and gave me a family and a home. I pride myself on serving this nation and on doing my part to make it a safer, better place for ourselves and for our children. I hope I will be able to work for another twenty-three years, so I take this award as an encouragement and reassurance. Thank you, George. Thank you all." He veered and hurried off the platform, his legs shaking violently now, and the faces before him were swimming. Somehow he was touched by his own little speech, which had come from deep within and caught him by surprise. His head was reeling with emotion. Indeed, after living in America for seventeen years, he'd begun to view it as his second country.

A reception followed on the seventh floor. Though this was just a work event, there were cocktails and wine at a bar, and also cheese and hors d'oeuvres carried around by six waitresses. People were trading pleasantries and making small talk, the whole lounge buzzing and humming. Gary reminded himself not to drink too much, because he'd have to pick up his daughter at the train station that evening. The girl was coming home from her prep school to have a molar pulled. Gary held a flute of champagne but only sipped it. Now and then he picked up a meatball or a giant olive stuffed with sun-dried tomato from the salvers floating around. He chatted at length with David Shuman about the Red model drama currently in vogue in China. David particularly liked the play called *Taking the Tiger Mountain by Strategies,* not for the lyrics or the subject matter but for the music and the scenery. He had watched the films of many contemporary Chinese plays and was becoming an expert on the revolutionary drama, even able to sing snatches of Beijing opera. He often chanted in Gary's presence: "Before going to the torture chamber / Let me drink a bowl of wine poured by you, my mother / To make me bold and unbreakable." Or: "Ah, this little rascal / Who has no manners whatsoever." It was too bad that David couldn't visit China (his name had appeared on Beijing's blacklist). Swirling his wine, he again brought up the topic of the Chinese government's recent objection to him as a member of an unofficial cultural delegation. Gary consoled him, saying, "Who knows, you might become a big diplomat someday. Life is unpredictable. Just follow your own interests and hang in there. I'm sure good opportunities will present themselves."

"Thanks," David said. "Besides, I enjoy what I've been doing and I'm paid to specialize in Chinese affairs. You can't beat that."

By now Gary's life was peaceful and materially comfortable. The previous fall his daughter had gone to prep school, and she was doing well there and should have no difficulty getting into a good college. Whenever he went to Boston on business, he'd rent a car and drive forty miles to Groton so he could spend a bit of time with Lilian. He loved her and would spare no cost for her education. If someday he returned to China, he hoped she would often visit him there. She was his deepest attachment to this land.

Before Christmas in 1972, Gary was informed by the CIA that he'd been given a thirteen-hundred-dollar raise. In the previous years his salary had been increased by three or four hundred dollars annually, just enough to keep up with inflation. This time the big raise delighted both him and Nellie. When she asked him why they were so generous to him, he merely said, "I worked hard and deserve it."

She smiled, rolling her eyes while stroking his hairless wrist. "You're such an arrogant man," she told him.

◈◈◈

Istill often heard from my niece Juli after her reunion with her parents in Fushan. She had just opened an electronics shop selling DVDs, video games, cell phones. She had attempted to order some iPads, but at the moment they were in short supply because too many young people were crazy about this new Apple product. There were some pirated iPads available, but they were almost as expensive as the genuine thing. Juli sent me a photo of her store, which was a few doors down the street from her mother's seamstress shop. Her parents were happy to have her home and tried every way to make her stay. The family had just bought a car, a red low-end Chery, which looked like a mini-compact sedan and cost over fifty thousand yuan, about eight thousand dollars. (I wondered if that was how she had spent the settlement money from Wuping.) Juli was the only one in the family who could drive, so she made deliveries for her mother's shop as well. She seemed to have calmed down and confided to me that she'd been giving two middle schoolers music lessons and was going to form a small band so they could perform in the evenings. She would just play the guitar because there were others who had better voices. "If the locals only could have more opportunities," Juli wrote. "Some of them are more talented than those people in my band in Guangzhou."

I was glad to see that she hadn't lost her passion for music. On behalf of her parents, Juli invited me to visit them the next summer. "Maybe my brother will come home too," she said. "We will have a big reunion." The family was pleased to know Ben was in America, near me. Without a second thought I accepted their invitation and was amazed by my prompt response, since in general I wasn't fond of travel. But I felt close to these relatives in China, even closer than to Aunt Marsha's family. Perhaps my presence would help improve the family's standing in the county town, because they could be known to have overseas relations, who are often viewed as opportunities. Unlike decades ago, nowadays officials try to cultivate foreign connections. Many of the rich send their children abroad for college, and people with enough means plan to emigrate because they feel insecure with their newfound wealth. In Beijing and Shanghai and Guangzhou it's fashionable to greet rich friends by saying, "Done with the emigration paperwork yet?"

I'd been working on a syllabus for a new course in the fall and had also been reading the books I would assign my class. I enjoyed the summer's peace and quiet, which was nourishing both mentally and physically, so I spent most of the daytime in my study while Henry was busy with the maintenance work. In late August he bought another five Intel chips for Ben. These were smaller than the previous batch but more expensive, costing nearly four thousand dollars total. The prospect of a bigger profit had Henry floating on air. He often whistled a tune while vacuuming the corridors of our building or wiping the windows in the lobby with a squeegee or hauling the wheeled trash cans between the backyard and the front street. But I was ill at ease about his little sideline, knowing Ben's business was shady. I wondered if I should talk Henry out of it but decided not to. In his whole life seldom had he been able to make money so easily, and I wouldn't spoil his mood. Let him be happy if he enjoyed helping Ben.

ON SUNDAY AFTERNOON BEFORE LABOR DAY, Ben called and asked if I'd heard from Sonya. "No," I said. "What happened to her?"

"She's gone. I looked for her everywhere and can't figure out where she might be. I emailed her, but she won't respond."

"Did you two have a fight?"

"Sort of."

"Is there a third party involved?"

"No, what made you say that?"

"Sonya said you gabbed too much with some women on your Weibo."

"That's because I'm supposed to set up a website. I have to find the people who can help me."

"Help you with what?"

"The website."

"What kind of website is that?"

"Mainly on weaponry and space technology. My company wants me to edit a magazine as well, using the information available online."

"So you and Sonya fell out over something else?"

"She's too headstrong. I asked her to give me a couple of weeks so I could make up my mind."

"About what?"

"Her pregnancy, what else?"

"Didn't I tell you to leave it to her?"

"I can't. A baby means a lifetime commitment. I can't let her bring a child into the world without the love and care of both parents. My mother and uncle had a terrible childhood growing up without a father, so I don't want that to happen to my children."

His words startled me as I realized that my assumptions about his hesitation had been simplistic. "Then what do you plan to do?" I asked.

"I must find her. I'm worried sick. You know I love her."

"If you do, propose to her. That might solve the trouble."

"It's not that simple. My life is still insecure. I must fix a few things before I can propose to her."

I didn't press him for more details and promised to look for Sonya as well. After I hung up, I wrote her an email and asked her to contact me without delay. I said Ben was worried, calling around looking for her. "Please don't run away like this," I pleaded. "If you want to keep the baby, you're obligated to give it a loving father. You mustn't leave Ben out of this, because the child has already bound you two together."

Late that night Sonya called and said she was staying with a cousin in Toronto. Her parents had asked her to return to Ukraine, but she would not and had to figure out where to live if Ben jilted her.

"For Christ's sake, he won't do that," I said.

"You never know, Lilian. He can be very cold, cold like an animal. I simply don't know what to make of him. Maybe he had a traumatized childhood."

"He just told me that to have a child means a lifetime commitment. If he were heartless, he wouldn't have said that, would he? If he had no feelings for you, he wouldn't be worried sick looking for you. Sonya, try to use your head. To my mind, he does love you. It looks to me as if, if he lets you have the child, he might propose to you. That's what makes him hesitate."

"You sure that's what he's thinking?"

"Pretty sure. If he wanted to wash his hands of you, he could use this opportunity to fire you. For whatever doubts you might have about him, he's a decent man at heart. I'm positive about that."

My words seemed to be soaking in, though she didn't say what she was going to do. I thought of calling Ben but decided not to. Probably Sonya would contact him soon, so I'd better let them sort things out by themselves.

As I'd expected, Ben called me the next evening, saying Sonya was with a relative of hers, a thirty-something studying sculpture in Canada. Ben had to attend to an urgent business matter and couldn't go to Toronto, but Sonya had promised to return within a few days and not to do anything drastic. I was glad to hear that but was still somewhat mystified by Ben, so I asked him why it was so hard for him to propose to Sonya. He paused, tiny bursts of static crackling. Then he said, "Because I must first figure out what happened to my grandfather. Only after that can I decide whether to settle down in America."

Surprised, I asked, "Why do you have to know more about him? Those articles I sent you give a pretty accurate picture of his life and activities here."

"There might be more than that. I must understand him thoroughly." Ben gave a nervous giggle. "Like Comrade Vladimir Lenin said, 'To forget the past amounts to betrayal.' I'm not a forgetful man."

I wondered why he didn't ask me for more articles on his grandfather or for Gary's diary. I offered, "I can FedEx you the book on my father, *The Chinese Spook*. It gives a good amount of information, but don't buy everything it says."

"That would be great. Please send it along. I'll read it carefully and make my own judgment."

I emailed Sonya, saying she should give Ben some time so he could decide whether to live in the States permanently. I added, "Keep in mind that he is working for a Chinese company and might be called back anytime."

She returned: "What's the big deal? I will be happy to live with him in China if he has to go back."

Seeing those words, I smiled and my eyes misted over. I hadn't thought she loved him so much that she was willing to settle down with him even in China, where life could be hard for Westerners.

1974–1975

I'm your whore, your shameless whore!" Suzie told Gary. "Heaven knows how I wish I could break up with you."

They were seated in her living room, the floor fan whirling while the chirring of cicadas surged fitfully in the sycamore outside the window screen. In recent months she had often lost her temper, but Gary was already accustomed to her outbursts. Today he clammed up, his body tense and his face averted as if ready to take a slap. Instead of leaving, he stayed on, waiting for her gust of anger to subside, because he had something on his mind and had to talk to her rationally.

Lately he'd been mulling over the idea of divulging his whole story to her in the hope that she might understand his predicament and help him find out about his family back in China. The past few years, every time he'd met with Bingwen in Hong Kong, the man would tell him that his family was well, that his children both had good jobs in a tractor factory. But Bingwen could never produce a current photo of them, always giving the excuse that he'd forgotten to ask Yufeng for it. As a result, Gary couldn't help but have misgivings about his family's actual condition. Yet he couldn't write to Yufeng directly—his letter would be intercepted for certain, nor could he bluntly demand photographic evidence from Bingwen, with whom he had to stay on cordial terms. He had tried hard to look for ways to get in touch with Yufeng, but to no avail. After weighing this matter for months, he had concluded that the only feasible option was to ask Suzie to help.

Today while she was sprawled on her sofa and seething with a folded hand towel over her face because of a headache, he went into her kitchen and brewed a pot of oolong tea. After pouring her a cup, he said, "Suzie, I'm going to tell you something extremely important, a matter of life and death."

"All right, go ahead."

"But first you must promise you'll never let it slip to anyone."

She sat up, astonished by the graveness of his voice. Her eyes flashed, then fixed on him. "Fine, I will always keep my mouth shut," she said. "I know you're full of secrets."

So he began telling her about his true identity and the history of his spying career, from his mission in Shanghai in 1949 to his current position in China's Ministry of National Security. He spoke without stopping, as if afraid she might interrupt him. In one hour he poured out everything. When he was done, he felt at once unburdened. He might be at her mercy from now on, because there was a remote possibility that she would use his secret to control him or make excessive demands. But to his amazement, she didn't seem shocked and just looked thoughtful, her face clouded with a frown. Perhaps through the years she had suspected something.

He then told her about his original family, about his wife and children in the countryside of Shandong, and about Bingwen's assurance every time they met in Hong Kong. He said he couldn't completely trust his handler and thought that their superiors might have instructed the man to tell him that his "backyard" was fully covered, so he would concentrate on his mission abroad. In recent years Gary had felt that Bingwen avoided mentioning his family and might have withheld information. If only he could contact Yufeng directly and find out the truth!

When he had finished speaking, Suzie asked, "Can I see what your twins look like? Do you have their photos?"

"I don't have one now. I had one, but it would have been too dangerous to keep it around, so I left it in Hong Kong. They're good kids and I miss them, although I've never seen them in the flesh or heard their voices. They know nothing about their daddy, I assume."

At that, Suzie broke into sobs, her narrow shoulders convulsing while her face contorted. "Why did I meet you in the first place?" she groaned. "I must have owed you something in my previous life, or how could I let you torment me like this? What good will come of this wretched affair? I wish I could start my life over without you or could pluck you out of my heart!"

He kept silent, somewhat soothed by her ravings. She wasn't thinking of abandoning him. He needed her. In this place she was the only friend he could rely on, and the revelation of his true identity, as he'd planned, would be a step toward another phase of their relationship. He reminded himself that from now on he'd have to accept whatever she might say or do to him. Let her blow off steam if she wanted to. She would become herself again. He trusted she loved him enough that she'd do her best to help him get in touch with his original family.

To Gary's relief, thereafter Suzie stopped lashing out at him. Neither did she drop hints or suggestions again, as though she had finally accepted him for who he was, with the heavy baggage he carried. They continued to see each other once a week, and their affair grew more stable—every Thursday afternoon he would arrive at her apartment and would leave around midnight. She would inquire after Nellie and Lilian, as though she had also accepted them as part of her life. Before Christmas, Suzie bought the girl a pair of patent-leather boots, knee high and each with three brass buttons on the top of the side, which Lilian loved but dared not wear at home.

When Suzie went back to Taiwan for the Spring Festival in February 1975, Gary asked her to go to mainland China via Hong Kong and to see if she could find his family there. He told her that she wouldn't have to speak at length with Yufeng or let her know who she was. Just take a look at their house and shoot a few photos of his family if possible, so that he could assess what their life was really like. Suzie promised to try her very best to look for them. But when she attempted to enter China from Hong Kong on the pretext that she wanted to see her bedridden uncle, she was stopped. Her name appeared on some kind of blacklist, probably because of her work at Voice of America. They rejected her application for a visa and told her that as a U.S. citizen she couldn't enter China, because the two countries hadn't formed a normal relationship yet and she'd have to get her papers from the States directly. No matter how she begged them, they wouldn't let her pass.

Suzie came back to DC in early March, harried and tired. She described to Gary the difficulties she had encountered in Hong Kong, saying, "I even told them that my uncle is hospitalized and I wanted to see him before he died, but they wouldn't relent, every one of them remained stone-faced. I felt as if I was bumping into an iron wall, and even if I had smashed my head into it, none of them would've given a damn. They were all like automatons. The next day I went to Bingwen Chu and asked him to help. He went berserk and blamed me for not notifying him beforehand. He said he couldn't do anything either, because I was a U.S. citizen and was not allowed to enter China unless I'd already got a visa. He urged me not to try again."

Gary became unsettled. "Did you tell him that you know about my family in Shandong?"

"Of course not. I only asked him to help me get through customs. I told him we were friends."

"He might've guessed your intention."

"Probably. I shouldn't have gone to him."

Gary regretted having given her Bingwen's contact information (to use in case of emergency). That was clearly a mistake. He feared that their superiors might learn of Suzie's attempt. Indeed, the following week he received a letter from his handler, who expressed his worries and insinuated that their higher-ups had been furious about Suzie's effort to sneak into China. They believed Gary must have gone out of his mind; otherwise he wouldn't have committed such a blunder, which might compromise his position at the CIA. They threatened to take disciplinary action against him if he continued to behave unprofessionally. That might imply they'd bust him down to colonel. "Please don't let your friend run such a risk again!" Bingwen pleaded. "It would be too dangerous for everyone."

The last sentence sent a shiver down Gary's spine as he realized that Suzie might have run into danger if she had stayed longer in Hong Kong. To protect his identity, the Chinese might have had her eliminated. He wouldn't let her get involved in this matter again, nor would he allow her to reenter Hong Kong. More than that, he gave up attempting to contact his original family.

THUS GARY'S LIFE RESUMED its old pattern. He was a man accustomed to loneliness and to the torment of qualms and could always keep a cool head. Had he let his guilt overcome him, he wouldn't have been able to function in his daily life. He had to convince himself that China was looking after his family's livelihood—everything was fine back home, and all he should do was focus on the mission here. As time went by, he again managed to put Yufeng and their children into a vault deep within him.

In his American home, life had grown peaceful. Rarely would he and Nellie raise their voices. His wife, though still embittered, stopped griping despite knowing that Gary saw Suzie regularly. Nellie even appreciated that he came home every night, given that their daughter was far away in Massachusetts. Indeed, over the years Gary had developed a greater attachment to Nellie. When she had been ill with gallstones three years before, he'd been so worried that he often skipped meals and lost sixteen pounds. Nowadays he often watched TV with her just as a way of keeping her company. For better or worse, this American woman had given him a child and a home, where she was the only person he could speak to if he had to say something. Deep inside, he was grateful, though he had never expressed this feeling to her.

Nellie wasn't troubled by his remoteness anymore, revolving in her own little sphere of life. She enjoyed working at the bakery and by now had become an expert in cookies and cakes. She'd get up early in the morning to be at work before five to start baking. When the store opened at seven, she'd take a breather and return home to make breakfast for Gary—she would cook poached eggs, or French toast with an omelet, or pancakes, or even a frittata. The two of them would eat together. During the day she kept flexible hours and spent a lot of time alone in the bakery's kitchen preparing the next batch of offerings. She would measure flour, sugar, and milk, knead bread, roll out piecrusts, blend in butter or grated cheese or sour cream if needed, and add chocolate chips or raisins or nuts to cookie dough. The bakery was less than half a mile from her home, so she felt comfortable about the work schedule and the walk back and forth, which she took as exercise. If she was pressed for time or the weather was foul, she'd drive. She had her own car, a burgundy Chevrolet coupe.

A Dunkin' Donuts had opened recently on a nearby street and attracted droves of customers, most of whom went to work early in the morning. Both Nellie and Peggy noticed the thriving shop and wondered what made it so popular. Sometimes cars would form a line stretching from the parking lot onto the street. Nellie went there one afternoon and bought a muffin and a bagel, which didn't taste at all better than those sold by their own bakery. Peggy and Nellie were both confident that they offered better baked goods. Then, what made that shop so successful?

Peggy wasn't terribly bothered, saying the donut shop was similar to McDonald's or Burger King, which couldn't compete with real restaurants and drew in only junk-food lovers. But Nellie wanted to figure out what made the coffee shop thrive. She mentioned this to Gary at breakfast one day. He said, "David Shuman stops by Dunkin' Donuts every morning too. He told me he was hooked."

"Is the shop on his way to work?" Nellie asked.

"That's part of it. David also said Dunkin' Donuts has the best coffee."

"Really? Then it must be the coffee that makes it tick."

"Maybe. Why not go try it and see if it's true?"

She looked at her big wristwatch. "My, I've got to run. Peggy's face will drop a mile if I'm too late."

On her way Nellie stopped by the Dunkin' Donuts and bought a cup of coffee, the original blend, which was indeed strong and fragrant. She let Peggy taste it too.

After a swallow, the old woman said, "Oh my, this could keep a grizzly awake for a whole day."

"We should offer better coffee too," Nellie suggested.

"We don't need to follow Dunkin' Donuts."

"But it could bring in more customers."

"We're a bakery, not a coffee shop. Don't be troubled by this. We can sell more bread instead of donuts and muffins. We don't need lots of bagel eaters for customers anyway."

"Peggy, you're a bad businesswoman," Nellie said with a straight face, which had been getting pretty in a gaunt way as she grew older, even her eyes more vivid than a decade before. "We can't let them take away our customers. I won't just sit tight doing nothing. Why not offer an extra few kinds of coffee and make them all strong? Just see what will happen."

Peggy shook her head. "A coffee bar will cost a pretty penny."

"But we must do our best to keep our business."

"All right, I'll grab some coffeemakers and put them there." Peggy pointed at the corner in the small dining area.

So the "coffee bar" was set up the following week, offering French vanilla, Colombian, hazelnut, and house blend, all twice as strong as before. To go with the coffees were whole milk, half-and-half, cinnamon powder, sugar, its substitutes, and bits of bread and pastry for sampling. The corner indeed looked like a tiny bar.

Morning after morning Peggy and Nellie could see that more people were now dropping by on their way to work.

Soon Peggy hired another full-timer, and the bakery continued thriving.

By the summer of 1975, Gary had grown tired of sourdough and developed a taste for Irish soda bread, so Nellie would bring one home every evening. He had quit relishing raw garlic long ago and was no longer a lusty meat eater; rarely would he have sausage. Like a senior general who needn't go to the front line anymore, he would no longer travel to Hong Kong in person (in part because he dreaded jet lag).

When on vacation, he would stay home, reading and writing. Lately he'd been translating Kurt Vonnegut's *Slaughterhouse-Five*. He knew this might infringe the copyright, but at the time no written works were covered by any rights in China, where foreign books were just translated and brought out without notifying the authors and the original publishers, so it might be possible for Gary to get his translation of the small novel published when he was back in his homeland. Ideally it would be a bilingual edition, with the original words and the Chinese characters printed on facing pages so that English majors could use it as a textbook for learning current American idioms. (Gary didn't feel comfortable with Briticisms, which sounded mannered to him but were still taught throughout China.) He kept reminding himself that the translation was just a pastime, and proceeded at his leisure, three or four paragraphs a day.

He wouldn't dig for intelligence anymore and preferred to just pick up whatever came through his hands. Of that there was plenty, because all the CIA's reports on China would be checked by him for accuracy and stylistic consistency before they were dispatched to the White House. At long last he could afford to take it easy, like an old angler who didn't care how many fish he caught and only settled in a beach chair, holding a rod while drifting in and out of sleep.

Nevertheless, every once in a while important information would come his way and he'd photograph the pages and provide his analyses. By now Gary's views and assessments were highly valued in Beijing—he had become China's ear to the heartbeat of the United States. He knew he was indispensable to the Chinese leaders thanks to the position he occupied. Whenever he had something to deliver, he'd drive to Father Murray's church in downtown Baltimore. Even in the absence of urgent business, he'd go out with the priest for lunch or dinner once a month. Neither of them bothered about the rule that prohibited such a no-delivery meeting. Having gone through so many years' fear and danger together, the two had become friends. Murray wouldn't eat red meat but loved seafood and cheese. He often told Gary stories of his childhood in the Philippines. He was estranged from his father, a burly white man, captain of a British ocean liner, who'd taken Kevin's mother as a "local wife" and had his legal family back in Manchester. The man provided for his Chinese-Filipina mistress, though; he also sent their son and daughter to an English school and then to an American college in Manila. "I hate my father," Kevin said, munching on a soft-shell crab sandwich. "He's a selfish asshole."

Gary chuckled. He listened to Murray attentively but didn't say anything about his own past, afraid that once he started, he might not be able to hold back the flood of emotions and memories.

✧✧✧

Ben came to College Park on the pretext of picking up the micro-chips that had just arrived. Again he paid Henry a one hundred percent profit, $3,920, which thrilled my husband. But Ben didn't look well; his eyes were slightly puffy and his face drawn, as though he were sleep-deprived. He told me that he had finished the book on his grandfather and then read more about Gary to figure out what actually happened to him. He came to see me because he'd been stonewalled in his investigation. He'd gone to the Boston Public Library and got hold of the microfilms of *The New York Times* and *The Washington Post* from the fall of 1980, and he had read all the articles on Gary's arrest and his espionage activities. But the deeper Ben delved into the case, the more misgivings he had about his grandfather, who was very different from the figure Ben had pictured.

We were seated in my study, just the two of us. Ben, his eyelids a little tremulous, asked about my father, "Do you think he missed his family back home?"

"He did," I said.

"Did he love my grandmother?"

"Of course. He missed her a lot, especially during the first years of their separation. He was always remote from things around him, and his heart was elsewhere. In his diary he mentioned that he dreamed of your grandmother every once in a while."

"But he married your mother and kept a mistress on the side," Ben said, an edge to his voice.

"He was a complicated man. He might have been traumatized."

"By what?"

"By the separation from his original family. Imagine how much he carried within him. In the beginning it must have been so hard for him. Then gradually he grew jaded and numbed. Still, he was human and couldn't possibly have suppressed his longings and pain all the time. The more I work on his story, the more terrible his life appears to me."

Ben lifted his cup of coffee and took a large sip. He went on, "Was he a good father to you?"

"Absolutely. He was gentle and loving and patient. I must have been the only person on earth he could hold close to his heart, but I went to a prep school when I was thirteen and then to college. I didn't spend enough time with him. He once told me that someday he and I would go visit his home village together. If only we could have done that."

"He never saw his son, my uncle, who died at the age of twelve. A couple of articles say Gary was a bigwig in China's intelligence service. Was he that big?"

"According to his diary, he was a vice minister of national security, holding the rank of major general."

"I can't believe this! My uncle starved to death while his father was a high official."

"I was told he had died of encephalitis."

"That was what the local clinic said. Some people also said he'd died of a twisted gut. But my grandmother told me he had actually starved to death, his belly sticking out like a balloon. During the famine the family had to eat wild herbs, elm bark, willow leaves, corncob flour, and whatnot. My uncle wasn't strong physically, but he was hungry all the time, shrunken to the bone. Once he was ill, there was no way his body could fight the illness."

"Your grandfather didn't get the big promotion until 1972, long after the famine."

"Still, we didn't benefit one bit from his high rank. My grandmother was terrified by the rumor flying around their hometown. It said that her husband had fled to Taiwan and then to the U.S. Some people even threatened to denounce her publicly and drag her through the streets. The true reason was, they were jealous of the money she received from the government every month. In the 1950s, a hundred yuan was a tidy sum. Grandma had no choice but to cut all the ties to her husband to protect the family. After she left Shandong, she didn't report her whereabouts to the government and stopped receiving his salary on purpose. She was too scared to be connected with him publicly. So the family had to start from scratch in a mud hole of a village and constantly struggled to make ends meet. My mom did all sorts of work in her teens, even collected manure and dug up sand to sell to a construction company. She also cut grass for a pig farm, and during the winter she sold frozen tofu in the county town, having to set off before daylight. After she and Dad got married, they both toiled in the fields like beasts of burden for many years. My dad almost got killed in a granite quarry, unable to work for months after an injury to his leg. Our family always lived hand to mouth until he became a clerk in the county administration."

"Would it be possible he got that job because of some official help?" I doubted that the government was really ignorant of where Yufeng was. It seemed to me that very few people could escape its surveillance.

"I doubt it," Ben said. "Before working in that office, Dad had taught elementary school briefly. He could write well, and the county administration needed someone like him for propaganda work. For many years nobody in our family would mention my grandfather, not until the mid-nineties, when we were informed that he had died in the line of duty overseas. In other words, officially our family had a clean history. When Grandma heard about that, she wept for a whole night."

I burst out, "The government ought to have paid her all the arrears—I mean Gary's salary had been accumulating since 1961."

"They did when she filed a petition. That's how our family got the funds for starting the seamstress shop."

I didn't know what to say and lowered my eyes, which were getting hot and watery. Unlike them, I was the main beneficiary of my father's small amount of wealth, which Nellie inherited and later bequeathed to me. (They'd been co-owners of the house.) Reluctant to let on to Ben that my mother had given me the down payment for our apartment building, I remained silent.

Ben continued, "Aunt Lilian, do you think my grandfather loved China to the end of his life?"

"I believe so. Otherwise it would have been unimaginable for him to live that kind of isolated existence for so many years while he was always determined to return to his homeland."

"He sacrificed a great deal for China, in other words. I respect that, but in his trial he claimed he loved America as well."

"That must have been also true. He had lived here for so many years that he couldn't help but develop some good feelings for this place. Besides, my mother and I were Americans."

"Truth be told, that's what I fear most."

"Fear what?"

"To love both places and be torn between them."

"Is that why you can't make up your mind about marrying Sonya and settling down here?"

"In some ways. Yes."

He didn't say more about his plight. I knew he was to some extent controlled by his company in China. In the back of my mind remained the suspicion that Ben might have been collecting intelligence for the Chinese military, though I wasn't sure how professional he was. I guessed he might be a petty spy specializing in industrial and technological information. Regardless, it was a dangerous business and he might get caught sooner or later.

He stayed with us for only one day and took the Acela Express back to Boston the next morning. I had let him take all six volumes of Gary's diary with him in the hope that they might shed some light on his investigation.

I urged my husband not to purchase microchips for Ben again. "What's the big deal?" Henry asked blithely.

"The chips are banned from export to China," I said. "And some Chinese companies might be their destinations."

"That's Ben's business. Mine is just to buy them."

"But that might make you an accomplice."

"Don't be such a worrywart, Lilian. I do everything legally, and I have no further connection with the chips once Ben has them. How the hell can I be charged for buying something entirely legal on the market? The truth is anybody can get them—if not from the U.S., you can buy them from places like Taiwan and Singapore."

"This gives me the willies."

"Sweetie, just take it easy. At this rate I'll pay off my debt and get rich pretty soon."

So I left it at that, but still I was agitated.

1978–1979

Twice a year Gary would pass a batch of films to Father Murray, and for every delivery a thousand dollars would be deposited into his bank account in Hong Kong. But he wouldn't withdraw cash directly from it, afraid of being noticed by the FBI. Since 1976, when the Cultural Revolution officially ended, he'd written to Bingwen regularly, addressing him as his cousin, as before. He asked him about Yufeng and their children, and the man would assure him that everything was fine back home. Bingwen also repeated the instruction that Gary must not attempt to contact his family in China again. That was unnecessary—he'd finally been informed that Yufeng had left their home village to join her brother's village in the northeast, and Gary couldn't possibly find out her current address.

He was heartened by the Chinese leadership after Mao. In his diary he wrote about Deng Xiaoping, the new chairman: "That short man can become a Napoleonic figure and should be able to keep China on the right track. He may even outshine Mao eventually. At least he is more prudent and more practical and understands economics."

For Lilian's education at Bryn Mawr, Gary had spent most of his savings. Now he was in his mid-fifties and in poor health, suffering from bursitis in one shoulder. Recently he'd been diagnosed with early-stage diabetes, and his doctor had urged him to watch out for starch and sugar in his diet—he had to avoid eating white bread and rice. At most he could have a slice of pumpernickel at a meal, or a bowl of oatmeal for breakfast; he ought to eat more vegetables and protein instead. So Gary had to quit munching all the fine pastries Nellie brought home. In fact, he suspected it was the sweet food that had made him ill. When shopping, at the sight of fresh coffee cakes, for only ninety-nine cents apiece, he'd be overtaken by such a rush of craving that both his mouth and eyes would water, and he'd have to drag himself away. Never had he been so full of self-pity, which he knew was ridiculous and might be a sign of feeblemindedness. During the daytime he often felt dizzy and thirsty, his limbs heavy. No matter what he ate or drank, there was always a bitter taste in his mouth. He noticed the change in his fingernails, flat and wider now, each a miniature spade. Even his eyesight was deteriorating—he saw more tadpoles and pearl drops swimming around whenever he opened a book or magazine. He got a pair of glasses, but he didn't like to wear them; most times he pushed them up on his forehead.

Gary's poor health made him ruminate about the possibility of an early retirement. He had read some books on spies and knew that most of them had come to grief, unable to evacuate before getting caught. Perhaps his failing health was a signal for the necessity of a clean withdrawal. Yet he also believed that once he retired from the CIA, he might become worthless to China, so he had to take care not to jeopardize his standing in his superiors' eyes. A useless man is less valuable than a pet, he would remind himself. Indeed, how frightening it would be to become a person no one wanted.

Over the years he had gathered information on the privileges that high-ranking officials in China enjoyed, and he knew that if he lived there, as a vice minister he could have a chauffeur, a secretary, an orderly, a chef, a nurse, special medical care. True, a senior official in China didn't pull in a handsome salary, only two or three hundred dollars a month, but his life was free from material worries—everything was provided by the state. In contrast, here he'd have to live an uncertain life, the prospect of which unnerved him. On his way to work he would pass a small nursing home, in front of which stood a tall pole flying a U.S. flag; just the sight of the place would remind him of the wretched final years of life that many Americans could not escape. Nellie's mother had died in 1974, and soon afterward her father went to a local nursing home. Luckily for the old man, he had only his debt-ridden vegetable farm to lose to the state of Florida. Gary and Nellie once drove down to visit Matt at that place, and the old man wouldn't stop blaming them for not bringing him a bottle of Jack Daniel's or Wild Turkey. Matt, frail and addled, claimed that his boy often came to visit him with a six-pack of beer and barbecued wings, though Jimmy, his only son, had fallen three decades ago in the Battle of Savo Island. On their drive back to DC, Gary told Nellie that he'd kill himself before he ended up in such a place. A wheelchair might be acceptable, but he would never be fed and washed by strangers. These days he couldn't help but be preoccupied with thoughts about his old age. If China didn't call him home, he'd be stuck in the existence of a lowly CIA translator and then in that of the senile elderly, so he'd better do something before it was too late.

THE PREVIOUS WINTER Peggy had slipped on her way to the bakery and sprained her ankle. She'd had a slight limp ever since and slowed down considerably. She often used a cane when walking. Lately she'd been saying she wanted to sell her business so she could move to New Orleans to join her daughter. One day Nellie asked her, "How much will you sell it for?"

"One hundred and twenty grand," Peggy said in a nasal, scratchy voice.

"That's a humongous amount for a bakery!"

"But it's worth it. We just updated most of the facilities last fall. We have a steady clientele and have been around for more than twenty years. This place is a small cash cow, you know."

"If I buy, will you sell it cheaper?"

"Well, business is business, we shall see." Peggy smiled, which seemed to imply this could be negotiable.

"Can you wait until I figure out how to get the money?"

"Okay, I can hold on to it for a while."

Since then, the two often talked about the price. They knew

each other well enough to banter casually, so they haggled back and forth. Three weeks later Peggy agreed to sell Nellie the bakery for $105,000, her final offer.

Nellie suggested taking out a home equity loan, but Gary disagreed. He said, "If we miss a few payments, we might lose the house. No, we mustn't run such a risk. What if I die? You might become homeless."

"Oh, c'mon, don't be so pessimistic. I'm more likely to croak before you." That was what she believed, because she'd always had health problems.

"Let me figure out a way, okay? For now, tell Peggy you're going to buy her bakery. Just make sure she won't sell it to others."

Gary had about forty thousand dollars in his Hong Kong bank account but would need another sixty-five grand. For days he'd been weighing his plan to get the money from China directly and thinking about the repercussions of such a demand. He calculated that such a move might tarnish his reputation in his superiors' eyes but wouldn't ruin him, because for better or worse he had made a considerable contribution to their motherland. There wouldn't be enough reason for them to strip him of his rank when he returned to China. Above all, he felt entitled to make such a request. So he wrote to Bingwen and asked for seventy thousand dollars, saying he needed the cash immediately for some important work here. Within a month the amount was deposited into his account at Hang Seng Bank. Bingwen didn't even ask how the money would be spent when he wrote back; he just informed Gary: "The goods were delivered."

Now came the more dangerous step: to transfer the cash to his bank account in the States. Gary knew that if he moved such a large sum all at once, the FBI would notice it, but he had to act now. He was the kind of man who could remain torpid, biding his time for decades, but the moment an opportunity came up, he'd spring to life and act with reckless resolve. There'd be some risk, he understood. But to his mind, this might be the last thing he did before clearing out of America, so he wouldn't care about what might come afterward. Every three or four days he wrote a check to transfer six or seven thousand dollars from Hang Seng Bank to his Citibank account.

The cash was ready six weeks later, and he gave Nellie a cashier's check for the bakery. Surprised, his wife asked, "Where did you get so much money?"

"I borrowed it from my cousin in Taiwan. An interest-free loan."

"Why don't we sign the contract together? You've spent so much for the bakery."

"I don't want to be any part of it."

"Why, Gary? You . . . you're mad at me?" Nellie stammered, sucking in her breath.

"No, I want you to have the business, so all the paperwork should be done under your name. It's better that way."

"I don't get it."

"Don't ask so many questions. I've had it with pastries that already made me diabetic. I just don't want to have anything to do with the bakery anymore."

Nellie looked in wonder at his pallid face, then burst into laughter. In spite of his gloominess, Gary did have a dry sense of humor, which would bubble up every now and then.

So Nellie bought the business from Peggy and signed the paperwork alone. The week after the purchase, Peggy left for New Orleans. Nellie kept the two staffers while considering whether to hire another hand, but she thought better of it. She changed the bakery's name to Nellie's Kitchen. She disliked the word "Kitchen" but dared not alter the original name too much for fear of ruining the luck. The business, small as it was, had been a good moneymaker.

She had noticed some Dunkin' Donuts products in supermarkets. From then on, her bakery began offering two Dunkin' Donuts coffees: Original Blend and Dunkin' Dark, besides three previous kinds. Determined to make Nellie's Kitchen into a combination of bakery and coffee shop, she had a sign hung beside the front door that announced: "We have Dunkin' coffee!" Unsure if that might get her in trouble, she talked to Gary about it. He assured her that it would be all right if the coffees were for sale in grocery stores.

Now that Nellie's life seemed secured for the future, Gary wrote a request to his Chinese superiors, asking to be called back. He said he was ill and exhausted and very likely to retire from the CIA before long, so it was about time to end his career, which had lasted three decades. During his years abroad he had served the Party and the country heart and soul. It was his sincere wish to return and join his family so he could spend his remaining years peacefully and die on his native soil. He even attached the latest report from his doctor, which stated that his fasting blood sugar count was 172, clearly a case of diabetes.

He delivered the request to Father Murray and asked him to have it sent to their higher-ups without delay. He told the clergyman, "I'm more homesick as I'm getting older. I hope I can go back soon."

"You're lucky to have a homeland to return to," Murray said, his eyes glazed over. His whiskered face was so pale that he might pass for a white; even his nostrils were oval, and there was hair on the backs of his hands. "I don't know where my home is," he continued. "It used to be the little pastel blue bungalow surrounded by a stone wall in the alley where my mother lived. After she died, the house changed hands, and Manila doesn't mean a thing to me anymore."

"How about your older sister?" Gary asked.

"She lives in New Zealand now."

"But you belong to your church, don't you? You're a padre, different from us earthlings." Gary had always admired the ease and equanimity with which the priest carried himself. Now he recognized another suffering man, another lonely soul.

Murray said, "I wish I were a believer."

"I see." Gary tried to fathom the depth of desolation that the priest must have suffered if he didn't believe in the church he'd been serving. Gary confessed, "I'm afraid my heart won't hold out for long and I might fall to pieces here." Again the numbing pain stirred in his chest while he tried hard not to laugh. Of late when he laughed out loud, he'd often lost control and couldn't stop his tears. He knew he had reached the point where the pressure might break him anytime.

"You'll be okay," Murray said. "You've done a great service to your motherland. I'm sure they'll welcome you home as an honored son. You deserve a grand return to your country."

"Which country is yours then?"

"I don't know. I've been helping China only out of ancestral loyalty and out of my disgust at colonialism and imperialism, but I wouldn't be able to live there."

"In a way, that's not bad," Gary said. "To have no home on earth. That can make you detached and more like a religious man."

"You know, for me, home's not a fixed entity but an emotion, a longing."

"I admire that—I mean you can find home within yourself."

"I don't know if I can, but I've been trying."

Gary managed a small laugh while Murray grinned.

Following that meeting came Gary's long wait for the official reply from Beijing.

◈◈◈

Henry and I were in the hallway of our apartment building hanging a large picture that I'd brought back from Beijing. It was an oil painting that showed clusters of blooming rainbow cacti. I'd just had it framed. Two tall men, one thirtyish and the other about fifty, came in through the front door, both in dark suits and sky-blue ties. One of them asked us where the Cohens' was.

"I'm Henry Cohen," my husband said and came down the stepladder.

The two men showed their FBI badges—one was named Simpson and the other Clifton. I glanced at their armpits and could tell they were bearing sidearms in shoulder holsters. The older one asked Henry, "Can you spare a minute? We have a few questions for you, Mr. Cohen."

"Okay, fire away."

"Can we talk somewhere else?" the man went on.

"Sure, but what d'you want to know?"

"About your recent purchases of some Intel chips."

Henry put his hand on my shoulder. "Can my wife come with me?"

I said, "Hi, I'm Lilian." I didn't hold out my hand, uncertain about their intention.

"Sure thing, she can join us," the younger man told Henry in a voice that indicated that he was not a mere sidekick to his colleague.

I felt a bit relieved as I realized this might not be an interrogation. They followed us down the hall to our apartment. Once we had sat down in the living room, Officer Clifton, the older one, said to Henry, "We would like to know how you have used the microchips you bought recently."

The younger officer, Simpson, added, "Or did you sell them to somebody?" He took out a pen and put a yellow legal pad on his lap.

"Well, I bought them for a friend," Henry said.

"Is it illegal to acquire them?" I asked.

"Not really," Clifton answered. "But they're items banned from export to certain countries."

"Henry bought them for my nephew, who had a computer company outside Boston."

"What's his name?" asked Simpson.

"Ben Liang," Henry said.

Clifton opened his briefcase and took out a manila folder. "Is this man your nephew?" He handed me a photo.

The snapshot showed a younger Ben, whose sweaty face still had a shadow of baby fat and who was wearing shorts and an undershirt, holding a basketball under his arm. "Yes, that's my nephew," I replied, reflecting on the photo, probably taken before he had come to the States.

"He's a fine young man," Henry said. "We're friends."

"Has it ever occurred to you that he might ship the chips to the People's Republic of China?" Clifton continued, squinting his eyes and tilting his square chin.

"I have no clue about their destinations at all," Henry said. "Look, Ben has a computer business, so it's natural for him to buy all sorts of parts. I never thought about the legality of the acquisitions because the chips were out there for sale. I just bought them on his behalf."

"Why wouldn't he purchase them by himself?" Clifton asked.

"He said his Chinese name, Liang, often incurred racial prejudice."

"Can you elaborate on that?" Simpson said and uncrossed his long legs.

"Ben's orders would arrive too late, and from time to time they simply didn't come. That's what he told me, and I believe it's true."

"Officers," I put in, "you ought to accept the fact that racism is still prevalent in America."

"That we don't deny," Clifton said. "But what we have here is something else, more like a crime."

"What's so criminal about buying microchips?" Henry asked.

Simpson answered in a snappy voice, "That depends on where the chips went. If they were exported to China, it's a crime."

Silence followed. I was pretty sure that Ben had shipped them out of the States. Seeing Henry speechless, I managed to say, "We wish we could tell you something about their destinations, but we really don't know."

The officers seemed satisfied with our answers and stood to leave. But before reaching the door, Clifton wheeled around and said to Henry, "One more question if you don't mind. How much did Ben Liang pay you each time?"

"Two hundred percent of the amount I spent," Henry told him.

"Can you be more specific?"

"If I spent one thousand bucks on the chips, he'd pay me two thousand."

"That's a profit of one hundred percent—a hell of a deal, isn't it?"

"We're friends and family, so Ben has been generous to me."

I was pleased by Henry's answers, which, in spite of his initial nervousness, came out clear and firm. Nevertheless, the officers' visit disturbed both of us. After they left, we went on talking about Ben. Knowing of my father's role as a Chinese spy, Henry began to see the implications of the FBI's investigation. He was worried about Ben, whom he couldn't help but suspect of spying for China.

"Do you think Ben is in the same line of work as your father?" Henry asked me, his face twisted a little.

"Probably, but my dad was a vice minister, a big shot. Ben is at most a small-time agent."

"You mean he might steal technological intelligence?"

"And also military stuff."

"What else might he have a hand in? Would he smuggle weapons?"

"No way. You have to have powerful backing if you sell weapons on the international market. Only some Chinese princelings can do that. It's an extremely lucrative business."

"Anyways, you shouldn't have invited him over to begin with."

"Damn it, Henry! You wanted to make money and ignored my warning."

"All right, I got greedy, I'm to blame myself. But don't you think we should try to stop Ben?"

"We should, but how?"

"Speak to him."

"I'm afraid his phones are tapped."

"By email then."

"That might not be safe either. Perhaps I should go to Boston next week."

"No, you should go as soon as you're done teaching for this week. Let him know of the danger he's already got himself into. He must quit working for the Communist government."

I thought to explain that Ben might have a spying mission and that I might not be able to sway him, but I checked myself and agreed to go see him that very week. There had to be something I didn't know about Ben, and I'd better talk with him in person again.

1980

In 1975, Chairman Mao had once burst out at his lying and bickering staffers, "Damn it, I know more about what's going on in Nixon's Oval Office than in my own quarters." Those words were leaked and set many heads in the U.S. intelligence community spinning with questions and speculations. Did Mao really mean what he'd said? Or was he just bragging, too senile to be cognizant of Nixon's resignation? Or was the U.S. government already infiltrated by the Chinese Communists? That seemed unlikely. Still, there couldn't be smoke without fire. Even if Mao's remark had only a grain of truth, it might imply that the Chinese had compromised the communications channels of the White House. To ensure there was no mole in their midst, the CIA required all its employees who had access to classified materials to take a lie-detector test. Gary had no choice but to follow his colleagues through the procedure. Over the decades, he'd taken the test several times, and now he passed again. He was shaken nonetheless. The instant he was unwired from the machine, he'd broken into a cold sweat, fearing he might have flunked it and be dismissed.

Ever since he'd wrangled seventy thousand dollars out of China, Gary had been anxious that his superiors might change their opinion of him. They'd given him the money because they believed his career at the CIA would last many more years. Then, as soon as he got the cash, he submitted his request for an early retirement. The higher-ups must have been caught off guard by his maneuver. Now, they might even have doubts about his loyalty, and some might suspect he was corrupted by the capitalist society and the American way of life, valuing money above everything. That might account for the long silence after he had sent off his request.

Meanwhile, Gary's diabetes had taken a turn for the worse. He was thirsty all the time and had to drink water constantly. As a result, he had to empty his bladder every hour. He felt dizzy and sluggish at work, unable to concentrate. At the end of the day he feared he might conk out while driving home. Worse yet, he had grown insomniac and could sleep for only two or three hours at night, which aggravated his symptoms during the day. His doctor prescribed insulin, which helped a lot—after a few injections, his forehead wasn't numb and tight anymore, his legs stopped itching, and even his taste buds were keen again. From then on, he would carry a syringe and some ampoules with him whenever he left home. He had mentioned the possibility of an early retirement to Thomas and his other colleagues, who had all noticed the sleepy look in his eyes. There'd be no problem with the CIA, much as it valued his linguistic expertise and his insights into Asian affairs. Yet he couldn't make up his mind, because the insulin injections seemed able to control his symptoms and because there was still no word from China.

He had also talked about his plan to Suzie, who urged him to go back and join his original family. To her mind, the sooner he quit espionage the better—she just wanted him to get out of danger. She even said she might retire to Taiwan eventually, and if so, she'd go visit him from time to time, since now American citizens could travel to China without restriction. Her words made him more inclined to quit the CIA.

Finally, in late July 1980, came the reply from Beijing: an early retirement was deemed inappropriate. Gary's superiors urged him to stay at the CIA as long as he could. They said the United States had the best medical technology and facilities, and diabetes was not a fatal illness, completely manageable with insulin and a proper diet, so he should string out his mission. He was only fifty-six and should be able to continue working at the CIA for a long time. Meanwhile, they'd make arrangements for his final return. They too would love to see him retired to their homeland, but he should give them time to arrange for his successor, for whom he too should cast around—ideally he could recruit someone within the CIA. They sounded reasonable and firm. The reply made Gary regret having asked for an early retirement. To make amends, he knew he'd have to pull himself together and bear his miseries for a few more years. Perhaps he'd have to outlive his usefulness here.

Yet lately he got homesick all the more. His mind could not escape wandering to a public bathhouse in his hometown, in which, three decades ago, he had often snoozed for an hour or so with a warm towel over his naked body after a hot bath. When he woke up, he'd drunk jasmine tea served by a teenage boy and conversed with an acquaintance or two. If only he could again lie in the steaming pool and then repose on a long bed, free from any care. He knew that most of the traditional bathhouses might have disappeared, but he couldn't curb his reveries. At the same time, his vision of home had grown cloudy, and it was no longer his village or hometown but somewhere vaguely in China, virtually any place his superiors might assign him to live. Nevertheless, his longing had been growing stronger and more tempestuous day by day.

He had no idea that ever since the hefty sum of money had been transferred stateside from Hong Kong, the FBI had been following him. They launched a thorough investigation, and all the findings enabled them to connect the dots: now they realized that Mao's remark about the Oval Office was by no means a joke or brag. The ghost spy had finally revealed his shadow. All attention was now focused on Gary Shang, and he was kept under strict surveillance, his mail and phone calls monitored and his bills examined. They also installed a secret camera near his home, in a neighbor's house across the street, whose top floor they had rented. The longer they followed him, the more amazed they were by his simple, casual fashion of conducting espionage. In many ways he seemed unprofessional. For instance, few spies would go to East Asia in person year after year and write to their handlers directly in the regular mail. His disregard for the general practice of spycraft, however, singled him out as an expert mole, who had succeeded in staying below the radar and concealing his trail for three decades. They concluded that he had to be stopped without delay; the damage he'd done already was unimaginable. If they didn't act now, Gary Shang, holding a U.S. passport, might flee abroad the minute he sensed danger. He could even bolt into the Chinese embassy.

They obtained an approval from the Justice Department for "interviewing" the suspect, and without informing the CIA, which they feared might interfere with the mole hunt, they went ahead. Three agents arrived at the Shangs' one afternoon in September, and Gary answered the doorbell. His wife was in Seattle to visit her sister, who'd just had cataract surgery, and their daughter was in Boston, a first-year grad student at BU. Gary appeared calm and let in the agents, as though he'd been expecting them all along. He must have assumed they had accumulated enough evidence against him, so this was the final hour he had to face, a scenario he had played out in his mind often enough that he was almost familiar with it. It was good he was home alone. He led the three men into the dining room and sat them at the table, while he took the seat at its head. He looked meek but undaunted.

One of the men started "the interview," speaking politely, as if out of respect for a senior colleague. But before answering, Gary said, "I will tell you all the truth on one condition." It was neither a demand nor a request, as though he was certain this should be the way for them to talk.

"What's that?" asked a man who had a pink face.

"My family and my girlfriend, Suzie Chao, know nothing about what I've been doing. Leave them out of your investigation."

They looked at each other. The pink-faced man, who must have been the head, smiled, drumming his fat fingers beside a pocket tape recorder on the table. He told Gary, "We'll do that as long as you cooperate."

Their agreement further convinced Gary that they possessed enough evidence against him, because they appeared to believe the truth that his family knew nothing about his real profession, that Suzie had never been involved in his espionage activities.

So the interrogation began. It lasted seven hours with a dinner break. (After asking about Gary's preference, the agents ordered from a Chinese restaurant sesame chicken, mapo tofu, and two seafood dishes, plus a platter of assorted appetizers. Gary meant to have a hearty meal like this in spite of his diabetes, believing he wouldn't be able to eat Chinese food again for a long time.) His answers were so clear and straightforward that the agents were amazed time and again. It never occurred to him that they might not have possessed enough evidence to incriminate him, partly because one of the agents had lied, saying they'd been following him for a good many years. It was also because Gary had never been fully trained as a spy, not knowing how to take advantage of legal protection.

Around ten p.m. the interrogation was over, and the suspect held out his wrists to let the agents cuff him. They did. They took him away in a cruiser and put him in the county jail in Arlington. From there they went to Baltimore to arrest Father Murray, but the man wasn't in when they arrived. Seeing that everything was neat in his room at the parsonage—even his teapot was still warm and two-thirds full, they waited for him to return. They stayed there for a good hour until they realized Murray was gone.

GARY'S ATTORNEY ADVISED HIM to plead guilty, and Nellie urged him to do the same, so that he might get a lighter sentence, but he refused and wanted to go through the trial, convinced that he'd done a significant service to both China and the United States. He might also have hoped against hope that the trial would end in a hung jury, giving China enough time to rescue him. The jurors, seven women and five men, were selected, and Gary was intent on fighting in court, not for escaping a life sentence but for the justice he believed he deserved. Everyone could see that he was deluded, but he couldn't be dissuaded.

The trial turned out to be a disaster. He was accused of spying for the People's Republic of China, selling intelligence for cash. His betrayal had done great damage to national security and caused the deaths of numerous people. God knew how much secret information he had funneled to the Chinese and what the long-term ramifications might be. Gary denied most of the charges, emphasizing that he was a patriot of both the United States and China. "The two countries are like parents to me," he said. "They are like father and mother, so as a son I cannot separate the two and I love them both. I can't possibly hurt one of them to promote the well-being of the other. It's true that I passed information to China, but it helped improve the Sino-U.S. relationship, from which both countries have benefited. As a matter of fact, I seized every opportunity to improve the mutual understanding and cooperation between the two countries. God knows, over the decades, how much vital intelligence I gathered for the United States through gleaning Chinese-language publications and reports. Sometimes I put in more than sixty hours a week. For my hard work I have received several commendations." In short, it was he who had helped bring the two countries together to shake hands like friends. For that kind of diligence and dedication he should be recognized as a valuable citizen, if not decorated with laurels. "I am an American and love this country like every one of you," he concluded in a strident voice.

In his testimony George Thomas, his domed forehead beaded with sweat, said, "To my mind, Gary Shang did help the United States reestablish a diplomatic relationship with China. In a perverse fashion he served both countries." While saying that, he avoided looking Gary's way, his dappled hands trembling a little.

David Shuman, his face still babyish at age forty-three in spite of his thick blond mustache and beer belly, told the court that he felt Gary might be a patriot. Blinking his camel eyes, he said, "I remembered when President Kennedy was assassinated, Gary

Shang collapsed in the office blubbering like a small boy. He was more heartbroken than the rest of us, you know. You can ask anyone in the CIA about him, and I can assure you that they'll all say he was a gentleman, easygoing and friendly. Of course, reflecting on the whole thing now, it gives me the creeps to think of Gary Shang as a Communist mole among us. You know, this really freaks me out."

Nonetheless, the jurors looked unconvinced, some shaking their heads, furrowing their brows, or scowling at the CIA officers. The government's attorney, a middle-aged man with cat eyes and scanty brows, began to cross-question the accused. The man straightened up and said in a smoky voice, "Mr. Shang, did you provide the names of more than a dozen defected Chinese POWs for the Communist regime in 1953?"

"That was due to—"

"Yes or no?"

"Yes."

"How much did you get paid for that?"

"Five hundred dollars."

"So for that paltry amount of money you sold more than a dozen lives to Communist China?"

"It didn't happen like that. I didn't know the consequences of the intelligence. I assumed those men would go to Taiwan anyway. That was the first time I passed information to China. Perhaps I might be guilty of an accidental act. But I never did that kind of thing again after I came to know about those returnees' incarceration and deaths."

"So you were aware that some of them had been executed?"

"Yes, later I was informed of that."

"Mr. Shang, did you reveal to Communist China the communications plans and the code names of the secret agents dispatched to destroy China's nuclear facilities in 1965?"

"Yes, I did. I had their mission stopped on purpose, because it might have started the Third World War. That prospect terrified me. What could the United States have gained from such a war? Nothing but destruction of lives and property and a waste of tax-payers' dollars. So I would do my damnedest to prevent that mission from being carried out. For that I don't feel one iota of guilt."

Some in the audience chuckled and a few cheered. The judge, his face turning puce and his goatee tilting up a little, banged the gavel for order. When the room was quiet again, the flat-cheeked cross-examiner went on to ask about the information on missiles and aircraft that the accused was charged with stealing. To the question of the technological secrets, Gary answered in a haughty tone, "I was interested only in strategic intelligence. I am not a petty thief—that sort of information is beneath me."

A pregnant silence filled the courtroom. It was drizzling outside, rivulets running intermittently down the windows, beyond which the pointed tips of cypresses swayed a little. The sky was so saturated it looked as though it was about to collapse in a downpour.

Without difficulty the jury reached their guilty verdict unanimously, and the judge gave Gary 121 years in prison and more than three million dollars in fines. The jurors also stated that they took umbrage at the attitudes of some CIA officers, who seemed to have stuck up for the Red spy, the monster of deception, but not for the truth or for the interests of our nation. One of them, a fortyish black woman with arched eyebrows, even voiced her suspicion of complicity.

The convicted man was stolid, his face expressionless, though his tired eyes appeared narrower and his temples were throbbing. He was biting his lip in order not to cry. For a brief moment everything went blurry around him. He leaned forward and clasped his head in his hands.

Afterward, in the lobby of the courthouse, when a woman reporter asked Gary what he'd like to say to the Chinese government, he cried out, "I appeal to Deng Xiaoping to intervene on my behalf. President Deng, please bring me home!"

Those words were published in several major newspapers the

next day. But at a news conference, the Chinese ambassador to Washington responded negatively to the question about Beijing's connection with Gary Shang, insisting, "Let me reiterate, I never heard of that man. China has no spy in the United States at all, so we have nothing to do with him. All the accusations against the Chinese government are baseless, fabricated by those people hostile to our country."

$\diamondsuit\diamondsuit\diamondsuit$

"id you go see your father in prison?" Ben asked me, his hands in his jeans pockets. We were strolling on Wollaston Beach with Boston's skyline in view, a bunch of skyscrapers partly obscured by the dissipating mist in the northwest. An airliner was descending noiselessly toward Logan Airport. The drizzle had let up, the clouds opening and revealing patches of blue.

I said, "I visited him once, in late November of that year, but I had to rush back to BU. I was teaching a course and had to meet my class. Dad didn't say much to me because a guard was standing beside him and there was glass and steel wire between us. We spoke over a phone. He kept saying 'I'm sorry' and was tearful. I went through the visit as if I were drugged, unable to find words. That was the first time I'd ever seen him in tears, and at the end of the meeting he blew me a kiss and forced a smile. My mother saw him more often and made sure that he received proper medication and also had his ulcerated gum treated. I wished I could have stayed home longer so that I could visit him again."

"He must've died miserably."

"I was devastated when I heard about his suicide. I had a breakdown and couldn't help my tears whenever I saw an older man."

Ben had read that Gary smothered himself with a trash bag tied around his neck with two connected shoestrings. (He had skipped breakfast so that his body might not be messy. He lay on his bed in the solitary cell and died without making any noise.) We had talked about his death the previous night, when Ben finally confessed he was indeed a Chinese spy, though a minor one.

The ebbing tide kept the bay flat. Ben continued, "What touched me most is this sentence he said to his cross-examiner: 'I am not a petty thief.' I wept when I read that. It reminded me that

I was a petty thief. Recently I acquired a pair of new night-vision goggles just issued to the U.S. Marines, an F-18 manual, a list of the public radio frequencies, and some other stuff. I've been stealing technological secrets—a petty thief indeed."

"On some level Gary was a conceited man."

"He had to have a high opinion of himself or how could he survive? A spy of his kind had to convince himself of the importance of his mission so that he could continue in the face of adversity."

Ben's words reminded me of a sentence in Gary's diary that had baffled me for a while: "For me, self-sacrifice is sweet." My father seemed to believe in the grandeur of what he was doing. In spite of his remarkable intelligence, he lived in a fog, possessed by an ancient emotion whose validity his reason couldn't penetrate. Indeed, an exalted vision or illusion might make pain bright and supportable.

Farther along the beach a little girl cried out. She was carrying a miniature saffron bucket with a spade in it and wobbling toward her mother, who was sitting on a boulder and flipping through a fashion magazine. The sun had come out, and the sand was turning whitish. Ben went on about Gary, "I still think he gave up too easily. China might have made a rescue effort to get him repatriated."

"You're too naïve," I said. "Didn't the Chinese ambassador deny that China had anything to do with him?"

"But that couldn't be the final word. My grandfather held at least the same rank as the ambassador, probably even higher. That is to say, the ambassador had no right to decide Gary's fate. The official denial might just have been routine bureaucracy. Once the media quieted down and the case was out of public view, there might have been a way to get him out of jail and back to China."

"But the ambassador represented the country."

"Look, even for small potatoes like me there's an exit plan in the event of emergency. My grandfather's case couldn't be that simple."

I was about to ask Ben how he could extricate himself, but I refrained. A pair of mottled seagulls took off from the teeth of the soft waves and let out sharp squawks. They were suspended in the air, their wings hardly moving. I said, "Maybe Suzie Chao knows more about this. Last winter when we talked, she said she hated the Communists because they had abandoned your grandfather."

"She's someone I'd like to meet. She seemed to remain loyal to him, to the very end."

"Maybe I should pay her another visit. Would you like to come if I go to see her again?"

"When do you plan to go?"

I thought about it and believed that the FBI might swoop down on Ben any minute, so I said, "The sooner the better. Let me give her a call."

I fished my cell phone out of my black suede purse and dialed Suzie's number. On the third ring her voice came on, halting as if I'd woken her up. I said, "Suzie, this is Lilian."

"Lilian who?"

"Gary's daughter."

"Oh, I thought you'd wiped me out of your mind long ago."

"How are you doing?"

"Still up and around."

"Listen, my nephew, Gary's grandson, and I would love to see you. Can we visit you if we come to Montreal?"

"Sure, anytime. I'll be happy to see you. You say you have a nephew, a Chinese?"

"Yes, he's from China. We'll speak more about this tonight, okay?"

"That's fine, call around nine."

I was pleased by her agreement. Putting away the phone, I turned to Ben. "Suzie can meet us anytime. Today is Friday. Maybe we should head to Montreal tomorrow. What do you think?"

"Well, I can't fly. The moment I board a plane, the FBI will know. Perhaps we should drive."

"Good idea, but don't you need a visa for crossing the border?"

"Not if I have a green card."

"Then let's drive."

"Should we rent a car or use mine? I just got my engine replaced. The car runs like new."

"We can drive your car. This should be safe."

On our walk back to his place, Ben talked more about how he'd gone into the espionage business. He said, "Most of my school-mates enrolled at the spy college in Luoyang because their parents or grandparents had been in the profession. We were told that we were the crème de la crème of our generation, handpicked by the Party, and we all pledged allegiance to the country and the revolutionary cause. In retrospect, I can see that the whole thing was quite sanctimonious, as if every one of us were a great man in the making. Our Party leaders even called us 'linchpins of the nation.'

"They chose me because my grandfather had been a top spy, so I was supposed to be cut out for the work as well. But in most ways I wasn't a good student. If anything, I was on the underperforming side. I couldn't shoot well or swim more than two miles. In bare-handed melee I usually lost to my opponents. But I had an ear for language, and my English was among the best in the class. I could reel off whatever we'd learned the previous day and could imitate all kinds of sounds and tones like a ventriloquist. What's more, I had interpersonal skills; I was able to strike up productive conversations with strangers. I was nicknamed Superglue, which meant I could always find ways to make a connection with others. During our training, whenever we were sent out to gather intelligence from folks in small towns, I would get more useful information than my classmates. That impressed our instructors. I also was good at analyzing intelligence and could see implications in small details. That's why they continued to train me after graduation, to prepare me for missions abroad. They let me enroll in a master's program and I got an MS in technology."

"What did they tell you about your grandfather?" I asked.

"They said he was a martyr who had fallen in the line of duty, so I was obliged to follow in his footsteps."

"In hindsight, do you resent that?"

"Sort of. But they also made me a more capable man, well off and privileged in some ways."

"Do you know you're in danger now? The FBI might move in on you at any moment."

"I'm aware of that and must act soon."

"But you have been passive for so long. Does Sonya know your true profession?"

"She might've sensed it, but I didn't tell her anything."

"You have a lot to decide. To be honest, few women can stand your kind of passivity."

"Actually, I asked my higher-ups for permission to marry her so that we could have the baby and live in America for some years, but they want to keep me more or less detached from this place. A baby born here will be a U.S. citizen, and that might bind me to America. My superiors reprimanded me for losing control of my sex life and told me to make Sonya have an abortion. I've been trying to figure out a solution. I can't force her to do anything."

When we arrived at his place, Sonya was cooking spaghetti and, with a wooden spoon, stirring the sauce of ground beef and black olives. She was wearing a mauve housedress like a maternity outfit, though her pregnancy wasn't showing yet. In spite of her smile, which accentuated a pimple on her nose, her roundish face was a picture of worries, her eyes a bit shadowy, but she still looked pretty, especially in profile. She'd been suffering from morning sickness, and her nose was congested. The previous evening she had confided to me, "I just can't figure Ben out. He seems sick of everything. He promised me this and that, but I'm not sure I can believe him."

After trying the sauce, I told Sonya, "This is delicious." Then I said in an undertone that we were going to Montreal the next morning, but she mustn't let anyone know of the trip.

"What for?" she asked.

"We're going to see an old friend of my father's. We'll be back on Sunday." I kept my voice low and assured her, "Don't worry too much. Everything will work out fine."

"I hope so." She breathed a feeble sigh. Another pot was coming to a boil. Sonya broke a bunch of angel-hair spaghetti in two, threw it into the water, and began stirring. I turned to wash the pans in the sink.

There was a gas station close by, so after dinner I took Ben's black Mustang there and filled the tank. Then he worked for a while on his car in the basement garage. He poured a bottle of fuel treatment into the tank, saying that was something he'd done every fall. He also checked all the lights and added fluids. I put two coats into the trunk, having heard that the temperature would plummet the following day. Back in his apartment, he and I avoided talking about his spying activities and the trip openly, not so much because of Sonya as because the place might have been bugged. In a way, I admired Ben for his composure. He seemed to have inherited Gary's ability to bear stress and uncertainty. Though knowing the FBI was after him, he was still clearheaded about everything—he must have gone through a considerable amount of mental training. In spite of my admiration, I feared he might not be able to find his way out of danger. Perhaps I should urge him to defect and file for political asylum, but we had to thoroughly consider the pros and cons of such a drastic move.

AFTER WE CHECKED IN to a motel outside Montreal, I phoned Suzie to let her know we had arrived. She said her apartment was too messy for us to meet there. I offered to take her to lunch in Chinatown, where she lived. She suggested Kam Fung, which I knew was a pricey Cantonese place where all the tables had tablecloths. We agreed to meet at eleven the next morning.

At the front desk of the motel, I'd thought Ben might feel

uncomfortable about sharing a room with me, but he had stopped me when I asked for two rooms. He said, "Let's have one room with two beds. This is more natural." I was pleased he felt that way. We didn't go to bed until midnight, even though the seven-hour trip had tired me out. We were talking about his family back in Fushan County and about my father. As our conversation continued, I managed to steer it to his current situation and even mentioned the possibility of turning himself in to the FBI. He shook his head and said, "You're too naïve, Aunt Lilian. Like most Americans, you think only in clear and straight ways. What will happen to my parents and siblings if I defect? China will grind them down, and they'll never forgive me."

"I didn't take them into account," I admitted.

"You met them and saw how well they were doing in a god-forsaken town. Do you think they could succeed like that just on their own? There've been powerful hands helping them ever since I started in my profession. If I betray my country, those hands can also destroy them."

"What should you do?"

"That's the question I've been grappling with these days. My business here is worth one and a half million dollars. It was the Chinese government's investment. If I surrender to the FBI, the business will be gone and I'll be blamed for the loss. Worse yet, I'd have to give the FBI a lot of information on Chinese espionage operations, especially in North America. Then to China I'll become a criminal guilty of high treason."

"Why can't you reverse the roles of the plaintiff and the accused? Why is a country always innocent and always right? Hasn't China used both you and your grandfather relentlessly? Hasn't your country betrayed you?"

He looked astonished, his eyebrows locked together. I continued, "Ben, things have been changing in China, where many people no longer depend on the state for their livelihood and survival. If your family's economic situation takes a downturn, I can send them money regularly. So for now, just think about what will be the best for you and Sonya." I had to mention money to fully convince him that his family's survival might not depend on the state anymore.

"Thank you, Aunt Lilian! This means a great deal to me. With your help I'll have my rear base covered. I will figure out a way."

He didn't go to sleep for a long time after I switched off the lights. He tossed and twisted in the bed close to the window, now and again letting out a faint sigh. My promise must have set his mind racing.

We checked out of the motel the next morning and drove into the city. It took just fifteen minutes to get to Chinatown. I liked Montreal for its easy traffic. After parking in an outside lot, we headed to Saint-Urbain Street, where Kam Fung was. No sooner had we sat down at a corner table than Suzie appeared, using a cane that had a thin leather strap attached to it. She was much frailer and more bent than ten months before and might have suffered from rheumatism and osteoporosis. Ben and I stood, he drew up a chair, and we sat her down. I hung her cane on the back of the chair. She took out a Kleenex and blew her nose. She tried to smile, but her effort only made her face look sickly. Her eyes were watery, the lower lids a little swollen.

I said, "Are you under the weather, Suzie?"

"No, it's just the withdrawal symptoms."

"Withdrawal from what?" I asked.

"Caffeine. I just quit coffee."

"Why did you do that?" The thought came to me that she might not have many years to live.

"I want to put my life together again."

"Have you been dating someone?" I asked in earnest.

"Get out of here!" She cackled. "I quit sex long ago. I just want to live longer. When I was young, I thought I'd die before sixty, and

I wouldn't mind that as long as I was happy when I was alive. But since I turned sixty, somehow the older I get, the longer I want to live. Guess I've got greedy."

"That's natural," I said. "Life has become more precious to you."

"What a smart girl. That's why I like you much more than your mom."

Ben poured her a cup of jasmine tea and said, "Here, drink this, Grandaunt, and you'll feel better."

Indeed, a few swallows later she returned to normal, relaxed with her legs folded under her. She grinned, and her face creased, showing a coating of makeup. She glanced sideways at Ben, blinking her eyes, which had lost their almond shape and were almost triangular now. "He's handsome like your dad," she said about Ben.

"You bet," I agreed. "He's also smart like him."

We ordered lunch. Suzie wanted only a bowl of wontons, saying she wasn't hungry and was happy just to see us. Indeed, she'd been beaming nonstop. We resumed making small talk.

When our food had come, I said to Suzie, "One question has been on my mind since we last met. How come my dad left his diary with you?"

"Gary had a feeling that something bad might happen to him. He told me to say nothing about his secret profession to the investigators. Just play the fool and deny knowing anything. He wanted me to keep the diary and let nobody know of its existence. He had a sixth sense for danger."

"He wanted you to pass it on to me?"

"He said nothing like that, but I assumed that could be his intention. Also, the diary could have become criminal evidence, so he wouldn't want the FBI to get hold of it."

"Grandaunt Suzie," Ben joined in, "one thing I can't figure out about my granddad—why did he commit suicide? There must have been ways China could rescue him."

"Baloney! China dumped him," she said, twisting her mouth a

little. "I got a note from Gary after he was in custody. He asked me to go to Beijing and beg Deng Xiaoping to swap some imprisoned U.S. spies for him."

"You received a letter from him?" I was so surprised that I put down my soup spoon.

"Yes, it came to me through the mail."

"How could he send you the letter from prison?" Ben asked.

"It's beyond me too. Guess there must've been a secret agent who smuggled the letter out of jail and dropped it into the mailbox. Or someone who visited Gary might have brought it out for him. In any event, the letter reached me without a glitch. So I went to Hong Kong right away and got in touch with Bingwen Chu, Gary's handler, who helped me cross the border into China. In Beijing I asked some officials to let me speak to Deng Xiaoping personally."

"Did you get to?" Again I was taken aback.

"Of course not. There was this man named Ding, a big shot in the Ministry of National Security. He received me in his office, but no matter how I begged, they wouldn't try to rescue Gary."

Ben put in, "That must have been Hao Ding, the minister of national security. He was in charge of China's intelligence service in the eighties. What did he tell you, Grandaunt?"

"He said his country had nothing to do with Gary Shang anymore. To them, Gary was a traitor, a blackmailer. Ding told me, 'He just extorted seventy thousand dollars from our country. What kind of money is that? Let me give you an idea: I make only two hundred dollars a month. That's thirty years' salary for me.' Another man jumped in, 'Gary Shang got rich in the U.S. He was rolling in cash and always drove a Buick, but he was corrupted by capitalism, greedy like a snake that wants to swallow an elephant.' The same man went on to say that Gary even had a bourgeois disease, because anyone who ate coarse grains and vegetables every day wouldn't suffer from diabetes. I realized there was no way I could reason with them, so again I asked to see Deng Xiaoping in person. They laughed in my face, saying I was out of my senses and that Chairman Deng had no time for such a trifle. I got furious and yelled at them.

"Seeing me distraught, Ding revealed to me, 'To tell you the truth, there's no need to make such a futile attempt. Chairman Deng was well informed of Gary Shang's case and already gave instructions: "Let that selfish man rot in an American prison together with his silly dream of being loyal to both countries." So Gary Shang blew his chance and the case is closed. Nobody can help him anymore.' Those were the final words I got from them."

"Then you came back and told my father that?" I asked.

"No, I wasn't a family member and couldn't go to the jailhouse to see him. Someone else must have passed the message on to him."

"I cannot believe this," Ben said, stupefied. "He held the rank of major general."

"A general is also a soldier," I told him. "Soldiers are all expendable."

"Everybody is," Suzie agreed.

"I have another question for you, Suzie," I said.

"Okay, go ahead."

"This might be personal and embarrassing, but I need to ask. Why was my dad so fond of you? Was it because of your common racial, cultural background? Or simply because you were good in bed? Or something else? To be honest, I don't think you were superior to my mother in every way."

Suzie smirked complacently. "Well, domesticity was never my thing, and I wasn't good at keeping a man happy at all. In the beginning it was mostly mutual attraction, but bit by bit Gary and I began to get along. When we were together we could talk endlessly, about everything, so after many years an affair grew into a friendship in spite of all the quarrels we had. Besides, compared to Nellie, I was more useful to him."

"In what way?" I asked, despite knowing of her secret trip to Hong Kong and her failed attempt to look for Yufeng.

Suzie said, "My uncle used to be a senior officer in Taiwan's intelligence service. That meant Gary could work for the Nationalists at any time. I advised him to do that, because if he was caught by the U.S. government, he could identify himself as a spy working for Taipei. That would make his crime a lot less serious because Taiwan was not an enemy country to the United States. In other words, I could be Gary's safety net."

"Did he ever work for the Nationalists?"

"No, never. He wasn't a triple agent. He would not betray the mainland because he didn't want to endanger his family there, also because he wouldn't get me embroiled in the espionage business. For that I was grateful. He never took advantage of me and just remained a good friend. A real gentleman."

"Did you tell your uncle about Gary's true identity?"

"Of course not. If the Nationalists had known of that, they could have tipped off the CIA. So Gary and I were faithful to each other to the very end. Wasn't that remarkable?"

I nodded while she broke down sobbing. I glanced at Ben, who was teary too. "Aunt Suzie," I murmured, "thank you for loving and helping my father. You allowed us to understand him better—he was at least loyal and decent in his own way."

"I still miss him," she mumbled, wiping her wrinkled face with a red napkin, her cheeks streaked with makeup.

After lunch we sent Suzie back to her apartment building, a kind of senior home. Then we hit Expressway 10, headed east. Ben was pensive and reticent while I was driving. When we'd begun cruising along with little traffic on the road, I asked him, "Do you think Minister Hao Ding had a point? I mean, as he said, your grandfather was a blackmailer?"

"No. That was just an excuse."

"How come? Seventy thousand dollars was a ton of money by Chinese standards then."

"It was a mere pittance in my grandfather's case. Remember what Mao said about him? 'This man is worth four armored divisions.' An armored division had more than two hundred tanks. A single tank was worth hundreds of thousands of dollars."

"But that was when Gary was still useful to them."

"True, they squeezed everything they could out of him. His case was a textbook example of stupidity and misjudgment. In a way, you can say it was his love for your mother that did him in."

"What makes you say that?"

"He got the money for her fucking bakery! That was like blowing his identity on purpose—no professional spy would make such a dangerous move. How could he have got that lax?"

"I'm not sure if he loved Nellie, but he must have meant to do right by her. After twenty-five years' living together, he must have developed some feelings for her. Now that he was going to leave America for good, he wanted to make sure she'd be able to survive without him around. We can call that love or honor or a sense of responsibility, whichever name it doesn't matter. What's essential is that he finally did something he felt right on his own, and was willing to pay the price."

Ben looked at me in astonishment. I added, "Don't you think my mother was also a victim?"

"I can see that. Let me say this then: it was his decency that ruined him."

"Also because he was ignorant of the nefarious nature of the power that used and manipulated him."

"You mean China?"

"Yes, what it did to your grandfather is evil. On the other hand, he allowed the country to take the moral high ground and to dictate how he lived his life. That's also a source of his tragedy."

"It wasn't that simple. How could he have separated himself from China, where he still had a good part of his family?"

"That's another source of his tragedy—he couldn't exist alone."

A lull followed. I kept driving in silence. Ben seemed to be dozing off in the reclined passenger seat, but I suspected he was just deep in thought trying to figure a way out of his plight, so I remained wordless.

It started sprinkling, the beads of rain rattling on the windshield, and I flipped on the wipers, which began swishing monotonously. I'd been driving sixty miles an hour, following a tanker truck at a distance of about five hundred feet.

As we were approaching Magog, Ben sat up, pulled a notepad out of his hip pocket, and scribbled on it. He ripped off the page and handed it to me. "Keep this, Aunt Lilian," he said.

"What is it?"

"An email address and a password. From now on we should communicate only through this account. I've already set it up. You just leave a message for me in the draft folder whenever you want to reach me. After I read it, I will delete every word. You must do the same. We must leave nothing in the account after we have read a message."

"Why should we do that?"

"This is a way to communicate without leaving any trace online. Email exchanges might not be safe. We just share the same account, known only to the two of us. Every time after you've read my message, delete the whole thing."

"Is this how you send intelligence to China?"

He chuckled. "It's one of the methods. There're more complex ways too, like classified codes and encrypted fax. For you and me this should be private enough."

Evidently he'd begun making arrangements. Whatever action he might take, it would be better than sitting tight with apprehension, so I didn't press him for details.

Back in College Park, I checked our shared email account a few times a day but found no words. I wrote Ben a note, saying I hoped everything was well. The message disappeared overnight, which meant he had read it. That put my mind somewhat at ease.

Henry and I dined out on Wednesday evening, September 21, to celebrate his birthday—he was sixty-two now. Again he talked about Ben, hoping he could get out of his trouble with the FBI soon and quit his shady computer business so he might work for us someday, and so we could live together like a family. Henry knew I would love that. Indeed, if that happened, I'd feel blessed. I always admired immigrant families that had parents and children, even grandchildren, living under the same roof, although I could see that it might be hard for the younger generation, who needed more space for themselves. But I said nothing to Henry about Ben's current situation, which must have been volatile. Longing for an early retirement, my husband wanted to collect his Social Security without delay. He was not afraid of losing some of his benefits since my employment at the university could cover him. I made no comment but wondered whether it would be good for him to be entirely unoccupied. His job wasn't that demanding and gave him a lot of free time. Still, he suggested we contract a handyman to lighten his maintenance work. I wouldn't mind if that was what he wanted, yet I told him that he should keep himself busy so that he could live longer. He laughed and said, "I prefer comfort to longevity—quality but not quantity of life."

When we came back that night, I booted up my computer and accessed the secret email account again. A message appeared:

Dear Aunt Lilian:

By the time you read this, Sonya and I are no longer in the Boston area. We are very fond of Massachusetts but unable to live there anymore. I just sold my business at a huge discount so that I could get some ready cash. I am not sure where Sonya and I will end up, but we have each other and will share all our good and bad fortunes. As long as she is with me, I can live anywhere and won't be lonesome. I will cherish her as my sole companion and will love her as my wife and the mother of my children.

There will be consequences for my family back in China on my account, and I won't be able to do anything for them for a long time, but I believe that with your help they will survive. Among my family members, I am most worried about Juli, who is, as I am, untamed at heart. I fear she might flee home again given that the provincial life can be prosaic and stifling. But as long as she is with our parents, she should be all right. So please always urge her to stay home. Also, don't let them know of my present situation yet. It's better to keep them in the dark for now.

I feel liberated as we are traveling along. For the first time in my life I am acting as an independent man, also as a man without a country. I have decided to grow a beard. Yes, let it get as thick as a forest so I will look older and a little fierce. Whether Sonya and I will be able to live decently, I am not sure, but we are willing to accept all the joys and sorrows that come our way. This is the true condition of freedom, isn't it?

Love from both of us,
Ben

PS: Originally I planned to come to DC next spring to pay my respects to your parents, but I will not be able to do that anymore. When you go visit them in the cemetery next time, please take along two bouquets, of white chrysanthemums or roses, on behalf of me and Sonya.

I felt that Ben's escape was a natural step, but he might have been rash to dispose of his business like that. On the other hand, that must have been his only way to get funds for the road.

I wondered about Ben and Sonya. Did they cross the border into Canada? That was unlikely. Ben had once said there was too much Chinese influence in Canada when I half-joked that he should consider immigrating to Quebec like a U.S. draft dodger. He and Sonya might still be in the States. Their immediate task was to elude the FBI and the Chinese investigators, so for now they might have to continue to travel. Wherever they went, I was certain they could survive.

I read Ben's message again, then deleted it. I couldn't help smiling about his decision to grow a beard, which sounded a shade eccentric. I supposed it could be his way to assert his manhood, at least in appearance. Ben didn't know my parents had been buried in different cemeteries, but I'd bring them flowers as he requested. I left him a message saying that he and Sonya must take care of each other and must avoid making friends for the time being.

My words got erased the next morning. That pleased me.

Through Juli I informed my sister and her husband that Ben was working on a special project that imposed strict isolation on him, but that he was well and they shouldn't worry. Juli wrote back and thanked me on behalf of her parents. She reminded me of the next summer's family reunion, to which I again promised to come.

Weeks have passed, and I still haven't heard another word from Ben. I try to stay undisturbed. The silence might mean everything is okay.

ACKNOWLEDGMENTS

I am grateful to LuAnn Walther, Catherine Tung, and Lane Zachary. Their comments and suggestions made this novel richer and stronger.

WAITING

In *Waiting*, Ha Jin draws on his intimate knowledge of contemporary China to create a novel of unexpected richness and feeling. This is the story of Lin Kong, a man living in two worlds, struggling with the claims of two utterly different women as he moves through the political minefields of a society designed to regulate his every move. For more than seventeen years, Lin has been in love with an educated, clever woman, Manna Wu. But back in his home village lives the wife his family chose for him—a humble and touchingly loyal woman, whom he visits in order to ask, again and again, for a divorce. In a culture in which the ancient ties of tradition and family still hold sway and where adultery discovered by the Party can ruin lives forever, Lin's passionate love is stretched ever more taut by the passing years. Ha Jin vividly conjures the texture of daily life in a place where the demands of human longing must contend with the weight of centuries of custom.

Fiction

WAR TRASH

Ha Jin casts a searchlight into a forgotten corner of modern history, the experience of Chinese soldiers held in U.S. POW camps during the Korean War. In 1951 Yu Yuan, a scholarly and self-effacing clerical officer in Mao's "volunteer" army, is taken prisoner south of the 38th Parallel. Because he speaks English, he soon becomes an intermediary between his compatriots and their American captors. With Yuan as guide, we are ushered into the secret world behind the barbed wire, a world where kindness alternates with blinding cruelty and one has infinitely more to fear from one's fellow prisoners than from the guards.

Fiction

NANJING REQUIEM

It's 1937, and the Japanese are poised to invade Nanjing. Minnie Vautrin, a missionary and the dean of Jinling Women's College, decides to remain at the school, convinced that her American citizenship will help her safeguard the welfare of the Chinese men and women who work there. She is painfully mistaken. In the aftermath of the invasion, the school becomes a refugee camp for more than ten thousand homeless women and children, and Vautrin must struggle to intercede on the behalf of the hapless victims.

Fiction

THE CRAZED

Ha Jin's seismically powerful novel is at once an unblinking look into the bell jar of communist Chinese society and a portrait of the eternal compromises and deceptions of the human state. When the venerable professor Yang has a stroke, his student Jian Wan is assigned to care for him. Since Jian plans to marry his mentor's beautiful, icy daughter, the job requires delicacy. Just how much delicacy becomes clear when Yang begins to rave. Are these just the outpourings of a broken mind, or is Yang speaking the truth—about his family, his colleagues, and his life's work? And will bearing witness to the truth end up breaking Jian's heart?

Fiction

A FREE LIFE

In *A Free Life*, Ha Jin follows the Wu family—father Nan, mother Pingping, and son Taotao—as they sever their ties with China in the aftermath of the 1989 massacre at Tiananmen Square and begin a new life in the United States. As Nan takes on a number of menial jobs, eventually operating a restaurant with Pingping, he struggles to adapt to the American way of life and to hold his family together, even as he pines for a woman he loved and lost in his youth. Ha Jin's talents are in full force as he brings to life the contemporary immigrant experience.

Fiction

IN THE POND

In the Pond is a darkly funny portrait of an amateur calligrapher who wields his artist's brush as a weapon. Shao Bin is a worker at the Harvest Fertilizer Plant by day and an aspiring artist by night. Passed over on the list to receive a decent apartment for his young family, Shao Bin chafes at his powerlessness. When he attempts to expose his corrupt superiors by circulating satirical cartoons, he provokes a series of counterattacks that send ripples beyond his small community. Suffused with earthy wit, *In the Pond* is a moving tale about humble lives caught up in larger social forces.

Fiction

OCEAN OF WORDS

The place is the chilly border between Russia and China. The time is the early 1970s. And the characters in this thrilling collection of stories are Chinese soldiers who must constantly scrutinize the enemy even as they themselves are watched for signs of the fatal disease of bourgeois liberalism. In *Ocean of Words*, Ha Jin explores the predicament of these simple, barely literate men with breathtaking concision and humanity. *Ocean of Words* is a triumphant volume, poignant, hilarious, and harrowing.

Short Stories

THE BRIDEGROOM

A collection of comical and deeply moving tales of contemporary China that are as warm and human as they are surprising, disturbing, and delightful. In the title story, the head of security at a factory is shocked, first when the handsomest worker proposes marriage to his homely adopted daughter, and again when his new son-in-law is arrested for the "crime" of homosexuality. In another story, the workers at an American-style fast food franchise receive a crash course in marketing, deep frying, and that capitalist dictum, "the customer is always right." Ha Jin has triumphed again with his unforgettable storytelling.

Short Stories

A GOOD FALL

National Book Award–winning author Ha Jin gives us a collection that delves into the experience of Chinese immigrants in America. A lonely composer takes comfort in the antics of his girlfriend's parakeet; young children decide to change their names so they might sound more "American," unaware of how deeply this will hurt their grandparents; a Chinese professor of English attempts to defect with the help of a reluctant former student. All of Ha Jin's characters struggle to remain loyal to their homeland and its traditions while also exploring the freedom that life in a new country offers. Stark, deeply moving, acutely insightful, and often strikingly humorous, *A Good Fall* reminds us once again of the storytelling prowess of this superb writer.

Short Stories

VINTAGE INTERNATIONAL
Available wherever books are sold.
www.vintagebooks.com